American Andarte
An OSS Commando Fights for Greece

American Andarte

An OSS Commando Fights for Greece

by

Steven James Hantzis

Alinet, LLC

Alexandria, Virginia USA

2025

American Andarte is a work of fiction. All incidents and dialogue, and all characters with the exception of some well-known historical figures, are products of the author's imagination and are not to be construed as real. Where real-life historical persons appear, the situations, incidents, and dialogues concerning those persons are entirely fictional and are not intended to depict actual events or to change the entirely fictional nature of the work. In all other respects, any resemblance to persons living or dead is entirely coincidental.

Alinet, LLC
P.O. Box 7353
Alexandria, VA 22307

ISBN: 9798998606748

Contents

Acknowledgements

American Andarte would never have been written but for my dear friend, high school classmate, fellow Indiana University alumni, and a highly-recruited neighborhood baseball star, Jill Renuart. In 2017, Jill sent me an article by Steve Frangos in The *National Herald* entitled "The Greek Battalion: Unravelling the Story of a Special Group of Greek Americans." The Greek Battalion, as you will read, was the US Army's forerunner to the Office of Strategic Services (OSS) Greek Operational Groups whose exploits in Nazi occupied Greece were classified Top Secret until recently. Thank you, Jill, greatly appreciated, way to light the fire.

Cover Photo: OSS Greek Operational Group 1944, OSS Society, Herndon, Virginia

Chapter 1

"He just died, Pop. I didn't touch him. I put the shell in my pocket, called an attendant, the doctor came, they pronounced him dead, and I flew back to Washington. He knew. I saw the fear in his eyes. He was frail, but he knew. Now he's gone, and he died thinking of Segundo."

Alex listened to his son's report as the two sat on the back porch of the family home in Creve Coeur. From their wooden Adirondack chairs, they watched the boaters on the lake as a warm summer breeze luffed sails and fanned the morning stillness.

Alex, gray-haired, fit and trim with a stubble beard, was a quiet, thoughtful, and determined man at age sixty-five. As he listened to his son's report, ancient memories stirred, thoughts and feelings churned in folds and recesses where they had rested for many years. The news pleased him but in a way that forced him to register an unfinished obligation, frustrating sadness, and deferred honor. Life in the four decades since Colorado held many distractions. But *the oath* persisted. A lingering commitment underlying the veneer of all other challenges.

Alex took another sip of coffee from his white porcelain mug. He returned it to the wide arm of the porch chair as Marta pushed open the sliding screen door with a tray of Italian sweets and a carafe.

"You came in so late last night that I didn't bother to get up. Was that the only flight you could book?" asked Marta. Not waiting for an answer, she continued, "We go to bed early these days and sleep as late as possible. Still, I'm thrilled you are home. We haven't seen our mystery man since . . . when? Greek Easter? April twenty-first? That was a good date, no? Both Easters on the same day? Two birds with one stone."

Alex pointed to the empty Adirondack next to Stavros. "Sit, Marta, our son has something to tell you."

Marta, graceful and composed, sat in the chair and crossed her legs at the ankles. She wore a light floral-print dress with her still luxuriant hair in a bun, now streaked with gray. She looked as radiant and well-put-together as ever.

Stavros repeated his account of visiting Linderfelt in San Diego and ended with the summation shared with his father. At the telling, Marta faintly gasped and crossed herself twice. Neither she nor Alex had any idea Stavros had been tracking the vile man, the tormentor of Stavros's birth mother. Marta said, "I cross myself for Eléni, not the swine," and she pretended to spit on the wooden decking.

"How did you find him? And how did he get to San Diego?" Marta asked.

"Mother," Stavros said in a tone both dismissive and knowing.

"Oh, that's right," answered Marta, "I forgot who you work for," and she dramatically placed her finger to her lips and shushed. A second later she added, "A proper use of the taxpayer's money. I approve."

Alex said, "I should feel happy, but I don't. I am relieved he is dead, but sad that he lived as long as he did." The dredging of old memories and the unexpected news from Stavros mixed in Alex's mind, and the results overwhelmed him. He did not break down—Alex was strong willed—but when Stavros looked over at his father, there were tears in his eyes. It was the first time in forty-five years Stavros had seen his father cry.

Marta said, "He was a pig and deserved to die *before* he killed Eléni. Now, it is done. What did Harry say? A beginning, a middle, and an end? So, this is the end. It was a long chapter, but now the book is *il fine* . . . a happy ending . . . just like an American movie.

"Now, we must tell the others so they, too, can be happy. Everyone will want to know—Harry, Dimitri, Yiorgos, everyone. Today is a good day, and, Stavros, you have made us proud. I know you have made Eléni proud. She birthed you, and we raised you, and everyone is proud.

"Tonight, we celebrate."

Alex would wait to call Harry and Dimitri until late that evening. But, after more coffee and a half of a toasted ham and cheese sandwich, he went to his writing desk in the room set aside for his business matters. There he began a letter to Yiorgos in Athens.

June 7, 1957

Dear Friend, Yiorgos,

I hope this letter finds you well and happy. Your work in the old country is commendable, and we can only hope that the situation there is improving. I'm certain with your help that things will be better soon.

Marta wishes you well, and she and I received an unexpected visit last evening from Stavros. He had news that we thought you would approve.

Linderfelt is dead. His black soul left his body to be judged by God as Stavros stood over him. His last thought was Segundo. Stavros reminded him as he lay in bed, fearing for his life at the sight of the grown man he had left as a pleading babe on the cold tent floor that night in Colorado.

Our obligation is done, and our pledge fulfilled. Perhaps in a way that none of us could have imagined when we took separate paths so long ago. But it is done.

Stavros hopes to be in Greece in the coming months, and he said he would get in touch, so he can tell you all the details. Can he still reach you through the Ministry of Education, Research, and Religious Affairs?

If there is a better way, please write with your information.

    Thank you for all the help you've been in my life, my friend. If it were not for you finding me work after the strike, I would never have been able to raise my son. Now, we can both be happy for his contributions, no?

Your friend always,

Alex

Chapter 2

Notoriety was not his friend. It was an occupational hazard. With apprehension, Stavros queued to board the gleaming, triple-tailed Lockheed L-1649 Starliner at Lambert Field for his flight back to Washington. He'd flown an older Lockheed Constellation, a Connie, to St. Louis. When he booked his trip, he did not know that he would be aboard the inaugural flight for the rollout of Trans World Airlines' sleek new plane.

Stavros navigated a line of press people and photographers to board the aircraft. He tipped his fedora and lowered his eyes. His dark glasses—aviators, the only style he'd worn since the war—remained in his breast pocket. Putting them on would have been stereotypical, like cheese in a trap for the curious media. Stavros was tall, good-looking, well-built, and well-dressed. And, since TWA's inaugural flight was going to Washington, DC, the press would be on the lookout for VIPs. They loved that angle. Photos of important people engaged in mundanity sold copy. The voyeuristic masses couldn't help themselves.

His precaution—staying in the background, uninteresting, and unnoticeable—was no longer a do-or-die part of his tradecraft since his promotion to headquarters in 1952. He was a bureaucrat, a knowledgeable, credible, and field-tempered one, but a bureaucrat, nevertheless. Still, old habits die hard. Especially the ones that extend your life expectancy. Although his operational days were behind him, his operational habits were not.

Stavros had gotten his promotion the old-fashioned way; he'd earned it. His employer, the Central Intelligence Agency, made the meritorious appointment soon after Greece joined the North Atlantic Treaty Organization (NATO) in February 1952. Stavros, with his midwestern roots and small college pedigree, joined the prep school, Ivy League majority at headquarters. The accession of Greece and Turkey to NATO anchored them on the Cold War chessboard, the ever-tilting bounds on which the Greeks had maneuvered since World War II. Stavros's time in the Office of Strategic Services (OSS) Greek American Operational Group attested to that.

For the previous five years, Stavros had worked as the primary point of contact, for Greek affairs with the CIA's station chief in Athens reporting to him. Stavros reported to the directorate chief of operations and through him to the director. Stavros had many friends and contacts in the old country, but no longer *ran* these relationships as assets of American intelligence. That was the job of case officers working through the station chief under diplomatic, academic, or commercial cover within the country. So said the official organizational chart.

With a mild midday breeze out of the southwest, TWA's latest-in-the-line Connie entered Washington, DC, Metropolitan Area Air Defense Identification Zone. Her seasoned crew set the bearing for National Airport's Runway 19 on a river visual approach. With the Potomac unwinding below, Stavros, seated on the starboard side, recognized Rosslyn, Arlington National Cemetery, and Columbia Island Marina, where he kept his boat. Just beyond the marina, the Pentagon splayed in the center of its vast parking lots. Then, the soft thud of grooved rubber tires racing in an instant from zero to 150 miles per hour announced terra firma. The Connie pulled up short of the river and taxied lazily to Terminal A. There, press and television cameras centered on a bunted podium just inside the terminal. Carter L. Burgess, the new president of the airline, held court answering questions before delivering his prepared statement. It was a good day for TWA public relations but fraught for a homebound spy.

Chapter 3

Penny was happy to see Stavros, all twenty-five pounds of her. She lived next door and seldom ventured farther than the adjoining porch stoops. She was a peaceful animal with a peaceful countenance, and the cat's biggest threat to mice and birds was her hard stares and twitching tail. Stavros put his key into the lock and, before he opened the door, leaned over to scratch her head between her tufted ears. The appreciative animal wound herself around his calves, and Stavros gently guided her out of the way. He turned the key, but before pushing the door open, he checked a small fleck of paint. It was the same color as the door surround. He had left it wedged between the door and the jam just below the lock. It was still in place. He opened the parking lot door of his two-story brick row house in the Belle View neighborhood just south of Old Town Alexandria, Virginia.

He entered the townhouse's small kitchen and walked through the narrow living room to the front door. The door opened on a grassy common where the postal service delivered through a slot. He reached down to gather a water bill, a shopping flyer, and a hand-addressed letter with no return postmarked airmail from Athens, Greece.

Stavros carried his travel bag upstairs to the bedroom. He changed out of his suit into blue jeans and a T-shirt and returned downstairs to the kitchen for a short glass of ouzo, water, ice, and lemon. Then he sat on the living room sofa to read his mail.

Using a small Case penknife, he sliced open the letter from Greece and caught a whiff of lavender. It was a pleasant association. He knew at once that the letter was from Dimitra.

Stavros first met Dimitra—a captivating, intelligent, raven-haired woman—in 1944 in the mountains of Western Greece, when both were in their early thirties. She reminded him of his stepmother, Marta, just as poised and beautiful but with the guile of a Greek. She was from Platanos, the principal village of the Aetolia-Acarnania municipality, the municipality of Chómori, the Hantzis family, and Harry, Stavros's honorary uncle.

Stavros and Dimitra were well-educated. Stavros held a Master of Arts in World History, and Dimitra was on her way to finishing her Masters in Archaeology at Aristotle University of Thessaloniki. War interrupted her studies when an Italian submarine torpedoed the Greek cruiser *Elli* at anchor off the island of Tinos on August 15, 1940.

The *Elli* took a direct hit at 8:25 a.m. as her crew prepared to go ashore as an honor guard for the Dormition of the Mother of God celebration. The explosion sent a plume into the clear Greek morning. The column of smoke and debris soared hundreds of feet, white and watery at its base and black as death at its peak. Its pall hung over ten thousand pilgrims awaiting ceremonies at the venerated Church of Panagia Evangelistria. There, in 1823, a visionary nun had uncovered a Byzantine-era icon of the Virgin Mary (Panagia) kneeling, head bent in prayer, reading from a book. The church opened its doors on the commanding hills above the harbor in 1825, when it became the holiest church in the country, and its icon the protector of all Greece. Pilgrims flocked there on holy days, making it the most popular *proskýnima* in the country.

The explosion from the warship and the detonation of more torpedoes in the peaceful harbor concussed and stunned sojourners. Pilgrims froze, crawling from the port to the church on their hands and knees. Seconds before, wishing only to wash in holy water, kiss the sacred icon, and offer supplications, the faithful redirected their prayers.

Mussolini had ordered an unprovoked attack that killed nine petty officers and wounded twenty-four aboard the *Elli*. Mussolini hoped to intimidate the Greeks. Instead, coming on a Catholic and Orthodox holy day, the attack was fuel on the fire. Dimitra knew war was coming, and she didn't return to the university that fall. She stayed with her family in Platanos and helped organize the Greek Army's call-up of reserve soldiers and other forces.

At 3:00 a.m. on October 28, Italy's ambassador in Athens, Emanuele Grazzi, handed an ultimatum from Mussolini to the Prime Minister of Greece, Ioannis Metaxas. The Italian despot demanded the cession of Greek territory.

Metaxas replied in French, "Alors, c'est la guerre." (Then, it's war.) The Greeks heard "Oxi!" (No!), and since then October 28 has been Oxi Day.[1]

At 5:30 a.m. before the ultimatum's deadline, Mussolini's fascist army of eight divisions, 140,000 troops, invaded from Albania. After early success, the Italians stalled before the hastily mobilized Greek Army and guerrilla fighters.[2] These guerrillas, forces Dimitra had helped organize, were the forerunners of the andartes. These were the fighters that Stavros, as an OSS commando, would team with in April 1944 to punish the Germans during their retreat from Greece. That was where Stavros met Dimitra.

By early November 1940, the Greeks had turned the tables at the Battle of Elaia–Kalamas in the Pindus Mountains to the north. During the harsh winter of 1940–41, the Greeks advanced, pushing the Italians back more than a third of the way into Albania. By then, Mussolini had bolstered his army to twenty-eight divisions, and still they lost ground to the Greek Army's fourteen divisions.[3] The Greeks registered the first defeat of an Axis power in World War II. But it didn't last. On April 13, 1941, Hitler and his Bulgarian allies came to the rescue of the Italians. The Germans launched a general offensive and a brutal, murderous occupation of Greece that lasted until October 1944. The Greek campaign caused Hitler to delay his invasion of Russia, stranding his forces late that year in the steppe's killing winter, a winter of killing in Greece, as well.

Stavros removed the neatly folded letter, inside of which was a two-page clipping from the journal *Archaeology in Greece*. He read the letter first.

15 May 1957, Athens

Dear Stavros,

When will you be back in Greece? I hope to see you soon as I hope your family is healthy and happy. Things in Greece are as they should be, chaotic and frantic, but it wouldn't be Greece otherwise, no? Our dig team had a stroke of luck earlier this spring, and I thought you might enjoy our fleeting notoriety as proclaimed in the enclosed clipping. If only they paid a bonus for clever work. I've been fortunate this semester because my team is all postgraduates. So, hurray, no babysitting and elemental instruction–this is your trowel, this is your trug, this is your brush, this is a grid. That part of my job is numbing. Nevertheless, I always remind myself that I, the glorious Dr. Dimitra, started as an immodest acolyte with a lofty ambition. This is true of all life, no?

Stavros, my darling fiancé, I so look forward to seeing you for other reasons than to allow me to brag. All Greeks brag, but Americans seem to listen when we do. You're a breath of fresh air, and I cherish our love. And that's enough sentiment.

Let me know when you plan to travel. Our current excavation is in Attica, and we shouldn't be too far from Athens, and our apartment.

Love and kisses,

Natasha

Stavros chuckled when he read Dimitra's signature. Natasha was Dimitra's nom de guerre, humorous because its Russian derivation was a play on her former affiliation with the Communist Party of Greece.

Stavros unfolded the clipping and glanced first at the second page, a page of six photographs of artifacts. At the bottom of the page, he read:

> *From the Athenian Agora a portrait head of Julia Domna, a pottery fragment by Myson from the RF Period (229–168 BC), and a stone-curbed repository. Then, from Corinth, a photo of the Diolkos, the trackway of limestone that runs across the narrow Isthmus where the ancients moved ships overland between the Aegean Sea and the Gulf of Corinth, from Salonica the head of a Roman cult statute, and from Lerna a squat piece of Neolithic ware.*

Dimitra had underlined the caption for the stone-curbed repository. When Stavros turned to the first page of the clipping, he read:

> *ATHENS AND ATTICA*
>
> *The Athenian Agora. The excavation of the Agora itself is now virtually completed. But last year a more thorough exploration was made of the north and northwest slopes of the Areopagus, clarifying the lines of several ancient roads, and proving that this was chiefly a residential district throughout ancient times. The earliest structural remains here are of the fifth and fourth centuries BC, but the most imposing belong to two large houses of the Early Christian period (fifth–sixth centuries AD). Finds from wells and other deposits in this area include some interesting pieces of sculpture, notably a portrait of Julia Domna, wife of the Emperor Septimius*

Severus, and some good fragments of early red-figure like the small oinochoe with a komos scene by Myson. A fragment of an opisthographic stele of the fourth century BC preserves regulations governing the selection and duties of officials connected with the Eleusinian mysteries. This came from a well about 50m west of the sanctuary which has been identified as the Eleusinian.

A curious stone-curbed underground repository came to light on the west side of the Panathenaic Way at a point just north of the Altar of Ares. The container was made of an old well-head of poros resting on a massive stone floor and had been sealed with a stopper hewn from a Doric capital of poros. "At some later date in antiquity, the stopper had been violently removed and the contents disturbed. The contents, insofar as may be inferred from a few remnants, comprised objects characteristic of votive deposits of the late seventh century BC: figurines, shields, and pinakes of terracotta, a few scraps of jewelry, a miniature hawk of faience. In the bottom of the pit lay a mass of charred animal bones and the horns of goats. The ceramic evidence and the style of the stonework would indicate that the deposit had been made, sealed and buried early in the fifth century BC. At this date, perhaps, some early sanctuary having been disturbed, characteristic relics of it were laid away in a ceremony that included a sacrifice. The very prominent position leaves no doubt that the establishment was of some importance, but no clue as yet has been found to a closer identification."

Dimitra had circled the second paragraph and, in clear penmanship, written in the right margin, *My team excavated the repository, and I personally, as the exalted team leader, confirmed the identification of goat horns. See, all those years in the university have paid off.*

Stavros chuckled again.

Perhaps it was the ouzo and the tang of lemon that stirred his memories. He was tired and longing for Dimitra. He stretched out on the sofa, fluffed a pillow behind his head, and closed his eyes. His thoughts anchored fifteen years before.

Chapter 4

Early December 1942

In the year since the attack on Pearl Harbor, all the news had been bad. But, on this bright Wednesday morning, the sky was clear, the air bracing, and Missouri Highway 45 to Leavenworth untraveled. The Ford's flathead V-8 engine hummed like a well-oiled sewing machine, and for a moment, Stavros thought about pulling to the roadside and lowering the convertible top. Then he thought better. He feared his arrival at the Command and General Staff College of the United States Army would be conspicuous. His enjoyment of the glorious day and his convertible might register as flippant during these dark days.

The semester was ending, and Stavros had two more lectures on his schedule before the New Year's break. Park College in Parkville, Missouri, where Stavros taught world history, had a collegial relationship with the Command and General Staff College, supplying lecturers and accredited classes. Today's lecture was on the 1571 Battle of Lepanto. The epic sea war in the western Gulf of Corinth involved six hundred rowed-galleys and sixty thousand soldiers. The battle ended the Ottoman's westward expansion into Christendom.

Stavros crossed the Missouri River into Kansas on a converted iron railroad bridge, then turned north into Fort Leavenworth. Leavenworth, the oldest operating Army base west of the Mississippi River, featured well-tended grounds, historic architecture, and a vantage on the Missouri River. Stavros stopped at the guard post, and the sergeant in charge recognized him and his black convertible. After a perfunctory greeting and questioning, Stavros continued north through the campus to Grant Hall.

Stavros loved history, and he loved teaching, but he was ready to join the military. College teachers were exempt from the draft and considered essential civilian employees, but that mattered less to Stavros than serving his country. Stavros was fit, educated, and intelligent. In his early thirties, he was unmarried and unattached. He should be carrying a weapon instead of sitting at a desk drafting curriculum.

Before his lecture began, one student, a lieutenant colonel named Brixton, approached Stavros at the lectern and asked if Stavros had a moment to meet after class. Stavros knew the man to be smart and participatory, but had never spoken with him one-on-one. Stavros agreed and suggested that they stay in the lecture hall after the others left.

When the lecture finished, Stavros talked with stragglers about the finer points of his presentation, and the room cleared but for two soldiers. Brixton waited at the rear of the hall with a young officer in a uniform that Stavros did not recognize. The Command and General Staff College hosted military personnel from many of America's allies.

As Brixton and the other man approached, Stavros walked around the lectern to the front row of seats for introductions. Brixton said, "Professor Theofanis, I'd like you to meet John Tsouderos, son of the Greek prime minister in exile."

Now he understood the different uniform and the Greek flag insignia on the shoulder.

Tsouderos said, "It's an honor to meet you, Professor. Colonel Brixton has many good things to say about you, and it is my pleasure to meet another Greek."

Stavros said, "It is a great honor to meet you, and I hope your family is safe in these difficult times."

Tsouderos replied, "Thank you for your concern. I can't tell you where the family is at this moment because I'm sure you understand it is a security matter, but I must believe they will be safe.

"Tell me, where is your family from?"

Stavros said, "I was born in Colorado, but my mother and father are from Crete."

"Ah, very good! Crete is a fabled part of our beloved country and my place of birth, too. Cretans are fighters, very brave."

Stavros nodded.

"How do you like your teaching position?" asked Tsouderos.

"Frankly, Captain, I love what I do, but I love my country. I believe it is time to relinquish my exemption and see what Uncle Sam can make of me."

The term *Uncle Sam* confused Tsouderos, and Colonel Brixton had to explain it was a personification for the United States and not an actual uncle.

Brixton said, "Professor, I am pleased to hear you speak of military service. The reason I asked to see you is that I'd like to share some confidential information. But, before I go on, this information is confidential within the meaning of national security and cannot be repeated to anyone. Can you honor that request?"

Stavros said, "Certainly."

Brixton went on, "I'm here as a recruiter. Later this spring, the United States Army will activate a Greek Battalion for special operations as needed. I can't be more specific than that. I want you to know that if you are interested, I can see to your bypassing the draft board and have you assigned to the outfit. Does that appeal to you?"

"This battalion will be Greek Americans? And they will serve somewhere that you cannot specify. Have I got that right?" asked Stavros.

"Yes," Brixton said, "But the unit will include Greek nationals as well as Greek Americans. All enlisted men and officers will speak Greek. You won't activate until later this spring.

"You don't have to tell me this minute, and you know how to get in touch. So, we can talk at your next lecture. Will that work?"

"Unnecessary," Stavros said. "Sign me up, Colonel. I'll let Park College know that I'll be leaving this spring."

Both men shook Stavros's hand, and all three left the lecture hall.

That weekend, Stavros drove to St. Louis and told Alex and Marta his plans. He didn't mention the Greek Battalion and said only that he would enter the service under a special sponsorship. Alex understood his son's motivation and did not object, but Marta did. Marta could not for the life of her understand his decision. Why would Stavros give up a good job, his PhD aspirations, his pick of any girl in Missouri? Why would he leave his family to fight in a war from which the government had excused him? She concluded, "I will come to understand the brain of a donkey before I understand men. Donkeys are smarter."

In Washington, DC, on December 12, 1942, Henry L. Stimson, Secretary of War, announced the formation of a Greek Battalion in the Army of the United States.[4] The cat had slipped the bag, and Marta fumed.

Chapter 5

"Put down 'GO' for Greek Orthodox," Stavros suggested.

The corporal stared up at him through thick eyeglasses from behind a long table and replied without emotion, "Your choices are 'C' for Roman Catholic, 'P' for Protestant, 'H' for Hebrew, or nothing."

After a repetition of his suggestion, Stavros left the ID station with a one-off 'GO' stamped on the bottom right of his dog tags. The corporal in charge decided not to waste time on Stavros with hundreds of inductees waiting in line. The US Army Chaplain Corps had no Greek Orthodox priests, anyway.

Stavros underwent military induction at Fort Leavenworth. He had recently taught commissioned officers world history in the scrubbed-clean confines of its hallowed lecture halls and classrooms. Now, the United States Army used the same Fort Leavenworth, this time in facilities not so scrubbed clean, to instruct Stavros in his coming life of service. One station, one corporal, one sergeant, one doctor, one dentist, one barber, one warrant officer at a time. Stavros shuffled along in an assembly line of hundreds of inductees from backgrounds as varied as the colors of the rainbow cast above the steaming showers. He was inoculated, tested for aptitude, tested for lice, tested for intelligence, prodded, poked, and stuck, indoctrinated and sworn. Then, after the US Army had taken his measure, he received two duffle bags for clothes and equipment and instructions to wait for transfer orders. Thanks to Colonel Brixton, that transfer would be to Camp Carson in Colorado Springs for training with the 122nd Infantry Battalion, the Greek Battalion. As of April 8, 1943, Stavros's top-down-convertible days were over, and his grist-to-the-mill days beginning. Fort Leavenworth was doing its job, turning out American soldiers, as it had since 1827.

Four days later, he waited under a giant chandelier and ornate ceiling in the Grand Hall of the vast Beaux Arts Kansas City Union Station. His freshly pressed and starched uniform crackled as he shifted on the wooden bench. Marta and Alex had visited from St. Louis, and Marta brought starch and an iron. She told Stavros that she did not approve of his decision to give up his draft exemption. She insisted that, for all his education and university background, certain barnyard animals were smarter than him. But she insisted he must look his best upon arrival, though she knew not where. He shook his head, thinking of his stepmother fretting over his appearance at age thirty-one. Marta had waged a never-ending battle against the barbarian coding of both Alex and Stavros, and Stavros thought she might have finally won. He wondered if she realized the United States Army would be her long-sought-after ally and carry on the battle from here. He smiled.

"Are you happy to be going?" came a voice from his right. It was a lanky young private Stavros recognized from the barracks at the induction center.

"Why do you ask?" replied Stavros.

"Because you're smiling, and that says you're happy about something," came the response.

"I guess I am . . . happy. But not to be leaving. Although, I suppose that's okay, too. I was thinking about someone in the family. How about you? Are you happy to be leaving?" asked Stavros.

"Yes-siree, I couldn't go another day smelling that Dettol . . . makes me sick to my stomach," said the young man.

Dettol disinfectant hung in the air of the induction center and barracks. The pungent compound of phenol and chlorine with pine oil, isopropyl alcohol, castor oil soap, caramel, and water assaulted the senses. Used to disinfect surfaces of vomit and other contagious agents, the smell lingered long after cleanup. Stavros cringed at the Dettol fetor as much as the tannic residue rafting from new footwear and the tinge of laundry powder and lye emitted by stacks of freshly issued clothing.

"I understand. I hope it's better when you get to where you're going," Stavros replied.

"Fort Lost in the Woods," said the young soldier, using the nickname for Fort Leonard Wood, Missouri. "And how about you?"

"Sorry, classified."

The young soldier nodded. "Well, best of luck, wherever that might be."

The giant arrival–departure board clicked and clacked as its split-flap display updated, and both men looked for their train numbers. Stavros saw the Santa Fe Railroad's *Centennial State* was boarding on Track 12. He gave the young soldier a quick salute, wished him well, and hoisted his duffels in the direction of the boarding platform. He was still smiling.

Stavros checked his duffels with the baggage porter and found a seat in first class. As he settled into the comfortable leather, he saw a neatly folded newspaper in the storage pocket. He pulled it out and saw it was a two-day-old copy of the *New York Daily News*. On page two, the headline in the right column caught his attention: "Spring Move to Open up Turkish Waters Is Seen." The column by Ervin S. Acel was an installment in a rumor and scuttlebutt series called *Something Cooking Here*.

> *Signs indicate that spring may see an Allied campaign to open the Dardanelles and the Bosporus Straits of Turkey for ships of the United Nations. This would create a junction between the Red Army in southern Russia and the Allied forces in North Africa, thus facilitating a coordinated offensive against the Axis in southeast Europe.*
>
> *The Dardanelles and Bosporus connect the Mediterranean and Black Seas. Through them, the*

United Nations could ship supplies direct to the southern regions of Russia, where the greatest battles of the war are being fought.

Something Cooking.

Undoubtedly something is cooking in Turkey and Greece–the two countries that dominate the straits. Turkey controls the shores of the Dardanelles and the Bosporus, while the approach to them from the Mediterranean runs through the Axis-held Greek Islands.

The Allies now have the friendship of Turkey. And they may—after the Axis is outset from Tunisia—as the next step invade Greece and the Greek Islands.

Lately there have been many hints to prepare the Turkish public for some startling move.

The leader of a group of Turkish newspapermen on a visit to India made a statement that the beginning of May is going to be a crucial period for Turkey.

Commenting on this puzzling prophecy, a semiofficial British periodical on the Middle East remarked that "Turkey could open the Dardanelles route for the United Nations." This would give her a decisive role in the war.

Controls Shipping.

According to the British commentator, the Montreux Convention, which has regulated shipping through the straits since 1936, gave Ankara complete control over the vital water route. Ankara can let through not only commercial ships, but even men-of-war— provided the Montreux Treaty is stretched with a little goodwill.

Another sign that the Dardanelles may soon become a war zone is the recent voyage to Egypt of King George of Greece and his premier, Emmanouil Tsouderos. Reportedly the entire Greek government will be transferred from London to Cairo.

King George, nominal commander of all Greek forces, wants to be on hand if fighting starts for the islands of Crete, the Dodecanese, and the Aegean Sea, which guard the approach to the straits.

There are three Greek divisions in the Near East, ready for action—to help in reconquering the Greek Islands or invading Greece proper. One Greek division that fought with Gen. Bernard Montgomery was recently withdrawn from Libya and sent to an unnamed station.

It is also significant that the Greek Navy has been reconstituted. The Greeks, in their heroic resistance against the Italians and Germans, lost twenty destroyers and numerous other small warships. All these have been replaced by British shipyards. In fact, the Greek Navy is stronger today than it was before the Battle of Greece.

The Greek Army and Navy are constantly strengthened by hundreds of adventurous refugees who have fled to Egypt in small boats from the Greek mainland and islands. In addition there are many recruits from the large Greek settlements in Egypt and other Near East countries.

Suited to Invasion.

The German High Command would be greatly handicapped in defending Greece. The little country, farthest away from Germany, is connected to the Nazi war base only by a second-class railway.

The rail line runs from Vienna to Athens via Belgrade and Salonika, through guerrilla-infested Yugoslavia. Most of the time, it is out of service. Many of its great bridges have been dynamited by Greek partisans.

The hilly, roadless Greek countryside is well suited for Allied invasion. The vast shoreline has innumerable bays to hide surprise landings. While the coast is accessible from the sea, the lack of rail service make it is hard to reach from inland towns. German defenders will be up against the same difficulties that the British encountered when they tried to hold the island of Crete in 1941.

The Allies also hope that Turkey will not be satisfied with the anemic role of merely allowing the passage of their ships through the straits. The Turkish President, Ismet Inonu, realizes that he now must choose sides to obtain the goodwill of the probable winners.

Turkey is a border country between Soviet Russia and the British Near East. Her history is a series of losing wars against the Tsars. Against future Russian expansion, she can depend only on Britain. By joining the Allied camp, she would assure Russian goodwill and British support for herself in the postwar world.

Chapter 6

On December 23, 1942, the Joint Chiefs of Staff authorized the OSS to organize Operational Groups (OGs) of highly trained commandos skilled in sabotage and small arms. Commandos would qualify as parachutists, speak the language of their assigned location, and maneuver in small units behind enemy lines.[5] It was a bitter pill the Joint Chiefs swallowed. The friction between the US Army and the upstart OSS, although highly classified, was no secret.

In June 1942, Bill Donovan's Office of the Coordination of Information (COI), became the Office of Strategic Services and employed twenty-three hundred, up from one hundred less than a year before. The new organization fell under the Joint Chiefs of Staff (JCS).

The Joint Chiefs, newly created in February 1942, looked to subsume the OSS under Army Intelligence (G-2). The Joint Chiefs, which undervalued covert action and unorthodox methods, wanted OSS subjugated to traditional armed service discipline and chain of command. They dismissed citizen soldiers and Donovan's authority to commission military ranks from lieutenant to colonel. Army Chief of Staff General George C. Marshall called such appointments "political generals." The problem for the Joint Chiefs was that Donavan and the OSS, although organizationally under the JCS, reported directly to President Roosevelt.

A bureaucratic truce prevailed with intermittent shoulder-bumping and turf battles. The OSS went about the business of unconventional operations and intelligence gathering. By the time Stavros had exfiltrated Greece in September 1944, the OSS employed thirteen thousand men and women, with thousands more passing through its ranks.[6] JCS and OSS politics percolated behind the scenes for the entire war. But when Stavros enlisted, he and his Greek brethren were US Army all the way. That would change.

Chapter 7

The train rolled and swayed over the endless plains of Kansas. The faint *clickety-clack* of the well-maintained right-of-way was a metallic metronome. Stavros read *For Whom the Bell Tolls*, Hemingway's fictional account of an American teacher working with Spanish Republican partisans during the Civil War. Their mission was to blow up an enemy-held bridge. The book was intriguing, historically correct, and fit Stavros's unexpressed expectations. Hollywood planned to release a blockbuster movie starring Gary Cooper and Ingrid Bergman in July.

Stavros was weary from his time in the barracks awaiting transfer orders. Strangers—their noises and smells—and sleeping on less than comfortable bunk beds left him dulled. Revelry didn't bother him. He was an early riser. But his adjustment to communal accommodations had yet to come. After two chapters of Hemingway's assertive prose and stilted Spanish, he fell asleep in the comfortable first-class seat.

When he woke up, still groggy, the train had slowed passing through Kanorado, Kansas. On the outskirts of the small town, Stavros saw a wooden sign held by two fieldstone pillars aside westbound Highway 24 welcoming travelers to Colorado.

The lingering daze of his still proximate nap, unguarded and unprotected, let his thoughts drift to a day in 1929 when he was sixteen years old. It was an unwelcome memory.

On a bitter winter day in St. Louis, Alex told Stavros the story of his mother, Eléni, and how she died. Before that day, Alex and Marta had maintained a fiction to shield Stavros from the harsh and bloody truth. Stavros believed his mother had died in childbirth but had always suspected there was more to the story. His stepbrother and sister were old enough to remember the commotion and fear of those days in Segundo and Pueblo. But they never talked about it.

Alex and Marta never returned to Colorado after the strike following the death of Marta's brother and the murder of Eléni. Marta left for St. Louis in late spring 1914 to be with her family and raise her brother's two children. Alex and Marta married a year and a half later, and Alex moved to St. Louis with Stavros. Stavros's return to Colorado triggered a painful remembrance, one that Stavros had lived with, dodged like a bull in a ring, and tried to avoid for fifteen years.

Alex and Eléni had lived in the strikers' tent colony in Segundo when Stavros was a babe in arms, less than a year old. One cold evening in December, and it was on the anniversary of Eléni's death that Alex recounted the events to Stavros, two invaders raped and murdered Eléni. One was a Greek spy for the Baldwin-Felts Detective Agency and the other an officer in the Colorado National Guard. That night, when Alex was in the hills with a detachment of armed Greeks, Eléni had been stabbed and left to die on the cold wooden floor of the tent. Stavros wailed nearby, swaddled and lying in a pool of his mother's blood. Marta, Eléni's best friend, had been first on the scene.

The Colorado authorities didn't care; their allegiance was to the Rockefeller-owned Colorado Fuel and Iron Company. So Eléni's family in Crete asked a favor of Harry Hantzis, an obligation of honor. Harry, the son of a Nafpaktian assassin, the village lawgiver in Chómori, owed his life to Eléni's brother, who had made the sacrifice on a hillside in Epirus where both were battling Turks in the Balkan War preceding the Colorado strike. Harry traveled to Colorado and, along with Alex and Dimitri, another war veteran and a good friend of both Harry and Alex, tracked Eléni's killers. The trio sought justice through the darkest days of the strike, through the horrendous massacre of women and children and the burning and looting of the Ludlow colony. They settled the score with the Greek spy. But the National Guard tormentor, Linderfelt, escaped. Settling scores with him was an unfinished obligation, one that Stavros mutely pledged when he heard the story.

"You ever been here?" asked a lanky GI who stood in the aisle and steadied himself on the seat back in front of Stavros, swaying with the motion of the train.

Stavros took a second to gather his thoughts after his plunge into the dark remembrance of his mother's murder. He said, "Here? You mean this state?"

The tall GI answered, "*Nai, edó*. Colorado."

Stavros sized up the young Greek. He was not from the Midwest, probably the East Coast. There was a certain swagger about Greeks who grew up in Greek-speaking enclaves with minimal American cultural influence. It was cockiness, a trait seldom seen in their assimilated countrymen to the west.

The tall GI said, "Costa Petropoulos . . . Gus. I saw your name tags on your duffels when you handed them to the porter. Theofanis, is it?"

Stavros smiled. "Right. Good eyes. Stavros, pleased to meet you, Gus."

Gus said, "We Greeks must be on the lookout for other Greeks. You never know when you might need a friend. Where are you headed, Stavros?"

"They say it's classified."

"Sure, me too," intoned Gus with a knowing smile. "So, you ever been here?"

Stavros returned to the earlier question and answered almost truthfully, leaving out that he had been born in Colorado. "Never. Kansas is as far west as I have been, and then only to Leavenworth, and one trip to Lawrence. How about you?"

"Never west of Baltimore until I got on this train. My family is from Queens in New York. Home of the world-famous New York Yankees. Where you from, Stavros?"

Stavros smiled. Gus had just served a soft pitch. This was the East Coast bravado Stavros knew well. Stavros said, "I'm from St. Louis." He watched crestfallen features spread across Gus's boyish face and his shoulders slump.

"Oh boy! Congratulations, I guess," Gus forced his words, and his reticence stifled the conversation. The Yankees had lost the World Series in five games the preceding fall to the St. Louis Cardinals.

"I'll hand it to your Cardinals, brother. That Beazley is a hell of a workhorse. Two complete games, two wins, then he picks off Gordon at second in the ninth and fans the final two for the win. He's your guy, you got to love him."

Stavros nodded and almost felt bad for him, but Gus had walked into a trap of his own making. This was the thing about East Coast Greeks, especially the young ones. Gus was only twenty. They often overextended and made assertions that came back to bite them. Stavros thought Midwestern Greeks more reserved. But Gus was engaging and a fellow Greek, so Stavros suggested they go to the café car for some coffee. Stavros assumed Gus was traveling to Camp Carson.

In the café car, the two GIs sat at a table watching the flat land of eastern Colorado roll by like frames in a boring movie. Colorado was much like Kansas, and so it would remain until near Denver. The African American porter in his white tunic brought the men each a cup and saucer, and poured their cups full from a silver carafe. The coffee's fresh aroma was pleasing. He asked, "Would you gentlemen like anything to eat? Would you like to see menus?"

Stavros and Gus looked at each other and shrugged. Then Stavros said, "Thanks, I think we're okay for now."

The porter nodded and withdrew to take an order for another table.

Stavros started with, "So, Gus, how did you come by your classified assignment, if you can tell me?"

Gus answered with a glint in his eye, "An uncle."

Stavros said, "Is his name Sam?"

"You bet. Sure was," came the sly reply.

Stavros nodded. "Yep, me too."

Gus asked, "So, what were you doing before the Army?"

"Teaching history at Park College just north of Kansas City and living the good life. How about you?" Stavros asked.

"Living in Queens with my mom and pop and two younger sisters, working at the Navy Yard in Brooklyn. I was a steamfitter apprentice and taking classes at Queens College. So, I guess we might have something in common, eh?" Gus asked with a smile.

"What's that?"

"We both gave up exemptions to get to our classified destinations. College teachers are exempt, right?" asked Gus.

Stavros nodded and held up his coffee cup to toast the revelation.

Stavros asked, "What were you studying at Queens College?"

"The girls," Gus replied without hesitation. "But when I had to choose a class, it was engineering or mathematics. After the war, I'll be a marine engineer. It's in the blood, you know, Greeks and sailing and all that history. It's in our blood. My pop has worked at the yard for twenty-five years. He works in the brass shop. It's good pay, and he's lucky, most of his work is inside. The yard can get cold, you know. That north wind whips off the East River down Wallabout Bay and right into the basin like a funnel pointed right at your . . . you know."

Stavros smiled and nodded.

Gus went on, "Everything around you is steel or cast or concrete. Freezing cold to the touch. Anyway, it's good pay and when I left, seventy thousand people were working there. Most of the new hires were women. They put some old guys to shame," Gus confided.

"Will your family be okay with you away?" asked Stavros.

"Oh, sure. Pop's still working, and Mom helps at my uncle's pizza joint, Nick's Pizza on Ascan Avenue in Forest Hills. It's the best pie in the Apple. They use real Greek olive oil, from Kalamata, and fresh mozzarella that Nick makes in the shop. They show the Italians a thing or two."

Gus beamed with pride.

"So, you're second generation?" asked Stavros.

"Yep. Mom and Pop came in the early twenties, had me, and have never been back. They talk about Greece all the time. They miss the family and the food and the holiday celebrations." Gus paused a second and went on, "But you know, my uncle may give me an all-expense-paid visit. The other uncle, not the pizza uncle."

Stavros smiled, then asked, "Where were they from?"

"The island of Milos. Ever heard of it?"

Stavros had heard of it. He remembered it from his studies of the origins of Greece. He recalled a lecture he'd given early in his teaching career:

To imagine the Greeks ever organizing into a nation is to contemplate time and space. In distant days before modern communications and speedy travel, the Greeks wove together a network of like-minded tribes. Sea and land separated them whose distance and difficulty befuddled most other cultures.

The key question is why they did it, not how. The how is simple: leaders, trade, nautical technology, a common religion, and skilled warriors. But why? Why would a disparate, isolated people not acquiesce to external pressure, the Persians, for example? Why did they invest in tenuous unity and come to see themselves as capable of implementing and nourishing democracy, a novelty, untried and untested?

Democracy is a leap, a qualitative step up to a higher level of societal organization and personal commitment. Democracy requires investment and maintenance, education, and critical thought. The leap was monumental.

At Sounion, the Temple of Poseidon rises high above the sea, bidding safe travels and wary minds to countless Greeks today as it has for two and a half millennia. But before Sounion, the land, the southernmost point of Attica, beckoned and released seabound Greeks for centuries before the temple. Sounion knows the price of democracy paid in the trepidation and death of those who plied the waters between the lands. The Greek lands.

Someone had to transport the obsidian from Milos before anyone spoke of 'the Hellenes' and the silver from Attica before the Delian League. Melian obsidian, the volcanic stone skilled craftsmen worked as sharp as glass, traded around the Mediterranean five thousand years before the Bronze Age. It found its way to Crete, Rhodes, and Italy. On the Peloponnesus, in the Franchthi Cave, the precious stone dated to eight thousand years before Christ.

These were his thoughts, but to Gus, he said only, "Sure, obsidian."

Gus cocked his head, "What's that?"

Chapter 8

"The operation the British speak of . . . it is to start in June? What are we to do until then? It is only April. It is the first quarter of a new moon. Our movement is risky. We must take care. But we can maneuver and attack all the same. When the moon is full, we will hide. This everyone knows. This is time that could be our advantage.

"Our raid on the collaborationist *chorofylaki* in Thermos yielded two *Maschinenpistoles* and two dozen ammunition clips. These with the Mauser *Karabiners* we liberated from the gendarmerie improved our weapons, did they not? And we took six pairs of boots. Not the best, but boots all the same. We should press our advantage to liberate more weapons while the iron is in the fire. This I offer in solidarity, Comrade Kapetánios, with due respect to you and the movement."

So spoke one of two lieutenants, the older and taller man with the unruly beard and a mass of long hair. He wore a thick, sky-gray, rough wool cape, the *samaroskouti* of Pindus mountain herdsmen. He looked like a Sarakatsani shepherd, a nomad indistinguishable but for his British combat boots. The shorter and younger man to his left likewise wore the dress of a herdsman but with trimmed hair and a mustache. He shifted and adjusted the sling of his Mauser carbine. His serious stare through his round, wire-framed glasses fell straight upon his commander.

"Comrade, I believe Yiorgos makes a good argument. We are stronger and better armed than before. And perhaps we have the tide running with us. But we are still few. We can muster only fifty capable fighters, eighty if we count the lesser ones, the old and weak-kneed. But I believe our movement suffers from a lack of discipline. We have conducted ourselves like village hunting clubs, as if we were hunting the boar in autumn. We care little about the strategy necessary for victory over the monarcho-fascists. We see the Italians; we ambush the Italians. We see the Germans; we ambush the Germans. Same for the Bulgarians, but here we do not see those devils.

"And now, we fight even among the Greeks. Are not we shooting Royalists in Evros? I know it is far away and, in these mountains, we are unchallenged, but is this smart? If someone wants to kill fascists, let them kill fascists. Then, when all the fascists are dead, we can settle our differences. If that requires more shooting, so be it. It is not something I wish for, but what do I know? We must do first things first and second things next. This is how we win and free our country.

"No, I do not trust the British. Nor do I believe they have Greece in their hearts. Lord Byron was the last Britisher to have that, and now we have his heart, no? The British would have the king return after the Germans. They would have us ruled by a *xenos*! Impossible!

"But the British are a great power with much to share, many weapons, many boots, much ammunition, and a powerful navy. They don't always do the right thing, but now they are friends. They say we fit in their plans, a grand campaign to destroy the fascists. You say they named these plans Operation Harling?" Vasilios shrugged.

"So be it. I feel we have no choice. We should respect their orders. We should stand down until the June operation, as they have asked. The British see the entire chessboard. Us . . . only a few squares. That is what I have to say, Comrade Kapetánios.

"And you, Comrade, what are your thoughts?"

Seated at a small wooden desk just inside the two-room, stone-walled schoolhouse, Dimitra rose and straightened her cartridge belt around her trim waist. She stood tall with exact posture. Her khaki combat blouse was buttoned to the top. It was ironed and creased, unlike her baggy trousers. She had trimmed her long raven hair soon after the Italian invasion when she first went into the mountains to join the resistance, the fighters she had organized in Platanos. Now, her hair reached to her shoulders and when outdoors, she wore an olive drab garrison cap embossed with ΕΛΑΣ but no rank. She picked up the cap from the table where it rested on a tattered map and swatted the palm of her left hand before she spoke. She was a beautiful woman, tall and poised, but would have none of it during this time of war and service. Her dark, intelligent eyes stared first at Yiorgos, the older man, then at Vasilios.

"Comrades, we have been at this now for a year. Together, we have seen death and sacrifice and joy and victory. We have knelt with our fallen fighters and wondered at the fascists' barbarity and cruelty. We have cleared villages of the corpses after the invaders despoiled them. We fight only to free our country and bring the days of equality and shared wealth. We are the ascendant side of history and human progress. I believe we should honor the British call. Here is why.

"Vasilios is correct. We cannot win without a strategy. Since a year ago, this very month, April 1942, EAM-ELAS has led the resistance to the fascist invaders. We are strong and getting stronger, but we act as though each band is conducting its own war. I fear we mistake vendetta for war. We kill fascists, they kill a few of us. Then the fascists kill the villagers and peasants, steal their food, and loot their homes. Then we kill them when we can . . . that is not war, that is revenge and retribution. Perhaps honorable in its own way, but not the path to freedom and revolution for Greece.

"Yiorgos, we have a few new weapons; the machine pistols are a welcome addition, but they fire nine-millimeter rounds, which are puny. These guns are best for close fighting, not something we do in an ambush. For an ambush, we need proper machine guns. We need big, heavy weapons. A *Knochensäge*, a bone saw as the Germans say. But these we must take from the Germans and not the local chorofylaki. Either way, we are not so equipped.

"The British are promising arms and training and supplies, and I believe it is wise to see if they can provide them. It will not hurt our force to stand down for three weeks. During this time, we can deepen our political studies and rest the fighters and animals. Easter falls late this year, on May second. We can make holiday plans, boost morale, and make it part of our stand-down. We will stay vigilant. There is to be no slackening of the sentries and reconnaissance patrols. We should extend the patrols by a kilometer, if possible, but no attacks, unless we're provoked by a heaven-sent opportunity. And, since heaven is a myth, so will be our opportunity."

The two lieutenants nodded their understanding, first Vasilios and then a reluctant Yiorgos.

"Now," continued Dimitra, "Let us discuss the literacy sessions and the political sessions. Shall we do that in the fresh air of this spring morning with our coffees in hand?"

"Better with raki," offered Yiorgos.

"It is still early, and you are on duty, Comrade," warned Dimitra.

"When am I not on duty? Do I know?" pleaded Yiorgos.

Dimitra and Vasilios smiled.

"There was a priest in Thermos," Yiorgos said. "After we dispatched the chorofylaki, he came to me. He said, 'You understand, I pray, it is my duty as a priest to give to the collaborationists the sacred rights of all men. But this does not mean that I am one of them.'

"I told him, 'Go about your business, Father. Today we are not hunting priests.' And then I almost blew his head off with my shotgun when he reached inside his cassock. He stopped with his hand under the garment. 'Nothing to worry, Comrade, I have a gift.' And he pulled from his vestment an *askós oínou* and handed the wineskin to me.

"I don't trust any priest. So, I demanded, 'What is it?' He said, 'Raki, among the finest in Greece. You will enjoy the anise. It is refined, better than the Turkish drink.'

"Still, I did not trust the priest. I said, 'First, you drink.' And he leveraged the cork from the bladder, took a swallow, and I watched the prominence on his neck to see he was not pretending. Then he pursed his lips, as I'm sure it burned going to his stomach. I then took a drink, but not enough to fade my judgment, Comrade Kapetánios, and it was good. The priest was right. The anise was distinct and refreshing. I accepted the gift on behalf of the movement, and the priest went about his duties."

"Perhaps later in the evening, Comrade, you might share this spoil with *the movement*, if any remains from your verification of the product," Dimitra chided.

To this, Yiorgos did not answer.

Rolling the map tight into a precise cylinder, Dimitra looked up at Yiorgos and shook her head. Then, holding the map like a baton, she motioned her lieutenants out of the schoolhouse. Together, the three walked along the paved stone road through the village of Chómori to the plateia.

Chapter 9

"Oh, they're healthy. You betcha. But I worry about 'em when they get over there . . . in Asia, Burma, India. They can get surra. It's a disease spread by horseflies. It can waste 'em so bad, they have to put 'em down. But they leave here healthy . . . raring to go," beamed the lanky staff sergeant, missing an incisor. Sergeant Miles was a Missouri mule man and proud of it. The 604th and 605th Field Artillery battalions broke and trained and cared for the animals. Miles was with the 604th.

The friendly sergeant responded to a compliment from Stavros, who stopped at the paddock fence to look over the mule barns on his way to Denver for Orthodox Easter. The Greek Battalion's forty-eight-hour leave was the first since his arrival at Camp Carson. They were off until reveille on Easter morning. Stavros had stopped on his way to the camp depot to join his Company B comrades. He looked sharp in polished shoes and his pressed field uniform.

"They ship out around a thousand to twelve hundred pounds. They can carry about one-third of their weight. We recommend keeping packs to a hundred eighty pounds. The big ones, the stout boys, we use them for the Howzers. It takes seven mules for a Howzer. The barrel alone weighs two hundred forty pounds. And the wranglers are special, too. They have to be at least six feet tall to load the custom packs. Each part of a seventy-five-millimeter cannon has a special attachment on the pack saddle designed for a certain mule. Gotta keep things balanced, or you'll hurt the mules and wear them out. We train 'em for a particular gait, too. Working with mules is as much science as art. They're like soldiers . . . only you can't order them to do things. You gotta train 'em. They gotta learn to work together as a team. And you gotta feed 'em right."

"What's he doing over there?" Stavros nodded to an older man in the near corral wearing a tattered *feldgrau* Afrika Korps tunic with the large white letters 'PW' stenciled on the back. The man was examining a mule's gums while the animal fretted, its ears laid back.

"That old guy is a POW who got captured in Libya. He's a veterinarian. Our guys checked him out. He's the real deal. He helps around here and seems to love it. He knows his stuff, and his English is good. He tended Rommel's camels and horses in North Africa.[7] He warned us about surra. It all checked out," answered the sergeant.

"Is anybody guarding him?" asked Stavros.

"I guess I am," said the sergeant. "But he ain't going anywhere. He's got it good here . . . clean barracks, good food, an interesting job. Heck, he makes eighty cents a day wages plus his officer's allowance. I think that's thirty or forty dollars a month.[8] Where's he gonna go? The mountains are to the west, and the plains are to the east. I guess he could try to cross into Mexico, but that's six hundred miles.

"I'm not kidding about the food. The Germans have their own mess and cooks. We hand over the produce, eggs, and meat, and they figure out what to do with it. They make some of the best food in camp.

"We're not supposed to fraternize with prisoners, but how you gonna talk to the guy about the mules? He cares about 'em, and so do we. We keep things friendly but always at arm's length.

"We sent about three hundred Germans up to Camp Hale at Leadville, the troublemakers, Rommel's brownshirt riffraff. They got 'em under tight security up there. Most POWs at Carson are tame. Still best to keep an eye on 'em."

Stavros leaned against the three-rail, unpainted wooden fence that surrounded and intersected the seven white wooden mule barns and their paddocks. The dust kicked up by the animals hung low on their legs and mixed with the smell of manure. But the bright spring day encouraged conversation. Stavros scanned the area, about the size of two football fields, and tried to estimate the number of animals. The long ears of the mules waved like flags above the mass of brown bodies. Then he spotted one animal in the second paddock that stood out. It was silvery white and larger than the rest. Stavros asked, "What's the story with the white one?"

The sergeant smiled. "That's Hamilton T. Bone. We just call him Hambone. He's a Missouri product. We've taught him to steeple. He competes with the horses. Beats 'em, too. He's got one hell of an arc. It's like he's showing off. He's smarter than your average mule. You gotta watch him. He knows how to unlock the paddock gate. He never runs off. He stays in camp and struts like he's brass. He's a character. His primary assignment is to ride the first sergeant of Fourth Field Artillery anywhere he wants to go. Hambone's got a real fan club around here."

Halfway through the sergeant's description of Hambone, the animal raised his head toward the two men, and his nearest ear rotated in their direction.

"How long have they been working mules here at Camp Carson?" asked Stavros.

"The first batch came from Nebraska in July 1942. We get a lot from Missouri, too, some from Tennessee," replied the sergeant.

"It looks like a couple thousand, at least. How many do you have?" asked Stavros.

The sergeant shook his head. "That's classified."

"Right," answered Stavros.

The two men stood and looked over the mulling mass for another minute, and Stavros said, "Well, I appreciate your time, Sergeant. Best of luck with your charges . . . men or mules."

The sergeant said, "Thanks, soldier. I see you're with the Hundred Twenty-Second. That's the Greeks, right?"

Stavros nodded.

"The word in camp is that you boys are a tough bunch. I guess you'll need to be when you get to wherever you're going. I bet you'll be handling some mules when you get there.

"Here's the thing about mules. They want to please you, but they gotta trust you. Never try to beat a mule into doing something. A mule will size up a situation. He'll be cautious and weigh the odds. If he trusts you, he'll perform. Him being cautious is not stubbornness, it's him sizing things up and thinking it over. A horse will react and bolt. But a mule . . . give him time. Then ask him nicely."

Stavros nodded. "Good to know. Thanks for the advice, Sergeant."

Camp Carson, six miles south of Colorado Springs and five miles east of Cheyenne Mountain, began with 60,000 acres in 1941 and grew from there. The first construction program employed 11,500 workers and raised 1,650 buildings, including 438 barracks, 181 mess halls, and 18 hospitals to support 30,000 to 40,000 troops. Another 375 buildings went up by the end of 1942. In 1943, when Stavros arrived, the post included a Prisoner of War camp for 3,000 POWs that expanded to 9,000, mainly Germans.[9] By the time Stavros left in late 1943, 43,000 military personnel called it home, and 104,165 troops trained there during the war.

Camp Carson activated 125 units during the war, including the Greek Battalion and an Italian ordnance company. But the camp's core specialty was mountain warfare, and it was home to the 10th, 71st, and 104th Mountain Infantry Divisions. At Camp Carson, you bunked at 6,000 feet and trained up from there. Cheyenne Mountain, the nearest summit, was 9,500 feet. Pike's Peak, at 14,000 feet, was fifteen miles northwest as the crow flies. Or, in the Rockies, an eagle.

Stavros and Gus were the only two soldiers to get off the train when it reached Denver's Union Station. From there, they boarded a local passenger service to Colorado Springs. A corporal in a Jeep drove them eight miles to the Headquarters Company of the 122nd Infantry Battalion. Both men drew a Company B assignment and shared a barracks. That was fine with both soldiers. Neither man knew anyone in the battalion, and they had begun an easy friendship from the train.

With their duffels and gear over their shoulders, the two men reported to a tidy white wooden barracks of seventy-four men. Each precisely spaced bunk looked sharp with bedrolls at the feet, fluffed white pillows, and sheets turned down by one foot over olive-green army blankets. There were footlockers at the end of the beds jutting into the walkway down the center of the barracks. A cast-and-nickel wood stove stood at the far end of the building, and its metal flu rose straight through the center of the roof. Bare electric light bulbs hung above the walkway on every third rafter tie. The building smelled of other men, disinfectant, and fresh wooden construction.

It was late afternoon when Stavros met two platoons who had finished training early. Most were Greek nationals, with Greek American soldiers in the minority. The Greek nationals were merchant marine sailors and Greek Army veterans who had fled to Egypt after the German occupation. Most were older than the GIs, many in their thirties, like Stavros.

That evening, in the mess with the full company, Stavros composed a mental picture of his future. Turning to the soldier sitting next to him on the wooden bench, he asked, "How do you get the Greek food, the olives, feta, and oregano?"

The soldier, a rough but friendly *mangas* from Piraeus, replied in Greek, "We trade rations with other units. Some we buy in Denver. Some we *find*. What do I know? On Sundays, we have avgolemono soup and a nice salad. We bake our own bread. We're Greeks, what do you expect?" Then he returned to cutting his pork chop, holding his knife and fork in the European manner.

When they checked in at Camp Carson, Gus and Stavros were excused from physical training for three days to acclimatize to the altitude. Stavros, in good physical condition, thought he should begin at once. The next morning, after reveille at 0430 hours, the demanding routine began.

Calisthenics is a Greek word, a combination of *kallos*, meaning beauty, and *sthenos*, meaning strength. In 480 BCE, Herodotus used the word to describe the Spartan warriors' training before their battle with the Persians at Thermopylae.[10] Stavros drew upon the historian's writing for his mental images and fascinations. Now the unvarnished truth of experience was upon him.

At Park College, Stavros ran, and played basketball, baseball, and sometimes football. He was always competitive. He was tall, lean, and well-fed. At 0500 hours and six thousand feet, with the sun still below the horizon, Company B formed up on a brisk April morning. Stavros breathed harder than expected doing jumping-jacks. Then the sit-ups, push-ups, mule-kicks, toe-touches, squats, lunges, and pull-ups taxed him further. When the all-business drill sergeant barked the order to fall in and run in their heavy combat boots, he was winded. His morning's effort was not graceful or exemplary. But by 0600 hours, he had recovered enough to find humor in the breakfast mess hall banter.

At 0630 hours, they marched and drilled and ran. Lunch was at noon, and by 1230 hours, they were again marching and drilling. Then they broke into smaller groups for specialized instruction. The soldiers practiced cleaning and loading and fieldstripping and reassembling their weapons. Later in the afternoon, on the firing range, they took the measure of their brand-new M1 Garand rifles, the smaller M1 Carbine, and their Colt .45 M1911 standard-issue sidearms. After familiarization with these weapons, Company B shouldered the M1918 Browning Automatic Rifle (BAR) and the Thompson submachine gun. These were tactical weapons. The Thompson, with its smaller sidearm-caliber ammo, was best for close-quarters combat. The BAR was best used to establish a broad field of fire, allowing soldiers armed with standard weapons to maneuver. At sixteen pounds plus ammo, it was awkward. But the BAR had great range and could lay down fire equal to five soldiers carrying M1s.

There was special training in detecting ambushes and disarming booby traps, reading maps and compasses, and using chemical warfare gear. They crawled over an uneven, pockmarked field under razor wire with live machine-gun rounds inches above their butts. They negotiated obstacle courses, working as teams. They practiced throwing live grenades and disarming antipersonnel mines. When the excitement ended, they dug foxholes and fought boredom on guard duty. Every evening after dinner at 1700 hours, their drill sergeant addressed the group about camp policies and performance deficiencies. Then everyone stood for mail call.

At 2000 hours, they had personal time. The men read their mail or a book, wrote letters home, did laundry, showered, cleaned their lockers, and cleaned the barracks. At 2100 hours, it was lights out. Stavros would look back on these first two weeks of training as easy.

Stavros arrived at Camp Carson on April 12. Major Peter Demosthenes Clainos summoned him to the Battalion HQ a week later. Stavros had heard the barracks lore about the major. Clainos was the first Greek-born American to graduate from the US Military Academy at West Point, class of 1933. Born in Sparta, his demanding character and no-nonsense countenance earned him respect.

The commander was thirty-six years old. Stavros had expected an older man. Clainos was handsome and fit, with cropped dark hair. His creased uniform was crisp and his hair trim and parted. He wore the golden oak leaf of a major rank on the right collar of his olive-green blouse and the crossed rifles of the infantry on his left. With his tie tucked under his second button and his deep-set brown eyes, he presented an intelligent and disciplined figure.

Clainos continued to note a document on his desk when Stavros entered his office. Stavros took two steps inside the room and stood at attention. After a minute, the major looked up. "At ease, soldier."

Stavros assumed a more relaxed posture and remained standing.

After another minute of writing, the major put away the document and looked at Stavros.

"Theofanis, Stavros Alexis. Born in Trinidad, Colorado, in 1912. Graduated high school in Saint Louis, Missouri, then graduated with honors from Park College earning a Bachelor of Arts, then a Master of Arts degrees in World History. Do I have that right, soldier?"

"Yes, sir," replied Stavros, keeping his eyes straight ahead.

"You have lectured United States Army officers in accredited college courses at the General Staff College, Fort Leavenworth, Kansas. There you came to the attention of a lieutenant colonel serving under Major General George Veazey Strong, US Army Deputy Chief of Staff for Intelligence, G-2. The lieutenant colonel recruited you into the Hundred Twenty-Second Infantry Combat Battalion, so named in honor of a hundred twenty-two years of Greek independence. Is that right?" continued the major.

"Yes, sir," offered Stavros.

"You speak modern Italian and Greek and scored 141 on the Army General Classification Test. That score, Professor Theofanis, elevates you into Class I with only seven percent of all other US Army personnel. That score would have you on your way to the Air Corps and Officer Candidate School. Instead, you are an enlisted man in the Hundred Twenty-Second Infantry Combat Battalion, so named for a hundred twenty-two years of

Greek independence. This is because you want to fight to free Greece of its fascist invaders. Have I got that right?" followed the rhetorical query.

"Yes, sir," answered Stavros.

"Now, soldier, I know that *Stavros Alexis* translates to *the defender of the cross*, an honorable avocation and your God-given prerogative."

The major looked at the Greek flag on his desk with its nine horizontal blue-and-white stripes and a white cross on a blue field in the canton.

"But the United States Army also has a prerogative, if not God-given, enforceable under the constitution of this great land. That prerogative is to put intelligent and accomplished recruits into jobs where they can best serve their country. Do I make myself clear?"

Not waiting for an answer, Major Clainos continued.

"Rather than eating dehydrated mutton on a mountain crag, dodging Germans, Italians, and Bulgarians who will shoot you on sight, might you rather apply for ninety-day-wonder officer training? From that, you will emerge a second lieutenant with the world as your oyster?"

Again, not waiting for an answer, Major Clainos went on.

"Speak freely, Mr. Theofanis."

"Yes, sir," answered Stavros, forming a succinct response.

"Sir, I have a Greek story like all others in the Hundred Twenty-Second. I left a deferred job to fight for Greece. I believe this battalion, so named for a hundred twenty-two years of Greek independence, will give me the best opportunity to do that. If I were to enter the Officer Candidate School and complete the program, I would ship to anywhere the Army needs a second lieutenant. I would rather fight for Greece with Greeks, if possible, sir."

Major Clainos nodded and glanced at the topological wall map to the right of his desk. He said, "We'll celebrate Easter in a few days. After that, you and your company will come to respect that map."

Stavros didn't grasp the implication.

The major rose from behind his desk. "Dismissed."

Major Clainos was proud of the Greek Battalion. He was proud of his Greek heritage and wanted the 122nd to be an example to all America of the courage and character of its Greek immigrant citizens. Greeks in America had not always fared well in the eyes of the native-born population. Now, with the Greek defeat of the Italians, the first defeat of any Axis power, and the unwavering resistance of the Greek people, America's press and public favored the Greeks.

But there were worries, whispers from the War Department. Whispers from staff and officers, people with reliable information concerning zones of influence and the mindset of the Big Three: Churchill, Stalin, and Roosevelt. Clainos weighed all elements and prospects for the 122nd as he prodded his men to the highest levels of physical and mental readiness.

His training routine was relentless, but he hiked and ran every step alongside his men. He sorted his recruits, weeding out the slackers, and transferring men who couldn't keep up. The result was a tight-knit, agile unit that looked as good on the parade ground as they did on mountain trails.

Less than two weeks after the major's interview with Stavros, on April 24, 1943, the Greek Battalion formed up on the Camp Carson parade grounds.[11] There they previewed a new "secret" weapon called the bazooka and marched in review as the camp orchestra played "The Army Goes Rolling Along." President Franklin D. Roosevelt waved his hat from the reviewing stand. Army Chief of Staff General George C. Marshall stood erect and attentive alongside Major Clainos. At the head of the column, rising above the dust kicked by their syncopated footfalls, an American flag flew to the right, and a

Greek flag to the left. Flanked on either side by riflemen, it was the first and only time a foreign flag had flown next to the Army's Stars and Stripes on American soil.[12]

Chapter 10

With his left sleeve pinned at the shoulder of his tunic, the former Abwehrkommando held a magnifying glass in his right hand and squinted through a rimmed monocle. He struggled to read a damp piece of paper under a bright desk lamp. He copied its words to a form in front of him on his desk. In stilted German, he wrote:

They number one thousand men organized into a battalion. They are Greeks of American birth and Greeks from Europe. Their commander, Clainos, is a Greek and a graduate of the American Military Academy. He is a major in rank. They train for fighting in the mountains and exhibit esprit de corps. [13]

The German Secret Intelligence Service, the Abwehr, filed and cross-filed this report from Camp Carson via secret message. The report was filed by date, source, POW Camp, service noted, and country of interest, in this case, Greece. These and a half a dozen other categories were standard protocol in the inflexible bureaucracy.

The personal letter with the secret message was from a captured homesick lieutenant to his abiding sweetheart in Berlin. Written on standard POW stationary, and screened by American censors the Red Cross delivered it to *die junge frau*, Renate. Its sentiments were predictable. I love you. I miss you. How is the family? Are you staying true?

Renate was an actual person at a proper address in Berlin. So was her uncle, an *oberstleutnant* working for Vice Admiral Wilhelm Canaris, chief of Abwehr. After his encounter with the Polish Armia Krajowa bomb and months of rehabilitation, Abwehr reassigned the disabled lieutenant colonel to Department I-Ht, technical army intelligence.

The POW method of secret writing was not sophisticated, and the Americans would catch on. But at the end of April 1943, they were still in the dark. The sender needed only water, two pieces of paper, a not-too-sharp pencil, a hard writing surface, and patience. He soaked the first piece of paper in water, then placed it on a hard writing surface, a mirror, smooth metal, glass, anything hard and smooth. Then he placed the dry paper on top of the soaked sheet and wrote his secret message. He pressed lightly to avoid poking through the damp top sheet and leaving a mark on the secret sheet.

Then, the secret sheet was dried to become stationary for an innocent, homesick, lovelorn missive. Once in the hands of the Abwehr and rehydrated, the secret message was deciphered, copied, and filed.

After the Americans uncovered the undercover message technique, they designed a special paper that would turn green when dampened. The Germans modified their indented message technique and found that by writing on a piece of waxed paper over the safety paper, they could still conceal their reports. In 1945, the Americans figured out the wax paper trick and began developing yet another fool-proof stationary. By then, the war in Europe was ending, and no number of secret communiqués could change Germany's fate.

Chapter 11

"It is the pine that flavors the lamb and gives the ancient taste. This is known to everyone. A metal *ovelos* makes the meat taste like a gun barrel," insisted the grizzled sage squatted next to the younger man.

"Bah," intoned the younger man. "You have drunk too much *tsipouro*. You could not taste the difference between lamb and pigeon, Christian. The metal ovelos you make only one time. The pine, every year. Metal is less work. Easter is a day of celebration, not work. Pine? Impossible!"

It was May 2, 1943, Easter in the Nafpaktian Mountains. The eight men tending the barbeque spit were never far from skins of tsipouro. The brandy energized their rapid rotation and lively conversation. They engaged in dialogue as old as Christ. Older still if considered in the category of Greeks discussing the best way to prepare food. In contention this chilly morning was the rod that skewered the lamb as it spun over glowing coals. The traditional ovelos was a straight. six-foot branch of pine bough with an S-shaped branch bound to the end with leather forming a handle. The new ovelos was a metal rod with its handle bent into its end, one piece of steel, tidy and durable. The lamb would take three hours cooked on either ovelos, so teams of spinners spelled each other. *Kokoretsi*, the smaller rotisserie of organ meat wrapped with intestine, cooked more quickly. Kokoretsi was the domain of women and previewed the meal to come.

The villagers of Chómori attended Mass at midnight, spread the light of Christ's resurrection in the darkened church, then returned to their homes. They broke the Great Lent fast with *mayiritsa*, an egg-lemon soup made from the intestine and offal of the sacrificial lambs. They toasted with wine, then played *tsougrisma*, exclaiming *"Christos Anesti!"* (Christ has risen!) and *"Alithos Anesti!"* (Indeed he has risen!). The tapping of hard-boiled, okra-tinted eggs, *kokkina avga*, assigned good fortune for the coming year. The holder of the final uncracked egg won the blessing. Most villagers were asleep by two in the morning, then the men were up at seven to start the coals in the spit and ready the lambs and kokoretsi. They spun the ovelos, drank tsipouro, talked and argued and chided one another for failings, both real and imagined.

Dimitra and her lieutenants stood in field dress on the road in front of the spit, unarmed but with their weapons near at hand. Hung behind them on the railing of the raised spit was a blue flag with a white cross and the letters ΕΛΑΣ (ELAS) centered in the cross. They exchanged Christian acknowledgments with the villagers, the men in rough clothing and worn shoes and the women barefoot in long black dresses. The villagers talked, fingered worry beads, and some spelled the men turning the ovelos. They nodded to Dimitra and her lieutenants. Dimitra met their gaze, but her male lieutenants looked on with practiced indifference.

ELAS, the Greek People's Liberation Army, was the leading resistance force in the Nafpaktian Mountains and in Greece. ELAS had supplied the four lambs sizzling on the spit, the product of a minor mission, more akin to extortion than banditry. Dimitra's lieutenant Yiorgos and a detachment of andartes had visited a well-off farmer on the road to Nafpaktos. The farmer supported George II, King of Greece, in exile. Yiorgos, from the village of Kato Dafni on the fertile banks of the Mornos River, knew the farmer and his wealthy family from before the days of occupation. Although he presented himself as a hill-bound shepherd in need of grooming, Yiorgos was the educated son of a well-off storekeeper, respected winemaker, and keeper of bees. Yiorgos and the farmer disagreed on politics, but their families remained friendly. Yiorgos had never denounced the farmer as a monarcho-fascist, an act that would have seen his property confiscated then him tied to a post and shot. The farmer, opposed to the Nazis and Italians, and especially the Bulgarians, tempered his support for the monarchy and tithed to ELAS. The lambs were tithing.

Tsipouro was a distilled spirit derived from the fermentation of the pomace residue in wine presses and sometimes flavored with anise. It was a potent, special occasion drink. Chómori's product was the classic variant, straight without anise.

Dimitra was also a local product. The striking young woman had grown up only a few miles from Chómori in the municipality of Platanos. Her village of eight hundred residents was large by Nafpaktian standards and served as the repository for official records in Aetolia-Acarnania, Western Greece. Her father oversaw the record-keeping, and her mother, Eva, a modern Greek woman raised in cosmopolitan Thessaloniki, taught stringed instruments to music students at the school. She made certain Dimitra received an excellent education and stood for the entrance exams at Aristotle University of Thessaloniki. Dimitra had been in her second year of graduate archaeology studies when war clouds gathered over Western Greece in the summer of 1940. She stayed in Platanos that fall to help with the call-up of the Greek Army. She recruited and mobilized irregular forces, the *andartiko*, who fought alongside the Hellenic infantry.

She was a gifted organizer and a physical presence among the male masses. The Greeks worshipped Athena as the exemplar warrior and built to her a temple and a mythology that stands to this day. So the men shrugged. If a woman could lead them, could organize them, could inspire them, then so be it. She built her credibility in the early days, and it earned her the elected position of *kapetánios*, the leader of the EAM-ELAS unit in her realm of the Nafpaktian Mountains.

She was a member of the Communist Party of Greece, KKE. She believed Greece must undergo a revolution to throw off oppression. She detested foreign kings and quisling rule of any sort—Italians, Nazis, Turks, and all historical villains that ravaged her country. She believed in sexual equality as well as equality between rich and poor. She was less enamored of the Soviet Union than many of her KKE comrades. But that disagreement could wait. Now was the war of liberation, and time for cultivating allies whenever and wherever possible. She honored the official call of the EAM, the Greek National Liberation Front, that required only that members resist the Axis invaders and support a postwar regime based on the will of the people as expressed in free elections.[14]

She knew that Greece, especially in its remote mountains, was backward, poor, and desperate. People lived lives of burden and poverty in a hand-to-mouth existence, as they had for centuries. In large cities, things were different. There, women had rights and educated people enjoyed an elevated culture. But, in the mountains, humans rose barely above the animals. The daily routine was stultifying. Material provisions were scant and subject to brigands or confiscation by the Italians and Germans. A Greek of the mountains was worth only as much as their flock of goats, their patch of potatoes, their dried herbs. If they were lucky, they lived in a stone-and-mortar hovel warmed by wood. Others sheltered in caves, burned dung, and survived on scraps and charity.

And the women. The women were beasts of burden. The men used women for transport when they feared injuring the mules. This was the darkness that Greece birthed alongside the illumination of its endless contributions to science, politics, philosophy, and human development.

Dimitra, a raven-haired living statue, was *in* this mountain world, but not *of* it. She found nothing in these hills and ravines romantic, folkloric, or redeemable. She was free to dream and organize and excel. She made herself that way, and she would make Greece in her image one day. Enlightenment required education and effort, and if that came at the end of a rifle barrel, then it was progress. Three years of fighting fascists, documenting atrocities, burying fallen comrades, and marshaling ill-equipped forces had distilled her theory of motivation. Hers was the tsipouro of leadership.

Determined, focused, and intelligent, Dimitra was perhaps too cerebral, too enlightened for the primal decisions she faced. She foresaw her weakness and chose her lieutenants accordingly.

ELAS, the military wing of the resistance movement EAM, included communists and other parties and operated as a top-down triad. Local ELAS fighters elected their commander, their kapetánios. ELAS allowed all fighters to vote, including women.[15] Dimitra, kapetánios, had served since the birth of ELAS in February 1942. Grizzly Yiorgos was the *stratiotikós* or military specialist. He was thirty-six years old and a *tagmatarkhis* or battalion commander in the Greek Army. He was not a communist but was affiliated with the Popular Democratic Union (ELD). Yiorgos was one of fifteen hundred commissioned officers, sixteen generals and thirty-four colonels working within EAM-ELAS (Greek National Liberation Front - People's Liberation Army).[16]

Teacherly Vasilios, thin, bespeckled and doctrinaire, was twenty-three years old and served as *politikós*, political leader and representative of EAM.

The lambs finished roasting by noon. The women carved and chopped the crispy carcasses and placed chunks of meat and bones in large wooden bowls. The heads remained intact and their delicacies enjoyed in situ. Women handed out choice pieces of charred fat as rewards to the spit attendees. Then the women carried the bowls up the hill to the open deck of the taverna for the feast. There, with potatoes, *horta*, boiled greens, and local table wine, the villagers ate and talked and laughed through the afternoon.

After the dancing and the shotguns and the reenactment of the Turkomachia, as the sun touched the western peaks, all sat transfixed. They listened with their hearts to the mournful pitch of the village *klarinetístas*, the aged and blind Konstantinos. His *klarino* or clarinet, the favored musical instrument in these mountains so near Epirus, formed at its worn ligature and released through its chipped and cracked bell a sad lament. Freed from the instrument, his staccato refrain sailed across the valley, over the creeks and crevasses, and echoed off the neighboring rises. His was the music of a patient Greece, a timeless Greece, and the theme of all existence.

Chapter 12

"The weekend was heaven, and today is hell," observed Gus. Stavros and Gus were marching side by side humping seventy-pound packs and eleven-pound M1s slung over their shoulders. Saturday, they had enjoyed the company of coquettish Greek girls at the Assumption of the Theotokos Cathedral resurrection service in Denver. A dose of religion, a dose of flirtation, and a dose of admiration had seen the men return to camp in high spirits. Sunday, the battalion made an undemanding march to an off-camp picnic area where they were greeted by Greek families from Denver and Colorado Springs. Their gracious hosts brought a priest and their daughters and barbequed twenty lambs. After the Paschal vespers service, the Greek women uncovered traditional holiday dishes on picnic tables, and the well-behaved GIs descended, fighting to contain the ravenous hyaenas within.

But the weekend was over. It was Monday, May 3, 1943. They were three miles into their first of many marches up Cheyenne Mountain. Major Clainos marched at the head of the column. He never ordered his men to do anything he couldn't. This earned him the respectful nickname *Leonidas of Thermopylae* and more than a few curses. Leonidas was a master of the march, but his men had yet to prove themselves.

Company B had orders to summit the mountain. They were to lunch on the grounds of a shuttered luxury resort, the Cheyenne Lodge, then return to Camp Carson, over thirty steep miles. They left camp at 0600 hours on dirt pathways through the tree line, and Gus made his comment to Stavros within the first mile. They returned to their barracks at 2000 hours, worn and humbled, and performed close-order drills until Clainos deemed them sharp enough to release.

During their thirty-minute lunch at the summit, Gus relived the weekend's events for Stavros. Looking to the east over the vast plains, he said, "You know, New York blacks out at night, everything's doused. It makes it harder for the U-boats to target the city. It was exciting to see the neon and Denver all lit up, ready to party. It felt like a big city.

"Sleeping in that bus's luggage rack on the trip back to camp was smart. I got two hours of solid shuteye. That's the way to travel, brother."

Stavros replied, "You needed the sleep because you exhausted yourself charming the ladies."

"Hey, it worked, didn't it? I got her name and number, right? I'll call the next time we get some leave. She's a cutie," Gus smiled.

"Her father had his eye on you. You didn't charm *him*," answered Stavros.

"Sure, but I'll win him over. I'm a red-blooded American Greek GI. What's not to love?"

Stavros shook his head.

They returned to camp by paved roads so ambulances could follow. Their gurneys were full by the end of the march.

Chapter 13

The skiff *Ana* bobbed on the rolling Gulf of Cádiz under an overcast sky, rendering Jose's job difficult. The onshore breeze and the rising sun made spotting sardines, fathoms below, a search for watery ghosts. Jose Antonio Rey Marias was the best at his work in Punta Umbria on the southwestern coast of Andalusia, Spain. But today, the shimmering shapes were undetectable. *La Calina*, a fishing boat with an antsy crew ready to set their horseshoe net, awaited Jose's signal. They had barely wet an oar, caching only a few anchovies and bream for their early morning outing. On this, the last day of April, with the weather warming and spring teasing, the sardine run was ending. The disappointed crew had hoped for a heavy haul and a quick return to port to sell their catch and recount their ventures in the café. But while the fishing was dreary, their morning would soon be memorable, and talk of it was part of the plan, part of Operation Mincemeat.[17]

Jose thought he saw a dead porpoise, but as he rowed near, his keen eyes defined the lump as a man's body. The corpse floated face down and wore a yellow life vest. The skin of the face had peeled, and the body gave off a stomach-turning stench. Jose was sick and tried not to breathe. He called to the *La Calina,* and when it pulled abeam, he told the crew to drop a line and haul the body onboard. But they wanted nothing to do with it.

Jose grabbed the collar of the life vest and drew the torso onto the stern of his small boat, leaving the legs dragging in the water. Then he rowed to shore. He dragged the tall man, dressed in a khaki tunic and a trench coat, to a sandy dune and into the shade of a pine tree. A black leather briefcase dragged along with the body chained to its waist. A Roman Catholic cross hung around its neck.

Jose told a snooping teenager to summon the Spanish Defense Unit drilling on the beach earlier that morning and now enjoying a siesta. The unit's officer posted two sentries and sent a messenger to summon his commander, unwittingly forging the first deception in an elaborate chain.

The British were good at deception. This ruse, first imagined in Room 13 of the Admiralty by Charles Cholmondeley, a British Intelligence officer, arose from a memo circulated in 1939. Attributed to Rear Admiral John Godfrey, the Director of Naval Intelligence, the memo was likely drafted by his Lieutenant Commander Ian Fleming. Charles Cholmondeley and Captain Ewen Montagu, a naval intelligence officer, planned Mincemeat with meticulous care and attention to detail. It worked. The corpse carried persuasive documents, including a personal letter from Lieutenant General Sir Archibald Nye to General Sir Harold Alexander. Nye worried the Germans were: *reinforcing and strengthening their defenses in Greece and Crete, and CIGS (Chief of the Imperial General Staff) felt that our forces for the assault were insufficient.*

The informal letter listed the coming Allied assaults on Cape Araxos and Kalamata. The deception percolated through the Spanish authorities into the Abwehr. It then continued up the chain of command to the desk of Adolf Hitler. Hitler ordered reinforcements to Greece to counter the coming Allied invasion. The Balkans were Hitler's preoccupation, with their indispensable oil, wheat, corn, timber, tobacco, cotton, currants, process fruits, wool, hides, copper, bauxite, iron ore, chrome, and labor force.

In May, Hitler told Mussolini to reinforce Sardinia and Corsica, with no mention of Sicily. The German high command ordered its prized 1st Panzer Division transferred from France to Thessaloniki. Then two more panzer divisions moved to the Balkans from the Eastern Front, and torpedo boats moved from Sicily to the Greek Islands. At the end of June, seven more German divisions transferred to Greece, bringing troop strength to eight divisions or 120,000 men. Hitler also reinforced

Yugoslavia with ten divisions fielding a Balkan-wide force of 270,000 men.[18]

On July 9, 1943, the Allies executed Operation Husky and went ashore five hundred miles to the east in Sicily with light resistance.

Chapter 14

"It is over a hundred kilometers. A five-day march with packs and mules. We will need two, maybe three days to reconnoiter and stage for an attack. They ask for fifty fighters. Can we muster fifty? Yes . . . capable fighters, but we also need boots. And arms and ammunition. And what of explosives? Will the British supply these? We know their use, but our stores are empty. Are we to coordinate with other units? You say they want 250 EAM-ELAS? Where are we to stage? There are many things to know before we leave.

"Kapetánios, with due respect to you and EAM-ELAS command, we have waited a month while we might prepare for this mission. Why are we ordered now? I will ready the fighters. But the command is . . . unexpected." Yiorgos uttered the last phrase with his arms raised, like he was pleading with the Almighty for the right word.

A frustrated but resigned Yiorgos continued, "Forgive me. It is no matter. I will ready the fighters. We can leave on your command, Comrade Kapetánios."

Yiorgos reacted to the sudden news of the EAM-ELAS high command order to action. The target was the Kournovo rail tunnel twenty miles northeast of Larissa, on the mainline from Athens to Salonika.

Dimitra said, "Make the fighters ready. We should not have to leave for a day, maybe two. I share your concerns, Yiorgos. But Major General Sarafis did not include me in his deliberations. We have orders. Is there anything else?"

"No, Comrade Kapetánios," answered Yiorgos.

Dimitra didn't share her thoughts with Yiorgos. She had her doubts about the mission. She had her doubts about Stefanos Sarafis.

The major general, formerly a colonel in the Hellenic Army, was a newcomer in EAM-ELAS ranks. He joined the resistance soon after German occupation, but he joined as a Republican, a conservative. He joined EDES, the National Republican Greek League. Then, in March 1943, just two months prior, EAM-ELAS had arrested him. In custody, he professed his admiration for ELAS's organizational skills and its large and disciplined membership.[19] He swore allegiance to EAM-ELAS but remained a member of the Liberal Party. To Dimitra, he was a political opportunist and suspect.

Dimitra admired Sarafis's talent for military organizing. She supported his notion of an EAM-ELAS organized along traditional military lines. But she worried he filtered decisions through a sieve of self-reward. She didn't like him. There was tension between them. She was young and attractive, and he lacked enlightenment or finesse. The struggle against the fascists had thrust unpleasant personalities into Dimitra's orbit, but she always put discipline and unity first. She knew her place in the pecking order. And now an interloper of regrettable personality was her superior officer.

Greek resistance revolved around two political centers. EDES, the smaller group based in the far northwestern mountains bordering Albania. And EAM-ELAS, which by December 1942, operated in four-fifths of the Greek mainland.

EDES, led by Napoleon Zervas, was conservative, supported a republican government, and tolerated supporters of the king in exile. EAM-ELAS, a coalition led by the Communist Party of Greece (KKE), demanded radical reforms. They had no use for the government in exile or the king. KKE, along with its Liberal and Socialist Party coalition partners, led EAM-ELAS. Within the Central Committee, the reticent and regimented communists held sway.

Stefanos Sarafis was commander in chief of ELAS, the military wing of EAM. Aris Velouchiotis, a legendary resistance fighter and founder of ELAS, commanded troops in the field. For clarity, this narrative will use EDES, EAM-ELAS, and alternatively, ELAS, to name these two rivals, organizations as likely to attack each other as they were Germans, Bulgarians, or Italians.[20]

EDES posed as a centrist opposition. Their founding doctrine declared their mission was "establishment in Greece of a republican regime of socialist form." On paper, EDES opposed the king and the corrupt prewar Metaxas dictatorship.[21] But EDES was welcoming territory for conservatives and reactionaries. The British favored EDES. The BBC broadcast supportive reports praising EDED and awarded high British decorations to its commanders.[22] By the summer of 1943, EDES had seven thousand fighters organized into sixteen to twenty battalions. Their headquarters and most of their fighters were in Epirus, with smaller groups in Thessaly and the Peloponnesus.

EAM-ELAS had seven divisions and twelve thousand fighters conducting attacks over the length of Greece. They ceded territory to EDES only in the Pindus Mountains. When Sarafis left EDES to head EAM-ELAS military operations, he was mounting, in midstream, a bigger, more organized horse.

EAM-ELAS deemed EDES collaborationists and didn't trust the British. The Nazis courted EDES in their attempt to set the two resistance groups against each other. The German 1st Mountain Division arrived in mid-1943, and the Germans offered EDES a truce. EDES turned them down, fearing they would alienate the British.

EAM-ELAS had reason to call EDES collaborationist. An EDES leader in Athens recruited young Hellenic Army officers into Security Battalions of Nazi sympathizers. Established by collaborationist Prime Minister Ioannis Rallis in the fall of 1943, the Security Battalions were the brainchild of the German Waffen-SS Lieutenant General Schimana.[23] In the summer of 1944, the Security Battalions joined the Nazis attacking EAM-ELAS in Athens.[24] Greeks hated the Security Battalions. They feared them less for their politics than for their cruelty, thievery, rape, and looting.[25]

Churchill and the British Foreign Office supported the return of the government in exile, and Churchill supported King George II. Churchill and the Foreign Office supported EDES. But the mood in Greece was neither pro-king nor pro-government in exile. Athens was starving. Germans corralled men on the streets and sent them to work and die in Axis industries and mines. Villages burned in the countryside. Thousands of innocent Greeks perished under the Nazi doctrine of "collective responsibility."

EAM-ELAS had a handle on Greek politics. They led a dynamic movement with popular and growing civic and cultural institutions. They ran educational and literacy programs and allowed women to vote. And pivotal for the British, EAM-ELAS andartes controlled most of Greece and the territory holding high-value targets.

For all the complexity and drama that was Greek resistance politics, the Greek railway network was easy to understand. There was a single standard-gauge mainline. It ran north from the Port of Piraeus through Athens to Thessaloniki in Greece; and from there to Sofia, Bulgaria; then Nis and Belgrade and Zagreb in Yugoslavia. At Zagreb, lines fanned out to Austria, Italy, and Hungary. The rail line carried forty-eight trains a day. It was part of an essential military line of communication that stretched from the industrial centers of Germany through Piraeus to the Libyan ports of Tobruk and Benghazi.[26] The Greek railroad was the only supply route with the ability to carry the weight of war. Over it rolled troops and supplies for the occupation of the Balkans and the resupply of Rommel's North Afrika Korps. The British took notice of the railroad's strategic importance. In the fall of 1942, they handed the problem to the Special Operations Executive (SOE), known as "The Baker Street Irregulars" or "Churchill's Secret Army."

On September 30, 1942, under a waning gibbous moon offering too much light for the stealth intended, Lt. Colonel Eddie Myers made a last check of men and supplies. Myers was a scrappy, assertive, thirty-six-year-old sapper from Kensington via the Middle East. The SOE team climbed into an American-crewed B-24 Liberator idling on the tarmac of Deversoir Aerodrome near the entrance of the Suez Canal.

Myers and three other SOE commandos boarded the first plane, and two more groups of four boarded two other planes. Each man, dressed in a British military uniform, carried an Enfield No. 2 Mk I .38 caliber revolver and a Fairbairn-Sykes commando dagger. They packed field dressings and a so-called Baker Street Kit. The kit contained a compass disguised as a button, a map on a silk scarf, a leather belt secreting two gold sovereigns, rations, torches, and suicide pills. They were parachuting into Greece. Their Sten submachine guns, grenades, and the detonators for their plastic explosives they dropped in metal pod canisters.[27]

They had done this before, two nights earlier. After flying four hours, eight hundred miles, over the Mediterranean into the mountains of Roumeli, Central Greece, they had turned away for Cairo. They had failed to spot signal fires positioned to look like a cross. Tonight was better. The pilot keyed the intercom and told Myers he thought he saw three fires burning in a valley below.

The snow on Mount Giona reflected the light of the moon and cast the palest glow on an alien world. The ancient name for Mount Giona is Aselinon Oros, or moonless mountain. Tonight, the name misled. The Liberator descended to just above the peaks as Myers opened the bottom hatch in the airplane's bay and jumped into the frigid darkness of the luminous unknown.

He fought updrafts from the mountain peaks. Buoyed and buffeted, he blew away from his intended valley and drifted toward a forest of fir trees. He fought his heavy pack but couldn't correct his descent. He landed high in a tall fir and crashed through its branches, ending on the ground with his parachute tangled above. His pack ripped from him in the fall, snagged on a stout limb and swung above. When he hit the ground, he sat for a few minutes in the snow and fir needles gathering his wits. The throbbing pulse of twelve fourteen-cylinder Pratt & Whitney engines faded into the void. The Liberators were going home. It was silent, and Myers was alone.

Myers had landed thirty-eight kilometers southeast of Chómori and Dimitra's andartes, on the edge of her zone of operation. But the EAM-ELAS intelligence network was fast, and she learned of the British team's arrival within hours.

There was no sign of the equipment pods or other commandos. Myers stood on the steep mountain slope, hardly able to move without tumbling forward, and tried to stay calm. First, he lit a flare, but that drew no attention. Then he lit a bonfire, with the same result. He stumbled toward the valley, using trees as braking points for his descent. In the valley, he met two Greek shepherds. Myers did not speak Greek, but the three pantomimed and worked out that they would stay put until dawn.

As the sun came up, Myers returned to the tree where he had landed, surprised that his parachute and pack were missing. That was when Tom Barnes, a New Zealander and one of Myers's team, appeared through the trees and approached Myers and the shepherds. He was unhurt. Barnes had received a signal from a third commando, Len Wilmot, and the two commandos went looking for him. The two shepherds went looking for the fourth commando, Denys Hamson, the only Greek-speaker in their group.

When the commandos and shepherds met at midday, the shepherds had found Hamson, and Wilmot appeared soon after. The team, one of three, was back together, intact, and Operation Harling was underway.

The second team, headed by Christopher Woodhouse, fared better. They landed seventeen kilometers north of Myers on the other side of Mount Giona. The four commandos landed without separation or injury. Then, Woodhouse's team encountered armed men. The tension lifted when the andartes saw they were British and not German. The leader was a Greek who said he was expecting a supply drop of explosives to collapse the walls of the Corinth Canal. With him were two Cypriots, escaped prisoners of war.[28]

The andartes led them to a village. There, Woodhouse, who went by Monty instead of Lord Terrington of Huddersfield, welcomed their equipment canisters retrieved by the villagers. But he watched in horror as children munched on the plastic explosive bars, thinking they were fudge. They got sick but survived. Woodhouse, an Oxford-educated classics scholar and fluent in Greek, came to understand the strangeness of occupied Greece, a country of scant resemblance to the land of Pericles.

Following the advice of a supportive villager, the Woodhouse team moved to a cave on the eastern slopes of Mount Giona on a plateau called Prophet Elias. The cave was enormous, large enough to shelter all three commando groups, but it was a three-day hike across a vast and rugged terrain. They trudged through deep snow in the valleys while the wind blew in gales, cutting like the icy steel of a knife. Woodhouse welcomed Myers and his team and the two shepherds into their grotto sanctuary two days after their arrival.

They knew the Italians were searching for them. The Italians had heard the Liberators on two nights. The SOE men moved to another cave that offered a better defense and tried to contact the third team.

The third team had not jumped with the other two on September 30. Failing to spot signal fires, they'd returned to Cairo. Three weeks later, they jumped blind and misjudged their location, dropping into the Karpenisi Valley near a large Italian garrison.[29] Aris Velouchiotis commanded an EAM-ELAS unit that rescued the SOE team from certain capture. It took the three SOE teams a month to reunite.

Meanwhile, Woodhouse and Myers had met the local EDES leader, Zervas, a short, rotund man of carefree persona underlying his reputation as a brigand. Zervas controlled one hundred fighters. Later, they met Aris, the EAM-ELAS commander. He was thin, lanky, and hard-eyed, always alert and examining his surroundings. Aris commanded a larger, more disciplined force. His andartes controlled the territory on which rose the primary target of Operation Harling, the Gorgopotamos Bridge. But before they could destroy one bridge, Myers had to build another.

To say EAM-ELAS and EDES were bitter rivals was to sugarcoat reality. Given provocation, both groups would not hesitate to attack and kill the other. Their politics clashed, and their leaders clashed. EAM-ELAS was better organized, disciplined, and larger. But British strategists leery of communist influence favored EDES. Myers and Woodhouse were to walk a diplomatic tightwire and forge a truce to carry out Operation Harling.

When they met with Aris of EAM-ELAS and Zervas of EDES, brandy helped to relax the grim Aris. The carrot of arms and ammunition, air support and resupply sweetened the British proposition. Still, Aris was less enthusiastic about the attack than Zervas. EAM-ELAS leadership decreed countryside military raids secondary to urban actions. Aris was under orders "not to attack formed bodies of the enemy."

But Aris bucked EAM-ELAS leadership and agreed to take part. With the shaking of hands all around and toasts to the pact, EAM-ELAS and EDES pledged to work together for the attack on the Gorgopotamos Bridge. The British saw this arrangement as perhaps the start of a lasting reconciliation and a budding alliance between the organizations. But in Greece, the old is never far from the present.

Operation Animals, set for June 21, 1943, called for an ambitious campaign of sabotage in Greece. SOE attacks with andarte support were to fool the Axis powers into believing that Greece, rather than Sicily, was the target of an Allied amphibious landing. Operation Animals was part of a broader campaign,

Operation Barclay. This plan involved twelve fake Allied divisions, bogus troop movements, and corresponding fake radio communications. The deception was to fool the Germans into reinforcing Greece and forget about Sicily. Operation Mincemeat, the corpse brought ashore in Spain, was part of Operation Barclay.

The British SOE commandos parachuted into Greece with three targets; bridges across the Papadia, Asopos, and Gorgopotamos Rivers, all Roumeli railroad viaducts. Colonel Myers, while waiting to reunite with Woodhouse, reconnoitered all three and found Gorgopotamos Bridge the best choice.

Constructed in 1905 and considered an engineering marvel, the Gorgopotamos Bridge is ninety-five miles northwest of Athens. The bridge rises 112 feet to span the gorge and churning river for seven hundred feet.[30] Gorgopotamos means "the rushing river" in Greek. Over it crossed a single line of railway, the lifeblood of Germany's campaigns in the Balkans and North Africa.

As Myers crawled to his vantage at dawn, he could see through powerful binoculars the seven sublinear spans supported by six pylons of the massive Gorgopotamos structure. The four central pylons were stone and would be impervious to the plastic explosives of the SOE. But iron piers, girders, and trusses supported either end. These would be the target for the four hundred pounds of shaped charges on the night of November 25, 1942.

One hundred Italians and five Germans guarded the bridge with pillboxes and heavy machine guns at either approach. With the SOE team, eighty-six fighters from EAM-ELAS and fifty-two from EDES, the attack would go forward with one hundred fifty fighters. The plan was simple, but the execution treacherous.

Before 1100 hours, small groups of andartes went up the rail line both north and south to cut communications wires, halt advancing trains, and block any attempt at reinforcement. Then, at 1114 hours, all hell broke loose as the andartes attacked pillboxes at either end of the bridge. The southern position fell first, with the Italians running to escape the attack. The northern defense fell when Myers sent his small contingent of reinforcements. As the attackers gained control of the bridge, the explosives team and eight mules made their way down the rough brush and slippery stones of the gorge. At the floor of the gorge, they waded into the powerful, unsettled currents of the river and across a narrow plank bridge.

At the base of the bridge, the explosives team shaped and reshaped their charges and attached them to the girders. At 0130 hours on the morning of November 26, the first explosion collapsed the two spans at either end of the bridge. The severed sections fell into the gorge with a crash to the cheers of fighters. An hour later, with leftover explosives, the SOE sappers demolished the fallen spans where they landed. With the sky lightening at the hint of dawn, a green Very light spread an eerie glow on the gray-rose palate and signaled the retreat. The attackers withdrew at 0430 hours for a fifteen-hour trek to their hideout. The andartes suffered only four casualties and none killed in action. The SOE men were untouched, and Myers estimated the Italian dead at thirty.[31]

At the hideout, Myers expressed his gratitude to both Zervas and Aris. He told them the attack could not have succeeded without them. Myers sent a messenger to Athens to arrange a supply drop of boots, clothing, arms, and whiskey for EDES and Zervas. Aris requested the same for EAM-ELAS, but Myers had no authority for the communist request. Instead, he gave Aris and EAM-ELAS 250 gold sovereigns.[32] Myers told Zervas and Aris that he had recommended them for decorations and commended them for their service to the Allied cause. Zervas was effusive, but Aris wanted none of it and told Myers he preferred boots for his fighters.

The German repair of the Gorgopotamos Bridge took six weeks, denying Rommel's Afrika Korps two thousand trainloads of supplies.[33] The repair to German respect for Italian courage under fire never happened. The Germans took over security for the entire railway system, straining their forces in Greece and the Balkans. Less than a month later, the 11th Luftwaffe Field Division moved into Attica north of Athens.[34]

On December 1, 1942, ten villagers from tiny Ypati, hands bound, were herded to the rubble of the Gorgopotamos Bridge, and gunned down by the Germans. Four days later, the Germans killed another six hostages in the same way.[35] It wasn't the first blood retribution for the Germans and their doctrine of collective responsibility, and it wouldn't be the last.

After Gorgopotamos, the Germans added *klouves* or crates to their trains. The Nazis filled these barbed-wire-fenced open railcars with innocent Greek civilians, often women and children. They coupled the cars ahead of the locomotives and shoved them first in line to discourage attack.[36] It is impossible to overstate Nazi barbarity. At the Nuremberg Trials following the war, the Greek government reported ninety-one thousand Greeks murdered as hostages and eight hundred villages and towns destroyed by the German occupation forces.[37]

Dimitra received her marching orders six months after the felling of Gorgopotamos Bridge. At Gorgopotamos, she and thirty EAM-ELAS andartes were the reinforcing group that secured the northern pillbox. After capturing the pillbox, her unit blocked a train full of Italian reinforcements from Lamia. This allowed the SOE demolition teams to place their charges. That night, the exhilaration of working with EDES was palpable, but the cooperation between EDES and EAM-ELAS had frayed. Now she feared a fratricide as unavoidable as a train on rails.

After Gorgopotamos, Colonel Eddie Myers and eleven SOE men trudged west over a hundred miles as the crow flies and twice that far over mountain trails. They walked the width of Greece under a false assumption. Upon leaving Cairo, they were told SOE would evacuate them after Operation Harling. That had been three months ago. Now, with Gorgopotamos destroyed and Harling a success, they made their way across the rugged, unforgiving landscape with the cold biting and the snow falling. They billeted with EAM-ELAS fighters, but food was scarce. They grew hungry and exhausted. When they reached their extraction point, a beach on the Ionian Coast five miles south of Parga, they hid in the daytime and signaled at night for a submarine that never signaled back.

Christmas Day broke sunny and bright, but depression reigned. A priest came to their hideout with gifts of brown bread lifting spirits. But later, as the men prepared to return to the rendezvous coordinates, a runner arrived with news from Woodhouse in Athens. The entire SOE contingent was to remain in Greece until further notice. Cairo had canceled the evacuation. Colonel Myers would remain in charge, with Woodhouse his second in command.

Soon after receiving orders to stay in Greece, the SOE commandos began planning another attack on the railroad, the same mainline serviced by Gorgopotamos. This time it would be the Asopos Viaduct, a three-hinged, truss-arch structure, 330 feet above a roiling river with waterfalls rising on sheer cliff sides. The Asopos Viaduct was the highest railway bridge in Greece.[38]

Tunnels bookended the bridge and six hundred feet of the railroad. There would be no approach through these. There were, however, narrow paths leading over the tunnels. But during the daytime, they were in full view of the German sentries and garrison. At night, powerful searchlights swept the paths. Avoiding their beams would be difficult and deadly.

Myers met with EAM-ELAS and EDES about a joint operation. Then EAM-ELAS arrested an EDES commander, complicating these talks. EAM-ELAS issued the captive commander an ultimatum to join or perish. It was a breach of the cooperation accord reached for the Gorgopotamos operation.

Myers threatened to cut off supplies to EAM-ELAS, and Aris agreed to help attack Asopos, but Dimitra's nemesis,

Sarafis, who outranked Aris, overruled him. Sarafis wanted no part of what he saw as an impossible mission, one requiring at least fifteen hundred fighters, heavy machine guns, and artillery. The Germans had in place concrete reinforced bunkers, barbed-wire entanglements, searchlights, and ambushes lurking on the approaches. Even with a powerful frontal attack on the German positions, they couldn't hold the bridge long enough for sappers to reach the base and plant their charges. The nearby German garrison would rush reinforcements. Sarafis proposed instead that EAM-ELAS destroy a tunnel seventy-five miles north of Asopos Bridge. After hesitation, worrying that blowing the Kournovo Tunnel would yield only brief inconvenience for the Germans, Myers agreed to supply EAM-ELAS with explosives. Sarafis thought he would need 250 fighters, and Dimitra received her orders soon after.

They moved at night. Dimitra rode a coal-coated mount, and Yiorgos's horse was a dapple gray with a sooty mane. Both animals were tall and healthy and gave their riders elevation for scouting. The horses complemented their riders with Dimitra's dark features and raven hair, and Yiorgos's grizzled gray hair and beard. They rode side by side on the narrow pathways when possible and single file when not. With the tethered mules and horses and fighters, the column stretched out for a hundred yards.

They rested in caves and under outcrops in the daylight, slept when they could, and hid from the German and Italian spotter planes. Even in late May, some valleys where the sun never shone had snow in their lowest passages. Their march to the rendezvous was taxing, but everyone made it healthy and ready to fight.

Dimitra's fighters arrived ready, willing, and able. During the briefing before the attack, she received a compliment from Aris for her organization and discipline. Sarafis was mute. It mattered not to Dimitra because she held Aris in higher esteem than Sarafis. Her unit and the special unit of EAM-ELAS explosives engineers had drawn the attention and admiration of the commander most respected by EAM-ELAS volunteers. When the briefing concluded, Aris sought out Dimitra before she could leave, "Kapetánios, do your fighters need anything? How are their boots? Do they need boots?"

Dimitra smiled and, looking the formidable man straight in the eye, answered, "Comrade, I must answer yes. Not all are so equipped, but they march all the same."

Aris nodded and went to the table where his weapon rested. When he returned to Dimitra, he said, "Comrade quartermaster will help with the boots. Tell him I ordered your men to all be properly fitted before they leave on the mission. And here, take this. It is a reward for your leadership and strength. May it be the death of many fascists." And with that, he handed Dimitra his Sten gun.

Dimitra reached for the weapon and held it in front of her for a moment, "Comrade, thank you, but this is your weapon. What will *you* use?"

"Worry not, Kapetánios. I have convinced a former EDES man to join with EAM-ELAS and bring his band, and along with his band came many British supplies. I will have no problem rearming." Then he smiled for just a second.

Dimitra again thanked her commander and slung the weapon over her shoulder. As she left the briefing, standing tall and poised, she carried the Sten on her left shoulder and her Mannlicher carbine in her right hand.

When Yiorgos met her outside, he said, "Comrade Kapetánios, you're looking well-armed today."

She replied, "It is our lucky day. Tell the fighters without proper boots to visit the quartermaster at once and tell the quartermaster that Comrade Aris has ordered their requisition."

"Yes, Kapetánios, at once. Today is starting well for us," replied Yiorgos.

Dimitra said only, "Let us hope."

On the night of June 1, 1943, the 250 EAM-ELAS explosives engineers and fighters split into two squads and went to either end of the 1,600-foot-long tunnel. The attackers passed a signal when a train loaded with ammunition and Italian soldiers on leave entered from the south. Both ends blew simultaneously.

Dimitra's fighters at the south end of the tunnel had little to do since there was no German security at the site. They waited in ambush for any reinforcements or sentries, but none ever showed.

The twin blasts and resulting wreck and fire killed two to three hundred Italians and seven Germans with another one hundred suffering disabling burns. The attack also killed sixty Greek prisoners of war, the engine crew of three Greek civilians, and forty Greek hostages shoved before the locomotive in a klouves.[39] It was the helpless, innocent faces, standing packed in the wire cage, holding its wooden frame for balance that haunted Dimitra for many nights.[40]

There was no permanent damage to the tunnel, and the Germans repaired the track in a week. On June 5, Italian Commander in Chief General Carlo Vecchiarelli, ordered 106 EAM-ELAS Greek prisoners of war moved from their concentration camp in Larissa. The next day, the Italians took them eighteen miles north of the Kournovo Tunnel entrance. Shepherds hidden in the hills watched as the Italians tied the hostages together, then mowed them down with machine-gun fire. The Italians stripped the bodies of their clothes, piled the corpses like sardines, and buried them in a pit.[41]

Early on June 21, 1943, six British SOE commandos carried out what Sarafis had declared impossible. For days they inched down sheer cliffs carrying packs, rations, weapons, and explosives. They traversed icy cold waterfalls and dodged German sentries. But when the spans of Asopos Viaduct fell into the rushing water, the SOE made their mark not only on Greece, but on the history of warfare. The United States Army Special Operations

Command today says that the attack on the Asopos Viaduct "was probably the single most spectacular exploit of its kind in World War II."[42] The Germans were so certain that the destruction of the Asopos Viaduct could only be an act of treachery that they shot the entire garrison guarding it that night.[43]

Using Polish and Greek forced labor, the Germans took two months to repair the viaduct. The first engine to cross the reconstructed bridge swayed and rocked, then plunged into the abyss when a faulty pier collapsed. The German reconstruction work was shoddy. Or sabotaged. It took the Germans another two months with stringent oversight to complete a repair. Colonel Myers and his small band of commandos cut the Axis powers' strategic communications for four months, a major contribution to Operation Barclay. They also birthed a legend for generations to come.

After the SOE team radioed of their success at Asopos to Cairo, an aged but flight-worthy RAF Martin Maryland light bomber circled the wreckage for reconnaissance. The SOE developed the photos into colored, stereoscopic prints that made Churchill chuckle.[44]

Chapter 15

"Where did you get this photograph?" asked Stavros.

"Did I mention I have diplomatic courtesies because of my father's service in the Greek government and through my commission in the Greek Army? I am *axiomatikós syndésmou*," answered John Tsouderos, grinning like the Cheshire cat.

"A liaison officer? I thought you were a buck private? No, you never mentioned it. I thought you were training with the battalion like the rest of us? I should have known you were . . . special. No offense. A recon photo from the RAF? Is it authentic?'

Tsouderos nodded.

"Where did they take it, and how did you get it?" continued Stavros.

"It's informal, my relationship with the United States Army and other government offices. Informal, but useful. Yet here I am before you as a private. That is why I have taken the name Giannakopoulos instead of Tsouderos. It's all very intriguing, isn't it? All very Greek, no? I wear the helmet, the leggings, the blouse, the same boots as you. I take the same orders, like you. I march in the mountains, do my push-ups, run, practice with my knife and rifle. I box. I am the same as you or any other American soldier. But to part of my story I must, as the Americans say, *give a deep six*," responded the young soldier.

"Right, John. I've known since we met after my lecture at Fort Leavenworth that you were a VIP. You wore a captain's rank then. You would have to be. I mean, the son of the Greek prime minister in exile? You are *somebody*. I get that. And I understand you don't want every Tom, Dick, and Harry to know who you are. But how in the hell did you get this photo? It's stamped *Most Secret* right here," and Stavros pointed to the lower right hand of the glossy print folded and cracked to fit into John's pocket. "Are we breaking any rules just looking at it?"

The two men were alone in the mess next to their barracks on guard duty. They were spelling the other two GIs from Company B assigned in rotation to patrol the perimeter. It was 0300 hours. They had retreated to the mess for coffee and could hear a cook scrubbing pans in the kitchen, getting ready for breakfast. But in the dining hall, they were alone.

Stavros liked John Tsouderos, no matter that he was the son of a prominent family. He was a young man. But Stavros found him mature and focused and as motivated as any in the battalion. Maybe more so. John yearned to fight for Greece. He could have had a soft life and gone to live with his family in London or Cairo. But he chose hard training and life among soldiers.

"Professor Theofanis," began John, who was at once cut off by Stavros.

"Just *Stavros*, John. Don't let the other GIs hear you call me Professor, or I'll get a nickname," Stavros pleaded.

John apologized and told Stavros that in Greece, it would be disrespectful not to use the honorific.

John started again. "Stavros, my friend and brother, the British SOE, shared this photograph with my father. He thought I would find it motivating. This viaduct, the Asopos, was the highest in Greece and thought impervious to attack. The Germans guarded both approaches with reinforced concrete pillboxes and powerful searchlights, and they believed the base of the foundation unassailable. The walls of the ravine are sheer, over one hundred meters. They rise like stone curtains. Waterfalls block all pathways. But the British did it! With only six men! With determination, patience, and daring. Six! Its destruction will interrupt German resupply for weeks or months.

"This is what we can do when we get to Greece, no? The Germans are vulnerable, and the Italians are even more so. I wish we were there today, at this very moment. The British parachuted a Special Operations Executive mission into Greece a year ago. They have a head start on the Americans. But the British are jealous of their influence in Greece. Maybe not jealous, let us say protective. They see Greece as their domain. They are colonialists. They worry that the seas of Greece will no longer give safe passage through Suez to India, Burma, and the Orient. A friendly Greece is to them a friendly sea. And the seas are to Britain the conveyance of their wealth. The SOE has been in Crete all along, but here in Roumeli and Asopos is where the Germans are most vulnerable, no? This is their supply line, their lifeblood. This is where we will go to fight them, no? But of that, I have no intelligence. It is only my wish."

John Tsouderos was twenty years old. He had been a scholarship student at Carleton College in Northfield, Minnesota, studying economics and political science, when the Italians invaded, and the Germans overran Greece. His family fled with King George II and had since rotated between Cairo and London. His father, the prime minister in exile, struggled to represent the people of Greece in the Allied capitals. He labored at the impossible task of maintaining political legitimacy in his abandoned country and among its displaced armed forces. John had only one request of his ever-so-connected father. *Let me fight for Greece.* His father, Emmanouil Tsouderos, told him to stay in America, and he would see to it. President Roosevelt asked for a Greek fighting unit, and the US Army complied. Now John Tsouderos was in the Greek Battalion under an assumed name. The first three digits of his fake serial number showed John was a draftee.[45] His was a false identity. But he was a godsend for the curious Stavros and a delight to be around. John was smart and mature, fit, and comfortable with the other recruits. He had the social skills of an American boy and the culture, depth, and knowledge of a Greek son of privilege.

Stavros was no slacker at Greek history, but John had lived it. During their twenty-minute coffee break, at 0300 hours in early July 1943, Tsouderos lectured the professor. He started in 1936.

In the spring of that year, Greek elections gave a handful of communists the balance of power between the Liberal and Royalist parties. When the parties failed to form a compromise government, the king declared a non-party government headed by a former Liberal, Constantine Demertzes. Demertzes died soon after that, and the king appointed his Vice-Premier, Ioannis Metaxas. Metaxas, Tsouderos noted, was a military man and a royalist and head of a minor political party called Freethinkers. They were very conservative.

In August 1936, soon after his appointment as premier, Metaxas declared the government suspended until new elections and assumed the authority to rule by decree. He appointed right-wing advisers and supporters to key posts, and this provoked a general strike. Metaxas used this unrest as an opportunity to declare a state of emergency, citing the communist danger. Metaxas declared that as of August 4, 1936, he held unbridled power to save Greece from catastrophe. He meant communists.

He banned all political parties and anti-Greek literature, including Plato's *Republic*. He prohibited strikes. He arrested opponents and tortured at will. He emulated the fascists. He was a known Germanophile who, during his studies in Berlin, admired Prussian militarism and embraced fascist earmarks. He instituted secret police, and a right-wing youth movement, and he rewarded Greeks who informed on fellow Greeks.

When Italy invaded in October 1940, Metaxas's dream of keeping Greece neutral vanished. By then, the Greek communists had built clandestine networks in the towns and cities over the previous four years. During that time, the party had two thousand members and supporters imprisoned or sentenced to internal exile. The fabric of their membership, infiltrated and compromised, was shredded and torn. But a disciplined nucleus survived. Compartmentalized and resilient, this core was primed to organize the occupation resistance. Practiced subversives and skilled operatives, the communists were professionals.

Early in the winter of 1941, with Greece overcoming the Italian forces in Epirus, Metaxas died of a blood infection in Athens. On January 29, King George II appointed Alexandros Koryzis, apolitical and formerly the Governor of the Bank of Greece, the new prime minister.

On April 6, 1941, Koryzis rejected a German demand to remove British troops from Greece. Two weeks later, the Germans rode to the salvation of the Italians, and Greece's defenses fell before them. After a desponding meeting with the king and Athens under martial law, Koryzis walked from the Grande Bretagne Hotel to his apartment. There he shot himself twice through the heart. He would not be the man to surrender Greece to the Germans.[46]

John's father, Emmanouil, accepted the prime ministership on April 21, 1941, the day following the Hellenic Army's unilateral surrender in Epirus. He was an excellent choice, noted John. His father was a Venizelist. Stavros knew that meant a parliamentarian. He was also an Anglophile from Crete, where they hoped to reestablish the government.

The British and the king's government retreated to Crete. Two weeks later, when Crete fell to the Germans, Emmanouil with his wife and John's two sisters fled with the king, first to the Middle East and then to London. John couldn't tell Stavros for security reasons, but his father was now in Cairo.

On September 27, 1941, in the shadow of German occupation and Waffen-SS spy networks, the Greek communists and three other left-leaning parties met in Phthia northwest of Athens. There in a small butcher shop, amid hanging lambs and hams, they founded EAM-ELAS, the leading resistance underground in the country.[47]

There was much John couldn't tell Stavros, things he didn't know and things he didn't want to mention. John's father had a tough job. He may have lived a life of relative luxury in secure surroundings, but responsibility burdened the prime minister of Greece in exile. By July 1943, the load had not lightened.

In April and May 1941, the Germans swept all before them in their occupation of Greece and then Crete. Thousands of Greek soldiers, and officers with navy vessels and aircraft, fled the fighting to the British-controlled Middle East. Many landed in Egypt, where they joined a force of six hundred Greek Egyptian volunteers. The British hoped to use these troops liberating the Italian-held Dodecanese islands.[48] The self-exiled soldiers from the Greek mainland and Crete began arriving in May. Soldiers of the Evros Regiment who had crossed the Turkish border from Macedonia joined them. Turkey, a neutral country, detained the Greeks under German protest. Then the Turks allowed them to travel on to the Middle East where, in October 1941, they joined the other forces numbering six thousand. These ill-equipped Greek armed forces in exile became the Royal Greek Middle East Forces (VESMA) and fell under British command.

From the beginning, these forces were top-heavy with a disproportionate number of officers and bristled with political backbiting. Divisions within the Greek military began as seething friction during the First World War when republican Venizelists fought royalists. When the Turkish contingent arrived, they brought a strain of political contagion. In the Greek Army, they called themselves the Antifascist Military Organization or ASO. In the Navy, they were the AON, and in the small Greek Air Force in exile, the AOA. The antifascist movement attracted younger recruits, often led by EAM-ELAS and Communist Party cadre.

The British were aghast at the level of political recrimination among the Greek troops in exile. The British Commander in Chief Middle East, Sir Claude Auchinleck, suggested that the Greeks were good only for digging entrenchments. The British Foreign Office overruled Auchinleck. In March 1942, John's father, prime minister in exile, signed an agreement with the British Foreign Secretary, Anthony Eden. *The Organization and Employment of the Greek Armed Forces* resolved their military chain of command, if not their employment.[49]

The British estimation of Greek readiness improved with Rommel's lightning advance on El Alamein in the fall of 1942. In August, General Headquarters Middle East ordered the VESMA First Brigade, now based in Syria, to the Egyptian desert just north of the Qattara Depression. On October 23, 1942, detachments of the Greek Brigade fighting with distinction and cohesion were the first to open fire on the advancing Germans and Italians. Brave though they proved themselves, their Greek nature prevailed, and incessant political divisions remained.

By February 1943, discontent in the ranks was rising. ASO created the Central Bureau of Antifascist Organizations, incorporating the merchant marine trade union and their communist leadership. ASO dissatisfaction roiled around the Greek Minister of Defense, Panayotis Kanellopoulos, an appointee of John's father. The leftists and anti-royalist in VESMA suspected Kanellopoulos was plotting to return the king and far-right-wing elements, as shown in his appointment of military officers.

On March 1, three VESMA battalions stationed in Lebanon mutinied and sent a list of demands. These included the removal of all "reactionary elements" and a fair and representative plebiscite before the king's return. Kanellopoulos's trip to Lebanon was rancorous, and at the lowest point, he barely escaped a frantic mob.[50] Mutinies would grow and become a common tactic among the disenchanted in uniform, fomented by both right and left.

The Greek government and armed forces in exile, led by John's father, were a cauldron of boiling politics and strife. It was hard enough juggling royalists and Venizelists. Now, with added communist influence and general dissatisfaction, the government in exile was near turmoil.

Greece was an unsettled predicament. The balancing act required of John's father was precarious. Still, with all of Cairo's intrigue and drama, it paled in deadly consequence to a Nazi sweep through a village in Roumeli.

Chapter 16

"It says right here, we're the next blow, the Hundred Twenty-Second, we're the right fist. Sicily was the left. The Greek Battalion will be the right . . . or at least a big part of it." Gus flipped the newspaper with his index finger.

"Right here in the *Coloradoan*, today's paper, Sunday, July eleventh, front page. Lewis Hawkins reporting from London. The headline is, 'Sicily Attack Only First of Series, Is Belief; Defending Force May Total Four Hundred Thousand Troops.' Then Hawkins writes, 'Allied forces smash against the Axis on Sicily was hailed in London yesterday as the first in a rain of invasion blows designed to batter the enemy to his knees.' He goes on, 'General Eisenhower landed a solid left on Sicily, one military man said, but his forces there comprise only one of the Allied fists in the Mediterranean. Our right menaces the Balkans, and we have other fists in the West, so the enemy cannot throw everything into countering the punch.'[51]

"I'm telling you, Stavros, we'll be in Greece by Labor Day. I will visit Pop's family on Milos and Mom's folks, too. We'll have a feast. I'll get to kiss all the village girls, and they'll give me a medal and a statue. It's all in the cards, brother. I can't wait."

Gus was excited. He and everyone in Greece thought, with the landing on Sicily, the Allies would take back Greece in a matter of weeks. They would free her citizenry of the food blockade, the torture, the hostage-taking, stop the villages burning, and banish the Bulgarians and Germans and Italians. The fascist invaders would scurry back to their homelands, tails between their legs, to await ultimate defeat and surrender.

Gus continued thoughtfully, his excited eyes penetrating Stavros's stare.

"How do you think we'll go in?" he asked.

Then, not waiting for an answer, he went on. "I bet we take Crete first. Yep, that's got to be right. We take Crete first and secure the airfields, then we got 'em beat. We can bomb the crap out of them. They'll never know what hit 'em.

"Then, I guess we'll come ashore somewhere on the Peloponnesus and march to Athens. That's the surest way. They should make me a general. I've got the plan. Do you like it?"

Stavros nodded, pretending to process Gus's military insight. The young GI was psyched, and Stavros didn't want to throw cold water on his enthusiasm. But Stavros was reticent. He knew that just because something appeared in a newspaper under a credible byline, that didn't make it so. No matter how much someone wished it to be. Stavros knew from his lectures at the General Staff College in Fort Leavenworth that disinformation, deception, and surprise were elements of war planning as much as troop movements. It pleased Stavros that the landing on Sicily had gone well. But what would come next was of a higher order than either he or Gus could get their heads around. He just kept nodding and repeated, "Plausible. It's plausible."

Stavros was right. Events shaping his and Gus's futures were percolating far from sight and out of mind. Even John Tsouderos's substantial connections would yield no enlightenment on such matters. As Gus and Stavros sat on their bunks talking under bare lightbulbs in their barracks that Sunday evening, another band was preparing to meet for similar discussions.

In the Pindus Mountains near the border of Albania and Greece, the tiny village of Pertouli was about to host the British Military Mission (BMM). These men, and especially their commander, Eddie Myers, were operating with better information than Gus and Stavros. In Greece, information was intimate and urgent.

The BMM had grown from the original twelve commandos who had parachuted into Roumeli in September a year before. Now numbering forty men, some of whom Myers had yet to meet, the call to confer at Pertouli looked to be an uplifting gathering. The BMM was a military success. But their political portfolio was less illustrious. Still, they met in a mood of understated pride.

Along with destroying the Gorgopotamos and Asopos viaducts, there were more modest, but still risky, missions. Like straight from a textbook, the SOE commandos ambushed supply columns, sabotaged mining and forestry operations, and stayed one step ahead of the Germans and Italians.

One step ahead was Nick Hammond. Hammond had traveled to Thessaloniki by bus disguised as a shepherd. On his return trip, with intelligence on a potential BMM airfield, he became an object of ridicule for two German soldiers. Defying all odds, he fooled them with his Cambridge University Greek and arrived a day late.

After introductions and a round of slapping backs, Myers got down to brass tacks. He told the men he had orders from Middle East Command through SOE HQ in Cairo. They were to lie low and train the andartes to the highest pitch possible. They were to limit activities to minor sabotage sufficient only to instruct recruits and maintain the morale of the andarte bands. They were to conduct reconnaissance so that, when the time arrived to invade Greece, they would begin another series of widespread sabotage. Then Myers delivered a gut punch. He told his SOE men that Greece would not be on the Allies' target list before the coming winter or early 1944. This timetable meant the commandos would be in Greece for another unforgiving winter. Another season of securing food and shelter and struggling to maintain andarte and SOE operations.[52]

Myers discussed another tricky development the next day. Italian Army officers had secretly approached BMM personnel about surrender. Two battalion commanders had reached out for surrender negotiation. Myers saw this as a positive development, but it had delicate repercussions. He told his men it would be best if formed bodies, battalions, or even divisions surrender with their officer corps and discipline intact. That way, the BMM could control the disposition of Italian arms and, when possible, integrate Italian forces into Allied military planning. He knew that EDES and EAM-ELAS would salivate at the prospect of Italian surrenders and the opportunity to appropriate their arms. The Italians had substantial weapons, artillery, armored vehicles, tanks, and heavy machine guns. The rapid arming of either group might instigate clashes. As the Italians withdrew, the vacuum could suck into it the fragile cooperation Myers, Woodhouse, and the BMM strived to nurture.

Myers was dealing with another problem brought on by the turning tide of war. But of this, he spoke only to Woodhouse. Former Hellenic Army officers and pro-Quisling politicians increasingly solicited the commander of the BMM. In very Greek fashion, sensing Axis defeat, these people now sought to switch sides. Some, Myers intoned, were bona fide patriotic Greeks who had stayed in Athens to help the cause of Free Greece as best they could. But many were suffering from a guilty conscience and running before the grasp of EAM-ELAS, who had vowed to prosecute all collaborationists. Myers sorted the wheat from the chaff. He handed a few to EAM-ELAS for people's justice, sent some to EDES for employment, and ran others as agents in the occupation bureaucracy. The administrative needs of the BMM were outpacing developments. Again, much like John Tsouderos's father in Cairo, the political juggling in Roumeli took place on a taut wire somewhere above the fray but with immediate consequences looming.

Chapter 17

Vasilios straddled a hand-cranked generator in the far corner of the Chómori schoolhouse. A stout power cable ran from the generator through an alternator-voltage-regulator to the receptacle of a battered American BC-1306 HF field radio. The radio was original equipment on a humble Jeep that had found its way to North Africa and then into the hands of SOE quartermasters. The Jeep retired from service after meeting a German landmine on patrol north of the Ruweisat Ridge in the days just before Rommel's final push. Colonel Myers had allowed the radio for an EDES band sheltering in the hills near Kommeno, fifty miles northwest of Chómori. Before it dropped from a gray camo-painted RAF Halifax under black parachutes into Epirus, EDES had liberated a radio and batteries from inattentive Italians. To EDES, the American radio was surplus. They could get another one from Myers upon request. So they traded. Dimitra's EAM-ELAS handed over three British gold sovereigns and two lambs from Yiorgos's friendly royalist farmer in Kato Dafni. Yiorgos facilitated the swap because he knew Alexandros, the EDES leader in Kommeno, from their service in the Hellenic Army.

The BC-1306 HF ran on six, twelve, or twenty-four-volt batteries, none of which were available in Chómori. Vasilios, cranking away as if he were reefing a sail on a racing yacht, was himself the battery.

The reason for Vasilios's sweaty effort was so Dimitra and her two lieutenants could listen to the BBC broadcast that warm evening of July 25, 1943. As Yiorgos selected the correct megacycles and fine-tuned the rotary dial, the radio vacuum tubes heated, and the set came alive. The broadcast crackled off the ionosphere but came through clear enough for all to hear.

The Italian dictator, Benito Mussolini, is reported to have stepped down as head of the armed forces and the government. King Victor Emmanuel has assumed control of the army and issued a statement saying his country would, through the valor of her troops and the determination of her civilian population, find, in the respect of her old institutions, the way of recovery.

Marshal Pietro Badoglio is the new prime minister. He said the war would go on, and he urged the people to rally round the king. He also gave a warning that any attempt to disrupt public order would be severely dealt with.

The resignation of Mussolini, Adolf Hitler's junior partner, will be seen as a blow to the Axis coming hot on the heels of the Allies' invasion of Sicily.

Reports from Sicily say most of the island is now in Allied hands, apart from the mountainous area in the northeast, where they are still meeting tough resistance from the German military.[53]

The three EAM-ELAS leaders listened, transfixed, to the details, then one segment provoked Yiorgos.

Rome Radio announced the news of Mussolini's departure. Afterward the Italian national anthem was played, rather than the Fascist hymn, "Giovenessa," which has previously ended all bulletins.

It is being seen as a further indication of the new Italian regime's wish to disassociate itself from the Fascist Party, the movement founded by Mussolini in 1919 as Fasci di Combattimento.

"Thank heaven, Saint Cecilia, and the ghost of Apollo," exclaimed the bearded fighter, raising his arms above his head and rocking back in his wooden chair. "'Giovenessa' is imperious donkey dung. That the fascists chose that discordant mishmash out of all the praiseworthy Italian music tells the story of their stupidity, their arrogance, and their complete lack of cultural bearing. Good riddance to the swine Mussolini if for no other reason than his choice of music."

Dimitra chuckled, less at Yiorgos's remarks and more at her astonishment that Yiorgos had musical sensitivities or any artistic sensitivities at all. She had fought beside the formidable man for three years and had never seen this side of him.

Yiorgos regained his composure. "I must apologize, Comrade Kapetánios. I was out of line to use harsh words in your presence. It is only that I . . . I hate that song."

Dimitra shrugged, "I, too, hate the song. But I did not know you were so in tune with the musical world. My mother, you know, is a teacher of music. I studied with her, the lyre of the Cretan style, but I had a better head for science and investigation, which is why I studied archeology. Please express your musical criticism. It is a welcome reprieve from our usual dialogue.

"Vasilios, do you object to Yiorgos commenting on music? You are the political minder. You must weigh in on cultural matters, no?"

Vasilios shook his head from behind the generator. With his arms still rotating, he called from the corner, "No, it is good we have credible critics among us to keep us on the correct path of proletarian redemption." Yiorgos and Dimitra smiled, noting the self-effacing irony in the young man's tone.

"How long, Yiorgos, before Italy surrenders?" asked Dimitra. "And what of their forces in Greece? Do you have a military opinion to accompany your musical thoughts?"

"The Italians will sign a surrender within a month, maybe two. Their ranks have no heart for empire. They could win this war if we fought with guitars, not rifles. But we must remember, the Germans are in Italy. They will fight to keep the Allies at arm's length. The Austrian border is in the north. The Germans will fight, and the Allies will find them dug in before the Alps. There is a route called the Brenner Pass through the mountains to Innsbruck. Once through, the Allies will have Munich in their sights.

"But I think not. I think the Allies have another plan. It may include Greece, but it may not. How am I to know? They will need a better route than through the Alps. They would find it hard to aggregate the troops and supplies needed to invade Germany. No. They will open another front. Should that be in Greece, to join with the Red Army and attack from the east? How am I to know? Perhaps they will invade France across the English Channel. That would be difficult, maybe impossible. But if they come from England to France, they will force Germany to fight on two fronts. That would be the best strategy, Comrade Kapetánios. In that case, Greece will be the poor orphan left in the manger, and we will continue to do what Greeks do best . . . wait."

"And what of the surrendering Italians, Yiorgos? What of the wretched invaders today in our midst and soon-to-be innocents?" Dimitra mouthed the last word with scorn.

"Kapetánios, you know, as I know, the Italians are ready to quit the fighting. We have seen a dozen enlisted men seek us out to surrender, and this we have obliged. We have sent them to Aris for integration should they prove worthy. And my friend in Kommeno told me that EDES has had many Italians come to them.

"The question, Kapetánios, is not the Italians, but their arms. It is a race, is it not? Who will get their arms? EAM-ELAS, EDES, the British, or the Germans. Once the Italians have surrendered, the Germans will be their enemy. The Germans will never see the Italians as neutral. They will want to secure Italian weapons before they fall into our deserving grasp. It is like an octopus with its many arms, no? In the dark waters of occupation, each limb flails, eager to grab the prize."

Dimitra was silent for a moment, considering Yiorgos's assessment, when Yiorgos continued.

"Comrade Kapetánios, I apologize. I forgot to mention this before. They have promoted Colonel Myers of the BMM. He is now Brigadier Myers. And a Major Wallace with the Foreign Office from London has joined his staff. What it means, only the British know. But this is the first time a man of the Foreign Office has come to Greece."[54]

Dimitra nodded. "Interesting. Why would Secretary Eden need to second-guess a brigadier? The British are uncertain of their information, perhaps? Is EAM-ELAS getting too much of their support? The British favor EDES, this we know. The British want the king to return and the monarcho-fascists to rule when the Germans leave. Perhaps Major Wallace is here to make certain EAM-ELAS goes on rations, eh? Over these matters, we have no control. But it is valuable information, Yiorgos. Did this come from Alexandros in Kommeno?"

Yiorgos nodded.

Dimitra raised her eyes from Yiorgos and looked to the corner and the younger man.

"Vasilios, with the broadcast over, you can stop cranking," Dimitra offered. "Comrade Political Officer, please tell me your thoughts on our civic and cultural programs. It is the Central Committee's direction that we are to increase our civic infrastructure and popular participation. Can you shed light on our status and plans?"

"Yes, Comrade Kapetánios." The young man rose from straddling the generator and walked to the desk where Dimitra sat. Yiorgos sat to her right with the radio before him and Vasilios stood to her left.

"As you know, earlier this month, the Central Committee directed all cells to increase their efforts in civil development. And when possible, to organize cultural programs for the workers and peasants. This initiative will build the prerequisite governmental structures on the people's power. This will ready us for the day when Greece belongs to those who work for a living. With the invasion of Italy, we hope this day to be not far.

"Our programs fall into three categories: institutions, communications, and infrastructure. Our infrastructure projects are the most obvious." Vasilios pointed to several locations on the map spread before Dimitra.

"You know of the road repairs and well digging, not only in Chómori but throughout our military district. These require taxation and employment of civilians, and most of the projects are in the hands of civilians. EAM-ELAS checks the quality of the work and the correct payment of wages. We have twelve projects underway and expect another twelve to fifteen to begin by fall. The biggest of these will be telephone lines between all villages in our military district.

"Our work with village institutions of government is also proceeding. Of the twenty-one villages in our district, half have already held elections for village president, boards of elders, and peoples' courts. The new election system includes women voters, and the new lower age limit is now eighteen. This is a tricky proposition in more traditional villages. We can't force people to vote. Voting is alien to the women. We must provide them with education and assurance before elections. Kapetánios, you are a fine example to the women, and we often point to your leadership to allay fears that this is not a trick. Village customs can, as you know, be their own worst enemy, no?

"Formal education of the young and literacy for the adults is a matter of teachers. EAM is soon to establish a training institute for teachers. I have been told sixty volunteers stand ready to attend. Most villages have at least a rudimentary schoolhouse or dedicated building. But like the one where we now meet, they can all be improved, and their books and materials updated.

"EPON, our student wing, is a priority, and we have many fine young people in the youth corps. It grows every day. EPON's cultural presentations in isolated villages are big attractions and give EAM-ELAS a ready audience every time they perform.

"So, I would say, Kapetánios, that we have yet to complete all the work required, but the direction of our efforts is positive. I am to meet with other political advisers late next month, and I will have a better idea of our national disposition when I return."

Dimitra again grew silent for a moment, considering the report. Then she said, "Comrade Political Officer, please tell me if I should visit any village where the women are reluctant to vote. Do not hesitate."

Vasilios nodded.

Then Dimitra looked to Yiorgos. "Now, Comrade Military Officer and Chief Music Critic, will you please tell me of your plans to ambush the Italian supply column? This action I find attractive, and considering your earlier assessment, we may need to schedule it soon, before the Italians disappoint us and withdraw from the fighting, no?"

Yiorgos rose and went to Dimitra's right side to point to coordinates on her map. He briefed his commander. He pointed out the defile where the Italians would be most vulnerable and explained the predictable schedule the Italians followed. He described where they placed their armored vehicles in the column. Then he showed the contour of the ridge and cover from which the attack would mount. He told her he would need fifty fighters. The ambush was straightforward, an action like many over the past three years. The difference now was Dimitra's andartes were better armed. Every fighter had boots, and they were tempered and disciplined.

Dimitra knew dismissing any military action as routine was inviting disaster. Complacency was deadly. She questioned elements, cover, and movements. Yiorgos understood her caution and answered all questions.

The EAM-ELAS leadership in Chómori fit together the pieces needed for a successful mission in the Nafpaktian

Mountains. In London and Cairo, other leaders made ready to solve a bigger puzzle.

Chapter 18

Four miles southwest of Karditsa, the mountains of Roumeli end, and the Plains of Thessaly begin. In July 1943, British Liaison Officer Denys Hanson looked upon this expanse and had other planes in mind: airplanes. On a level plateau at an elevation of thirty-five hundred feet, Hanson found a strip of land two thousand yards long. It was cultivated but otherwise unused and undetected.[55] With Myers's approval, Hanson began preparing the land using villagers, mostly women. They worked in small groups, two shifts a day, clearing large rocks and obstacles, filling in ditches, cutting down trees and shrubs. As the work progressed, so did the ambitions of the SOE in Cairo.

Myers reported to Cairo HQ a potential airfield capable of handling small, single-engine aircraft. Cairo soon escalated the project to a tactical military facility for landing and launching Liberator and Halifax bombers. For the bombers, the runway had to be at least eighteen hundred yards.

As the villagers cleared the strip, they brought cartloads of fir branches from the hillsides. They stuck these in the ground to look like normal growth and break up visual cues that might reveal construction work from the air. They left their carts camouflaged to look like haystacks. They cleared everything when the strip was in use and replaced it when it wasn't.

For quality control, the RAF sent an officer to supervise landing and take-off arrangements and to test the runway's surface. He did this from an automobile gauging ride comfort between twenty and forty miles per hour. Then he made certain the car would freewheel for one hundred yards from a speed of twenty miles per hour.

The grand opening of the aerodrome came August 9, 1943, at 2200 hours, with the low drone of a black Douglas C-47 Dakota. The andartes hurried to their assignments. They had practiced lighting the runway, and just as important, dousing flames. This time, it was real. At the sound of the Dakota, the landing officer flashed wind and weather reports skyward with an Aldis lamp. Once acknowledged by the flight crew, two bonfires ignited at the approach to the strip. Andartes, lying prone on both sides of the runway, lit oil lamps spaced every 150 yards.

The landing was perfect, and the waiting andartes offloaded supplies. At 2212 hours, the Dakota rose into the blackness with a bearing for Cairo. Onboard was the future of Greece.

To say the visit to Cairo didn't go well would be charitable. The six men who flew with Brigadier Myers were ranking officials in the three leading resistance organizations, EAM-ELAS, EDES, and the smaller, left-leaning EKKA, allied with EAM-ELAS. These men thought they were going to a grand conference to resolve sticky political differences. Differences between not only their resistance groups but differences with the king and the government in exile. They thought this because that's what Myers told them. He was repeating what the Foreign Office had told him. The six resistance leaders aboard the Dakota were a collection of rivals. They were not on the same political score. But they found a common opponent in the king's government. At a minimum, the resistance groups wanted a plebiscite before the king's return to Greece, if he were ever to return at all.

The British Foreign Office displayed none of their hallmark diplomacy. They offered no balm to heal divisions and forge consensus. They did just the opposite. They provoked the resistance leaders with an unbending line about the primacy of the constitution and the legitimacy of the king's government. But legitimacy reined only on King Charles Street in London, not in the mountains of Greece. Whether this affront was by design or miscalculation, the results were disastrous. Monty Woodhouse sized things up in a first-person account from his book, *Apple of Discord.*

The situation was unprecedented and needed to be handled delicately. What was especially confusing was the collision of a political atmosphere permeated by the Communist question with one permeated by the King's matter. In occupied Greece, the latter had none of the urgency of the former; in Egypt, the import of the former had scarcely begun to be realized. The conversations which took place in Egypt were therefore carried on at cross-purposes. The alignments which formed themselves within the group of characters reassembled on the Egyptian stage were complicated. From occupied Greece had come six Greeks united on the King's matter, and potentially divided on the Communist question, to meet Greek authorities divided upon the former but potentially united on the latter as soon as they became aware of its menace."[56]

The Americans were nowhere. The British failed to invite their Allies even though the American equivalent of the SOE, the OSS, was about to join the British in Greece. John Tsouderos's father, the Greek prime minister in exile, was in touch with five American senators visiting Cairo during the meeting, but the senators remained uninvited.

The most organized were the communists. Thus, the KKE's agenda became the default for the resistance organizations. But there was no peace or consensus to come from Cairo. The parties signed inconsequential papers, but no agreement of substance emerged. Mutinies in the Greek armed forces flared, and when the six resistance leaders returned to the mountains on the night of September 17, bloody conflict was inevitable.

EAM-ELAS collected overwhelming stocks of weapons from retreating Italians and successful raids on the Germans. They expected the war in Greece to end soon. They believed the British would restore the king, and those they derided as monarcho-fascists. Thus, the Greek Communist Party (KKE) began planning the seizure of power.

The British Foreign Office prompted the sacking of Brigadier Myers. He never returned to Greece. The Foreign Office thought him too cozy with EAM-ELAS. Monty Woodhouse took his place. Among those who climbed from the returning Dakota onto the Plains of Thessaly that night in September were the first two American OSS officers.

Chapter 19

The chaos in Cairo played out in Colorado. The villain, the perpetrator or force majeure, was the British Foreign Office. American politics, too, were in play. Actions in London and Washington were reactions to the global truth of 1943. This truth changed with troop movements, the rise and fall of expectations, and the whims and wishes of Churchill, Roosevelt, and Stalin. The British did not want a communist Greece, fearing the loss of friendly sea lanes. They worried naïve America didn't understand Greece, as did Britain, with her years of experience and colonial forbearance. Britain claimed Greece. They considered it within their sphere of influence. This they would formalize with Stalin a year later in the Percentage Agreement.

Meanwhile, the last thing the British wanted was an American combat battalion maneuvering on Greek soil. They wanted no passionate Greeks with little loyalty or respect for King George II, armed by the indefatigable United States to complicate his restoration.

"What do you think this is about?" asked Gus.

"Stavros shook his head as he finished making his bunk and without looking up said, "No idea. But I saw some dire looking faces in camp this morning. If we were shipping out, I'd expect to see more smiles and grins. Your idea is as good as mine, that's for sure."

The entire battalion, six hundred men, mustered on the parade ground before the viewing stand. Men shook their heads in response to their comrades' questions about what the heck was going on. It was a warm morning. The sun had just taken on the character of a fired furnace. But the men left in the battalion, after seven months of grueling exercises, marathon conditioning, and robust weeding out, were unfazed.

Major Clainos and three unknown men climbed the steps to the riser. The men snapped to attention and shouted in unison, *"Eletheria e Thanatos!"* Liberty or Death! Clainos spoke without a microphone, in a voice clear to every ear on the parade ground. He said, "The Hundred Twenty-Second Combat Infantry Battalion will be disbanded effective within a month."

Stavros and Gus heard GIs in the ranks mutter, "What?" And *"Ti?"*

The major went on, "The men with me are representatives of the Office of Strategic Services. They are here to gather volunteers from this battalion. Volunteers will face a selection process and, if accepted, receive special training. They will deploy behind enemy lines into Greece by parachute and there operate as commandos with native Greek resistance units. These selected men can expect hazardous duty and high casualty rates. Selectees must speak Greek and display the highest physical and mental abilities."

In the ranks, heads swiveled as GIs looked to their buddies, trying to understand what was happening.

The major went on, "Gentlemen, let me say that it is my honor to have served as your commander, an honor I will take to my grave. Now, it will be my honor to be the first to volunteer for service in the OSS." The major raised his right hand and looked back over his left shoulder to the other men on the stand.

As soon as the major raised his hand, men in the ranks began shooting theirs into the air, and within seconds, all hands were aloft. Gus's hand flew into the air a half-second before Stavros.

Major Clainos had foreseen the dissolution of the battalion he worked so hard to create. The shadowy impetus for the Greek Battalion may well lead back to John Tsouderos's father.[57] Some believe that Emmanouil Tsouderos put the bug in FDR's ear about creating a combat unit composed of Greeks and

Greek Americans. If Tsouderos was the origin, he may too have ushered in its demise.

President Roosevelt signed the order in January 1943, establishing the 122nd Infantry Battalion. FDR was a friend and supporter of the Greeks and a member of the American Hellenic Educational Progressive Association (AHEPA) Delphi Chapter Number 25 in Manhattan, New York City. AHEPA was the leading Greek American society and a political player. Because of its community influence, the OSS kept a close watch on AHEPA's publications and the political leanings of its leadership.[58]

American Greeks didn't like an American combat unit supporting the reinstallation of King George II and the government in exile. This AHEPA wrote about, spoke about, and promoted in the Greek community. Reports to the Foreign Nationals Branch (FNB) of the OSS detailed AHEPA's politics. On December 30, 1942, FNB received a report entitled "AHEPA Concern over Possible Political Use of Greek Battalion."[59] Another report followed on February 6, 1943, "Greek Unit in the US Army and the American Greek Community." These were the tip of the intelligence iceberg. The FNB had many, many reports on Greek Americans, including speeches, lectures, radio broadcasts, meetings, and current religious and political newspapers, journals, and leaflets. The FNB collected thousands upon thousands of reports on all domestic ethnic communities, especially Europeans. The *US Office of Strategic Services Foreign Nationals Branch Files, 1942–1945 Index,* contains 457 pages and over 41,000 reports. Each report details something someone said or wrote or broadcast.[60]

Major Clainos knew when he took command of the 122nd that "the Greek Battalion in American uniforms would never go to Greece. They would allow no American unit in the Balkans because it was the British domain."[61] Because the major knew this, he kept the battalion below maximum strength, hoping to avoid the calamity of the 122nd deploying somewhere other than

Greece. If the battalion deployed elsewhere, perhaps Asia, Clainos feared desertions and demoralization. The prospect of ridicule of Greek character and loyalty haunted him.

The OSS Board of Officers sent to recruit at Camp Carson had their pick of the litter. They selected 160 men for OSS commando training and dubbed the new unit Company C, 2671 Special Reconnaissance Battalion, or Greek Operational Group (OG). The new battalion would form with six groups. Stavros and Gus drew Group II. Those not selected for OSS service transferred into other US Army units. Stavros and Gus received two weeks' leave and orders to report to Building Q in Washington, DC, on October 8, 1943.

Chapter 20

Trained and conditioned for unforgiving survival, Stavros was a proud product of Camp Carson. His body was lean and hard. He could kill another man with his hands, a knife, or a gun. He could run five miles in full kit in the heat of summer or lay in a sniper's hide for hours on end without registering movement. He had seen men fail and leave. He had seen other men best him on mountain trails and the rifle range. He knew his capabilities. He responded without thought to commands and marched crisply in formation. The routine at Camp Carson was confining and the training all-consuming. Life in camp was not liberating. Instead, what grew in him was not the personal freedom he had given up, but the new freedom of collective confidence. It was a confidence in who he was and freedom of association in a group of like minds.

It was Sunday, August 15, 1943, Dekapentavgoustos, the celebration of Mary's repose. A week before, the battalion had formed on the parade grounds and learned of its disbandment. Stavros started OSS interviews the following day. The OSS had reviewed the personnel files of the battalion before traveling to Colorado. Stavros was a recruiting target. He fit the OSS informal candidate criteria often attributed to the director, William "Wild Bill" Donovan, "A PhD who can win a bar fight."[62] Stavros passed a panel of psychological evaluations. He passed language and aptitude tests. He was fit. Three weeks later, the OSS enrolled him. He received orders to report to Washington after two weeks' leave.

The battalion had Dekapentavgoustos off. Following Alex's suggestion, Stavros traveled to Pueblo to meet his childhood.

Stavros wrote to Alex and Marta every week. He wrote nothing to alarm Marta. But he wrote enough he was certain his father could read between the lines. He sent photographs scrubbed clean in dress uniform to ally Marta's fear of hardship or deprivation, his actual condition at Camp Carson. And the family wrote back.

At the end of July, Alex wrote to his son that Stavros might want to visit friends in Pueblo, should he have the chance. Dekapentavgoustos was the perfect opportunity. Alex told Stavros that the people in Pueblo, Domna and Peter Georgallas, and Yiorgos Vedros, had helped Alex in 1914 after Eléni's death. Alex was circumspect; it was his nature. These three people had been more than friends. Their support of Alex during the strike and years following saved Stavros from adoption or an orphanage. Now, thirty years on, Stavros neared a reunion that none could have predicted.

Stavros stepped from the passenger car onto the boarding platform of Pueblo's Union Depot. He looked like a thousand other GIs in dress uniform. Domna recognized him at first glance. At the back of the crowd milling on the platform, Stavros saw a Greek woman in her sixties. She wore a black dress and a blue scarf and was crossing herself and muttering to the two men on either side. The older and taller man, Peter, was her husband, and the well-dressed man with the trim mustache standing to her left was Yiorgos. Yiorgos waved to Stavros. Stavros assumed Marta had sent a photograph, and that was how they recognized him. Domna said later that she didn't need a photo. She knew him, though she had not seen him since he was three years old.

Stavros smiled and offered warm and energetic handshakes and a respectful hug for Domna. The foursome issued a torrent of exclamations in Greek, inching their way into the station. Smiling all the while, Domna continued to cross herself every few minutes. Inside the station, they engaged in small talk, then made their way to Peter's car and to the Georgallas's house for a lavish holiday feast. Stavros, arriving at noon, missed the morning mass and prayers. Now it was homecoming and celebration. All the same, the Italian attack on the cruiser *Elli* on Dekapentavgoustos in 1940 had left painful memories, and talk of war soon followed.

When they arrived at Peter and Domna's house, the same house where Stavros stayed as a babe, there was something familiar about the place. Stavros recognized the smell and the light playing against the plaster walls in the living room. Peter motioned for Stavros to sit in a high-backed chair, and Peter and Yiorgos sat on the sofa across the room. Domna excused herself and returned with a serving tray and three short glasses of ouzo, water, and lemon slices. The men were gracious, and the conversation began. Domna again excused herself and entered the kitchen.

Yiorgos began, "Stavros, your father is one of the bravest men I know. I can see his character in you. You are taller, but the character is unmistakable."

Stavros smiled and blushed. In the Greek community, younger men defer to older one, so Stavros said only, "Thank you."

"Those years . . . that time . . . they were hard for the Greeks. You can't imagine. This state was like the Wild West. It *was* the Wild West! I'm sorry, I don't mean to bring up old ghosts. But know that your father and his friends, Harry and Dimitri, were brave men and never once foreswore their honor," intoned Yiorgos.

"My father says the same of you, Yiorgos, and Peter," answered Stavros.

"Yes, but Stavros, we only gave you sanctuary. It was your father and the others who fought evil in the hills to the south. I ran my flower shop and did what I could from here," answered Peter.

Yiorgos nodded.

"But Peter, you knew my mother. You knew Eléni?" Stavros ventured.

Peter nodded. "I stood up for them at their wedding. Your mother was like a dream—young, good-looking, smart as could be, and a pleasure to be around. Your father married well." Then added, "Twice! We arranged the second from this very house! Arranged by the woman now arranging the feast!"

Peter's comment and his chuckle lightened the conversation. Everyone loved Eléni, this Marta insisted. Eléni had been Marta's best friend in the coal camp at Segundo.

The men talked through the early afternoon, and the conversation flowed in friendly and respectful but guarded tones. Peter and Yiorgos and Domna lived through the terrible times in 1913–14. Times of more domestic bloodshed and disruption than any since the American Civil War. They lived in proximity, but Alex, Dimitri, and Harry lived in it. They were in the thick of the fighting. They saw death on both sides and the misery families endured in flimsy tent cities on the cold, windswept plains and hills. The three men hunted and rendered justice to one of Eléni's killers and stalked the other until their scant resources forced a return to their working lives. The problem for Peter and Yiorgos was that they were uncertain about how much Alex had shared with Stavros. So, they played it safe and talked about how hard things were, how Alex tricked the railroad foreman into thinking he was Swedish to get his job as a trackman. How Dimitri kept telling everyone, while he was penniless, that he was a born businessman, and look at him now. How Harry, a man of few words, always said the right thing at the right time to bring into focus the next task and the correct path. Peter talked about how Domna had engineered the marriage and combination of families for Alex and Marta. This, he thought, was well-done because Marta always complained how barbaric were the Greeks, and Alex was the most "mountain man" of them all. They all laughed when Stavros told them his adopted mother still tried to shepherd Alex toward civilization. He told them that her job at the Municipal Theatre, the Muny, had been a joy because she could attend the plays and operas. He said even in retirement, Marta had privileges. She took pleasure in making Alex shave, get his haircut, and put on a suit and tie to escort her to productions.

The thought of Alex in a suit and tie made Yiorgos and Peter chuckle.

Stavros, too, guarded his words. The news of the Greek Battalion's disbandment was not public. As far as the Greek community knew, the US Army was still in the business of training Greeks to fight in the old country. Stavros had yet to tell Alex and Marta about his pending transfer to the OSS. The conversation was pleasant, informative, and provided Stavros with sketches and outlines. Still, some narratives lacked completion and color, and he stored questions away for later illumination.

The men spoke about the war and the Allies in Italy. Like many Greeks in America and most of the Greeks in Greece, they assumed the Allies would liberate Greece on the heels of a victory in Italy. Everyone had a good reason why this must be so except Stavros, who held back and didn't endorse the "Greece is next" supposition. Stavros knew the OSS had a longer timetable, and he expected the Allies might delay their recapture of Greece. It was just a feeling.

Domna entered the living room, wiping her hands on her apron. She waited for a lull in the conversation and announced that the feast was ready. They were eating early because Stavros had to catch the 8:30 p.m. train. Peter and Domna's son and daughter arrived for dinner and brought their spouses and three grandchildren. Peter's son managed the flower business in Pueblo, and their daughter was a science teacher. The small children were well-behaved but never far from the center of attention.

The meal was extravagant. Stavros imagined Domna must have been preparing it for a week. He was right. Stavros ate full helpings of roast leg of lamb, chicken in tomato sauce, stuffed peppers, and the ever-delightful roasted potatoes with lemon and garlic. The avgolemono soup and dessert treats were almost unassailable. He loved every morsel, and when the meal was over, Domna insisted Stavros take a box of cookies for the train. He required little persuasion.

He rode to Union Depot with Peter and Yiorgos. They parked the car, and the three men walked to the waiting room and took seats. When the stationmaster called the train to Denver, they rose, shook hands, and Stavros saw glistening tears in both men's eyes.

It took Stavros the entire trip back to Colorado Springs and Camp Carson to sort his feelings and catalog insights. His time in Colorado had made him tough, but the trip to Pueblo left him curious and uncertain. He knew his father, Dimitri, and Harry had made one man who raped and killed his mother pay with his life. He knew another man remained too distant for them to reach. Now, he knew from Yiorgos, who was well-placed at Colorado Fuel and Iron, that the man was Karl Linderfelt, a military ruffian with a checkered history in the Colorado National Guard. He filed this away and vowed that, when the time was right, he would find Linderfelt.

Stavros's time in Colorado was like a play at the Muny. Act I, Camp Carson, set the stage. Act II, Pueblo, added immediacy and depth to the characters. Act III was yet to be written. First would come Greece.

Chapter 21

The village slept late. Only the older women were awake in the early hours, preparing for the day. Scattered in the fields and orange groves in their black dresses and aprons, they orbited Kommeno gathering firewood. Some collected fish from traps on the Arachthos Potamos, and others picked fruits and herbs from the marshy groves along the riverbank. The day before had been the feast of the repose of Mary. And for added festivities, the village of six hundred celebrated a wedding. The lambs from Chómori, traded in good faith for the American radio earlier that month, made their star appearance to the appreciation of all.

As the old women went about their chores, a pair gathering firewood near the village center noticed movement in the groves beyond. These were troops of the 12 Company of GebirgsJäger Regiment 98 under the command of Oberstleutnant Josef Salminger. They were light infantry of the German First Mountain Division.

Two days before, the Wehrmacht sent a reconnaissance team to the village. The villagers noticed their approach and their abrupt retreat without entering the village center. This worried the villagers, and that night they slept in the fields fearing an attack. The next day, the village president traveled to the Italian commander in Arta with a delegation. He explained andartes had visited, but that they were there seeking food, and billeted elsewhere. The villagers had a good relationship with the Italian authorities, who thanked them for coming forward and promised the villagers there would be no consequences. Reassured, the delegation returned to Kommeno to prepare for the holiday and wedding.

The German scouts reported seeing a small group of andartes to Wehrmacht divisional headquarters in Ioannina. The men they saw were members of the EDES band under the command of Yiorgos's friend Alexandros. They were preparing the spit for the holiday lamb roast.

At dawn, on August 16, 1943, 120 German troops surrounded the village and covered escape routes. When signal flares lit the sky, the soldiers moved in with orders to "leave nothing standing." The first to fall was the village priest. Lieutenant Röser, the leader of the assault, shot him point-blank in the head as he pleaded for his church. As the priest slumped to the ground, grenades toppled houses and indiscriminate killing erupted throughout the peaceful village. In the chaos, the Germans left an escape route to the river unguarded. Half of the village fled to its banks through cane thickets and took to fishing caïques or swam the churning current to the far side. Alexandros never returned fire, nor did any andartes. Outnumbered and outgunned, they took flight to the Arachthos.

Six hours later, the Germans withdrew from the burning rubble, carting off loot and livestock. They left behind 317 dead villagers—men, women, and children, seventy-four under the age of ten.[63] The Germans desecrated the bodies, all bodies, in the most humiliating and vile ways imaginable. The sickening details of their inhumanity will not see new life in these pages.

Chapter 22

October can be pleasant in Washington, DC, a reprieve from the punishment of summer. Stavros arrived to a light breeze, low humidity, and temperature in the sixties. He detrained at Union Station on an overnight from St. Louis. He had never visited before. He wished he could see more of the scenery, the historic architecture, and the scintillating ebb and flow of young women on their way to offices. But the canvas covering the GMC deuce-and-a-half truck bed where he sat on a wooden bench, shoulder-to-shoulder, had no windows. His view was through the open flap above the tailgate, a view he shared with fourteen men as the truck bumped and jarred over streetcar rails and potholes. Just a few blocks into their tour, the truck pulled to the curb, and a uniformed man without rank insignia climbed out of the cab. He walked to the rear, and, offering no explanation, lowered the tailgate. In the darkness of his canvas confines, Stavros foresaw the cave of secrets that would be his life.

Stavros arrived at 0800 hours at 2430 E Street, NW, OSS Headquarters. The uniformed guards at the gate directed him to Q Building. In Q Building, he was interviewed and briefed, then filled out forms and releases. Now, late in the afternoon, he was on his way to Area F with fourteen other soon-to-be American commandos. And should anyone ask, he couldn't tell them.

The dispatching officer at Q Building, headquarters for the Operational Groups, made Area F sound posh. "You will love it, boys, golf and swimming, great food, quiet nights. Love it."

No one in an Operational Group would ever swing a golf club.

Area F was the Congressional Country Club in the tony suburb of Bethesda, Maryland, twelve miles from downtown Washington. The patriotic members of the Congress of the United States of America had loaned their prime real estate to national security. They turned it over with élan and grace, happy to do their part for the war. So it seemed. Stavros learned more from the chief of grounds maintenance.

In March, the board passed a lofty resolution declaring, in part, "Whereas the members of the Congressional Country Club Inc. wish to do everything within their power to cooperate with the government in the war's prosecution. . . ." The patriotic clubbers signed a lease with OSS promising $4,000 a month rent and a guarantee that the grounds be returned to existing conditions after the war.[64] The club was broke. Membership had declined, and gas rationing had taken its toll on visitors. In January 1943, the board announced the club had hosted only five guests the weekend before.

The club had no shortage of *guests* now. From 1943 to 1945, Area F hosted twenty-five hundred soldiers training two hundred per rotation. It hosted all OSS Operational Groups for basic commando training. Not just the Greeks but Norwegians, French, Italians, Austrians, Germans, Dutch, Hungarians, Spaniards, Poles, Czech-Slovaks, Yugoslavs, Chinese, Koreans, and Thais.[65] Regardless of nationality, the "guests" were there to learn the basics of "dirty fighting," much of it taught by well-practiced British Special Operations Executive officers.

The GMC rumbled through the tall iron gates of the club's entrance, passing a guard post in the center of the roadway with sandbagged machine guns on either side. Stavros rocked in his dark confines and considered what he had signed up for. The OSS had hidden nothing from him. They had shown him explicit photographs and movie reel clips of combat and presented real-life scenarios in vivid and disturbing detail. The OSS selection process did everything it could to rattle candidates and reveal the "guts, savoir faire, and intelligence desired for OSS agents."[66] Psychologists engineered innocent social encounters designed to stress or surprise recruits, then observed their responses. They had waiters and kitchen staff drop plates nearby out of sight to spook men and watch reactions. They told volunteers that casualty rates could run as high as 90 percent. Stavros plunged ahead. He signed the last documents at Q Building, placing him in the 10 percent of volunteers who advanced into Operational Groups. Now he was processing not only his new surroundings, but his additional responsibility. The OSS, an organization with carte blanche commissioning authority, made Stavros a first lieutenant and put him in charge of OG II.

OSS Operational Groups comprised twenty-two enlisted men, with no ranks below corporal and two officers. Each OG had two section leaders and four squad leaders. Each section had two squads, and each squad had five men.[67] Stavros would be the commanding officer in Greek OG II. Gus slapped him on the back when he learned the news, then gave Stavros a proper salute. Gus, now a noncommissioned officer, a sergeant, also drew Group II.

Area F was four hundred acres of bucolic Maryland real estate. The OSS blew up, booby-trapped, camouflaged, ambushed, reconnoitered, and put it to the precise use for which it was never intended. Ear-splitting detonations and small arms fire replaced the lingering cluck of geese on the Potomac River. Instead of scrubbed golfers settling in for a short putt, commando trainees squirmed in the dirt and sand and mud, lying in wait for an enemy. Nighttime was no reprieve. Nighttime was for serious training. Spies, saboteurs, undercover agents, and commandos were nocturnal by design.

There were quiet times, times when William Ewart Fairbairn of the British Royal Marines taught silent killing. Fairbairn was fond of the Fairbairn-Sykes Fighting Knife. There were other silent methods, neck-breaking, suffocation, but the knife was the most efficient. When quiet killing was uncalled for, Fairbairn taught a style of fighting he called *Defendu*. This hand-to-hand style mixed jujitsu and boxing, wrestling, savate, judo and street fighting. Fairbairn refined this unique method during his police work fighting criminal gangs in 1930s Shanghai, the roughest city in the world. Fairbairn and his good friend E.A. Sykes engaged in two hundred documented incidents of violent close combat in that city. They knew their stuff. Defendu was a unique martial art where trainees didn't learn to parry or block. Fairbairn only believed in offense, initiative, and artifice. The SOE syllabus advised, "Don't stop just because an opponent is crippled. If you have broken his arm, for instance, that is only of value because it is then easier to kill."[68] Fairbairn was ungentlemanly and unpredictable, but his results were inevitable.

Fairbairn taught an innovative handgun technique where the pistol, in this case, a .45 caliber Colt M1911 was not sighted but pointed. Sighting takes time, and in close quarters, time is not your friend. Only on a shooting range do you have time to draw, sight, and shoot. Mastering this style of shooting required instinct and practice, lots of practice. The commandos drilled in chaotic, noisy, and confusing situations where decisions arose in a blink. Then they practiced at night with one arm tied. Then the other arm tied. Fairbairn learned his lessons in dim Shanghai alleyways where it was kill or be killed. This urgency he shared and drilled into commandos on both sides of the Atlantic. Fairbairn's books, *Scientific Self-Defence, Shooting to Live,* and *Get Tough! How to Win in Hand-to-Hand Fighting, as Taught to the British Commandos and the US Armed Forces,* circulate in special operations training courses worldwide to this day.

All of Fairbairn's wisdom and much more awaited Stavros and the men of Greek Operational Group II. The GMC rolled to a stop, and as the driver parted the canvas flap, he said, "Watch your step, boys. Welcome to Malice in Wonderland."

The passengers left the truck before a massive, white, Mediterranean-inspired clubhouse. It was a fantasy in brick and granite, landscaped like a fastidious model train layout. Longer than a football field, the six-story building was the largest clubhouse in the United States. On the evening of October 8, 1943, with the setting sun just touching the wooded rise above Great Falls on the Potomac River, Stavros surveyed the incongruity.

He looked south toward the tenth tee and the water trap beyond. To the left, he spotted a shooting range where the driving range should be. Trainees were blasting away with an assortment of weaponry, including some he'd never seen before. Then, beyond the first water trap, he watched in astonishment as a mortar shell hit twenty yards short of a white rain shelter. The errant shell threw fist-sized divots of manicured turf high into the air. The next shell blew the wooden shelter to smithereens. Five hundred yards downrange, on the fairway for the first hole, he watched as a dozen men in uniforms crawled over the cropped grass. Just above their heads zinged the rounds of an MG 42 German machine gun, a weapon Dimitra coveted. The gun's high rate of cyclic firing gave it a unique signature and earned it the nickname *Knochensäge* or bone saw. To the right of the machine gun, he saw barbed-wire barriers and an obstacle course incorporating the water and sand traps and assorted difficulties. To the far left, he saw a mock-up of a C-47 airplane fuselage. There, one group of men were leaping from its door and rolling when they hit the ground, and nearby another group was fighting hand-to-hand. Or rather, hand-to-hand, feet-to-hand, and any combination thereof.

Stavros also registered what he did not see. He did not see units marching in formation or any rank insignia on the uniforms.

The truck driver interrupted the group's gawking. He announced, "Gentlemen, chow is served in the castle," and he pointed to the clubhouse in case someone didn't get the message. "You'll bunk in the cabin tents on the tennis courts and along the entrance drive. There are seventy, and they are numbered. They've got coal-fired potbelly stoves and wooden floors. Better accommodations than wherever you're headed. Reveille is 0630 hours. Please see the facilities officer in the clubhouse for instructions. Have a great vacation. Oh, and Maryland snakes won't kill you, but machine guns will. If you happen across one on your crawl, stay down. We lost a man last week when he bolted."[69]

Area F training lasted two weeks. It was less physically demanding than Camp Carson but mentally arduous. The men no longer faced thirty-five-mile mountain hikes with full packs and gear. They no longer maneuvered all week, bivouacked in the wild, foraged for food, hunted rabbits, and found water. Instead, the men learned field craft, map reading, battle tactics, defensive and attack formations, and compass reading. They maneuvered at night, and most of their training took place in darkness with the Maryland sky far enough from Washington that the stars flickered bright and clear. They navigated using the pole star, constellations, and moss on trees.

The guns and mortars and explosives training were riveting. The hand-to-hand combat was exhilarating and bruising. These lessons the men readily absorbed. They found the conceptual maneuvering and fighting formations more challenging. All men, officers, and noncoms studied what was officer-level advanced material. Classes met in the stupendous, ornate, converted clubhouse ballroom and open-air locations scattered across the grounds. Along with the American and British instructors, they learned from French resistance leaders. Their two-week rotation flashed by, but still they had time to visit Washington.

The men shed their US Army fatigues for the latest military fashion, including the brand-new, fur-lined Eisenhower jackets and paratroop jump boots. The only thing missing was unit patches. They were a secret unit, and the OSS wanted to keep it that way.

They cut dashing figures in their new jackets and boots. They knew it, and they were full of themselves when they visited the Stage Door Canteen near Lafayette Park across from the White House. The canteen, attached to the American Theater Wing, was a magnet for Hollywood and Broadway stars who came to serve "the boys" and be a part of the war effort. It was a magnificent spot for a celebrity press photo-op.

The night the Greeks showed up, they listened spellbound to "The Band That Plays the Blues," the ever-popular Woody Herman and His Orchestra. Their stiff, high-laced paratrooper boots didn't keep them from the dance floor. Then, Herman slowed things down. The band leader cut into his new release, "Do Nothin' Till You Hear from Me." The men who couldn't find a USO hostess partner stood on the floor and swayed in time, lost in the melancholy.

Stavros liked the OG's fresh look, and he noted the energy and attitude of the younger men. He was proud of the uniform, and so were they. To Stavros, the uniform symbolized achievement and fighting status. But to the younger men, most nineteen or twenty years old, it also justified cockiness.

The mountains of Greece would cure that.

Chapter 23

"Here's an update, then I'll let you get back to your rabbit hunting." The men chuckled at the inside joke.

"The Greeks think they're done with the Germans, so now they are fighting each other. Last month, the Brits held a big meeting in Cairo to iron out the politics between the resistance groups and the government in exile. But that didn't work. So, when the resistance leaders returned to Greece, the largest resistance organization, EAM-ELAS, took control. The Brits did not invite Americans to the Cairo meeting.

"When the Italians caved in and signed the September armistice, EAM-ELAS incorporated the Pinerolo Division, twelve thousand men and most of their arms, including their mountain artillery. This division was the only unit that didn't surrender to the Germans. EAM-ELAS scattered the division's units to disrupt their concentrations. Many of those units folded in and are fighting with EAM-ELAS. They are lightly armed and no threat to EAM-ELAS.

"The Germans may have extended EAM-ELAS a ceasefire, but that is unconfirmed. It's just something we've heard from the Red Cross. The Germans have played resistance groups against each other since they goose-stepped into Greece.

"The Germans would love to clear out EDES. EDES is a smaller resistance group in the western mountains with some royalists and monarchists. EAM-ELAS is much larger and widely deployed. EAM-ELAS has the support of populations where it operates. It is disposed to the influence of communists, the KKE. Both groups have determined fighters, but the EAM-ELAS units are more disciplined and now better armed, even without British support.

"We have limited sources in Greece, and this information comes from friendly SOE contacts and other sources. We have a couple of OSS officers on the ground assigned to what we now call the Allied Military Mission, the AMM. But the Brits are walling us off. They've been in Greece for over a year. They are the primary supporters of the Greek government in exile. The British are touchy about American military power in what they consider a British zone of influence. Their men on the ground, seasoned SOE officers, are top-rate soldiers, but the politics are messy. The Brits fired the head of their military mission, Myers, back in September. The new man, Woodhouse, is a smart chap, friendly, but he will not buck the folks in Cairo or London.

"So, the Germans may have laid a trap, and the Greeks may have fallen for it. The German intelligence network, Abwehr, is spreading rumors in the countryside and in Athens about an impending German withdrawal. Everybody in Greece wants to believe that the Germans are on their way out. And who could blame them? The Germans, Bulgarians, and Italians have savaged that country. But the Germans aren't leaving. Not yet.

"From what we know, the Germans have six hundred thousand troops in Greece. They moved a few formations north, supply and transportation companies, but not their heavy hitters. And the Germans gave up control of two small Aegean Islands, but nothing strategic. The Germans are capable and willing to go into the mountains into EAM-ELAS strongholds and do damage. We are receiving reports of just such an offensive getting underway. This entire episode may be EAM-ELAS and KKE overreach.

"You will receive more briefings as you get closer to Greece, and when you're assigned areas of operation, you'll get details. For now, this will have to do, and as always, anything you've heard this morning is top secret. Don't talk to anybody about this, not even the British instructors. Is that clear?"

The six Operational Groups, one hundred and eighty-two enlisted men and eighteen officers, sat on a grassy clearing before a wooden riser. In the dense woods of Western Maryland's Catoctin Mountains arose a resounding, "Yes, sir!"[70]

The Greek OGs had just received their first intelligence briefing. The unidentified OSS major stepped off the riser without taking questions, then left in a black Chevrolet with two armed escorts minutes later.

The truck driver was right, Area F was a vacation compared to their new assignment. Catoctin Mountain Park, nine thousand acres of wooded hills and ravines, is sixty miles northeast of the Congressional Country Club. The Marylanders living in these hills would never be mistaken for those of Bethesda. The New Deal's Works Progress Administration (WPA) and the Civilian Conservation Corps (CCC) built the work camp, rustic cabins, kitchens, dining halls, and outbuildings in the late 1930s. The War Department leased the property from the Department of the Interior in March 1942, and the OSS dubbed it Area B in April and opened it for training. Area B hosted three hundred trainees per rotation and seventy-five station cadre and instructors.[71]

Area B introduced the men to every firearm America could get its hands on. They practiced with .45 caliber Colts, bazookas, 50 caliber machine guns, and everything in between. They fired mortars, learned to shape blasting charges, practiced defusing mines and booby traps, and blew simulated targets sky-high. They worked with blasting caps, time fuses, and primer cord, and in their free time, they practice hand-to-hand combat.

Area B was well suited for raiding and maneuvering in five-man squads. Instructors trucked the men over rutted fire trails to unfamiliar territory and dropped them off. They were to reach their target by a specific time using only their compasses, their wits, and the landmarks on their maps.

Catoctin is part of the Blue Ridge Mountains, and its dense hardwood forest covers 95 percent of the park. Massive oak, hickory, and poplar trees, along with elm, ash, and maple, reach to the sky. Mountain laurel, spicebush, low blueberry, and viburnum crowd the understory and the forest edge. Bears, bobcats, beavers, skunks, raccoons, rabbits, squirrels, foxes, and deer love it there. And the rushing creeks that cut through the greenery like chaotic seams in the landscape are trout havens. The men had no problem supplementing their camp diet. No problem, except their neighbors.

Besides the OSS, Catoctin was home to a secret presidential retreat, Camp #3, Hi-Catoctin, now called Camp David. But in 1943 it was known by another name, not known by many.[72] Upon his first visit on April 22, 1942, Franklin D. Roosevelt, so taken by the majestic view and bracing air, named it Shangri-La from James Hilton's 1933 novel, *Lost Horizon.*

The Greek OGs had, in the most basic ways, become self-sufficient. They could scrounge, hunt, pilfer, and trap their meals, find drinkable water, sleep in mud, and shelter outdoors when no building was handy. Area B was bountiful, and the game was plentiful and easy to flush. But one hunting expedition rousted a surprise. Two tall, plain-clothed men, dressed in long black coats, suits, and ties, and armed with Thompsons, appeared out of the woods like movie characters. They confronted the Greek hunters. The lead man ordered, "Please identify yourselves."

The Greeks said they were with an Army unit training nearby. The men were under orders to always answer that they were Army, not OSS.

The man in the long coat said, "We are Secret Service. Your president is resting nearby. Please return to your camp."

And return they did. But there were other neighbors in the woods of Catoctin.

"Well, that sure can't be the target. Hell, people live there!" exclaimed Stavros in a whisper.

"Right, I think the coordinates are north of here. Geez, Stavros, look at that place! If I didn't see it with my own eyes, I'd think it was from a Li'l Abner comic strip. That girl's wearing a potato sack. What's she, ten years old?"

Stavros just shook his head.

Gus whispered, "All that's missing is a blue tick hound dog."

At that instant, as if on cue, a deep woeful baying issued from the far side of the cabin. The two men looked at each other, stunned.

As the rest of the squad arrived at the edge of the clearing and saw the dilapidated log cabin, collapsing clothesline, and rickety outhouse, every man had the same reaction.

A woman, gray-haired in her fifties, walked from inside the cabin onto the front porch in a tattered gown, barefoot with a broom. She called to the little girl. But the men, in cover and out of sight, couldn't make out what she said. They couldn't understand her words.

Gus said, "I had no idea people lived like that in America."

Stavros said, "We better keep moving if we want to make our timetable."

"And if we stick around here, we may get a backside full of buckshot," added Gus.

The squad, faces painted, fatigues and helmets camouflaged with scrubs and brush, took compass readings, and headed out unseen and unheard.

Chapter 24

A funereal pall of cigarette smoke hung in the chilly room frosted by solemnity. Dimitra stood tall before Aris, her garrison cap held in front of her with ΕΛΑΣ facing outward. She stared at the hard man seated behind the table strewn with maps. Aris Velouchiotis was no taller than Dimitra. But with his full beard, piercing eyes, and reputation for demanding discipline, she stood anxious in his presence. She didn't show her feelings. Her speech was flat and her intonation resolute and reverent. She respected Aris. She knew his history.

Aris, ten years older than Dimitra, had been born in Lamia, the son of a lawyer. His family was well-off. His was much the same background as Dimitra. He graduated from the Geoponic School of Larissa and moved to Athens, where he joined the party in the 1920s. He became the editor of the communist newspaper *Rizospastis* and for that, he was jailed and tortured during the Metaxas dictatorship.

He had been a private in the Hellenic Army assigned to mountain artillery on the Albanian front when the Germans invaded. Dimitra first met the man in Platanos after the disintegration of his artillery unit. Dimitra was the local chief of organizing for the irregular forces, guerrillas who, along with the Hellenic Army, forced the invading Italians back into Albania. She joined KKE in December 1941.

That month, Aris traveled to Roumeli under orders from the KKE to organize the Greek People's Liberation Army, ELAS. He was successful. He started with fifteen brigands, klephts who knew the mountains but nothing of Karl Marx. Now, his fifty-thousand-fighter army included infantry, explosives specialists, mounted cavalry, and medical units. Aris was as close to an idol as egalitarian communist ideology allowed. Dimitra respected the man and knew the key to his success was his insistence on iron discipline. That was what she hoped to bend on this chilly morning in December 1943.

"Comrade Kapetánios, Dimitra, we go back, no? We both know the days of despair when villagers would run from us, thinking we were bandits and thieves. Together, with the strength of our party, we have built a powerful movement and one that will someday soon, we hope, govern all Greece. Is that not our dream and mission, comrade?" asked Aris.

"Yes, comrade. That is our mission," Dimitra answered.

"I wish you to speak freely, Dimitra. I may be your superior officer, but I need to hear from you all that you can share. We must speak honestly since a man's life is on the line. And a good man at that. But discipline is not negotiable and does not know the difference between this fighter and that. Between a likable man and a man who makes us retch. Am I speaking a truth on which we agree?" asked Aris.

"Yes, Comrade Commander."

Aris continued, "Discipline strengthens us. It unites us as a movement and an army. The stronger we are, the fewer people will die over the long course of our struggle. Is this not logic? If one man dies to ensure discipline, that lesson may save the lives of dozens more. If, for instance, in a battle, we face overwhelming odds, but a commander sees a path forward. Then the fighters hesitate for faulty discipline? Or, if we harbor a criminal in our ranks who robs from the people like the swine in the Security Battalions? Is it not best to make an immediate example? It is a lesson in times of war that will go unheeded if delayed. War demands immediacy. Reward comes to those who react at once, and doomed are those who equivocate.

"Listen to me. I sit before you lecturing like a stuffy professor. I apologize. Where was it you studied? Aristotle? University of Thessaloniki? I apologize. You have lived all these lessons, and you need not hear them from me. You know what is at stake. You are an accomplished leader, and a warrior, and, as a woman, doubly burdened to take your prominence among men.

This I know, and respect. So, please, tell me your thoughts, and together, we will try to satisfy the demands of our movement."

Aris unfolded his interlaced fingers and spread his arms on the desktop. His right hand moved toward his smoldering cigarette balanced in a brass tray, and his left toward his black fur Cossack cap. He waited for a second to make sure Dimitra registered his gesture. He picked up the smoldering cigarette, flicked the long ash, and put it to his lips. Dimitra understood his gesture, but she guarded her words, though she had no reason to mistrust Aris.

Dimitra began, "Comrade Commander, it is my understanding that Comrade Yiorgos, the commander of forces in the Chómori military district, stands accused of insubordination and cowardice."

Aris nodded, then recited, "The military commander of the Karpenissi District preferred written charges against your commander, alleging insubordination, cowardice, and sabotage of the movement for liberation. I asked that he withdraw the written document and allow me to judge informally first. This he has allowed. We are here today to decide Yiorgos's fate. If I decide that discipline is warranted, we will proceed with the written charges and formally adjudicate your commander. I don't have to tell you the penalty if the case against him stands."

Dimitra nodded, then resolutely responded, "Comrade, you have asked me to speak freely, and I will try. But I find this difficult. You are a figure of tremendous importance in our movement, and I am only a district Kapetánios. I have supported you and your programs whenever called upon in party discussions and debates. I support your resolute discipline. I have watched it shape our forces into iron wings, ready to fly upon command. Your contribution is unequaled. You have seen many battles and know their generalities and their exceptions. Today, I would like to tell you a case exceptional.

"Yiorgos has been my stratiotikós since we first elected district officers at the founding of ELAS. He is a masterful tactician, and there is no one, except yourself, that I would rather stand beside in a fight. He is not only fearless but unmovable, like the granite of these mountains.

"This you know about Yiorgos, Comrade Commander." Dimitra paused while Aris nodded.

"I will only remind you of his role at Gorgopotamos, where he led the reinforcements that rescued the EDES fighters who could not dislodge the Italians in the north position."

Aris held up his left hand and interrupted. "Comrade Dimitra, I was there, and I know you led the unit sent to reinforce the attack. Please do not give up your glory today when you fought valiantly on that day."

"Yes, Commander, and thank you. I had command of the reinforcements. That is true. But Yiorgos was the man who, armed with the Sten gun you gave me earlier, ran like a bull into the teeth of the firing. By some sleight of hand, he was not cut in half. He ran right to the concrete bunker and tossed in the first, second, and third grenades. It was only then that the Italians fled the fortification like rabbits. Most of them we shot like practice targets."

Dimitra related this to her commander with emotion in her voice.

"This story is new to me," confided Aris.

"Yiorgos is not a man who seeks notice. I arranged a celebration to honor him when we returned to Chómori. But he dodged the acclaim and spotlight like a shy schoolboy. He wished not to be elevated and praised as someone better than those around him. He is a humble man. But that only speaks to his character.

"I think there is another way to view his. . . ." Dimitra searched for words. "His actions or inaction concerning the EDES band of Kommeno.

"As you know, comrade, Yiorgos is not a party member. He is with the Popular Democratic Union. But he has never failed to follow military discipline. He is a fine example for others in the ELD of how they can work within EAM-ELAS as equals. Sometimes, I think the only reason he has declined party membership is because of his family's ancient friendship with a monarchist in his village. I have never pried.

"Yiorgos has a dear friend in Kommeno. I know him only as Alexandros. It was with him we traded for our American radio, and we have traded at other times for supplies and arms. More in the early days than now since our requisition of the Italian armory.

"Yiorgos has, over the months, tried to persuade Alexandros to bring his band to EAM-ELAS. He and Alexandros were both tagmatarchis in the Hellenic Army, and I believe they grew up together in Kato Dafni. I have never met Alexandros, so I cannot speak of his character. But Yiorgos has spoken of him as an honorable man willing to listen to logic, and a man impressed by our capture of so many Italian arms. As you know, EDES is well-supplied by the British, and Alexandros has said that he does not enjoy being a child of Britain. He told Yiorgos that one day the British will tell EDES to put away their toys and come in from the playground.

"Yiorgos came to me when he received an order to rendezvous with our forces from Karpenissi. You did not sign that order, Comrade Commander. The order was issued by the stratiotikós of Karpenissi district. Yiorgos brought it to me. I told him it was an order, yes, but one stratiotikós did not outrank another. It seemed more an invitation to discussion. I told him to muster the fighters and rendezvous. Once in contact with the Karpenissi commander, to begin a discussion. I told Yiorgos there may be something he did not know that might sway him. I told him to share in strict confidence our attempt to recruit Alexandros and his band to EAM-ELAS.

"Yiorgos was beside himself when we received news of the German attack on Kommeno this past August. He asked that we mobilize every fighter in the district and attack the fascist headquarters in Ioannina. I told him that was impossible. He was sullen for days afterward. I think he may have lost family in the attack. There was a wedding underway in the village and forty people who died were travelers just visiting for the ceremony. I think his family may have been in that group.

"I believe, Comrade Commander, that Yiorgos thought an attack on the EDES band in Kommeno was unnecessary. He believed he could win them and their supplies by persuasion, not force. He weighed the fighters we might lose in an attack and the fighters we might kill, all of which could someday fight on our side. And I agree. I think Yiorgos was right not to support an attack, and since the order was a lateral document, I think he used responsible discretion by declining to join in.

"As you know, the EDES band has since declared their allegiance to EAM-ELAS. This extends our area of military control fifty miles to the west. Their recruitment will prove valuable when we muster to attack the Germans in Ioannina. And, if you have not heard, Alexandros's defection has earned him a death warrant from Zervas.

"That is what I know of this matter, Comrade Commander."

Dimitra rested her case.

Aris inhaled on his nearly extinguished cigarette; the coal so close to his finger Dimitra wondered if he were displaying his imperviousness to pain. Then he spoke, "I heard about the defection and the death warrant. If I have my way, Zervas will die before his former lieutenant.

"Yiorgos's character is not an issue. Even before our dialogue, before I knew of his bravery at the viaduct, I held him in high regard. It is not the character of the man in question.

"I believe the charges against Commander Yiorgos are flawed. I believe the misunderstanding is this. The stratiotikós of the Karpenissi district is a party member and a member in high standing. I believe he may have had his feathers ruffled by a non-party commander questioning his plan. Sometimes it is difficult to separate the party protocols from the EAM-ELAS requirements, no? EAM-ELAS is a coalition where all members are equals, are they not?"

Dimitra knew the Karpenissi stratiotikós. He was the nephew of a KKE Central Committee member. She resented the young man's swagger and impudence. The KKE was egalitarian and within its ranks, the sexes treated equally. But this man behaved like the son of a Turkish pasha let loose in his father's harem.

"I agree that the 'order' was not valid. And you were correct to ask Yiorgos to rendezvous, dialogue, and synthesize a plan. I am only now hearing of this, and I have decided that Yiorgos is not guilty of the charges. He should receive another celebration for his recruitment. Tell him I send my best wishes. I will notify Karpenissi of my decision and you should not bother with this further."

Aris rocked back in his chair and Dimitra exhaled. Just then came a knock at Aris's door. The commander raised his voice and acknowledged the entrant. A young fighter pushed open the door, stepped inside, and stood at attention. Dimitra recognized him as one of the Cypriot prisoners of war from an earlier mission. He set his eyes on the wall above and behind Aris. When the commander nodded in his direction, the Cypriot spoke, "The people's court has rendered their verdict, comrade. They found the thief guilty."

"What were his transgressions?" asked Aris.

"He has confessed to stealing hogs and goats from three villages, sir. There was also testimony he sold them to the Germans. But this he denies."

Aris shook his head then looked at Dimitra. "Please pardon my departure, Comrade Dimitra. This matter is expedient. I know you will want to start your return to beautiful Chómori, no? I am pleased we talked and cleared matters. *Eftychisméno to néo étos* and may all the problems of 1944 be as simple as the ones today. Travel safely, comrade."

"Happy New Year to you, Comrade Commander," answered Dimitra, stiffening her posture.

And with those words, Aris rose and reached for his tall hat. He squared it on his head, and its black wool melded with his heavy mustache and bushy beard. He resembled the bringer of death. He drew the .45 Colt from his holster and stepped through the doorway with the young fighter. Seconds later, as she gathered her things to leave, Dimitra heard the metallic signature of his weapon charging, then the fatal report.

Chapter 25

January 28, 1944

Dear M&P,

We're about to board another boat, this one a step up from the recommissioned troop carrier we crossed the Atlantic on. Names are something I cannot share, but I think this ship will keep water on the outside and this trip should be shorter than the first. You know what I'll miss? I'll miss the fresh seafood scooped up in our torpedo netting and the ambitious Greeks who climbed overboard to harvest it. This ship we are about to board is not so equipped and crewed. Its sides are much higher.

I won't miss Cairo. The Greek community here is not friendly, and I don't know why. I think they may have a good thing going, business-wise, with the war. They are prosperous. But boy, are they stand-offish and rude! I don't understand it. Did you know a Greek owns the Grand Hotel, one of the top spots in Cairo? We heard they were hosting a *choroesperida* on the hotel's roof garden, so a bunch of us went. Marta, do you know I couldn't get a single Greek girl to dance with me? Not one. Help me, I'm losing my charm. They only danced the American style. There were no line dances, no *kalamatianos*. Cairo is a strange place for Greeks.

We beat the best basketball team that Camp Huckstep could muster. We've got top-flight young guys in this group. That's the biggest news I can think of, other than I'm now a paratrooper. I can't go into details, but the British who are in charge over here rounded us up one day and said they needed two teams to get qualified. I'm still uncertain how they chose our group. We traveled to a base in the Holy Land and five days later, we were paratroopers. The Brits don't waste time. The same training takes ninety days in the American jump school. I'll tell all when I get home. Marta, do not worry about me jumping out of airplanes. It's very worked out and not that hairy.

Pop, do you remember telling me that Greeks are the world's best sailors? Now, I know what you mean. I can't say where, but along the way to where we are, we ran into a nasty storm. The captain was smart and a good man, but he was sailing with a short crew. Things started rolling around on deck, and spray came over the bow and sides like a firehose. A few things washed into the drink. Who came to the rescue? The Greek nationals in our unit.

We have Greeks who are ex-merchant marine. They jumped ship in New York or another port of call and tried to enlist in the US Army when war came. The Army made them go to Canada and reenter the US legally before they accepted them. No joke.

When the storm hit, these ex-sailors went to the captain to volunteer. They shuttled around the deck like pros, and thanks to their deft hands and smart knots, things tightened up pronto. We rocked and rolled but made it through without major loss or damage.

Then they surprised me again. The Greek merchant men ran up semaphores, waved their shirts, came to attention, and saluted when we passed the *Averoff* in a canal I can't mention. They were proud of the Greek Navy's flagship. You could see it on their faces. The Greeks shouted, "By the power of God and the wishes of our king and in the name of justice, I sail toward the victory against the enemy of the nation."

Do you know that quotation? I think it's from the Balkan Wars. Harry or Dimitri might know. After we passed the battleship, one of the men in our unit told me every Greek should honor *Barba Yiorgis*. Papa George? Then he said, "The *Averoff*, she is Greece on the waves."

We will transport to our ship in an hour. I need to get my things together. I'll write when we get set up. I guess you should continue to use the same APO as always. Somehow the mail finds us.

I miss you both, and I miss sitting on the porch and feasting on Marta's minestrone alla Milanese and osso buco. There might be Italian cooking in my future, but I doubt I'll see dishes from as far north as Lombardia.

Love and kisses,

Stavros

"They'll censor Huckstep," offered Gus. "Maybe even jump school. Who knows?"

"Are you reading over my shoulder?" asked Stavros.

"Maybe." Gus shrugged. "Are you worried you're losing your charm? You weren't the only one they wouldn't dance with. I mean, if they turned me down, you're in the same boat. Hell, they turned down everybody who went that night. And it beats me. We're a good-looking bunch of Americans. What's not to like?"

Stavros stared at Gus. "Are you asking me to analyze why Egyptian Greek girls do not find you interesting? Two words in that formulation tell the tale . . . Egyptian and girls. What did the old man tell us when we landed at Port Suez? Be cautious of the food and ladies in these foreign lands. Remember?"

"Right. I listened. I have eaten no camel souvlaki. But women are my specialty," crowed Gus. "And I'll tell you this. Those Egyptian Greek girls are stuck on themselves. That's all there is to it. Hey, you didn't tell your folks about the plague and how we ended up in Cairo."

"No, I don't want them to worry. The plague's old news now, we hope," answered Stavros.

Gus went on without missing a beat. "I'm glad we got to see the pyramids and Heliopolis, but I'm done with this country. We dodged the plague in Port Said, but Cairo and Huckstep have been a bust. I mean, pretending to be a unit of truck drivers? Really? Who came up with that? Hell, nobody on base believes it. I'm ready for Italy. Bring on the pizzas and *giovani donne*. Or is it *signorina*? What's the plural for the young unmarried girls?"

"*Signorinas* or *signorine*," answered Stavros.

"Right, bring 'em on. Hey, what's the scuttlebutt? Where are we shipping out to?" asked Gus.

"No word until we're aboard. That's the drill," answered Stavros.

"Well, at least we've got a proper ship for this trip. The *Dilwara*? Too bad we didn't have her for the trip across the Atlantic instead of the *Pierre L'Enfant. Pierre* was a rust bucket. *Dilwara* is an Indian luxury liner, right? All we have to do is dodge the Luftwaffe in Bomb Alley for a few days, then we'll be ashore in *bel paese*," said Gus.

"Your grasp of Italian is impressive, sergeant, but I recommend you use a gesture when you say 'bel paese.' Something like. . . ." Stavros waved his arms to show he meant his surroundings, the world around him. "Otherwise, Sergeant, Italians might think you came ashore onto a soft cheese of Lombardy. Your hands will tell them you are speaking of their resplendent country and not fascinated by cheese."

"Right. Thanks for the tip," answered Gus.

"An Italian stepmother from Lombardy got me started early," offered Stavros.

"Have you seen the weather for the next couple of days? Are we going to get clouds? Or rain? We're a big target. We need cover from the Kraut flyboys. We were lucky on the way over. Bomb Alley is a shooting gallery when it's clear. Heck, the Germans are still bombing the southern coast of Italy. That's the scuttlebutt. Any word?"

"The only briefing I've received was sea state nominal, waves running one to three feet, wind speed twelve knots from the west to southwest. Visibility clear to light cover. No storms on the way. We'll get air escort out of Deversoir, that's why we're shoving off from Port Said," answered Stavros.

"Right. Well, we've got lifeboats. You know, here's something to consider, since you are an officer and part of the brain trust. Why the heck didn't we get swimming lessons? They trained us for every other imaginable scenario, but not swimming? What's with that?"

Stavros, not looking up, suggested, "Mae West vests are cheaper?"

Chapter 26

"A runner arrived this morning."

Dimitra handed Yiorgos a folded communiqué.

It is from Sarafis to Aris to me and now to you. It is from the Allied Military Mission to EAM-ELAS commanders in the field."

Yiorgos unfolded the document. It was a brief note. Yiorgos squinted and nodded as he read. He folded the note and handed it back to Dimitra, his logical mind already working out details.

He said, "We will need four days to reach Parga. Of the request for mules, we can bring one hundred, maybe more. Of the fighters, we can muster the fifty they ask. With the recruitment of the andartes from Kommeno and the resignation of the Italians, we should not face enemy patrols until north of Arta. If we travel at night, the Germans will leave us alone.

"The Americans bring with them many supplies, no? This is good. We can use all we can get. If not today, then in reserve.

"Of the American fighters, we are to billet twenty-four, no? I suggest we clear our fighters from the Monastery of the Sacred Mother. This will keep the Americans close but away from the village center. Our fighters can scatter to other billets. I think we only have twelve fighters there now.

"We can leave after Easter, perhaps the following day, April seventeenth. We can leave late in the day so that those who have celebrated the most can walk straight. That should give time for rendezvous with the Kommeno fighters and our travel on to Parga by the last week of April. The new moon rises April twenty-second. If the Americans are wise, they will travel then, no?

"I expect they will travel by boat from Italy, but what do I know? The shore at Parga is good for such a landing once past

Paxos. Between Paxos and Antipaxos, there is a channel, but it is narrow. Between the land is two kilometers, but the channel slithers like a serpent. Still, that is the best approach to Parga. The British have used this approach before. This I know. But the wind and tide can play the devil. If they arrive in a proper landing craft, they should be able to motor to shore and unload there instead of using small boats. If we unload on shore, we can make quick work of the supplies and begin the trip back to Chómori the same night."

Yiorgos paused, "What do we know of the Americans?"

Dimitra hesitated and shook her head. "I have no experience with them. I understand they are Greek Americans and other Greeks who fled Greece before the fascists. I expect many will speak Greek.

"I expect they are well-trained, much like the British SOE officers. But of their combat experience. . . ." Dimitra shrugged. "We in Chómori are an experiment, no?"

"Comrade Kapetánios, America is a place of wonder to Greeks. I have family who went there in the twenties and are well-off today. They write about America like it is a land where anything is possible," offered Yiorgos.

"Yes, I know those letters. My family, too, has wayward branches in America. Where did your family settle in America, Yiorgos?" asked Dimitra.

"First, they went to New York and then on to . . . I have a problem remembering the place. It is the city where they have the grand automobile race. It has a Greek name," he puzzled.

"Yes. Indianapolis, I suspect," offered Dimitra.

"Yes, that is it. It is a city where many men from these mountains have gone. They have a social club, the Nafpaktian Brotherhood. Like a gangster movie, no?" Then Yiorgos crouched and made like he was firing a Thompson submachine gun from his hip.

Dimitra chuckled.

Yiorgos went on, "Do you think the children of the diaspora will understand our ways? The Americans will be young men, and young men everywhere are full of themselves, no?"

Dimitra nodded, then offered, "The truth is yet to be told. We will learn about them when and if they arrive. Until then, we will prepare as gracious Greek hosts."

Yiorgos nodded, but Dimitra noted a skepticism in his prejudgment of the Americans. His was the prejudice one might have against children spoiled by weak parents.

"Do we know more about the truce with EDES?" inquired Yiorgos.

Dimitra shook her head. "No. We are not to attack any of their units. We may defend ourselves if attacked. That is the last instruction. I am pleased to obey it, as I know you are."

Yiorgos nodded. Then he asked, "What, comrade, do we know of the Mountain Government? I hear the fighters talk of this formation. Comrade political officer is away at his conference, can you tell me more?"

"All I know is that the Political Committee of National Liberation, PEEA, is to be a broad governing organization, elected by Greek citizens, including women. This will be our country's first national election where women enjoy such rights. Elections will be in late April. There will be an assembly in Evrytania in the middle of May. I have been ordered to attend," answered Dimitra.

"Then," continued Yiorgos, "PEEA will be the forerunner of our new government when the Germans leave. Is it that simple?"

"Simple? In Greece?" chided Dimitra.

"No, no, I understand." Yiorgos laughed. "We have a government in Egypt, and a king, no less, who believe, as do their British tenders, that they represent Greece. This they believe, though they have yet to kill a single fascist in a mountain ambush or blow up any bridgework known to date."

"Yes," replied Dimitra, "that is the problem. We control these mountains. The politicians seek to control the rest."

Yiorgos reflected, "Since you will attend the PEEA Mountain Government, will you not be a politician as well?"

Dimitra cocked her head and drilled a piercing stare through her grizzled comrade. Yiorgos shrugged, pursed his lips, and retreated from the schoolhouse.

Chapter 27

"No way! That's nuts!" whispered Stavros.

"What?" Gus whispered back.

"I'll tell you after the briefing. This is nuts!" repeated Stavros.

The briefing in Bari, Italy, was in a small building marked SBS for Strategic Balkan Services. Two OSS officers from Force 133 stood before Greek Operational Group II with maps and enlarged photographs behind them. The title banner above the maps and photos read OPERATION NOAH'S ARK. The briefers waved long pointers to critical coordinates that men noted and memorized. This was their final briefing before embarkation. This briefing was for Group II only and gave details on who they would work with, EAM-ELAS guerrillas; where they would base, Chómori; and their mission. Their mission was to work with and motivate the local andartes, blow things up, and deny the Germans a fast and painless retreat from Greece. Slowing down the Germans and thinning their ranks would hamper concentration of enemy forces to the west and diminish aggregation of a repelling force for the fast-approaching June D Day invasion. The part about D Day went unsaid.

After the briefing, Gus stepped into the hallway and lit a cigarette. He leaned against the wall to wait for Stavros, as the briefers had held the officers of OG II back for a private discussion. Gus was halfway through his Marlboro when Stavros came out. Gus asked, "What was that all about? What spooked you so bad?"

"I wasn't spooked, just shocked. Chómori, our base camp . . . I know people there, sort of," Stavros answered.

"What? You have family there?" asked Gus.

"No. Not exactly. Maybe an honorary uncle . . . it's a long story. Out of all the villages in Greece, they assign us Chómori . . . where I may know someone? That's crazy, don't you think?"

"Okay, okay, it's crazy. But whatever you do, do not tell them! If you tell the brass, they may move you to another group. Or worse, they may reassign us to another location, and we'll get delayed. I mean, we got to get to Greece and get in the fight before things cool off. So don't tell the brass. Okay?" insisted Gus.

"Right. You're right. Besides, I don't have any actual family there, and I don't know anybody there, so . . . I was just surprised that we drew Chómori. It's a small dot in a lot of mountains. What are the chances?" asked Stavros.

Gus piped up, "The chances are a million to one. That's about the same as they give us against the Germans. What did the briefing officer tell us? There will be no withdrawal route. No replacements. No supply lines. And you'll be there until the end of the war or until Jerry withdraws. But they plan to drop us mail and gold. Mail and gold. Why not pizza and beer?"

Stavros chuckled.

Chapter 28

Stavros rolled on his cot. The musty castle at the base of Monte Sant'Angelo in Manfredonia wasn't a bad billet. He had a room to himself. But tonight, the ghost of Bianca Lancia d'Agliano, the mistress and last wife of Emperor Frederick II, stirred and roused. The castle, haunted or not, was a hundred kilometers north of OSS HQ at Bari, and another forty kilometers north of Monopoli. There, at the end of the Appian Way and Via Traiana, at Trajan's doorstep to Greece, an overloaded Landing Craft Infantry tugged at its mooring lines. Docked among the bombed and sunken relics in the harbor, she awaited the new moon and OG II.

It wasn't the predicted two days at sea in the shallow draft LCI or Gus's story about almost getting married that kept Stavros awake. Nor was it the three enlisted men in his charge, disciplined for defacing the uniforms of Italian Army veterans of the Albanian and Greek campaigns, with their wearers still in them. The three hotheads with their quick-draw stilettos and decoration popping nonsense got the OG kicked out of Bari. But that was old news.

What was on Stavros's mind was dark and personal. Their assignment to Chómori triggered a train of thought that rumbled his consciousness. There were parts of his life Stavros did not know. Big parts. His insomnia in the early hours of April 20, 1944, was an attack of curiosity.

Alex had told him of Eléni's death, and Stavros knew it was ugly. He knew from the things Alex would not say. And, since talking to Yorgos and Peter and Domna in Pueblo, other questions stirred. How did they find the killers? Who killed the one they trapped? What did they do with the body? How did Marta fit in? How did Stavros, as a babe, fit in? How old was he when he went to Pueblo to live with Peter and Domna?

While they searched for Eléni's killers, the Greeks fought a war with the coal barons. What was that like? He knew that Harry Hantzis, the man whom Eléni's sister asked to find Eléni's killers, was a Balkan War veteran and the son of the village assassin. Was the assassin still in Chómori?

He wondered if Chómori held any answers. And if this tiny speck in the Nafpaktian Mountains held answers, how could he coax them to the surface? Still, his focus had to be on the mission and the lives of his men. Answers could wait.

Stavros was a smart man. He was an educated man. But where he was, where he was going, what he didn't know, and what might be in store was tonight overwhelming. It was 0240 hours before curiosity lost its grip.

Chapter 29

The drone of the four Detroit Diesels modulated as they plowed the waves. The Bora wind raced down the western face of the Dinaric Alps of Croatia, onto the Adriatic, then south, pushing the sea before it. The wind and waves drove against the incoming tide, building a watery wall of discomfort. One hundred miles south of Monopoli, halfway to their landing, the hardened OSS passengers on LCI 137 were wondering just how tough they were. The ship was thirty-five miles west of Vlorë, making ready to enter the Strait of Otranto, the narrowest part of the sea between the boot heel of Italy and Albania. There the captain would adjust course to the south. putting the sea chop dead ahead and offering slight relief.

LCI 137 was 158 feet of workhorse, nothing about her designed for comfort. She and her 922 sister ships plied waters around the globe and in every theater, every campaign. Innovations and modifications had changed the way she fought, but never her ride. She was a flat-bottom lander that rode atop the waves and bobbed like a cork but got the men and their machines to wherever the plan called. They might be green around the gills when they arrived, but they arrived.

She could make a steady twelve knots in almost any sea, so once they turned south, they would be ten hours from landing at Parga. That should put the men ashore around midnight, barring enemy patrols or surprises at sea.

Stavros and Gus worked through a chow line at the stern of the ship on her lower level. Today's lunch was ham sandwiches, as it was too rough for the cooks to prepare a hot meal. They listened to the seamen kitchen helpers cleaning vegetables as they stood in line. The enlisted men complained about the ship's boatswain and their frequent assignment in the galley.

Stavros and Gus filled their trays with sandwiches, canned peaches, and coffee and carried them topside midship to benches at the base of the conning tower. The men faced west, and the first rays of the afternoon sun warmed their faces.

Gus said, "It's better up here. I can't take the smell of diesel below. I don't know how the crew does it. I'd jump ship in the first port of call."

Stavros said, "You'd tough it out just like them. Hell, you are going to be a marine engineer, right? You'll smell more diesel than Rockefeller if that's your trade."

"Right. I may have to reconsider. I may go straight into bank robbery or arson, or building and bridge demolition, since the Oh So Secret has trained me in those fields. Hey, do we get a diploma at the end of this?" Gus asked with a straight face.

"Don't be disappointed, but Wild Bill will never hand you a sheepskin for a Bachelor of Sabotage and Mayhem. Hell, we can't even tell our families what we do."

Gus nodded.

"So, tell me about almost getting married. You mentioned it at the castle, but I need details. Who was she?" coaxed Stavros.

"All right. I met her at the post office, and she was a looker. Beautiful face, long wavy dark hair, twenty years old, and she spoke English. Her name is Sophia. I'm serious, Stavros. She was the most exquisite woman I've ever met.

"I asked her if she would like to get an espresso, and she said yes. We walked down Via Campanile to the waterfront and this sailing club, Lega Navale Italiana. Her uncle works in the little café there. She introduces me! We just met, and I'm meeting the family!

"We sat and watched the harbor and talked, and it's getting to be late in the afternoon. So, I say, what are you doing for dinner?

"She says she wants me to come to her house for dinner. I said, no, I don't want to put you out. I mean, she wasn't somebody special, she wasn't wearing anything fancy, only normal clothes. I figured she's not poor, but not rich, either. So, I say I'd like to come, but I want to help pay. I don't want to put you out. She asks if I have any American cigarettes. I do. I'm carrying three packs and I give them to her.

"She tells me her address and says to come by at 2000 hours. So, now I'm wondering if I've been had? Did she con me? I mean, she just walked off with three packs of cigarettes. Is she straight? I know she's beautiful, but I don't know if she's straight, right?

"So, that evening, I pack my Beretta under my jacket and go to find her house. She lives up toward Monticchio. It looks like a decent neighborhood. I knock on her door. She answers, and when I step inside, she introduces me to her entire family. There's the mother, the father, two sisters, a younger brother, and her uncle from the boat club. I mean, I'm getting the third degree, right?

"Her mother, who doesn't speak a word of English, had prepared chicken, fresh bread, pasta, fish, greens, potatoes, and we had a great red wine. It shocked me. I told Sophia that she had spent too much, and that I didn't mean to put them out. She said, no, she got it all with the three packs of cigarettes!

"But I'm telling you . . . I was there for a marriage inspection. I think I passed. I've got her address, and I'll look her up when we get back. But I told her I didn't know where we were going or if we would ever return.

"She said, 'You must only write, and I will come to you.' That's what she said, I think I'm engaged!"

The two friends chuckled in the warm sun at the base of the LCI pilot house under a life-size likeness of Lauren Bacall *au naturel*. While they were still laughing, the ship's communications officer called down from the conning station, "Lieutenant, you have a code from Bari. You can read it in the radio room."

Stavros waved to the officer, then said to Gus, "I wonder what this is?"

Gus shrugged.

Stavros climbed the stairs to the pilothouse entrance hatch and found the small radio room. A sailor wearing a set of headphones handed him a note from OSS HQ in Bari.

Be advised per BI that Sergeant Giannakopoulos is to return on LCI 137. He is not to remain in Greece.

Stavros's first thought was, *Boy, that's rough news for John.* Sergeant Giannakopoulos was, in fact, John Tsoudheros. And his second thought was, *Damn, now we're down a man and we haven't even set foot in Greece.* BI was an abbreviation for British Intelligence.

Stavros found John in the galley with two other Greek nationals, talking politics and smoking. Stavros interrupted the conversation, and John followed him topside. Once on the deck, Stavros leaned on the railing looking west over the endless blue toward Italy, with John to his right. He looked at the young man. "John, I've got bad news."

John Tsoudheros asked, "Is it my father? Is the family all right?"

"No, no," answered Stavros. "Everybody's all right, as far as I know. Everything's okay. But I got a code from Bari, and British Intelligence said they want you to return on the lander. They don't want you to stay in Greece."

"What? What the hell is that about?" asked John.

"I have no idea. You'll have to talk to the Brits when you get back to Bari. I only have orders, John, no details," answered Stavros.

John cursed in Greek, one that Stavros had never heard. Stavros offered, "Sorry, John. The group will miss you. And I'll miss you as a friend."

The young Greek shook his head and remained silent, staring into the blue of the water and the sky above, his thoughts absorbed by an indifferent sea.

Chapter 30

Two bonfires blazed and crackled on the stony beach casting a golden glow and deep shadows on the faces of men and mules. Yiorgos peered into the darkness, using his hand to shield the glare of the fire. Around him, andartes, villagers, a British detachment, countless mules and horses, and bedraggled Russian prisoners of war waited for LCI 137.

The ship was late. It was well past midnight. Yiorgos heard something and waved for everyone to be silent. In the stillness, he registered the cautious approach of idling diesels. The racket of the freewheeling anchor winch running out rode from the stern two hundred yards offshore confirmed her approach. The bow of the lander rose like a phantom in the darkness as the ship tugged against its anchor line, inching toward shore. Then the powerful searchlight atop the ship's conning tower blazed, blinding the pageant ashore. Mules and horses on the cliff above the beach bolted in surprise, but their handlers restrained them. The ship's hull grated against the submerged shore. Then the clang of davits on either side of the cathead presaged the lowering of dual gangways.

The first OSS man to touch Greek soil was John Tsoudheros, a bittersweet arrival. Stavros had pushed him to the front of the line as the ship came to a stop. Stavros's orders said nothing about Tsoudheros landing in Greece, only that he had to return.

When Stavros's boots touched Greek soil, he kneeled, steadied his pack and Thompson, and dug his right hand into the wet sandy gravel. He rose from his crouch, letting the cool, hard mix dribble through his fingers. A grizzled andarte shouldering an ancient Mannlicher said, *"Pístis i patrída!"* Faith and fatherland! Stavros nodded, then clasped hands with Yiorgos.

As the OSS men disembarked using the starboard gangway, the supply offloading began on the port side. Andartes and villagers hauled crates and sacks from the ship's hold to the shore, where the pliant mules accepted loads and lumbered away, led by trusted masters.

The ship was late. Under the waxing moon, their search for Aphrodite's Cave, the rendezvous at Parga, turned episodic. The last forty miles had passed warily as LCI 137 repeatedly killed her noisy Detroit Diesel engines to dodge German patrol boats. Dead in the water, the unyielding northern currents of the eastern Adriatic carried her off course. An hour later, with the lethal game of cat and mouse over, her captain powered the engines. He took his bearings, then wove an improvised course through the tricky narrow straights between the islands of Paxos and Antipaxos to the signal fires on the mainland. Now, ashore and unloading, the vital part of her mission was complete. The return to Italy would begin the minute the last Greek-bound cargo cleared her deck, the evacuees were boarded, and the load of six hundred returning parachutes stowed.

She had no time to waste tethered to shore, motionless and vulnerable.[73] She had a narrow window for a safe departure. Just as her inbound approach was timely, so was her exit. The Germans occupied Corfu one hundred kilometers north, and to sail in daylight was to invite attack. As 0200 hours approached, LCI 137 was on the uneasy side of a closing window.

Stavros stood with Yiorgos and counted the OSS men as they waddled down the gangway with their arms and packs. Yiorgos said, "Your men should go to the cliff top and wait there. The cove is not safe if the Germans come. I see a British officer over there," he added, pointing to the north end of the beach. "I believe he will want to talk with you, no? We will muster on the cliff road and begin our journey."

Stavros asked, "How far is it to Chómori?"

Yiorgos shrugged. "Three days, maybe four, maybe five. How am I to know?" Then he walked away to organize his men and mules.

Stavros, puzzled by the andarte's departure, walked to the British officer, saluted, and introduced himself.

Colonel Tom Barnes was a blond, stocky built New Zealander and one of the first SOE commandos into Greece. He had blown up Gorgopotamos and Asopos and dozens of bridges, viaducts, mines, and roadways. He had seen it all. He looked to Stavros strong as a bull. He spoke politely to Stavros, "How was your ride, Lieutenant?"

Stavros bobbed his head. "Little challenging, sir."

"Ah yes, she is not a pleasure craft, is she? She gets the job done.

"Lieutenant, I trust you received orders about your man Tsoudheros?"

Stavros replied, "Yes, sir. He reboarded after touching Greek soil. That was the least we could do."

"A shame, isn't it? A man trains for a mission, sweat and blood and all that, and then at the last count, they pull the rug out from under him. Still, it is for the best. The politics in Greece are unforgiving. It is my understanding the planners in Cairo may have something for him later in the game."

"I'm sure he will look forward to that," said Stavros.

"Lieutenant, I will be your commanding officer in the field. I report to Monty Woodhouse, our mission commander, here in Greece. Brigadier Woodhouse is head of what was the BMM. Now, with your unit's arrival, it is the Allied Military Mission. We'll be in touch by radio or runner, Germans and weather permitting. I'll get your radioman the codes and details."

"Yes, sir," said Stavros.

"Oh, and, Lieutenant, we don't stand on formalities here in Greece. As you can see around you, things are a bit . . . informal. If you call me Tom, you will not stand for report."

Stavros answered, "Yes, sir. Tom. And, Tom, you may call me Stavros."

"One last thing, Stavros. I can assign a translator if you need one," offered Barnes.

Stavros replied, "Unnecessary, sir. I mean, Tom. We all speak Greek, and three of the men are Greek nationals."

"Very well. That should leave you in good stead. Language can be a real problem for nonspeakers. Anything else I might offer?" asked the colonel.

"No, sir, Tom. We should be fine and ready to fight," Stavros answered.

"One last matter, Lieutenant. Your man, Yiorgos. He is a good fighter and smart. He is what the EAM-ELAS call a stratiotikós, the head military man for his district. He is not, however, a communist. He is a social democrat. Your Kapetánios, however, is KKE. She and the politikós, the political officer, are both KKE. Just a word to the wise, son," confided Barnes.

"She?" wondered Stavros out loud.

"Yes, son. And she's a rising star in the political firmament. She is smart and as brave as any man and much more pleasing to look at. Her name is Dimitra, and she also goes by Natasha. The second name is playful. The Greek fighters take a nom de guerre, and some take it more seriously than others.

"Right. Truth be told, the women do most of the work in Greece. You will see them in the snow on the mountains carrying supplies to this or that cave. Never the men. It is sad to say the women are used like mules. Our friend Dimitra is not of that breed.

"Will there be anything else, Lieutenant?"

"No, sir, thank you," answered Stavros. "I'll send the radioman, and we'll be in contact."

Stavros left Colonel Barnes, found the radioman, and started up the steep slope to the path above the cove. When he finished his climb, he heard Yiorgos dispatching two andartes to the north, telling them to release the roadblock south of Glyki at daybreak. They were to meet the main body of fighters past Arta in two days.

Then Yiorgos turned to Stavros. "We will travel to Louros tonight. There we will wait until darkness to travel on since our next leg will bring us close to Arta. The Germans send patrols from Arta. But they will not bother us at night. From there, we will see what comes.

"Our scouts are underway. We can begin as soon as your men are ready. Now, here is a trick of the mountains you will want to share with your men. Our path is narrow and unmarked. The moon is low. It is best that they hold a mule's tail for guidance when they cannot see the way. The mules know the path, and I've never heard them complain."

Stavros said, "Thanks for the tip." Then he turned to brief his men, who were standing in a group to the north. As he approached them, he heard the diesels of LCI 137 come to life and the powerful anchor winch on the stern began reeling in rode. Her departure was textbook, thanks to the skill of her crew, the offloading of tons of supplies, and the Ionian rising tide.

Gus piped up, "Say goodbye to our cruise ship. I'll miss the Manhattans."

Stavros ignored his friend. "We are marching through the night to a camp where we will rest until tomorrow night. Grab a mule tail when you can't tell the way. We will move out shortly. Our lead man, Yiorgos, says the Germans will not bother us at night but be alert and be ready. Questions?"

Hearing none, Stavros signaled Yiorgos at the head of the column, mounted on his dapple gray with the sooty mane. Over one hundred fighters, two hundred mules, and twenty-three antsy, combat-green American andartes ventured into the darkness led by mules and men of the mountains.

Chapter 31

The main road on the west coast of Greece, Ionia Odos, ran from Igoumenitsa in the north to Nafpaktos in the south. West of Nafpaktos, the Gulf of Corinth narrows. From there, people and cargo ferried two kilometers south to the Peloponnese and on to the Port of Patras. This was a vital line of communications for any occupying force, as it had been for the Italians, and was now for the Germans. It was not an option for the andartes. German mobile ground unit patrols and Messerschmitt and Focke-Wulf fighter overflights guaranteed casualties if not annihilation.

Yiorgos crossed the road only once. There was a shorter, easier route that crossed twice, but these crossings were in plain view of patrols. The safer way added time and denied the andarte train the flatter land along the east coast of the Ambracian Gulf. But it was the smart thing to do. If Yiorgos had with him fewer and more experienced fighters and not the essential supplies from LCI 137, he might have risked the quicker route. On the second night, south of Arta, the train crossed the Ionia Odos into the mountains. From there, they traveled over jagged rocks and steep hillsides for the next five days and four nights to reach Chómori.

They traveled at night in the German-controlled areas near major roads, larger villages, and the territory north of Arta. Once past German patrols and air surveillance, they traveled by day. They rose at 0400 hours, dispatched scouts, and then set off an hour later. They marched until late morning, then waited for the mules to catch up. The mules were slower and didn't arrive until late afternoon, sometimes after dark.

When the andarte scouts arrived at a village, they negotiated for food. In the evening, the fighters ate whatever the scouts had bought or bartered. The andartes carried bread and goat cheese and coffee. The Americans packed unappetizing dehydrated mutton. The andartes bought food with sovs or sovereigns, and the Americans soon realized they were underfunded.

On the afternoon of the third day, the fighters forded the Achelous River and stopped in the village of Loutra. The spring rains had filled the river's banks, and the fifty meters of submerged rock pathway proved treacherous. The men lifted their weapons, packs, and sleeping bags above their heads and waded. Everyone except those riding horses were soaked to their belts. In Loutra, Stavros noticed the women wore dresses pinned on their right shoulders. He asked Yiorgos.

"They pin their dresses so that the Germans won't rip and tear them as they have before. The Germans check their shoulders for bruises. They see a bruise . . . they shoot the woman. Or hang her or detain her. The bruises are proof to the Germans that they fired rifles. The only women firing rifles are andartes and reserves."

The mountain trails, *monopátia*, were tedious. Small *exoklísia* shrines rising alongside punctuated the monotony. Made of stones and sticks, the memorials were waist high with an icon or two under covered tops. On the bigger paths and the roads leading to villages, they found *kandylákia* shrines. Made of masonry stone and set on posts, kandylákia resembled model churches with oil offerings, worry beads, and enclosed icons.

To counter boredom, the Greek nationals sang "Koroido Mousolini" or "Mussolini, You Fool."

> With a smile on their lips,
> Our soldiers march forward
> And the Italians have become a ridicule
> Because their hearts aren't brave enough
>
> Mussolini, you fool
> None of you will be left standing.
> You and Italy,
> Your ridiculous country,

Are all afraid of the khaki color,

You have no honor.
And when we march in,
Even in Rome, we will raise
The Greek blue and white flag.[74]

They approached Lapses at the top of a rise north of Thermos, and it surprised the Americans to find stone steps. They were out of place in an otherwise undeveloped area. Later in the day, Yiorgos told Stavros, "The steps have been there since the early days of the Turks, hundreds of years ago. The villagers laid them so they could hear the hoofs of the mules and horses as they approached. That gave them time to run from the invaders and hide their livestock and valuables."

South of Lapses before Thermos, the train moved on easy trails along the shores of Limni Trichonida, the largest natural lake in Greece. Here were ducks and birds and an invitation to bathe in clean, chilly waters. There were fish, and a dozen floated to the surface after an andarte lobbed in a grenade. Yiorgos reproached the man, "Idiot! Do not waste explosives on fish! Tonight, we will eat well at our hide near Thermos. This everyone knows, idiot!"

The men gathered the fish with sticks and kept marching.

That night, while the Americans settled in, the OG discussed Colorado and Greece and the asperity of their mountains. Gus, sitting on his bedroll with a circle of men around a campfire, began, "Colorado mountains are steeper. We've climbed higher mountains before. We are tuckered out because we went soft in Italy. We spent two and a half months getting soft. Sure, we did PT, and we ran, but we got soft. That's the problem."

Sergeant Petropoulos, a Greek national, listened. The older Greek nationals thought Gus a braggart. Petropoulos lifted a burning twig to light his cigarette, casting shadows on his sunken features. He exhaled. In his resonant baritone, he offered, "The truth will be the number of hobnails on the soles of your fine paratroop boots by the end of this march, no?

"In Colorado, the mountains are steep. That is true. And here, maybe not so high. But in Colorado, the trails were wide and simple, no rocks, no slate, no gravel. A hike instead of a march, no?

"In Greece, the mountains are not so high, but they are rugged. The loose stones and slate and the cliffs, they are your companion. Always your companion, no? Better you are an eagle in Greece, not a man. In Greece, you are worn out after a kilometer of marching. More than you are in Colorado. So, we are worn. It was not Italy's fault. Many things are Italy's fault. But our weary bones and tired feet are not among them, my young friend."

The stocky Greek national sitting next to Petropoulos, Corporal Vedros, added, "Here in Greece you carry an added weight; you carry the burden of history. This country that we love requires our soul and dedication. These are a high price, no? To every man, there is a price. We sing the songs and tell the stories and hope to live as our fathers and grandfathers, but there is a price. We are lucky that history has chosen us to defend her. But no matter how brave this makes us, we carry an equal burden. This is the burden in these mountains, and this we owe to Greece."

A detachment of andartes and their supplies split off from the main train near Thermos. Fifty fighters with one hundred mules and supplies turned south for their military district near Missolonghi, a town that carried the burden of Greek history as no other. Its Garden of the Heroes, a cemetery with monuments to those who fought and fell in the Exodus of Missolonghi, is sacred ground. The year-long siege that ended in Greek defeat by the overwhelming Ottoman and Egyptian forces stirred the Western powers to Greece's side. With the help of Russia, England, and France, the Ottomans fled, ending the eight-year

War of Greek Independence. In the garden are dozens of honorable statuaries, the most memorable to Lord Byron, who died in Missolonghi in 1824 during the Exodus. Byron's body returned to England, but buried in the garden is his heart.

Stavros noted the villagers' reaction to the EAM-ELAS andartes. In every village, the people went about their business without fear or intimidation. The Greeks were, by nature, earnest hosts, and they greeted strangers in self-effacement and humble pride. The women seldom spoke and never looked the men in the eye. The men went about their business or sat and talked and took notice only when they were part of a project, like arranging the evening's food. And there again, the women did the work after the men negotiated the arrangements.

Upon entering a village, one of the first people to greet the andartes was the village president. His was a traditional office that put him at the center of village affairs. Without fail, these men were forthcoming and supportive. In Stavros's estimation, EAM-ELAS and Yiorgos were well-respected. What surprised Stavros was that the andartes did not hide. Their arrival was a secret shared with everyone in the village, and Yiorgos was unconcerned that they might tell the Germans or, as he learned later, the dreaded Greek Security Battalions.

When Stavros offered these observations to Yiorgos, the hardened fighter replied, "We are their friends. What is there to say? Now they know that. In the early days, it was not so plain. We were their friends, but we had to earn their trust. They thought we were klephts, brigands, bandits, rapists, thieves. Those were the only people in these mountains that looked like us. And early, when we first began our fight, we killed many brigands, many. Some we recruited. They were a tougher enemy than the Italians."

Then Yiorgos let out a barrel laugh. It was the first laugh Stavros had heard from the man.

"These people hate Metaxas. He was a dictator, yes? But worse, he killed their goats.[75] He shot their goats. He shot millions of them, but who knows? Some say he was right. They eat the forest, and the trees are valuable. But to the farmers in the villages, they were meat and milk and cheese and bladders and wineskins. Goats were practical items, no? They hated Metaxas. This was a hatred ELAS shared. The democratic people of Greece hated Metaxas, and some the king as well.

"The villagers cared less that Metaxas was a dictator, that he tortured his opponents and ordered them to exile than that he had the goats killed. That is history. Now they side with us. Simple, no? They fear the king's return will mean another Metaxas. How am I to know? They care only that we will fight the king and any Metaxas on their behalf.

"We ask for their support, food, secrecy, and shelter, and this most give. Where we move, the rules are plain, and this the people value. Soon, we will hold nationwide elections, and that will be a first. In them, the women will vote. This, too, will be a first. We are still explaining to the women how this works. Much of what we do is new to the people. But these ways should have been taught years ago. Greece is old in its ways, no? You will see."

Stavros nodded through Yiorgos's explanation and tried to form in his mind a social pattern. A pattern in which he and his men could maneuver. There was much to learn, and it had little to do with blowing up bridges or staging ambushes. These military skills only needed application and practice. The skills Stavros sought were those of an anthropologist. To understand Greece, he needed not only know how to read a map or how to contact HQ; he needed to know her people and their ways.

The people in the mountains were different. They weren't like the Greeks Stavros knew in America. They weren't like the Greek nationals in the Greek Battalion. Most of the nationals were seafarers, literate and worldly. The afternoon the train arrived in Loutra, a timid old man hunched over a water crock tending a small flock of chickens questioned Stavros. The old man asked Stavros if the flag on his shoulder was Russian.

Stavros said it was the flag of the United States of America. The old man asked if America was far away. Stavros told him it was beyond the ocean. The old man asked, is that more than two days?

The journey to Chómori hardened his body but softened his preconceptions. Stavros knew the mountains of Greece were a world apart, a world at which he could only guess. The disparity between what he imagined and the truth was as vast as the ocean that befuddled the old man.

Chapter 32

Dimitra stood tall before the gathered Americans. The plateia was alive with the bloom of spring. The tableau beyond the granite patio and iron railing was of bountiful mountains. Apple blossoms wafted on the cool morning breeze, their faint trace nature's perfume. Unending spring waters splashed in the three-spigot fountain underwriting the songs of excited birds. Clanging bells on grazing goats in the valley echoed and peppered the aural landscape. The jagged crowing of a tardy rooster was the only incongruity.

The OSS men sat on simple metal chairs, restrained and polite. No small feat thanks to the contrast of an engaging, poised woman before them in a country that, to this point, had presented its women as beasts of burden. Dimitra wore a creased khaki blouse with dark green combat pants and British combat boots. A Beretta M 1934 .380 pistol hung under her left shoulder. The scuffed holster was standard Italian Army issue, its bulky, awkward flap cut away and replaced with a thin leather strap. A rectangular slot on the body of the holster held an extra clip.

Dimitra's raven hair hung above her shoulders and fluttered in the light breeze. She removed her garrison cap and held it folded in front of her with the white cross on the blue field facing forward.

Stavros had briefed the OSS men upon arriving at the monastery. Yiorgos has seen to their needs and arranged a welcome evening meal of cheese, bread, and chicken. As the men ate, Stavros told them of the EAM-ELAS leadership and that the Kapetánios, the officer in charge of this military district, was a woman. This set heads bobbing and prompted questioning looks. Stavros said, "We will meet Commander Dimitra tomorrow morning at 0800 hours. So, get your rest and be sharp. And please, gentlemen, be gentlemen."

It was a short walk to the plateia. Along the way, Stavros saw a well-kept, two-level home with a tidy stone courtyard and ancient grape trellises flourishing alongside. A well-maintained terracotta roof crowned its intricate taupe stonework. Etched into the arched keystone above its green door was a Greek Orthodox Cross, and *1881 Σεπτεμβρ 18*, September 18, 1881. Stavros, with much on his mind, noted the home. It seemed propitious.

Dimitra stood in front of the iron railing with the mountain vista behind. Yiorgos and Vasilios sat to her right, facing the OSS men. To her left, beyond the OSS men, stood two grim andartes armed with British Sten guns. Stavros walked onto the plateia, went to the front row, and saluted first Yiorgos, then Dimitra. Yiorgos offered a less than formal salute, and Dimitra nodded acknowledgment. Stavros was the last to sit. Just before Dimitra spoke, an eagle plunged from the unseen heavens to take a pigeon out of midair fifty yards beyond the plateia. Dimitra saw the attack, as did the OSS men.

A screech echoed off the mountains, and feathers floated to the valley floor. Then she began, "Like that hungry eagle, we are here to pounce upon prey, no?"

She received chuckles and nods.

"Thank you on behalf of the Greek people and our liberation movement, EAM-ELAS. You honor us with your sacrifice and toil that you might take this dangerous journey to help beloved Greece in our time of peril. If you please, I will introduce our elected leadership.

"The man you know here is Yiorgos. Yiorgos is our stratiotikós. He is the head of military operations in this district. He plans our movements and campaigns and leads with my concurrence. I will not tell you of his courage, for he will show you if he has not already. Listen to Yiorgos if you want to kill Germans and live to tell.

"Vasilios is our politikós, the political officer in this district. Do not let his youth fool you. He is wise beyond his years. Talk with Vasilios of the villages or areas in which you look to move and maneuver. Here, we are in safe EAM-ELAS territory, but quirks await in every village and valley, no? Surprises, yes?"

Dimitra looked at Vasilios, who nodded.

As Dimitra spoke, she looked straight into the eyes of the Americans. She left no doubt she was in charge and a capable leader. She was obviously intelligent and savvy. Preconceptions floated away like pigeon feathers.

"You are in Greece, so we must talk history. Here is a short course in our movement in this district.

"When the Italians invaded, I worked with the authorities in Platanos, the village you passed through yesterday. I organized guerrillas to fight alongside the Hellenic Army. The Italians outnumbered us and had more modern equipment. But they fought with less conviction, less heart. We drove the Italians out of Greece and back into Albania. They were in retreat. Then came the Germans.

"When our defenses fell, many Hellenic Army officers stayed in Greece to fight the invaders, as did Yiorgos, whose rank is of battalion commander, tagmatarkhis. He is from a village south of here near Nafpaktos, so it was natural we stayed here to fight.

"In September 1941, EAM-ELAS grew from a meeting in Athens of the resistance leaders. In January 1942, the people elected the three of us to EAM-ELAS leadership for this district. You may call this the Chómori district. Our border to the south is the Nafpaktos district, to the north Karpenissi, to the west Kommeno, and to the east Mount Giona. These boundaries are flexible and offer only a general rule for military actions. The political responsibilities are more defined.

"As you were traveling from Parga, we concluded our Political Committee of National Liberation elections. These are the first free, secret-ballot elections in occupied Greece. The first elections where women can vote. This is a glorious landmark on the road to Greek liberation. There is to be a conference in May to review our results and form a representative government.

"Over the three years EAM-ELAS has operated in this district, we have trained and equipped our fighters to the best of our resources. In the early days, we were ill-equipped and fought with our hearts. Now, we are well-equipped and more disciplined, and the credit goes to Yiorgos and Commander Aris, the commander of EAM-ELAS military forces.

"Fighters from this district have engaged in large demolition campaigns at Gorgopotamos and Kournovo. They have conducted many raids and ambushes and attacks on mines and forestry operations. We have explosives and bomb experts, but your training and materials will be welcome. I have been fortunate to join in many actions and fortunate to fight beside Yiorgos. I will let him explain the details of military operations and entertain you with tales of what the British call 'blood and thunder.' I will leave you with the following thoughts.

"The Germans are ruthless. Kill them before they kill you. In Greece, this is the only way. Do not hesitate, or you will wind up at the bottom of a ravine with crows picking out your eyes. You will hear stories of Germans killing villagers in retribution, and they are true. But don't let those stories stop you from killing Germans. They are invaders and bear the burden of their crimes.

"Again, we welcome you to our village and our struggle. Long live Greece and the revolution!"

With those words, Dimitra nodded to Yiorgos, squared her garrison cap, and left the plateia without taking questions or further acknowledging the OSS men. The andartes fell in alongside Dimitra, and the men watched the threesome walk up the narrow stone roadway to the schoolhouse.

Yiorgos stood and faced the group. With his usual bluntness, he said "The Germans are leaving. We know not when, but we know they are going. Now arise two schools of thought. Some in our movement say, "Let them go, do not hamper their retreat, for it will only delay their departure and our liberation." Others, and with this school, I agree, say, "Kill them. Kill them all, the sooner the better." This is a strategy that will teach the barbarians a lesson of history and will slow the fascists' concentration to the west. The Allies will come to Europe from the west, no?

"For now, the EAM-ELAS command has ordered that we save fighters and material and allow the Germans to leave unimpeded. We may defend ourselves. And we may attack when we can see a gain in material resources. So, if we see a convoy that we can plunder to secure weapons, we may do so.

"You are coordinating with the British to delay the German withdrawal, no? This I understand. If I wore your boots, I would see it the same. You have a grand strategy, and this I respect. But you will come to respect the movement in Greece.

"In operations where we stand to gain supplies, even a few Mausers, let us talk of combining our forces. In other operations that are only sabotage to delay retreat, we may not be so helpful. This we will discuss, no? First, you talk with AMM, and then we talk.

"The Kapetánios spoke the truth. Kill Germans. They will not hesitate to kill you. In these mountains, it is no more to them than shooting rabbits. Your uniforms and American flags will protect you even less. Hitler has ordered you dead. A bullet from your own weapon is preferable to capture. The British even carry pills for such."

Then Yiorgos looked at Stavros. "Lieutenant, can we talk? Can you and your second come to the schoolhouse?"

Stavros nodded. "Yes, sir."

Then Stavros turned to his men, "Return to the monastery and police the grounds, clean your weapons, sharpen your knives, and sort our gear. Radioman, get the news from AMM. Yanni, you're with me. Dismissed."

Yannis Georgakas, like Stavros, was older, in his thirties. He had grown up in Pittsburgh, Pennsylvania, where he and his immigrant father and two brothers worked at the massive Jones and Laughlin Steel Works on the south side of the Monongahela River. Yannis went into the mills after high school, and in five years had worked his way up from a blast furnace tender into a boilermaker's apprenticeship. He was in his third year and one year from journeyman when the Japanese attacked Pearl Harbor. Like all steelworkers, he was military exempt, but in February 1942, he enlisted in the United States Marine Corps. He scored high on aptitude testing and shipped to Quantico for Officer Candidates School. In November, he went ashore on Guadalcanal as a freshly minted second lieutenant with the 97th Field Artillery Battalion.

The OSS came across Yannis by chance. Yannis was shipboard on the USS *McCawley* in November, awaiting the landing at Bougainville, when he met an OSS officer on his way to China. The OSS was building a network of weather stations and training Chinese guerrillas to rescue downed Allied airmen. Yannis impressed the OSS man with his Greek language skills and steadfast bearing. The OSS man, aware of the Operational Group recruiting, reported his find back up his chain of command. Just before Yannis was to jump off to take a beachhead on Torokina, he received orders to stand down and await instructions. He stayed with the *McCawley* until late November. when she docked in Wellington, New Zealand, for overhaul. It was there that he interviewed with the OSS. He told the recruiters he wanted to stay with his unit until they were ready to train OGs, and he did. In July 1944, he was ready to go ashore in Guam when he received orders to report to Washington, DC, Q Building.

Yanni was a tested man. Even before the war and the battles he'd survived, he was solid, immovable, and just plain tough. He was shorter than Stavros and stocky, and from somewhere—Stavros knew not where—he found ratty cigars, unlit, that he chewed as part of his persona. He had a dry sense of humor and a direct continence. And if something didn't strike him as right, he seldom held his tongue. Stavros and Yanni were the same OSS rank, first lieutenants, with Stavros chosen as the group leader. Yanni was his second in command. They were distinct personalities with different histories. But since meeting in Washington, the men had worked well together and ironed out their disagreements. They weren't close friends, but Stavros enjoyed Yanni's company and respected his combat experience. Stavros leaned on Yanni for that experience.

As the two men walked the short distance from the plateia to the schoolhouse, Yanni began, "Well, we know who's in charge. She made that plain."

Stavros replied, "She's impressive. Seems to run a tight ship."

"I like her man Yiorgos. He's no bullshitter. What'd she say? He was a captain in the Greek Army?" asked Yanni.

"That's the way I heard it," answered Stavros.

"Well, he sure handled that march from Parga like a pro. He read that guy who dynamited the fish the riot act. I bet his ass is still sore," chuckled Yanni.

"Right. He embarrassed the hell out of him when he made him hand over his other grenades. Greeks hate public humiliation, even in America," offered Stavros.

"Right," replied Yanni.

The OSS men reached the schoolhouse where the two andartes from the earlier meeting stood guard at the top of the steps. One opened the door for them. Stavros and Yanni nodded.

Made of assorted stone and brick, the schoolhouse looked much like all the buildings in Chómori. What distinguished it was the playground across the road with its swing sets. Four wavy windows let a smoky light into a two-room interior, and kerosene lamps burned on Dimitra's desk and a mantel at the far end of the larger room.

Dimitra sat at her heavy wooden desk with Yiorgos to her right and Vasilios to her left. She motioned to two battered wooden chairs. Stavros and Yanni took their seats.

She began, "Comrades . . . or rather . . . gentlemen, I wanted to give you a chance to ask questions about our activity. And now I speak informally. Not for quotation. We stand ready to join in your actions. We will join you, but we must obey the wishes of our command, no? Yiorgos and I are of the same mind. We have not finished killing Germans. Our leaders think we have killed enough, and now is the time for the Germans to leave without harassment and delay. Yiorgos explained how this must appear. We wish not to step out of line, no?"

Stavros and Yanni nodded.

"Then, if you please, I ask that you share as much as you can of your Allied Military Mission's intentions. Our EAM-ELAS contacts with AMM are ragged and rough, not at all smooth. As you know, the British support EDES, and EDES supports the reactionary government abroad. The British support the return of the king and his lackeys. EAM-ELAS is still a part of the AMM, but we are, let us say, on the outs. I believe that is an American idiom, no?

"Now, it is time for you to talk. Do you have questions?"

Stavros looked at Yanni, then began, "Kapetánios. . . ."

Dimitra waved her hand, "Lieutenant, when we are not before our troops, we can speak casually. You are free to call me Dimitra or, like the comics in our band, Natasha. I prefer Dimitra."

At the mention of Natasha, Yiorgos and Vasilios smirked.

Stavros said, "We are Stavros and Yanni."

Dimitra prompted, "Lieutenant Stavros, tell me first about your family. Where are they from? And you, Yanni? We have plenty of time for other matters."

Stavros, caught off guard, blurted, "Sure. Yanni, you go first."

Yanni glanced at Stavros as though Stavros had just thrown him a hot potato. He took the unlit cigar out of his mouth, "Kapetánios, Dimitra. My father came to America in 1906 from

Kithnos. He was a sailor and jumped ship in Philadelphia. He went to Pittsburgh because of the jobs in the steel industry, and that is where he worked until three years ago. My mother came later, in 1912, from a village near Corinth called Perigiali. She came with her family, and she met my father in her family's confectionery shop, where she worked. They got married, I was born, went to school, got a job in the mills, and then joined the United States Marines. The OSS found me somewhere in the Pacific and introduced me to the likes of him." He nodded to Stavros.

Stavros smiled at the fast handoff, then began. "My mother and father are from a village in Crete, Loutra, near Rethymno. They came to America in 1910, and my father went to work in the coal mines of Colorado. I was born in 1912, and my mother died in 1913."

Stavros skipped the delicate parts, the violence of the strike and his mother's murder. He continued without skipping a beat, "My father remarried in 1916 to a Northern Italian, moved to St. Louis, and began developing and selling restaurants. I went to high school in St. Louis, then moved to Kansas City where I went to college. I was teaching history at Park College and the US Army General Staff College when I heard of the Greek Battalion. That unit disbanded in August, and the OSS took me aboard. So here I am in Chómori, a village not unfamiliar."

Dimitra cocked her head. "Not unfamiliar?"

Stavros waved. "We can talk later. It's a long story. And it has nothing to do with killing Germans."

Dimitra narrowed her gaze at Stavros and hesitated before continuing. "Family is important. My family is from Platanos, and Yiorgos is from Kato Dafni. This I mentioned on the plateia. Vasilios is our big city cousin; he and his family are from Athens. He was attending university when the Germans came, as was I. He was studying economics and I archaeology, and here we all are. From the mines and universities and confectionery shops. We are history's choice to kill Germans."

The five combatants talked for another hour. They discussed the most promising targets and the best routes of retreat. They talked of how to attack rail movement. Is it best to attack the train or the locomotive? They discussed the best way to destroy rail freight cars and German armored cars. They talked of attacking convoys and the best vantage points and pinch-points for ambushes. They debated the best way to destroy a truck. It impressed Yiorgos that the Americans had bazookas. He recommended that, if the truck were carrying barrels of petroleum, the attackers pepper the barrels with rifle fire in the instant before firing the bazooka. He assured the Americans this made for a bigger explosion and fire.

They had a long discussion about blowing up bridges and the distinction between rail viaducts and roadway bridgework. The OSS had the latest C-2 plastic explosives. Again, this impressed Yiorgos. They talked of attacks on factories and petrochemical dumps and that the attacking forces should stage to the windward to avoid any noxious fumes from fires and explosions. They talked of mining roadways, something that the andartes seldom did—they preferred booby traps using trip wires—though this discussion was premature because neither force had mines. They discussed the best way to blow up a railroad track and how many yards of destruction were necessary to cause a particular period of delay. Both groups agreed that destroying switch points slowed the repair work.

They discussed direct assaults on garrisons and pillboxes, with both groups agreeing that this was only productive if the strongholds guarded a target of value. They agreed that the attacking force should outnumber the defenders by at least two to one. It was better, they agreed, to ambush the Germans on patrol or in convoy because neither the Americans nor the andartes could muster artillery for direct attacks. Mortars, yes, but field artillery, no. Mortars didn't have the range for large German encampments. The Germans were careful. They cleared and patrolled the zone around their forces to remove cover for mortar teams. Yiorgos told the Americans that, thanks to the recent retirement of the Italian forces into the EAM-ELAS, they hoped soon to have operational mountain artillery units. He didn't mention that field artillery was the ultimate piece in his hoped-for attack on the German headquarters in Ioannina. This was the command that ordered the attack on Kommeno, killing six of his family as they attended a wedding.

The meeting broke before noon. Yiorgos left to inspect his forces billeted near Platanos. The andarte sentries had his dapple gray saddled and ready, and two more mounted andartes joined him for the trip. Vasilios took leave and went to the smaller room in the schoolhouse, where Stavros and Yanni saw him sorting papers on a small desk.

Dimitra, Stavros, and Yanni left the schoolhouse and descended the steps to the stone roadway. Dimitra again thanked the OSS men for coming to Greece. Then, just before they parted company, as the two Americans stepped away, she said in English, "Professor Stavros. You and I must talk of your knowledge of Chómori, no?"

Stavros looked at Yanni, gobsmacked, then sputtered, "Yes, ma'am . . . Kapetánios . . . I mean . . . Dimitra."

She dismissed this with a shake of her head.

When the Americans were out of earshot, Yanni, a cigar between his lips, looked straight ahead and observed, "Boy, that was suave."

Stavros shook his head.

Chapter 33

The first German Stavros killed was a teenage boy who never saw it coming. He was operating a BMW R75 motorcycle with a sidecar carrying another young soldier manning a MG 42 machine gun. The machine gunner was the second German Stavros killed. The third man riding behind the operator fled when the vehicle crashed into the stony wall of the narrow defile. He carried only a Walther. Stavros saw he was an officer. The three soldiers were at the head of a mechanized column northbound from the supply dump in Arta, their diesel, gasoline, and aviation fuel destined for German HQ in Ioannina. By the time the officer fled, all hell had broken loose.

Four motorcycles escorted the column of eight trucks, four fuel haulers, and four troop transports. The column diverted from Ionia Odos, the main road between Igoumenitsa and Patras, onto a narrow mountain bypass at Kastrosika. They were detouring because a team of Kommeno andarte saboteurs had dynamited a culvert bridge the night before, cutting the road to truck traffic. It would take the Germans little time to repair the damage, but the goal was diversion, not damage. The trap was set when the German column changed course to the narrow road through the hills. The detour between Kastrosika and Riza Prevezas was only five kilometers. The risk seemed minor compared to the wrath of German HQ, which demanded that the fuel arrive on time. The young oberleutnant in charge of the column ordered the detour, and three kilometers later, he was running for his life.

Stavros, Yanni, and Yiorgos planned the attack. Operational Group II brought three of its four teams and two officers for seventeen men. Yiorgos brought fifty andartes, and the Kommeno team was five men. The attackers had first-rate cover and elevation. They attacked from five meters above the column with an excellent line of fire and a fifty-meter killing zone.

The Germans had thirty-two men in transports and twelve men on motorcycles. The MG 42s on the motorcycles were the biggest threat to the andartes. They were also the prize most coveted in Chómori.

With Stavros's shot from his M1 Garand, the attackers broke cover and rained down bullets. The andartes at the south end of the ambush dropped the two trailing motorcycle operators before they could bring their machine guns to bear. At the north end, the motorcycle behind the lead that Stavros had neutralized, turned and tried to maneuver to fire on the attackers. The bazooka round that destroyed the bike and its riders ignited a brush fire on the side of the roadway. The smoke from the burning BMW and brush cloaked the infantry dismounting from the trucks. Following the bazooka attack on the motorcycle, a second M9 launched its M6A3 solid fuel, 2.3-inch rocket into the lead fuel hauler in the middle of the column. Gus, the bazooka triggerman, was well within the thirty yards of optimal range. He whooped and yelled when the truck exploded in orange-and-yellow flames, sending a wall of heat toward the ambushers. The driver of the truck scrambled from the fiery cab, flailing and fanning his own flames. Billowing smoke further obscured the battle, allowing the German infantry to dismount and begin returning fire.

Andartes positioned a hundred meters north and south felled trees across the roadway at the sound of the attack, preventing motorized escape. When Stavros asked Yiorgos why his men carried heavy axes on their five-day march to the ambush. Yiorgos replied, "Trees are fighters, too."

The OSS men and andartes fired on the fleeing Germans with deadly effect. Half the soldiers fell within thirty seconds. The smoke made it difficult to target the remainder. A group of three Germans tried to run away to the south. The andarte lumberjacks cut them down with spray from their Sten guns. The remaining dozen Germans returned fire scattered over the length of the kill zone.

Gus fired his bazooka again and another fuel hauler burst into flames. The explosion set afire the trees and brush cover used by the three Germans who had to move or burn alive. Through the smoke and flames, Yanni made out the silhouette of one soldier and dropped the sights of his Garand onto the center of his chest. He pulled the trigger, and the German stumbled forward a few feet and collapsed. The other two Germans trying to escape the flames died by a well-thrown grenade from the andarte that Yiorgos had berated at Limni Trichonida. Yiorgos, who was firing his Mannlicher next to Stavros, saw the grenadier and smiled at Stavros.

Yiorgos yelled above the firing, "We need to begin our retreat in ten minutes. Fighters will be in the air soon if the Germans radioed. We must destroy the remaining fuel and recover the two machine guns." He nodded to the two disabled motorcycles that had been at the head of the column.

Stavros said, "Roger."

Stavros put his fingers to his lips and whistled. Two OSS men, Greek nationals, appeared at his side. He said, "We need those two buzz saws. Can you get 'em?"

The nationals looked at each other, then back to Stavros and nodded.

Stavros said, "Good. Wait until we light up those fuel haulers. Then make your move. Got it?"

The nationals nodded again.

Stavros shuttled through cover to the first bazooka man and his loader. He yelled above the firing, "Get with Gus and light up those two haulers so we can get out of here!"

The commando said, "Yes, sir."

Five minutes later, with Yiorgos growing nervous, the first remaining fuel hauler went up in flames, followed a second later by the last one. The two nationals descended into the roadway, and Stavros yelled at his men for covering fire. They removed the weapons from their mounts and shouldered them back up the hillside. When the nationals returned, Stavros nodded to Yiorgos. The andarte leader rolled onto his back and drew a Very pistol and shell from his bandolier. He opened the breech, loaded a green flare, and fired the signal for retreat.

The rally point was a cave near a nameless settlement only a kilometer to the east. There, the band would hide before traveling overland at night. They would head east, cross the Arachthos River at the Tzari Bridge, and take a northern route back to Chómori.

Yanni gathered his gear. The last thing he did before leaving was to crumple an empty carton of American cigarettes and place it on the wrecked motorcycle. This surprised Stavros. Yanni didn't smoke. Stavros looked puzzled. Yanni said, "Business card."

The ambush was a success: the fuel destroyed, machine guns pilfered, and seventeen Germans dead with more wounded. A bullet grazed an andarte's shoulder, and another fighter stumbled and sprained his wrist, running after a fleeing German. The bolting soldier enjoyed freedom until the andarte lumberjacks manning the north barricade mowed him down with their Stens.

Stavros and the OSS men fought well. Everybody kept their heads and did their jobs. When Stavros briefed the group on plans for the attack, there was unease. The OG had never fought before, and they had never maneuvered with the andartes. Yiorgos had insisted that the OSS men go with his andartes on their first mission. He told Stavros that the mission would be simple and allow the OSS men to season to the fighting. He compared the OSS men to olives on a tree, nice to look at but of no use until pressed.

Yiorgos did not tell Stavros that the ambush would be the closest attack ever to the German 1st Mountain Division

Headquarters in Ioannina. He did not tell Stavros of the division commander's September 20, 1943, order:

> *In order to oppose energetically the continued raids on convoys and members of the Wehrmacht, it is ordered that from 20 September 1943 onward, for every German soldier wounded or killed by insurgents or civilians, ten Greeks from all classes of the population are to be shot to death. This order must be carried out consistently in order to achieve a deterrent effect.*

Nor did Yiorgos tell Stavros of the October 25, 1943, superseding order:

> *If a member of the German Wehrmacht is killed by either attack or murder in a territory considered pacified, fifty Greeks (male) are to be shot for one murdered German.*[76]

Yiorgos did not know and could not tell Stavros something else. A month before the Americans arrived, the Germans had rounded up Ioannina's two thousand Romaniote and Sephardi Jews, herded them into railcars, and sent them to death camps.[77]

Yiorgos cared not for the legalities of fighting the Germans. After years of burying mutilated corpses, smelling their stench, and walking amid carnage and misery, he wanted them all dead. He had hated the Germans even before August 1943 in Kommeno. Now, he burned with an inner fire to avenge the murder of his family. Today's ambush was, in Yiorgos's mind, a prelude to destroying the Germans in their lair.

Ioannina and German HQ were thirty-five kilometers north of the ambush. An insurmountable German ground force could cover the distance in less than two hours, and fighter aircraft from Igoumenitsa in only minutes. There were in EDES territory, disputed though that might be. This was the land of

Albanian Chams. The Chams were Muslim collaborationists who had fallen for the fascist propaganda that, after the war, Chameria would be granted independence. The andartes, staging their ambush so near Ioannina, no longer swam in a friendly sea. Now they were tempting fate in shark-infested waters, and welcoming territory east of the Arachthos River was two days away.

Chapter 34

The sun rose red above the eastern mountains and Oros Kerasovouni as seven mounted andartes left Chómori. It was a two-hour ride to Platanos. The andartes' arrivals and departures were so common that the villagers paid them no mind. But this morning, an older woman hanging her wash took note. As the Kapetános passed her house, she offered a robust *asfalí taxídia!* Safe travels! Then she crossed herself twice. Dimitra nodded and offered a broad smile.

Dimitra rode her coal-coat stallion and was not in uniform. She wore a black dress and a nondescript, well-worn coat with the simple, ankle-high footwear of village women. A laced scarf covered her dark hair. Dimitra cut a striking figure, even in disguise. Two male andartes, masquerading as shepherds, wore bulky capes to conceal their Stens. The other four female andartes dressed in EAM-ELAS uniforms and shouldered British Lee-Enfield rifles. Dimitra carried a knife and her Beretta.

The andartes armed only for defense. This was not a military mission. Dimitra was traveling to Platanos for two reasons. She wanted to see her mother and to meet with Maria Svolou, a leading feminist in the resistance. Maria had plans for Dimitra.

In the 1920s, Maria had been secretary of the League for Women's Rights. She advocated for women's night schools and campaigned against prostitution. At the Labor Ministry, she had worked as an inspector, exposing poor housing and working conditions. She'd edited a dissident magazine, *Woman's Struggle.* Her editorial leanings and her husband's political transgressions earned them the ire of Metaxas and exile from Greece in 1936. The couple returned to Greece in 1940, and Maria volunteered as a nurse on the Albanian front. When the Germans occupied Greece, she joined EAM-ELAS and worked with the Red Cross to feed the starving children of Athens. Now, on her way to Platanos to meet Dimitra, she was a member of the National Council, the Central Committee of the formative Mountain Government. Maria sympathized with the communist movement but never joined the party. Still, she believed only a revolution could free the women of Greece.

In 1923 she married Alexandros Svolos, an ELD (Union of People's Democracy) socialist legal scholar. They had met at a University of Athens symposium on Alexandros's doctoral thesis about the rights of Greek workers. Alexandros was the president-in-waiting for PEEA, the Political Committee of National Liberation. In three weeks, he would head the Mountain Government, one of three regimes claiming Greece.

Maria traveled with Red Cross authorization papers and a young driver from Athens. They motored in a faded-sage-green 1939 Austin 12 saloon. A Red Cross banner fluttered on a make-shift staff wired to its flying *A* hood ornament. Both Maria and her driver wore Red Cross armbands. Maria had requested the meeting with Dimitra. They had to meet in Platanos because washouts and rockslides made it impossible to drive to Chómori.

Maria took the northern route from Athens to Platanos. The road was worse than the principal route that crossed into the Peloponnese at Corinth and ferried back across the Gulf at Rio. But the northern route through Central Greece was less patrolled, and while Maria had travel papers, she hoped to avoid confrontation.

She spent the night at a supporter's home in Nafpaktos and left for their meeting even earlier than Dimitra. The tired Austin struggled to pull its three thousand pounds up the Nafpaktian hillsides, overworking its sixteen-horsepower engine. Twice, they stopped to let the motor cool.

Dimitra left two female andartes a kilometer north of Platanos. There they would watch the approach for enemy movements and signal with a Very pistol if Dimitra were in danger. When the remaining five reached the town square, the other two female andartes continued on to set another watch point a kilometer south. The two "shepherds" with Dimitra took up casual positions at a street-side table in the courtyard, smoking cigarettes and drinking coffee. Dimitra waited inside the regional government office on the square in view of the shepherds. It was from this office that Dimitra had organized the guerrilla fighters to resist the Italians in Albania. Her father had once worked there. She was a welcome visitor.

The Germans had no permanent units in Platanos, nor any of the villages in the Chómori district. They sent mechanized patrols through the town, but it had been months since the last reported contact. The Germans knew what awaited them in these mountains, and since the territory was of little strategic importance, they gave Platanos a wide berth. Dimitra and her detachment were prudent. They deployed for defense, expecting the worst, hoping for the best.

The old Austin pulled into Platanos thirty minutes later. The driver parked across from the town square, opened the rear door for his passenger, and stayed with the car. Maria Svolos walked the short distance to the square, and Dimitra met her at the street. It was their first meeting.

Maria Svolos was fifty-two years old and reminded Dimitra of an earnest librarian or a *dimotiko* schoolteacher. She was shorter than Dimitra and slight of build, with shoulder-length, wavy brown hair. Her eyes conveyed intelligence and conviction from behind her round frames and thick lenses. She wore a heavy, double-breasted, gray wool coat over a forest-green dress with four large, round, fabric-covered buttons above her black leather belt. She wore no jewelry or wedding ring.

Dimitra greeted her with a formal *Kaliméra sýntrofos* and a nod of her head. Maria answered, "And good morning to you, comrade. It is a fine day, no? I'm so happy we can talk. I worried that your mountains would best our car. Better to come by horse, eh?"

Dimitra nodded and smiled. "We can sit here in the square if you like. The morning is fair, and the coffee is good. Will this table be all right?" She nodded toward a table in the center of the square.

"This is a lovely spot. May I ask, are you alone? You are an EAM-ELAS Kapetánios with a German price on your head," inquired Maria.

Dimitra nodded to the two shepherds at the table near the road.

Maria turned to look. "Oh, I see."

Dimitra said, "We will be safe here. We have sentries posted on the approaches. They will signal if there is a threat."

Maria said, "Of course."

Maria was a Greek of the city. She had spent a few months in the mountains after the German occupation, but her preconceptions had been formed in Athens.

The women sat at a small iron table in iron chairs. Both women sat erect and proper. Dimitra asked the café owner's wife to bring two Greek coffees, Dimitra's *sketos* and Maria's *metrios*. The server asked if the women would like *galaktoboureko*. Dimitra and Maria succumbed to the phyllo and custard sweet, Dimitra's favorite since childhood.

When the coffee and pastry arrived, the women began their discussion. Maria asked, "What do you see for yourself after the Germans leave? You're an impressive leader. By all reports, the women in this district look up to you. They have voted at the highest percentage of any district. And the men respect you. You have done much. You should be proud."

Dimitra knew flattery when she heard it. Still, she respected Maria's work for women and her reputation for political savvy. Dimitra had looked forward to meeting the woman and was honored that Maria had sought her out.

Dimitra considered Maria's question. "I will return to university and continue my studies in archaeology. I was to start the second year of my master's course when the Italians invaded. I deferred to help organize our fighters here in Platanos."

Maria said, "Yes, I know. I have read your background. Does your mother still live here?"

Dimitra worried that someone somewhere had a file on her that Maria could read. But she continued unfazed. "Yes, she lives just north of here by the school. She is a teacher."

"And your father?" asked Maria.

"He is dead. He died two years ago," said Dimitra, closing the painful episode.

Maria returned to her subject. "I believe you should look toward political leadership when the time is right. Greek women need strong female leaders to bring them out of their medieval dungeons. I don't have to tell you about their condition. You know better than I, since the worst enslavement is here."

Maria waved her hand at the surrounding mountains, then continued, "In these mountains and valleys, they live no better than pack animals, no?"

"Yes, that is true," offered Dimitra. "These mountains condition the women to accept their burden, and their illiteracy leaves them uninspired. Many do not think things could ever be better. Not here, not in the mountains. Perhaps in Athens? But here, the cycle is vicious. One day follows another. The Italians come, then they go. Now the Germans come, and they too will leave. Soon we hope. But the mountains stay the same, in their minds, so must they."

"May I tell you of my experience?" asked Dimitra.

"Oh, by all means. I would love to hear it," answered Maria.

Dimitra asked rhetorically, "The EAM-ELAS edict that grants women the vote, it is emancipation, no?"

Maria nodded.

Dimitra continued, "I imagine the Central Committee foresaw the desperate women of the mountains dancing with joy when they learned of our proclamation.

"We posted the notices in all villages in our district. A week later, our political officer reported not only were the women subdued by the news, but they were frightened. They worried the Germans would shoot them if they voted. They worried the men of the village would run them out of their homes if they voted. They worried their tax burden would increase. They had a thousand reasons they should not vote. Why did they not embrace change and progress?

"Here is how change came. The political officer and I went to each village, twenty in all. We entered the village and called the president to the commons. There we held a meeting and assured the women that they could vote. We promised them that if anyone interfered, EAM-ELAS would punish them. They know EAM-ELAS will make good on such a promise. I attended these meetings in uniform with a Mannlicher on my shoulder. Then, and only then, did the women come to embrace their liberation and the men respect change. And in some villages, there is still apprehension.

"My point is only this, Comrade Maria. Change comes when backed by arms. And, with all due respect, politicians reek with self-appointed importance and offer shallow and untrustworthy personalities. I doubt it is a world I would do well in."

"Ah, but you underestimate yourself, Comrade Dimitra. I agree that too many personalities in politics are, perhaps we say, regrettable? But there are good people, too. People who come from situations like yours and see the need to bring light to a dark cave. Politics is like combat . . . but your weapons are not explosives, rifles, and bullets. They are reason, perseverance, and organization. These last four years we have used bullets to define our politics. But soon, that will change."

Dimitra stared at Maria, registering her lack of concurrence.

Maria went on, "There is a young woman in France, Simone de Beauvoir, who is about your age. Have you heard of her?"

Dimitra shook her head. Her interests were ancient ruins and military organization, not French philosophers.

"She says women wallow in immanence. Do you take her meaning?" asked Maria.

Maria, certified in French Studies from the University of Athens and a former teacher, slipped into the pedantic. Dimitra felt she was in a classroom. Dimitra recognized in Maria something of her mother.

Dimitra played along and answered, "Perhaps Comrade de Beauvoir means women live inside of themselves, not allowing the outer world to reach them."

"Yes! That is what I think, too," said Maria. "So, how are they to escape their self-imposed prison and see the world that is? And the world that can be? By example, young lady! By example! You, my Kapetánios, are a splendid example. You burn like a beacon above the fog.

"Here is what I ask of you. I know the KKE has listed you as a delegate to the conference in Koryschades. And I know you must follow party discipline. I support the party, Dimitra, but my husband and I are not Leninists. Nor are many Greeks. All I ask of you is that you counsel those in your party of the primacy of women's concerns, that is all. And I hope you and the party will put your full backing behind Alexandros as president. More than lip service, Dimitra. Alexandros is our only hope for keeping the movement together and establishing a foothold in the new government following the Germans. The KKE is brave and bold, a veritable force. Of this, there is no doubt. But they cannot fend off the British and the backward Greeks who see them as Russian dolls. Alexandros, a socialist, can carry that burden and bring Greece to a place where peace and reason can win the day.

"Dimitra, we will spend years rebuilding our country and years depending upon richer nations to help us. A communist government will not win us friends, not even in Russia. We saw the Russians bend to the British most recently when EAM-ELAS tried to eliminate EDES, no? Did the Russians help? Did the Russians send weapons or material?

"The way forward for Greece is through democracy and socialism, not a dictatorship of the proletariat. One can only imagine a proletariat in Greece, let alone a class ready to exercise power.

"The KKE has done Greece a great and historic service with their resistance to the fascists. This everyone knows. But the organization needed to fight a war is not the organization needed to win the peace. There will come a time to put down your Mannlicher.

"I only ask that you consider my words. You are smart and analytical, and your leadership is invaluable to the future of Greece."

Dimitra recognized Maria's logic. She was right. Only a small segment of the KKE believed, like religious zealots, in the Leninist line. Members of the KKE were Greeks who wanted to fight the fascists. The KKE was the best way to do it. But they were Greeks first.

After a pause, she said to Maria, "I will consider your words. They carry weight. When I mounted Diávolos this fine morning, my plans were humble. I hope someday to study ancient artifacts and read archaeology journals. Perhaps I might publish. I relished the hope that I might never again suffer through a rhetoric-laden Central Committee position paper on the ethnic rights of Macedonians and self-determination."

Maria chuckled and nodded. Then, without missing a beat, she said, "I want you to stand for the National Council."

Dimitra cocked her head and stared at Maria. "Me? A politician? Impossible! I have enough to manage with EAM-ELAS and now the Americans. And the party has not assigned this to me. It would be a breach."

Maria said, "I think we can help with that. My husband and I are not without friends in KKE. We have discussed your candidacy, and you can stand if you choose."

"I know nothing of the National Council. Just that we are to elect in Koryschades," said Dimitra. "I have not studied these proceedings, only mobilized the women in the district to vote. It has not been my focus. Am I to pretend I know what is happening?"

Maria said, "The National Council will be a body of two hundred who will work with the administration. The Council will advance political initiatives and resolutions and act as authenticators for decisions of the administration. It will require meetings only so often. No one knows the exact schedule. You will stand for election in Koryschades. The Council will meet there. The Council will adopt a charter or some other founding document and vote on resolutions.

"You will be one of the first elected women in Greece, Dimitra. You will make history."

"What if I am not elected?" asked Dimitra.

"They will elect you. I assure this. You will have my husband's support and KKE's support. It is arranged," answered Maria.

Dimitra leaned back in her chair with a muffled, "Hmm."

Maria continued, "Comrade, the time is running short. The conference begins six days from now. We need to know your mind."

Dimitra noted the plural *we.* She said, "I will make my decision tomorrow and contact you in Athens. Will this be soon enough?"

"It should be. I will return to Athens today, Austin willing," replied Maria.

Dimitra said, "A messenger will contact you tomorrow with my decision. They will authenticate with the phrase *Sounion is fogged in.*"

The two women sat in the courtyard talking of the famine in Athens, then of the government in exile. They discussed Emmanouil Tsouderos's ouster as prime minister and the ascendance of Sofoklis Venizelos of the Liberal Party. Then, Venizelos's departure only a week later for Georgios Papandreou, the founder of the Democratic Socialist Party. They agreed that the change would make no difference in the British campaign to return King George II to Greece. Papandreou professed anti-royalist leanings, but the king concurred with his choice in Egypt. The British, they agreed, planned to subjugate Greece following the German retreat, whatever form the government might take.

Tsouderos's ouster came only two days before the Americans arrived, and Maria wondered if the two events connected. Dimitra had her doubts. According to EAM-ELAS intelligence reports, the Americans had no animus to the KKE or EAM-ELAS. The Americans were friends of the British and under their command, but independent.

Dimitra shared her impression of the Americans. She said, "They have just returned from their first mission. They lost no one. Yiorgos, our military commander, reported that they fought well. They were disciplined and kept up on the march. He said they were well-led. He likes both their commander and their second. They returned with two German bone saws. So, our weapons cache is happy, no?"

Maria did not know the slang for the prized German machine guns. But she listened without interruption.

"Americans are more glamorous than the British. Their weapons and equipment are the best in the world. They look like a film-director's idea of commando troops. They speak of the war in picturesque terms. They use tough words and sometimes bravado. Their officers discourage bravado. The Americans are of distinct personalities and have no pretense of rank and class. To them, the world is theirs to shape and mold. Like pottery. They presume this they will do and have a grand party afterward.

"They are easy to live with. They include you in their circles. They are friendly and generous, and they assume you to be the same. In this way, they are infectious."

"What of their officers?" asked Maria. "Are they of the bourgeoisie?"

"Oh, no. Far from it. Both officers are from working families, Greeks of the diaspora. The second officer is from the steel mills of Pittsburgh, and the commander is from a family in St. Louis. His father was a coal miner in Colorado. I think there is more to his story, but we have yet to discuss it. His mother died young, and his father remarried a Northern Italian. He speaks three languages. All the Americans speak Greek.

"The commander was a professor with a master's in history before the war. But he does not display the pedagogic arrogance of some in university instruction. He is far from bourgeois."

With her description of Stavros, in Dimitra percolated a curiosity. She wanted to know more about Stavros, and in time, she would.

The two women finished talking, and Maria began the journey back to Athens. Dimitra embraced her at the car, then walked to the kafeneion. She came out with a tray and three servings of galaktoboureko, two on plates and one wrapped. She took the tray to her shepherd escorts and told them she would visit her mother. The house was near, and she told them to stay in the courtyard and enjoy the morning. She would return in an hour. She took the wrapped pastry and walked the two blocks to the school, then another block to her mother's.

Dimitra's mother, Eva, was the same age as Maria. But there, the similarities ended. Eva was vivacious and full of life. She was shorter than Dimitra but trim and fit, with a complexion that told of her love of the outdoors. She worked a large garden on the side and back of her house, one that Dimitra's father tended. Dimitra thought it was too much for Eva, but Eva brushed her off. The garden was Eva's way of keeping her husband alive in her mind.

Eva wore a long, light-green dress with a cream-colored sweater over her shoulders. She had the same dark features as her daughter and gave Dimitra a forceful hug when she arrived. Then Eva said, "My daughter, it pleases me to see you. But your dress and coat are an embarrassment. Even your uniform is much better."

Dimitra said only, "Yes, Mother."

Then she handed Eva the wrapped pastry. Eva said, "What is this? As if I didn't know. You are too kind. Thank you, Daughter."

"How have you been, Mother?" asked Dimitra.

"Good days, bad days, in between days, you know. Such is the time, no? What else can we do?" answered Eva.

"You look good. You are eating well, and I see from your tan, you are working in the garden. I apologize for not visiting. What has it been, a month? We were preparing for the election, and then the Americans arrived," said Dimitra.

"Oh, the Americans, how are they? Did they send you a husband?" Eva asked, returning to a frequent concern. "You, my precious daughter, are lovely. But you do not grow any younger."

"Mother, this is a matter for after the war, no? Now is the time for worries other than marriage," Dimitra said, deflecting her mother's persistence.

"Yes, yes, of course. Of course. Come, we can sit. We can talk while I eat my galaktoboureko," instructed Eva.

Mother and daughter entered their home arm in arm.

Chapter 35

Stavros waited on the schoolhouse steps and tried to shoot the breeze with Dimitra's two sentries. It wasn't going well. The men were polite but taciturn. Large and taciturn. They prevented Stavros from going into the building with the explanation that Dimitra was teaching. The class, they said, had started late because of an urgent radio message. The class would finish in a few minutes.

Stavros offered both andartes American cigarettes. They accepted. Stavros didn't smoke, but like most Americans, he kept cigarettes with him as tokens of goodwill and currency. The andarte on Stavros's right lit his at once and the fellow on the left put his in his shirt pocket.

Stavros tried again to make conversation. He asked, "Are you guys from Chómori?"

The andarte to his right exhaled a lung full with a pleasurable smile, "No. Nafpaktos."

The fellow on the left just said, "No."

Stavros decided the andarte on his right was the conversationalist. He probed, "What did you do in Nafpaktos, if you don't mind me asking?"

The andarte replied, "Fisherman."

Stavros was interested. Fishermen have boats, and Stavros had envisioned a mission that might require one. He asked, "Do you have a boat there?"

The andarte answered, "Perhaps. But what do I know?"

Stavros sensed he may have hit a wall with his boat inquiry. He tacked. "What did you catch?"

The andarte scowled, "Fish. Mostly fish."

Stavros looked puzzled. The other andarte caught his expression and piped in, "He means he caught fish, yes. But he also caught octopus."

"Oh, okay," said Stavros.

The two andartes looked at each other, shrugged and nodded.

The schoolhouse door opened from the inside, and seven girls in long khaki jumpers with red bandannas skipped from the building. Each carried a used green reader. Stavros guessed their ages between twelve and seventeen. Dimitra followed them to the threshold and called, "We will read the lesson aloud on Tuesday. This we must do correctly *before* we practice our dancing. Is this understood, girls?"

A hail, "Yes, Kapetánios!" arose from the cohort as they ran to the enticing swing sets on the playground across the road.

Dimitra smiled and motioned Stavros in. As he stepped past the andartes he said, "It's been nice talking."

Dimitra returned to her desk and motioned for Stavros to sit. He pulled a wooden chair from the circle and placed it in front of the desk.

As he settled, Dimitra asked, "How have you been? Are your men comfortable? How did you find your first action?"

Stavros replied, "Your hospitality is first-rate, thank you. Yes, we are comfortable, and we appreciate all you are doing to help us on our missions. Yiorgos is a fine leader, and you are fortunate he is with you."

"Yes, he is a fine leader and a bull in battle, no?" answered Dimitra.

Stavros, still learning the subtle Greek idioms, answered, "No. I mean, yes, Kapetánios."

Dimitra said, "Dimitra, please."

Stavros nodded.

Dimitra asked, "And your first action in combat. How did that go?"

Stavros said, "Good, I believe. The men stuck to the plan, performed well, and no wounded or dead. We killed some Germans, blew up some fuel, and returned with two buzz saws."

"Bone saws," corrected Dimitra. "The Greeks call them bone saws. And thank you. They are superior weapons, no?"

"Yes, they are. It's best to be on the stock end and not the muzzle end, right?" offered Stavros.

Dimitra did not react to Stavros's humor.

Stavros continued, "Again, thank you for sending Yiorgos and your men with us. They are brave fighters and excellent instructors."

Dimitra nodded and held her tongue.

Stavros segued, "I see you are an instructor, too. Do you enjoy teaching?"

Dimitra said, "Yes, it is fulfilling, but only as a sideline. My mother is a teacher of music in Platanos. I could not teach all the time. I lack patience. It is part of my duties. It is part of our program. We are working to end illiteracy in these mountains. The most illiterate are the girls. They grow up to become illiterate women, subjugated women, no? We teach them to dance, but first they must learn to read.

"Those children you saw leaving are members of EPON, that is our youth organization. They will take their dancing and literacy to small villages, perform to the applause of people who know little entertainment, and then read to them from classical works. They are youth ambassadors. Models for other young women."

With her reference to female role models, Dimitra transitioned into her reason for meeting with Stavros. Dimitra said, "I will leave Chómori in four days to attend a conference in Koryschades. I will be away for a week, perhaps longer. Yiorgos will be in charge while I am gone. Vasilios will travel with me.

"Koryschades is near Karpenissi, two days north. We will travel in EAM-ELAS territory, but I will take with me a small detachment of fighters. Still, there will remain here enough fighters for you and Yiorgos to fashion your plans and execute missions."

Stavros nodded. "Can we be any help for your journey? Can we send a detachment?"

"No, no," said Dimitra. "This meeting is political, and I believe your command has ordered you to stay out of Greek politics, no?"

Stavros wondered how Dimitra knew of the standing noninterference order for OSS commandos.

She continued, "It is best that this conference is only Greeks. Our purpose is to form a government based on our secret-ballot elections last month. Oh, and of these elections, I am proud to say we have counted one and a half million votes. An extraordinary number for these times, no?"

Stavros caught on. "Yes, yes. Extraordinary."

"Professor Stavros," Dimitra beamed, "Professor, would you like to be a teacher in our school program?"

This caught Stavros off guard. He stammered, "Ah, yes. Maybe. But please, don't call me *Professor*, especially in front of my men. Americans are apt to hang nicknames, and I don't want to get stuck with *Professor*."

Dimitra smiled. "Like Natasha?"

"Yes, yes, like Natasha. But Natasha is not derogatory. Professor has a certain remoteness to it. In America we deride people for being ivory-towered professors, someone detached from the everyday world."

"Natasha, to Greeks, is a Russian name. Derogatory? Maybe. To a Greek, any nationality other than Greek is derogatory," replied Dimitra. "Still, you are a professor, no? So, you are qualified to teach, and perhaps learn while you teach?"

"Yes, but we will need to discuss this further when you return from your conference. I'm not sure my take on world history fits with your curriculum," answered Stavros. What he really wondered was if his take on history fit with KKE doctrine.

"Then it is decided. I will tell the conference that we have an American history professor instructing our andartes and villagers," announced Dimitra.

Stavros, mindful of the OSS directive to play nice with the locals, said, "Sure, honored to help when we're not maneuvering."

"Yes, fighting comes first. How else will we keep our schoolhouse?" intoned Dimitra.

Dimitra's comment sent a flash through Stavros. He thought how lucky Americans were to live far from occupiers and fascists so they might advance thought and science and culture. While interviewing at Q Building, Stavros picked up a July 1943 issue of *Psychological Review.* He presumed the journal had been left behind by the testing staff. As he waited alone in yet another small cubicle for yet another interview, he read "A Theory of Human Motivation." The two magazines in the cubicle, *Psychological Review*, with its bland blue, featureless cover, and *Time*, with a full-face color portrait of a determined General Eisenhower, had been a test. Behind a small translucent portrait of Wild Bill Donovan, an unseen researcher in the adjoining cubicle noted his choice.

In the article, an American psychologist, Abraham Maslow, offered a visualization of human motivation as a layered pyramid, what Maslow called a hierarchy of needs. He argued that psychology is progressive and regressive. When the most predominant need is realized, the next higher need emerges.

Maslow placed the elemental need for Physiological Survival at the base of the pyramid. The next layer he called Safety. The third layer was Love and Belonging. The fourth, Esteem. And, at the peak of the pyramid, Self-Actualization. Maslow argued humans could not advance to higher needs with unmet lower needs.

Dimitra asked Stavros to help with a higher need, education, while reminding him of the elemental, the security of the schoolhouse. The request seemed incongruous, yet he felt enlightened. He felt a warmth and respect for Dimitra's clarity and insight. The professor might still learn, and the Kapetánios had more to teach.

Dimitra brought him out of his thoughts, "When I return from Koryschades, we will talk more about your knowledge of Chómori, no?"

Stavros nodded. "Do you know a family in the village named Hantzis?"

Dimitra said, "Yes, they are prominent. The Italians killed George Hantzis in July last year. He was a lieutenant in our band."

Stavros asked, "Is the family still here?"

Dimitra said, "Yes. The patriarch, Demitris Konstantinos Hantzis, lives on the road to the monastery. You pass the house when you come here. It is the property beyond the lamb spit with the green door. He is old, in his eighties, I believe. He has seen much. He was alive when we drove the Turks into the sea in 1913. His son Harry fought in that Army with distinction.

"How do you know this family?"

Stavros pursed his lips and exhaled. "It is a long story. They helped my family many years ago. It is best we talk when we have more time. I told our men we would discuss some missions at noon. It's almost time."

"Yes," said Dimitra, "Missions come first."

As he stood to leave, Stavros said, "Oh. There's one thing more. Will you take your security detail to Koryschades? I might need the help of the fellow from Nafpaktos while you are away."

Chapter 36

What was Venetian Lepanto in 1571 became Greek Nafpaktos in 1944. The Battle of Lepanto inspired Stavros. He had spent hours in McFee Library at Park College poring over volumes depicting the epic clash. He distilled a lecture on the battle for the Command and General Staff College. When he learned OG II would stage nearby, in Chómori, he grew curious, even excited. Crossing the Adriatic, on the march to Chómori, at their first ambush, a notion percolated in him. It was now clear. Stavros wanted to sink a ferry.

Lepanto was the historical namesake of the sea battle that halted the Muslim Ottoman drive west and saved European Christendom. It was the last major naval clash fought with rowed warships, vessels much like the indomitable triremes of Pericles.

Battle tactics were straightforward. The six hundred Christian and Ottoman galleys and galliots were floating islands from which infantry launched assaults. Attacking vessel used the wind and rowers to advantage, rammed the enemy, then unleashed armored warriors onto the defenders. After the killing, capturing, and mayhem, the victors seized the defeated vessel or set it aflame.

On October 7, 1571, Christian forces captured 117 galleys and twenty galliots and sunk or burned fifty other ships, the bulk of the Ottoman fleet. They captured thousands of Turks and rescued thousands of Christian slaves. The Christians lost seventy-five hundred men and the Ottomans thirty thousand. It was an overwhelming victory for the West.[78] If OG II could sink a ferry, they would add another wreck to the ancient galleys that lay below the mesmerizing blue of the timeless Gulf of Corinth, this one teaming with Germans and their supplies.

The ferry from Antirrio on the northern shore to Rio on the southern motored two and a half kilometers across the Gulf at its narrowest point. Stavros learned from andartes that the

Germans often loaded a ferry with thirty trucks, sometimes artillery, and hundreds of troops. The ferry was the only way to travel northbound to Igoumenitsa or southbound to Patras. The first thing would be to scout Nafpaktos, the ports, and the ferry operation.

Nafpaktos was a day's march from Chómori, a half day on horseback. Besides its postcard-worthy port and tall stonework breakwaters, in Nafpaktos rose an ancient fortification first noted in 455 BCE. Built on a two-hundred-meter rise, the fort provided a lethal field of fire to the Gulf. There, the Germans deployed an artillery company of 250 men billeted in the old Venetian castle. Foot soldiers and motorized units patrolled the city streets. But the Germans weren't the only problem.

Collaborationist Prime Minister Ioannis Rallis had supporters in Nafpaktos. Security Battalions patrolled the harbor and strutted the narrow streets in their floppy berets. They extorted tribute from shop owners, taverna keepers, and hoteliers and menaced anyone for any reason. Nafpaktos was enemy territory.

Antirrio, the northern ferry terminus, was eleven kilometers west of Nafpaktos. Germans guarded the loading and storage and docking areas day and night. High fences crowned with razor wire ringed the terminus, and the approaches were mined. Dog patrols and searing searchlights made the port resemble a prison. Rio, the terminus on the southern shore, enjoyed no less security.

Stavros had never seen Nafpaktos or the ferry ports. Everything Stavros knew was secondhand. An attack on a German-laden, ferry while ambitious, had yet to gel. As he convened the mission meeting, Stavros refrained from bringing it up. Now was the time for practical plans, not daydreams.

Yiorgos offered a grounded and realistic suggestion. Yiorgos knew that the OSS men needed seasoning and tutelage in the Greek way. For their second mission and the first exposure for OG Squad Four, he proposed a railway target. Not the main line from Athens to Thessaloniki, but a narrow-gauge line. The railway Yiorgos had in mind connected the Port of Missolonghi on the Gulf of Patras to the agricultural center of Agrinio, forty kilometers north.

The rail line ran northwest from Missolonghi, skirting the heights of Ano Mousoura along the shores of brackish Aitoliko Lagoon. Past the lagoon, the line continued northwest to the Achelous River to avoid the rugged Zygos Mountains. At the river, the line turned due east across the fertile plains to Agrinio.

There was a branch from Missolonghi to the small port of Kryoneri, fourteen kilometers east. But here the land was flat and open, and Kryoneri, which handled scant traffic, was close to the Germans at Antirrio. The freight on this section was marginal, unlike the thousands of Papastratos cigarettes and cured tobacco arriving from Agrinio at Missolonghi. Yiorgos ruled out the Kryoneri branch for attack. Instead, the attack would be best between Missolonghi and Agrinio.

The railway had opened for business in 1888. In 1943, the Italians prohibited passenger service and began a northward extension to Amfilochia on the Ambracian Gulf. They never finished the work. The line from Agrinio to Missolonghi carried few German troops and no civilian passengers, except stowaways. It transported pigs and sheep and goats, tobacco and olives. The narrow-gauge rolling stock was old and the trains slow.

The village of Angelokastro rested in the foothills on the northwestern tip of the Zygos Mountains. A kilometer north of the village, the railroad crossed the Dimikos River. This tributary carried the overflow from Limni Trichonida and its smaller sister lake, Limni Lysimachia, to the Achelous River. A kilometer north of Angelokastro, a fifty-meter-long trestle spanned the Dimikos. Constructed of iron, it was well suited for OSS C2 explosives. This was the target Yiorgos recommended for the unseasoned explosive specialists of Squad Four. A simple mission in a friendly territory with a minor risk of German interference.

Yiorgos used a long stick to draw a staging map in the soft soil of the monastery courtyard. Around him kneeled Stavros, Yanni, the two OSS section leaders and the four squad leaders. Also, in the circle was Yiorgos's lieutenant, Nikolas, who remained standing with Yiorgos. He would guide the OSS men unofficially since Yiorgos did not want to contravene EAM-ELAS orders by engaging in a sabotage operation. Yiorgos would be in charge when Dimitra left for her conference in two days and needed to stay in Chómori.

Nikolas was younger than Yiorgos and less grizzled. He wore the rough beard and full mustache of most fighters, but his dark hair showed no gray and was shorter under his garrison cap. He carried himself with confidence and walked with a limp on his right side. He was tall and well-built, and other than the limp, he looked like he could handle anything or anyone that came his way.

Nikolas was the veteran of dozens of attacks and ambushes. He had joined the Chómori band just before the felling of Gorgopotamos in the fall of 1942 and was part of Dimitra's reinforcements that secured the Northern Italian pillbox in that attack. Yiorgos noted his bravery when Nikolas followed Yiorgos to the pillbox giving covering fire. It was Nikolas who tossed Yiorgos the grenades that Yiorgos unpinned and rolled over the pillbox slits, sending the Italians running.

Nikolas was from Missolonghi. His family pressed olives in a small plant on the lagoon. He knew the territory from there to Agrinio well. A former *sminias* or sergeant in the Greek Army, he respected Yiorgos's demand for discipline.

Stavros liked Nikolas. He was smart, and although Stavros never asked, he assumed Nikolas was a lyceum graduate. The Greek was a man of few words, but he knew a little English and liked to practice. He especially liked American slang idioms.

Stavros and Yanni agreed that Squad One would remain in Chómori to guard their supplies. That meant OG II would muster three squads, two section leaders, and two officers, along with Nikolas, a detachment of twenty. They would need six mules for supplies. The officers and Nikolas would ride horses. Yiorgos suggested they allow two days to travel to Moni Pantokratoros, a monastery north of Angelokastro. The fighters would billet there and reconnoiter on the third night. The fourth night they would set charges and blow the bridge, then retreat three kilometers into the forested hills to the southeast. There they would hide until nightfall the following day, when they would start their return to Chómori.

Yiorgos saw two weaknesses in this plan, and he offered them without sugar coating. First, their movement would happen during a waning gibbous moon offering too much light for full stealth. The new moon was two weeks away. This was both good and bad. The moonlight would help the detachment on the rugged trails. But should they meet Germans, they would be easy targets. Second, the kilometer from the monastery to the bridge was flat and open. The detachment would have no cover for reconnaissance or placing the charges. This meant that the entire detachment would have to maneuver for reconnaissance. It was the only way to protect the men sent to inspect the bridge.

Yiorgos and Nikolas described the bridge as fifty meters of steel-through-truss with stone abutments. The OG knew this common construction. They had practiced demolition dozens of times. But it was only practice. The flow of the Dimikos River could be fast, and the water under the bridge was three meters or more. Squad Four knew this meant they would have to suspend from the bridge to set charges. This was a less practiced routine, requiring rigging and harnesses. The attack sounded workable, but challenges lingered.

Yiorgos and Nikolas agreed a route to the south of Limni Trichonida and Limni Lysimachia was best. The detachment would retrace their route to Thermos, the same route that brought them to Chómori from Parga. But at Thermos, they would bear south and follow the shores of the two lakes for forty-five kilometers to the monastery. The marching would be on level ground, and the detachment could bolt into the mountains to the south should they need cover.

The most dangerous part of their route came at the eastern edge of Limni Lysimachia. There they would cross the Odos Riou-Agriniou, the main road connecting Agrinio to Antirrio. Agrinio was the hub of a major agricultural region, and Antirrio was the ferry gateway to the largest port on the Ionian Coast, Patras. They could dodge patrols by crossing at night. Here, Nikolas would be indispensable. To cross the road at a right angle for the briefest duration, the detachment would have to move off the shoreline and into the northern Zygos Mountains. A little-known pathway cut hours off the march, but it was hard to find, especially in the dark. But the time saved would make it worthwhile.

Nikolas knew the way. If the timetable went as planned, they should cross around midnight on the second night. After crossing Odos Riou-Agriniou, they would remain in the Zygos Mountains until reaching the monastery. Their retreat would be along the same route, bypassing the monastery with necessary adjustments for the Germans.

With the route and timetable set, the explosives men of Squad Four began planning. How much C2 would they need? How should they fashion the harnesses? How many harnesses would they need? Should they use a delay detonator? How long a delay? Should they detonate with a plunger? How much cable would they need to clear the blast? Could they use a pressure-sensitive A-3 detonator? The British SOE recommended this detonator for railroad sabotage. It fired when the weight of the train depressed the rails, sending a charge to the explosives. The advantage of a pressure-sensitive detonator was that the explosion damaged the rail and the train. But nobody knew the railroad timetable. Someone would have to wait at the bridge to verify the destruction. That was too risky. They ruled out this type of detonator.

Yiorgos told Squad Four to keep it simple. He recommended a British timed delay detonator that his andartes used. The OSS men had trained on the Number 10 delay switch or "Timing Pencil" in Maryland. They had a supply in camp. Yiorgos suggested a fifteen-minute delay to allow the sappers to take cover. The problem with the Timing Pencil was that there was no way to chain a charge. Felling the bridge would take multiple synchronized charges. The men of Squad Four agreed. A tried and trusted plunger detonator with parallel wiring was best.

The detachment would retreat to the woods once they set the charges. Two sappers would remain near enough to the bridge to man the detonator. They would blow the bridge, then join the detachment in the woods for retreat. Yiorgos told the OSS men they could destroy trains another time and the likelihood of night rail traffic was remote. He saw no need to complicate the mission. With nodding all around, the plan was set. Details still needed working out, but the detachment would leave Chómori in three days, on May 12.

Chapter 37

The next morning, Stavros went to see Dimitra at the schoolhouse. He exchanged greetings with her security detail and offered cigarettes. He told the andarte from Nafpaktos he might need his help and got a begrudging nod. Dimitra came to the door and invited Stavros inside.

"I understand you have another mission in the planning. Please come in and tell me about it. I apologize, I am gathering papers for the conference. I did not know people could write so much about so little. Vasilios is here too. I hope you don't mind."

"No, no. That's fine. I'll be quick," said Stavros.

Stavros pulled a chair in front of Dimitra's desk. Vasilios sat to her left, shuffling stacks of papers and pamphlets. Stavros looked at him, "Desk job, eh? You'll be a staff sergeant soon."

GI humor went over Vasilios's head. Through his round, wire-framed glasses, the young man looked puzzled.

Dimitra said, "Yiorgos tells me you are heading west to Agrinio."

"We'll be working just north of Angelokastro," Stavros corrected.

"Yes, yes, that is what he said. The railroad runs to Agrinio. If your mission is successful, you will anger many Greeks, no? You will deprive them of their god-awful Papastratos. Those vile things smell like burning boot leather. Have your friends at OSS airdrop American cigarettes, or our andartes will revolt," chided Dimitra.

Stavros chuckled. "I guess we didn't think it through."

"I am only joking. It is a suitable target. The Germans confiscate agricultural products, tobacco, pigs, and sheep. It is good to disrupt their supplies. That track carries forestry products, too. Although not so much. The Germans use the lumber for construction. Taking that away will benefit us," said Dimitra.

Stavros said, "We will shove off on the twelfth in three days. But I have an idea I would like to run by you."

"An idea? Yes. Tell me your thoughts," she invited.

Stavros glanced at Vasilios. Dimitra caught his look.

"Vasilios is trustworthy, Lieutenant. Have no fear of speaking in his presence."

Stavros noted Dimitra's change of tone with the use of *Lieutenant*, "Sorry, Kapetánios, our training in the States taught us need-to-know communications."

"Well, now you are in Greece, and Vasilios is my confidant. That is what *you* need to know," answered Dimitra.

"Yes," answered Stavros. He offered a tight-lipped smile to Vasilios, who didn't react.

Dimitra softened, "Stavros, tell me what is on your mind. Let us hope it is more entertaining than the drudgery of these papers."

"Right," answered Stavros. Then he launched into his formative idea. He said, "I'd like to sink a ferry. One loaded with Germans and their supplies."

Dimitra held up her right hand. She said, "A ferry? The ferry from Antirrio to Rio?"

"Yes."

Dimitra thought for a moment, "How do you propose to do this? Do you have a navy?"

"No, Kapetánios. No navy. Just an idea. I need to reconnoiter the ferry operation firsthand. I've heard about it from your fighters, but I need to see it. Can I borrow Yiorgos and your man from Nafpaktos for a day? I'd like to take Yanni, and we will need horses. Is that possible?"

Dimitra was cautious. She didn't want to encourage a wild idea, and a reconnaissance trip was risky. Still, these were Americans. She knew they thought in grand concepts and could muster equipment and forces she only dreamed of. Dimitra noted elegance in the proposal. The Germans, concentrated and predictable, were vulnerable aboard the ferry. That logic was sound. Retributive notions stirred deep in her Greek sensitivities. That the Germans should perish in the watery grave of vanquished invaders was the poetry of history.

She said, "Tell Yiorgos of your idea. If he does not laugh you out of Chómori, you may borrow my men and the horses. But I tell you this. If you travel to Nafpaktos, be aware of the Security Battalions. They are the worst swine, worse than the Germans. They are Greek traitors. Cut their throats if you have a chance, no regrets. Is this clear?"

Stavros nodded.

Dimitra said, "I am sorry to rush. Vasilios and I need to finish this unforgiving chore. Vasilios finds these papers enthralling. I am an archeologist. I see only a dig site for excavation. Nothing more. Somewhere, buried in detritus, there is enlightenment, no?"

Vasilios looked up at Dimitra and smiled.

Chapter 38

Yiorgos listened to Stavros like the professional skeptic he was. He didn't laugh Stavros out of Chómori. No, he gazed through the American like he was transparent, all the time processing the risks and rewards and balancing the practical with the suicidal. Sinking a ferry full of Germans was, to Yiorgos, equal to an attack on their HQ in Ioannina or destroying their port in Igoumenitsa. Yiorgos had toyed with Stavros's idea but dismissed it as unworkable. The Germans would sink any vessel approaching the ferry in mid-Gulf, even disguised as a fishing craft. The Germans would sink any boat without hesitation. The fishermen from Nafpaktos knew well to avoid the Germans.

As he listened, Yiorgos played out other attacks. He thought about hiding a bomb in the ferry for detonation when the Germans boarded. The problem was that they didn't know the German schedule. German crossings were unpredictable. The best information predicted a major crossing every two days. But that was variable. No andarte had ever watched the crossing for long enough to develop a pattern. Unlike the Italians, the Germans knew the value of inconsistency in their movements. So, hiding a bomb and waiting for the Germans presented a sticky problem, perhaps an insurmountable one.

Stavros continued to talk, and Yiorgos continued to think. Could the andartes disguise a bomber and place him aboard with the Germans? The bomber would have to be a crew member. The Germans did not allow locals aboard when they moved big loads. But how would a bomber escape? The Germans would spot anybody in the water. They would be shot or left to drown. And any man overboard would trigger a security response alerting the Germans.

Stavros stopped talking, and Yiorgos rejoined the conversation. He said, "Your idea has merit. I too have thought about such an attack and dismissed it as impossible."

Stavros said, "Maybe if we go to Nafpaktos and Antirrio and look around, we will see something we are missing."

Yiorgos dismissed this with a wave. "Bah. What you are missing, Lieutenant, is that guards are everywhere. There is a castle fort on the point of Antirrio where the ferry ties up. At Rio, the same thing. Another fort. Germans crawl in these forts like beetles on carrion. At no point in the water journey is the ferry left unguarded. Better you radio a US Navy submarine to come to our rescue. But even then, the waters in the narrows are swift, and a torpedo attack difficult. The ferry is not a craft that draws much water. It displaces perhaps three meters under the water. Not a big target.

"You should call your bomber aircraft. A better weapon, no?"

Stavros thought about the air corps, but he knew the OSS limited OG air support to resupply. He had been told in Italy not to expect fighters or bombers over Greece.

He asked Yiorgos again, "If we look, we might see an approach. I agree the ferry is well guarded. But every operation has vulnerabilities, right?"

Then Stavros remembered. He should have added "No?" to end his question as the local idiom required.

Yiorgos cautioned, "Looking is not without risk. The Germans and Security Battalions patrol in Nafpaktos and Antirrio. They are on guard and wary. You are too tall to disguise as a fisherman or a shepherd. With a haircut and shave, better to disguise you as a German. And your Greek . . . it is not so bad, but you cannot hide that you are American."

Then Yiorgos stopped talking, and a minute of silence fell between the men.

"Better you go as a priest. Only the two of us. You on a donkey and me on foot. You are celibate and silent. You have your sacred vows, no? I will speak and explain your religious requirement if questioned. Under your vestment carry a Colt, and I will hide a Sten. That is the only way.

"We will ride the horses to Kato Dafni, then change to the donkey and foot. I will lead the donkey like you are my charge. We must travel the main street through Nafpaktos. It is the quickest way, and a priest would do such. Do you know any blessing?" asked Yiorgos.

Stavros reeled from the suggestion. He stammered, "Ah . . . blessings. Sure, um? But I thought I couldn't talk?"

"Yes, but you might have to say something. Something a priest with his head in the clouds might say," answered Yiorgos. Then he went on, "Say this, '*To pséftiko kai móno to psévdos mas chorízei apó to Theó.*'"

"Falsehood and only falsehood separate us from God?" asked Stavros.

"Yes, yes," said Yiorgos. "Very priestly, no? Practice it like a Greek. Speak harsh and put the inflection on God. Very priestly."

"Where did this come from? Is this in the Bible?" asked Stavros.

"No, no. It is Serbian, Saint Nicholas. But what do I know?" replied Yiorgos, leaving Stavros with more questions than answers.

Yiorgos continued, "We must leave this afternoon. We will stay in Kato Dafni with my family and leave the horses there. We can borrow a donkey there, maybe two. I might ride, but what do I know? Best that we go through Nafpaktos early in the morning. Before sunrise. The Security Battalions drink most of the night and sleep late. We will travel around Nafpaktos, in the hills, for our return from Antirrio."

Stavros, processing the plan, asked, "Where will I get a priest's garb?"

Yiorgos said, "You live in a monastery, no?"

Chapter 39

His cassock was short and his *skufia* tall. The soft, black folding hat, its creases forming a cross, was sized for a smaller head and hard to balance. Yiorgos, dressed in his Sarakatsani shepherd disguise, wore a bulky samaroskouti flowing cape to conceal his Sten. He and Stavros were both on donkeys. Yiorgos led Stavros's mount by its reins, and it appeared the tandem was delivering a priest to a high ceremony. The sun peeked above the Gulf of Corinth, its shimmering reflection off the silvery waters a spiritual encounter more worthy than the riders.

The two followed the Mornos River road from Kato Dafni to the Gulf, then turned west toward Nafpaktos. This route gave Stavros and Yiorgos the best view of the Gulf and the city waterfront. Nafpaktos spreads out along the apex of a semicircular bay on the north shore of the Gulf, two kilometers across. At the top of this bay is a protected harbor, another semicircle, this one much smaller. The Old Harbor of Nafpaktos is only one hundred meters across, and the domain of fishing craft and rowing boats used to tend large vessels anchored beyond.

Overlooking the Old Harbor atop the west seawall is an iron statue of the Spanish novelist, poet, and playwright, Miguel de Cervantes. Cervantes had been twenty-three in 1571, serving with the Spanish infantry. Sailing aboard the galley *Marquesa*, Cervantes stood for a volley from an Ottoman harquebus that tore through his body in three places. The Spanish boarded and captured the Ottoman galley, but Cervantes lost his left arm.[79]

The main street through the town, Kannagou, passes within a block of the waterfront and along the north side of the town plateia. It was here that an early risen or late lingering Security Battalion thug waved for the tandem to stop. He was alone, and the street was empty. He was a big man, fat and slovenly uniformed. He approached with a carbine in hand. "Where are you two going this early in the morning?"

He was looking to extort some money to cover what he had spent the night before on women and wine.

Yiorgos dismounted and doffed his hat. Then, looking down at the street, answered, "My priest is going to Patras, there to finish a holy retreat, if it pleases you, sir."

It was hard for Yiorgos to be differential. But he kept up the act, hat in hand.

"I am not sure it pleases me. He is not much of a priest. His beard is not so long."

Yiorgos replied, "He trimmed it for lice."

The thug asked, "What have you to say, priest? You are someone I have not seen. Where are you coming from?" asked the man.

Yiorgos interjected, "He cannot speak, sir. He has taken a vow of silence until his retreat is finished."

The Security Battalion man looked up at Stavros, "Cannot speak? He is not much of a priest then, is he? What say you priest, can you make your own. . . ?"

He never finished the sentence. From under his cape, Yiorgos drew a knife, and when the man turned to Stavros, he grabbed him from behind. With his left hand over his mouth, he plunged the blade into his back. Then, as the man stiffened in shock, Yiorgos cut his throat from ear to ear.

The body fell limp to the street and Yiorgos said, "Help me put him in this truck."

Stavros dismounted and grabbed the man's feet, Yiorgos his shoulders. Then the two raised the body into the back of a covered lorry parked in front of the plateia. Yiorgos pitched the carbine in with the body. The truck was loaded with netting and other fishing gear. Yiorgos assumed the lory belonged to a fisherman out on the Gulf and it would be afternoon before anyone noticed.

"We must hurry now. See what you must and let's be gone. There are more swine. They will look for their lost piglet," warned Yiorgos.

The two recomposed and carried on at as quick a pace as the donkeys could muster. Two hours later, they were at the Church of Agios Panteleimon, a kilometer from the ferry dock. The land around Antirrio was flat, but the church sat on a small hill that rose thirty meters.

Yiorgos negotiated with the priest. They talked for what seemed to Stavros a long time. Yiorgos tithed three sovereigns, and the two men climbed the bell tower. Stavros used the powerful OSS binoculars and cataloged the target. Yiorgos took his turn with the glasses. While they were watching, a ferry from Rio docked. This gave the pair information about the size and operation of the ship. It was a single-ended design with a shallow hull about fifty meters long. The vehicle area on the deck looked like it could hold thirty trucks but, on this trip, there were only eighteen vehicles, all civilian.

Stavros pulled a notebook from under his cassock. Before he could write, Yiorgos stopped him. He said, "No notes. Not smart."

Stavros nodded. "Right."

The two men watched for another thirty minutes, then Yiorgos thought it best they leave. They returned to Kato Dafni through the hills north of Nafpaktos and retrieved their horses. They were back in Chómori late that evening.

They ate a satisfying meal of roasted chicken, potatoes, and horta with Yiorgos's family before leaving Kato Dafni. A kilometer into their ride back to Chómori, Stavros asked, "Where did you get that knife?"

Yiorgos said, "Mr. Fairbairn and Sykes. The British are good for some things, no?"

Chapter 40

A stream ran below the monastery, flowing with clear water from the mountains. OG II used it for drinking water and to make coffee. Coffee was on Stavros's mind after his late arrival from Nafpaktos the night before.

The morning was still, and only doves cooing in the trees preempted the peace. Stavros followed the pathway to the stream and kneeled on its bank. While the cool water burbled into his canteen, a voice to his side asked, "Are you a friend of the morning?"

Stavros looked to his left. Dimitra smiled at him. She was sitting on a flat bolder alongside the stream, stretched out and leaning back on her arms. She was wearing her fatigues without her garrison cap.

"A friend of the morning? I don't take your meaning."

Dimitra said, "Do you like the mornings? They are my favorite time of day. The world is at peace, my mind is unclouded, and the possibilities are ahead. Anything can be true by the day's end, no?"

Stavros said, "Sure. I like mornings. Just like you said. But an OSS schedule means mornings come and go like any other time of the day. Sometimes mornings come at the end of a day. We sleep in the day and maneuver at night."

"Dimitra considered then said, "Still, mornings are my favorite time of the day. In springtime, the earth is lush and replenishing from the ruin of winter. It is no wonder the beauty of spring inspired the ancients to myth. Do you know Persephone? Perhaps you know her as Kore?"

"Ah, Persephone, daughter of Demeter and Zeus?" answered Stavros.

"Yes, you are correct, Professor," Dimitra with a smile.

"Poor Persephone, a child lost to Hades, himself captive to Eros. During the long dark months she reined in the underworld, her mother let nothing grow above. No beauty, no life, no vitality. The world turned cold and barren. Even in the underworld, Persephone darkens, her hair turns black and her eyes become liquid voids.

"Then, thanks to the rule of not-eaten pomegranate seeds, Persephone ascends, now a fair-haired beauty with eyes as blue as the sea. She waves her elegant arm at heaven, and flowers bloom, animals mate, birds sing, and all is again magnificent. Until it isn't."

Stavros said, "That's beautiful. I like a good myth."

Dimitra pursed her lips and looked up through the trees at the sky. "Yes, it is beautiful. But, as with all of Greece and every Greek, there is more, no?

"The narrative is itself instruction. Eleusinian if you please. Kore suffers a loss in her descent. Then comes the search for her. The search for eiréné. Do you know that word?" asked Dimitra.

Stavros said, "It's religious. I think it means together?"

"Yes, yes, together, wholeness, completeness, unity . . . all of those words. But Kore's lessons continue. She undertakes an ascent. Her descent, her search, and her ascent. These are the lessons beyond the myth, no? A pattern, no?

"We Greeks are in the middle of this pattern thanks to the Italians and the Nazis. They caused our descent. Now we search to rid ourselves of their intemperate burden. Tomorrow, who knows? We will ascend, and life will return with beauty and love. Maybe eiréné."

"You sound philosophical. I thought you studied archeology?" asked Stavros.

"I did and I plan to continue upon ascent. You don't have to study philosophy to understand patterns. Archaeologists are good at seeing patterns, no? That is our job.

"Here is the water." Dimitra pointed to the stream before them.

"There are the trees." She pointed to the surrounding woods.

"Here are the stones. Maybe flint for knapping, no?" She opened her hand and waved over the earth.

"I can see a pattern: water, wood, and stones. People might have lived here. They had babies here. They buried their dead here. Perhaps they built temples and markets and fashioned spears and swords. Perhaps they studied mathematics and politics. Perhaps, perhaps, perhaps. Time to dig and find out, no?" Then she smiled, and Stavros was engaged beyond the obvious. Stavros liked this woman.

Stavros was still processing this unfamiliar warmth when Dimitra stood on the rock and jumped to the pathway. She landed lithe and balanced. She dusted off her baggy pants and pulled her garrison cap from her back pocket. She squared the hat on her head. As she did, Stavros asked, "You mentioned politics. May I ask how preparation for the conference goes?"

"We leave tomorrow, and I wish it were already over. I have neither mind nor patience for political debate. The papers are endless and the theory of this or that . . . so removed. There are more '*ites*' and '*ists*' and traitors to the cause and class enemies. I'm not cut of that cloth. Vasilios swims in it. He loves the distinctions between socialists and liberals and monarcho-fascist and reactionary collaborationists. It is his world."

Stavros asked, "Have you talked to Yiorgos since we returned from Nafpaktos?"

"No, I haven't seen him. You must have had a good trip. You are still alive." She smiled.

"Yes, a good trip. And the world has one less reactionary collaborationist to worry about," said Stavros.

"Really? You killed a collaborationist?" she quizzed.

"Not me, Yiorgos got him. With his knife. I'll let him tell you about it," said Stavros.

"How did this come about?" she asked, her voice officious.

Stavros said, "He didn't respect the church."

Chapter 41

Diávolos snorted his impatience. His fiery breath steamed in the morning chill. His eyes wide and his nostrils flaring, he looked to Dimitra like a storybook monster. She stroked his forehead where a streak of white formed a suggestive lightning bolt. "Be patient, Diávolos. Time will come. We have two days to ride. Time will come."

Diávolos was impatient because other horses were moving past him and he stood tethered, his reins looped around the schoolhouse fence. The three departing horses carried Stavros, Yanni, and Nikolas. Fifteen OG II men followed, six of them leading mules. Diávolos wanted to join the parade.

Dimitra waved to the departing detachment, and Stavros thought her gaze lingered on him. He expunged the fantasy and returned to commanding OG II. He waved back to Dimitra. "Safe travels, Kapetánios."

"And to you and your men. Remember, do not hesitate."

Stavros saluted, then returned his eyes forward.

Dimitra nodded.

Once the OG II detachment had cleared, Dimitra's party formed up. Dimitra was traveling with Vasilios and four andartes, two of them women. Everyone was in uniform, mounted, and well-armed. The two andartes at the end of the train, the two men, led mules on long tethers.

Dimitra's party followed the OG II detachment for four kilometers, then she took a route north to Krikello and Koryschades. OG II headed south to Platanos and on to Thermos.

Chapter 42

The Zygos Mountains were not the highest in Greece, but OG II did not need high. They needed cover. Rising to four hundred meters south of Lakes Trichonida and Lysimachia, their wooded lower levels were ideal concealment.

They entered the Zygos foothills just beyond Pappadates, a village at the western shore of Limni Trichonida. Their path took them through endless olive groves. The delicate clusters of yellow-and-white blossoms on the rows of squat trees reflected the pale moonlight, setting the groves aglow. It was mesmerizing and eerie.

Nikolas found the hidden turnoff before midnight on their second day from Chómori. The detachment left the level route along the lakeshore and groves and climbed into the tricky terrain. The sky was cloudy, and the moon faint. The men on foot followed Yiorgos's advice and held the mules' tails. The men on horses dismounted and led their animals.

Nikolas told Stavros and Yanni, "This path is only three kilometers, maybe less. After this, we will be on a better path to the monastery."

Nikolas was right. As the men climbed higher into the mountains, the trail challenged them. Men began slipping and stumbling and some fell, but no one was injured. Around 0200 hours, the men connected to a better pathway and an hour later, they crossed the Odos Riou-Agriniou and met no traffic and no Germans, just as planned.

South of Mourstiano on clear paths, the detachment veered west through a gap in the hills that delivered them into more olive groves and rolling terrain. The final four kilometers to the monastery skirted the foothills through groves and fields. This was fertile land, and the detachment arrived before sunrise.

Moni Pantokratoros was a large monastery, much larger than the one where the men billeted in Chómori. The Monastery of Panagia Kavadiotissa in Chómori was a single square stone building set into the hills, with a simple courtyard and only twenty alcoves for the dedicated. Here, in Angelokastro, the buildings were large and pristine, whitewashed with terracotta roofs set against the verdant hills and fields. The two principal buildings rose four levels, with a bell tower and verandas to view the vistas. Built in the Byzantine Era and renovated in 1746, the monastery remained unviolated by the fascists.

An expansive courtyard and plateia extended above the surrounding fields, with a stable on the lower plateau. This is where the men bunked and rested their animals after Nikolas met with the Igoúmenos, the head ascetic. The abbot knew Nikolas's family.

The men ate from their rations and later received bread and cheese and olives from their hosts. They talked about reconnoitering the bridge, then bunked down for some rest. Guards stood watch outside the stables on two-hour shifts.

While the men were stretching out to get some sleep, Stavros said to Nikolas, "It is good your family knows the head man here."

Nikolas responded, "It is good for this mission. I agree."

Stavros sensed something missing. He prodded, "Has your family known the Igoúmenos for a long time?"

"No. Not so long."

Reluctantly, Nikolas continued, "My brother stayed here until he died. He wanted to be a devout monk. Very religious. He was this way since his birth. He was my younger brother. I knew him well. Always he said. God can do this, God can do that . . . I thought he was soft in the head when we were young. He finished lyceum and the next day went to this monastery and applied for postulancy with this very Igoúmenos. He was three years a novitiate and ready for *kourá*. Do you know that word?"

Stavros shook his head.

"Kourá is when the devout may cut their hair in the fashion of an ordained monk. It is a graduation and means a novitiate is professed."

"How did he die?"

"After the Germans took Greece, the Italians became bold. My brother, his name was Christos. So, what chance did he have but to become a monk, no? Christos received permission to help with our work at the *ergostásio*. It was late September 1942. Only my mother and father and I were there to press the harvest. It is the busiest time of the year, and we had no help. The Italians and the Germans took all the laborers and shipped them to the West."

Stavros asked, "Is this the plant in Missolonghi?"

"Yes, but it is north of there on the lagoon, just above Aitoliko. It is not a large ergostásio, but it was our only income. My father's father built it after the war with Turkey, and many farmers brought us their crops.

"Christos was a dutiful son. They allowed him to leave the monastery to help the family. This is the way of things.

"The morning he died, we were loading from a wagon to the chute, and an Italian patrol arrived in a truck. There were six soldiers. We were unarmed. We were no threat to them. Their leader was a *tenente* no older than me. He asked why we were not with the conscripted labor, and he pointed to me and Christos. My father told him he needed us to work at the factory, and the tenente said that was no excuse. My father tried to reason with him and said the Italians would enjoy the oil we were pressing. But the tenente would have none of his reasoning.

"He ordered me and Christos into the truck. We marched in that direction. He turned his back on my father. He did not know that my mother was inside. When he faced the street, my mother came to the door with my father's double-barrel shotgun and shot the tenente from three meters. Then she shot the man next to him. The other soldiers were not ready, their weapons still slung.

"I grabbed the tenente's Beretta MAB 38 where he had fallen on it. I sprayed the truck and the four other soldiers, but not before they shot my brother in the chest and me in the leg. Christos died in our mother's arms. He looked like Christ on the cross lying in the dirt. I drove my parents to the church with my brother's body. I have never been back to the plant, but I know the Italians burned it.

"My family is now in a village, far from the lagoon. There they live like the others, with a small garden, some trees, and grapes. It is in EAM-ELAS territory, and they are safe. That is all that matters now.

"The next day, after my brother died, a doctor came and took the bullet from my leg. The wound is not so bad, but it pains me to carry my weight. I waited with my family for a week. Then I went to Chómori and joined with Yiorgos. And I brought my Beretta."

Nikolas reached for the submachine gun lying on his bedroll and patted it on the wooden stock.

Stavros said, "I'm sorry about your brother."

Nikolas lit a cigarette from a pack Stavros had given him earlier. "It is a sad story. There are many sad stories in Greece. What would an American say?"

Stavros thought for a moment. He wanted to indulge Nikolas's fascination in American slang and not insult the man. He said in his humblest voice, "They would say your story is a tearjerker."

Nikolas nodded, repeating, "Tearjerker. Yes. I understand. Like pulling tears from someone's eyes. Yes, yes."

The detachment slept most of the day, with only stirring animals and chiming bells interrupting their peace. They rousted at sunset, ate from their provisions, fed and watered their animals, and checked their gear. Tonight's maneuver would be on foot. Two guards would stay with the animals at the monastery, leaving sixteen men for recon.

They left the stables at midnight. Nikolas, Stavros and Yanni were in the lead as the column wove the kilometer and a half to the railroad bridge through groves and fields, over ditches and little used roadways. Other than barking farm dogs, the detachment moved in stealth.

The men stopped their advance in a small woods one hundred and fifty meters from the bridge alongside the railroad. The men of Squads Two and Three spread out to form a perimeter to watch for movement toward the bridge. They would be the shield for the two scouts from Squad Four who would follow the railroad to the bridge and size up the target.

Stavros sent two men two hundred meters to the right flank. These men watched the main roadway that curved across the Dimikos River one hundred and fifty meters above the railroad bridge. With everyone in position, the two sappers from Squad Four sprinted in a crouch up the railroad to the bridge.

What they found was about what they expected. The bridge was steel-through-truss with abutments of stone, just like Yiorgos and Nikolas had reported. It was a fifty-meter-long rectangle five meters tall with diagonal bracing crisscrossing the sides. There was no obvious security, no pillboxes, no machine-gun emplacements.

Two men, one atop the other's shoulders, could set charges at the critical points of attachment where the steel connected to the stone abutments. That would require a pair of two-man teams. Those charges would be enough to fell the bridge. But the three-meter drop to the base of the abutments would leave the structure intact and allow the Germans easy repair. To destroy the bridge, the sappers needed to set four pairs of charges, one at each end and two in the middle. That would cut the bridge into four sections, fell it into the river, and make it hard to reuse. Setting the two middle charges would require men lowered on harnesses above the river. Eight men would need fifteen minutes on the bridge to rig it for proper demolition. This is what the scouts had reported to Stavros upon returning to the monastery at 0300 hours. Stavros told his men to check their gear, start shaping charges, then bunk down and get their rest. Their next visit to the bridge would be showtime.

Stavros met with Yanni and Nikolas to work out assignments for the attack. They were twenty men. They would need the five men of Squad Four, the sappers, and three more to set the charges. That left ten men. Two men would take the animals to the rendezvous point in the hills beyond the monastery. Of the eight remaining, six would guard the south approach and two would advance over the bridge and guard the north approach. When a team of sappers finished setting their charge, that team would fall back to the southern base of the bridge and wait for the other teams. When all charges were set, the two lookouts to the north would cross the rigged bridge. When the bridge was clear of men, all twenty would make for the rendezvous, wait for the explosion, then melt into the hills for their retreat.

Yanni and Nikolas agreed with the outline of the attack. Yanni noted that the men crossing the river and guarding the north approach would need to know how to swim, just in case. Stavros nodded and remarked, "Good thinking."

Nikolas told Yanni and Stavros the Germans seldom patrolled at night. But he thought it was unusual they left the bridge without guards. "Perhaps they do not believe it is worth it. Or maybe they patrol in the daytime and that is all. We will be wise to watch for them or a trick, maybe a booby-trap. Tell the men to step only where they are certain. Every footfall. Maybe mines. Maybe wires."

Stavros nodded. "I will warn them."

"Tell them not to pick up anything from the ground. Nothing. They may see the Hope Diamond, but do not touch it. I have seen these tricks leave men without arms."

"Roger. Thanks, Nikolas, I'll let them know," said Stavros.

Stavros felt good about the mission preparation. The plan was workable and his men trained. As the sun's faint glow backlit the eastern hills, Stavros stepped outside the stable to check his guards. Both men were alert and poised. He asked them if they had a rotation, and they assured him all was set. With all the pieces in place and a plan in motion, Stavros bunked down on his bedroll. The soft hay of the manger and the warmth of his sleeping bag were welcome respite. Before he slept, he wondered about Dimitra and her journey. She should be in Koryschades by now.

Chapter 43

The demotiko schoolhouse knew the shuffle of children. But today was different. Now crammed into its halls and classrooms flowed a sea of men. Not men dressed as andartes, as was she, but men in suits and Sunday finest, politicians. Andartes moved in the mass like out-of-place soldiers at a festival of flowers.

Dimitra was not without friends. Aris arrived in Koryschades as a star attraction. Maria was there, always engaged in discussion, always persuading. Sarafis was there, and although he acknowledged Dimitra, she did not count him as a friend. Maria introduced Dimitra to her husband, Alexandros Svolos, the president of the Mountain Government. He was friendly and spoke with Dimitra longer than she expected. He assured Dimitra he supported all measures to free Greek women from bondage and subjugation. He complimented her as a shining role model, telling her she had a bright political future. It all reminded Dimitra of a university where the students were older, and the only courses taught were politics and economics.

General Sarafis described Free Greece late in the first day at a plenary session. He addressed the jam-packed auditorium opposite a three-meter wall map under a banner declaring DEATH TO FASCISM! He said Greece had 7.3 million people with three million living in cities. Sarafis said that 2.5 million people lived in Free Greece from the country's northern boundary to the Peloponnesus, an area larger than Switzerland.[80]

Dimitra sat through lectures and symposia recounting the history of the resistance movement, economic challenges, and taxation schemes. She sat in caucuses with other KKE delegates. They discussed the other parties—the Liberal Party, the Union of People's Democracy, the Socialist Party of Greece, the Agricultural Party of Greece, and on it went. The KKE derided former members of the Greek Parliament in attendance. These recently enlightened politicians came from right-wing parties like the General Popular Union, the Popular Party, and the Reform National Party.[81]

Dimitra listened while the KKE Central Committee explained why the party must be an "all-people's party" and broaden its recruiting base. This engendered concern and counterarguments, worries of diluting party purity. One local KKE leader from Thessaly reported that entire villages—the rich, old men and women, juveniles, adventurers, goat-thieves, Trotskyists, the well-to-do, and ignoramuses—had joined.[82]

But the party needed qualified tenders of the envisioned state. A state within a state. How else would KKE attract the teachers, lawyers, judges, and former state employees who would run Free Greece? The Liberal Party and socialists attracted skilled and educated people to their less rigorous ideology and discipline. These were critical recruits, people who would administer the new state. They were in short supply in KKE.

Meetings went on day after numbing day. Dimitra wanted to leave by the end of the third day. When she told Vasilios, he listened, then offered a rebuttal. He said, "These are preliminary meetings, and everyone is puffing out their chests. The election for National Council delegates will come later this week, and you will win. Then you can voice your concerns. Others will listen. You will exchange drafts of legislation. Some will give here, some will give there, then you will sign documents that will change people's lives. This is the game, this is the way of things, no? You should be proud you can play.

"Think of this time as a class you didn't want to study at university. Let us say, Medieval German literature. You require this to complete your degree, nothing more. This too will pass."

Then he added a clincher: "This will make your mother proud."

She stared straight through him at the mention of her mother. But Vasilios was right. Eva would be proud.

The next morning, Dimitra sat in a packed hall listening to a historical assessment of the economic challenges confronting the Mountain Government. The speaker said ELAS had grown from five hundred fighters in December 1942 to over ten thousand in April 1943. By the summer of 1943, ELAS counted thirty thousand in its ranks. The speaker, an ELAS Wing Commander, explained that daily food consumption for ELAS's thirty-five thousand regular fighters came to 64.1 metric tons. The ELAS logistics arm, ETA, required the services of fifteen thousand men, many women, and two thousand pack animals to provision these fighters.[83]

He told the room that when the movement was young, Commander Aris had seized the agricultural harvest gathered by the state in warehouses and redistributed it to farmers, subtracting a small part for ELAS's needs. The Battle of the Harvest had worked well. It cemented the support of the producers and provisioned Aris's forces. But the scale of the struggle had overtaken these tactics.

The logistician said that Free Greece was a war economy, and the needs of the army had to come first. He said that the Mountain Government must transform local village support for provisioning fighters into a countrywide coordinated network. This meant a fair tax on agricultural producers. ELAS headquarters issued Order 1222 in November 1943. This was the current authority ELAS used to requisition supplies. He told the attendees that this order needed updating and reformulation, so it did not dissuade local support or encourage black marketing. He suggested a progressive tax.

Dimitra saw in this a challenge, her first concrete engagement at the conference. She knew numbers, she knew the producers, and she had an opinion.

The primary schoolhouse in Koryschades was a large building. It was thirty meters long, two stories, and built of beige stone blocks. The roof was terracotta, and nine chimneys rose around its perimeter. It was warm in May, and they needed no fires. Delegates packed the meeting rooms. The stale air was unpleasant even with the windows open. Dimitra counted 130 participants in a session crammed into a room designed for fifty children. She often stepped outside the building to revive her attention. The courtyard in front of the school was a stone circle with rows of stone bleacher seats to the left. This is where Dimitra sat on the top row enjoying the fresh air and flowering plants when Maria asked if she could join her. Dimitra motioned to the stone row next to her, and Maria sat.

Maria said, "The elections are tomorrow. A big day, no? I see you have been meeting with the Taxation and Logistics Committee. That, along with Women's Affairs, is keeping you busy, no?"

Dimitra said, "It is not the work that wears me, it is the endless talking and discussion and meeting people and pretending to listen to their bad ideas.

"The work is interesting. The fighters need food. We know how much. We know the crops, and we only need a fair formula that will not displease the people and weaken our support. Wealthy producers can afford a greater tax, and the small farmers will pay less.

"I do not understand the need to debate agrarian reform and redistribution of land, all things we must do, but things that are future decisions. Why must we explore the deep water when we can fish in the shallow?"

Maria smiled at Dimitra's frustration, "Are you happy with the draft of Article Five?"

Maria was asking about the women's equal rights article in the Mountain Government's founding charter.

Dimitra replied, "It is better than before, no? It is something where before there was nothing. What is the final wording?"

"All Greeks, men and women, have equal political and civil rights," answered Maria.

"It is good. No equivocation. I support it."

Maria nodded.

"Dimitra, I'd like to talk to you about your affiliation . . . confidentially."

"We may discuss anything," answered Dimitra.

Maria went on, "You would be a better socialist than a communist and here is why. I have watched you and admired your independence, your independence of thought. I know you are rigorous within ELAS, and I respect your military discipline. Battle is no time for debate. But here, among these people, I have watched your thoughts form and listened to you express them. You are not doctrinaire or dogmatic. You are informed and thoughtful. I think you would flourish in the Socialist Party, no longer beholden to Soviet orders and whims. I know the Greek KKE is not a Soviet puppet. Even so, Mother Russia is a big bear lording over her cubs, and Greece is a cub.

"Greece will need friends to rebuild after this war. The Socialist Party believes we are more likely to find friends in the West. We already have friends there, no?

"You know I work with the Red Cross. The Germans steal our grain to feed their troops and send it back to Germany for their workforce. The winter following German occupation saw a hundred thousand Greeks die from hunger. Maybe more. Who can count? Do you know where Red Cross gets food?"

Maria did not wait for an answer. "The Americans. All this food, the milk and wheat, they grow it in Canada, then ship on Swedish vessels to Piraeus. All of it paid for by the United States. How much from the Soviets? Nyet! They are themselves receiving aid. Much of it paid for by the United States.[84]

"Do you see Dimitra? The Americans and the West will be our friends. You are with them today, in Chómori, no? Do they ask anything of you? Nothing more than the usual welcome of any visitors, no? Do they interfere in your politics? These are our friends. We will need them even more after this war."

Dimitra nodded. Everything Maria said was true.

Maria went on, "Greece is paying the Nazis for our occupation. Did you know that? We are paying for German soldiers to burn our villages and kill our citizens. We pay in money from our treasury and in timber, chrome, aluminum, agricultural products, tobacco, olive oil, we pay them. Did you know that in 1942, the Germans forced us . . . poor Greece . . . to give to them an interest free loan of four hundred seventy-six million Reichsmarks! A loan! From poor Greece![85]

"We will need friends after the war, Dimitra. Socialists will be friendly with the Soviets, but we will not be their junior cubs. Our friends are in the West."

Dimitra considered this. "In the beginning, I was organizing the fighters in Platanos. Then I met Aris. He was on his way to form the first ELAS. I was not a party member, and he said to me, 'Fights are won by people of steel, not wood. The party is the metal with which we shape our victory.' And he was right. We are at this conference today because we acted with the rigidity of metal. Discipline and valor, that is what the KKE preached, and for this we bled. Our blood flowed while others tried to talk their ways into favor with the invaders. Still others tried to fight, but they were ill-led and unprepared. It is this characteristic I respect and this history that I honor.

"What you say has weight, Maria. I will consider your arguments. But you must know, leaving the party is not an inconsequential matter. You are asking me to breach discipline. There are trials and penalties for this offense."

"Dimitra, everyone, even opponents of the party, respect its leadership of the resistance. Did you know this conference plans to name a mountain for Aris? Look. You can see it now." Maria stood and pointed to the snow-covered peak of Mount Timfristos seven kilometers to the north, rising eighteen hundred meters and dominating the skyline.

"Everyone respects the KKE. But times change, and we must change with them. I fear the KKE will not adjust well, and I do not want to see your talents go to waste."

The following day, the conference elected Dimitra to the National Council. She was one of five women councilors in a body of 208. It was the first time in modern Greek history for women to serve in nationally elected office.

Chapter 44

The first across the bridge were the two north access lookouts. The moon behind clouds revealed little in its faint glow. They moved guardedly over the open trestle, matching their footfalls to the railroad ties. One slip and they would fall into the river or break a leg if it caught between the ties. At the north end of the bridge, the two lookouts advanced another fifty meters up the railroad. There they fanned out, took positions in the trees lining the right-of-way, and signaled with a flashlight. Eight sappers advanced to set the charges while the two south approach lookouts took up their positions.

Movement over the bridge was slower than planned, every step calculated to fall on a tie. The four men setting the mid-bridge charges advanced. They carried weapons, wire, charges, harnesses, and squibs, and moved deliberately.

The sappers setting charges on the north abutment crossed the bridge in the same fashion. Once across, they shuffled down a dirt embankment and under the bridge. One sapper climbed on the other's shoulders and began placing the charges, coiling wire, then wiring squibs and inserting them into the blocks of C2. The sappers at the south abutment did the same with no need to cross the bridge.

The mid-bridge sappers tied their harnesses to cross members and eased over the bridge. They set their charges the same way, but they had to do it swinging free and working above their heads.

Stavros timed them. It took twenty-two minutes from when the north outlooks moved out until the ready-set signal from the Squad Four team leader. Stavros flashed his light for retreat. When all the sappers were clear of the bridge, the two north outlooks began their trip back.

It happened mid-bridge. The lookout in the lead fell between the ties and dropped his M1 into the river. Stavros heard a faint *shit!* Then a splash. He knew something was wrong, but he couldn't see. The second lookout hauled his partner from between the ties and helped him to his feet. The injured man stood but could not put weight on his left leg. A sapper waiting with the plunger detonator saw the problem and ran onto the bridge to help. Together, the two helpers, one under either shoulder, moved the injured man off the bridge. Once on solid ground, another sapper replaced the detonator man and helped the injured man to the rally point.

Stavros saw the problem. This would slow things down.

When the teams were clear and everyone but the detonator sappers at the rally point, Stavros signaled to blow the bridge. The first sapper wired the cable leads to the Livens Projector blasting machine terminals, whose carefully oiled bearings and gears they had tended before leaving Chómori. The sappers lubricated the commutator and armature shaft with graphite and cleaned the commutator and copper brushes. After confirming the circuit-breaker contacts were bright, they padded and packed the detonator for transport.

The first sapper gave thumbs up to the second commando, who dropped his weight on the machine's rack bar handle. The man knew the plunger would depress easily for the first period of travel, then meet greater resistance. He did not let up his force and rammed the plunger bar deep into the wooden case.

The bridge blew. All eight charges went off in an instant and four tidy sections fell into the Dimikos, leaving a billowing cloud of smoke and dust. It was 0013 hours when the detonator team rejoined the detachment. OG II began their retreat with the injured commando riding Stavros's horse.

The explosion woke the small village north of the Dimikos. Among those rocked into consciousness was a railroad bridge-tender and switchman. His only duties along this sleepy section were to inspect the bridge daily and throw switches if a train needed to enter a siding to let another pass. Tonight, he was a sentinel.

Two hundred meters north of the bridge stood a small wood-framed tarpaper railroad shack. It was unremarkable except for its telephone service to the railroad terminus in Agrinio. After inspecting the damage, the tender rushed to the shack and called Agrinio. The trainmaster in Agrinio informed the German officer attending.

The Germans billeted a company of light infantry from their 1st Mountain Division in Agrinio. Agrinio was a large town and an important commercial hub. The Germans had their hands full. They had little support in the city and only a month before, on Good Friday, they had hanged three suspected resistance fighters from lamp posts in Bellou Square.[86]

The Germans posted 180 men in Agrinio. A platoon of those men, four squads of ten men each, were on a two-day rest and recuperation furlough at the Sokou Thermal Springs resort. The resort comprised twenty stone cabins north of Mourstiano on the southern shore of Lake Lysimachia. The pools of the resort filled with the flow from the substrata of the Zygos Mountains seeping through cracks and underground tunnels. As these waters percolated through the stone, they absorbed volcanic elements and gases. The pools stayed warm year round, and the hydrogen sulfide and sodium salts gave off a heavy, foul odor. Their smell aside, locals believed the baths to remedy skin and rheumatic diseases and to relieve stiffness, neuralgia, and arthritis.

Each of the stone cabins had a freshwater shower to remove the odor after a therapeutic session. They could not, however, remove the schnapps and other liquors freely drunk while soaking.

At 0107 hours, the *oberjäger* manning the radio woke from a boozy fog to receive the message from company HQ in Agrinio. The platoon was to mobilize at once and intercept a band of saboteurs, strength unknown. The bandits were eastbound through the Zygos Mountains due south of the baths. The oberjäger relayed the message to the four oberleutnant squad leaders asleep in a cabin reserved for officers.

It was difficult to rouse the enlisted men. They anticipated another day of drinking and soaking before returning to duty, so they had been unrestrained on their first night of leave. Many struggled for balance when they stood to put on their boots. Ordered to fall in, their ranks wobbled as they tried to stand at attention in front of their cabins.

The platoon traveled in three vehicles, two covered trucks for the infantry and an open *Kübelwagen* for the officers. They moved through the night with blacked-out headlamps to a six-kilometer section of Odos Riou-Agriniou that bisected the Zygos Mountains. They were only fifteen kilometers away. The Germans split their platoon at the northern end of the section and sent one truck south to patrol the lower three kilometers. The other truck was to patrol the northern end. The Kübelwagen would cycle the entire six kilometers. The first to contact the saboteurs would radio the others who would converge on their location.

Stavros and the detachment planned to cross Odos Riou-Agriniou as before, across the section now patrolled. They had discussed this possibility in the planning stages and decided it was best to cross on the first night, no matter how late, so long it was dark. Yiorgos, Nikolas and Yanni agreed that getting stuck west of the Odos Riou-Agriniou meant that they would have a limited area in which to hide and maneuver. The Germans, with substantial forces in Agrinio, could make their lives hell if they were trapped there.

It was 0315 hours when the OSS detachment reached the crossing point dead center in the six-kilometer section of road. Their scouts, about half a kilometer ahead of the train, reported back that the Germans were running motorize patrols and could muster forty or fifty men.

Stavros ordered his men to break out the two bazookas and told the two men with BARs to make weapons ready. The scouts returned to the roadway.

Stavros talked with Yanni and Nikolas. They had options. They could try to sneak across undetected, or they could set an ambush and attack the Germans on their own terms. Either way, time was not on their side.

Yanni was cautious. He thought it would be impossible to cross undetected. He noted that on their trip west, it had taken the train fifteen minutes to clear the roadway. The likelihood that the Germans would see the detachment was high. Then, if they had to fight, they would be out of position and have no advantage or surprise on their side.

Nikolas said, "The Greek way is to fight. Force the crossing after an ambush. One bazooka and one BAR cross to the east side with two riflemen. They will give crossfire. We will need to move north one hundred meters where there is no path, but we will have elevation. We will not need to kill all of them, just stun them enough that we can get across. They will not follow at night on foot. They have not the heart."

Stavros ordered Gus with his bazooka and the BAR man from his squad to catch up with the scouts and tell them the plan. Gus and the other three were to cross and set firing positions on the east side of the roadway, a hundred meters north of the path. Stavros told them to stay in cover until they heard firing from the west side.

Stavros assigned two men and the casualty to stay with the mounts. He asked the injured man if he could walk, but he was too hurt. Stavros assumed he had a broken tibia and ordered another commando to splint his leg for support.

The other eleven commandos took positions along the elevation above the roadway, with the BAR and bazooka in the middle. Stavros, Yanni, and Nikolas took the far north position to wait on the patrolling Germans.

The first mistake the Germans made was not rolling up the canvas sides of their troop trucks. Stavros heard the labored knocking of the Borgward B 3000 diesel engine two hundred meters away. The detachment had by a stroke of luck positioned at the midpoint of the patrol routes. The truck slowed as it approached the ambush, still fifty meters away, not yet in the kill zone. It began a slow and awkward backing maneuver to turn around and head back to the north. The truck was out of range for the bazooka. Thirty meters was optimal for that weapon. He ordered the BAR man forward and told him to fire when the truck was broadside in the road.

The BAR man lowered the weapon on its bipod, and as the Borgward was coming about, Stavros saw movement to the south. It was the cycling Kübelwagen with two officers. The Kübelwagen was in the kill zone. He ordered the BAR man to open fire and told the bazooka to target the Kübelwagen.

Hell rained down an instant later. The BAR ripped into the side of the Borgward as Gus's men took up the attack from the east side. The Borgward was dead in the roadway and the men in it scrambled over the tailgate, every other one falling where he hit the ground. The Kübelwagen tried to reverse. After backing ten meters, Gus's bazooka round lifted it from the roadway and it overturned in flames. The blast killed one officer. The other officer tried to take cover, but Nikolas cut him down with his Beretta.

The fight was now with the dozen foot soldiers who had made it away from the riddled wreckage. These soldiers sought cover behind the Borgward. But the BAR man on the east side expected their move. Once the Kübelwagen was out of the game, he moved fifty meters north and positioned to fire on the other side of the truck. When he opened up, the deep pounding of the BAR from somewhere behind them was the last thing seven of the remaining Germans heard. One scout, who had advanced with the BAR man, picked off two more with his M1 before lobbing a grenade into the truck's open driver's cabin and setting it ablaze.

Just when the detachment had things under control, Stavros heard another noisy diesel approach from the south. This truck pulled up well short of the kill zone. Men began dismounting from the rear and taking cover along the sides of the roadway and in the surrounding woods. They did not advance.

Nikolas told Stavros, "They will not advance without an officer. We may have killed their man in the Jeep. We should attack and they will scatter."

Stavros said, "I count about twenty. We can send only ten of ours."

Nikolas said, "Send the BAR man with me. I will go. Then position your bazooka to take their truck. They will be without a retreat and melt into the woods."

Stavros ordered the BAR man forward and the bazooka to take the truck. He told Squad Three to advance to the south, and Stavros went with them. He told Yanni to get the animals and their tenders ready to cross, and when he got the signal from Stavros, to move out pronto.

Nikolas led the way down the top of the rise toward their crossing point, the BAR man following right behind. Twenty yards from the parked truck, they drew fire. Nikolas loaded a white flare in his Very gun and sent it aloft. The light exposed the Germans in the thin cover along the roadside. The BAR man and Nikolas opened fire together, Nikolas swept the nearside, and the BAR pummeled the far side. The men of Squad Three began picking targets with their M1s. Germans fell like ducks in a shooting gallery. There were ten Germans still firing when the bazooka round entered the radiator of the Borgward. The big truck rocked up onto its rear axle, then dropped back onto the roadway in orange flames. After that, the German fire stopped as the foot soldiers scramble to retreat down the road to the south and into the adjoining woods.

When the firing stopped, the two scouts on the east side descended into the roadway to guard the north approach, using the overturned Kübelwagen as cover. Two men from Squad Three took up lookout positions on either side of the burning truck. Stavros gave the order to cross and the tenders with the animals moved out with the injured man on Stavros's horse. When they were across the road, Stavros signaled for the rest of the detachment to move east. The lookouts joined the train at Stavros's signal, and at 0341 hours, they were again homebound for Chómori.

Chapter 45

It was a long trip back to Chómori. OG II veered deep into the Zygos Mountains, avoiding the easy pathways along the lake shores. After the ambush, they walked six hours to a tiny village south of Oros Arakinthos in the heart of the range. The longer route meant an extra day of travel, but guaranteed they would avoid the Germans. The pathways were not bad, just longer. It was 1000 hours when they bunked down in the Chapel of Prophet Elias, west of Melikineika.

The next night they marched south, then followed the Evinos River north to Sitaralona, a village on the eastern shore on Lake Trichonida. They bunked down in a small church dedicated to Saint Raphael, the healing saint. Stavros thought the site propitious. They could use a little healing.

Now, well within EAM-ELAS territory, the detachment moved in the daytime. They ate rations upon arriving at the church and bunked down for five hours of rest. They left the church at 1400 hours for the three-hour march to Kato Chrisovitsa, where they spent the night in the Church of Saint Nikolas. They woke the next morning to a pleasant day and began their eight-hour return to Chómori.

While the detachment made ready to shove off, Nikolas came to Stavros. "I think we should take your man to the doctor in Platanos. The doctor has worked with us many times. I think your man will need his leg set. I can stay with him and the rest go on to Chómori. Then I will find you later."

Stavros said, "If you think it is best and you trust the doctor. Should we assign an OSS man to stay behind? For security?"

Nikolas waved his hand. "No need. Platanos has its own security. We have twenty reserves there and all of them excellent fighters. Many are older men, but they have no fear. They are friends of our Kapetánios, men known to her family. Her mother still lives in the village and teaches at the school. They guard her. We have had no trouble in Platanos since the Kapetános's father died. That was two years ago. Your man will be safe. When he is ready to move, our reserves will bring him to Chómori. Do not worry."

"Okay. I'll let him know."

Stavros found the injured man being helped on his horse. Johnny, the unlucky commando who found the hole in the railroad bridge, looked at Stavros. "Did you come to reclaim your horse, Lieutenant?"

Stavros said, "How's the leg?"

Johnny, tall and blond, was one of the younger commandos. He was from California. He said, "It hurts like hell, sir. But the morphine helps. They taped me up with a splint, but it is hard to put weight on it."

Stavros said, "Okay. We're taking you to a doctor in Platanos. He can fix you up. Nikolas will stay with you while the doctor is attending. You will remain in Platanos until you are ready to move. Nikolas will return to Chómori. Nikolas says EAM-ELAS has good men in the village and you should not be in danger. The doctor has worked on andartes before. So, this visit will not be a surprise. Questions?"

Johnny said, "No, sir. Whatever you think is best. And, sir? Thanks for the horse and sorry about the rifle. What's that gonna' cost me?"

"When you can stand upright, you'll be the camp cook."

Johnny said, "Ah, geez."

"You think my horse is free?"

Johnny chuckled and grimaced.

Stavros was glad to see Johnny in a positive mood. Johnny was a good soldier, and his youth came through with his enthusiasm. He had an infectious personality. He was the same age as Gus, and Stavros thought of the two young men as case studies. Gus was the brash exhibitionist from the East Coast and Johnny the mellow, smiling, congenial kid from the West Coast.

Both were Greeks of serious mettle, but as different as night and day.

OG II moved out at 0900 hours and reached Platanos at 1400 hours. Nikolas found the doctor in his office on the plateia. He at once diagnosed Johnny with a broken tibia. He said the break was clean but would need to be set and put in a cast.

Stavros bid farewell to Nikolas, and OG II marched the final three hours to Chómori.

Johnny went to sleep in a cloud of ether and awoke with a straightened leg and a heavy plaster cast from just above the knee. It still hurt like hell, but he was on the mend.

Nikolas asked the doctor how long the recovery would take. The doctor said, "He is a healthy young man. He is strong. If he rests for a week before trying to move, he can remove the cast in five weeks. He should be able to stand on the leg after a week, maybe two. But no fighting. He would be an easy target for the Germans. A *kounéli* at dusk. No fighting.

"It would be best for him to stay in Platanos where I can check on him. I suggest you ask Dimitra's mother, Eva, if he can stay with her. She has the space, and her house is quiet. She is a woman who tends things. It is her nature."

Then the doctor spoke to his nurse. "Please run to Eva's house and see if this man can stay with her for a week. He is a fighter who needs to rest and recover."

The young nurse nodded and left the office.

She returned a few minutes later and said Eva was happy to help.

The doctor, his nurse, and Nikolas mounted a woozy Johnny on Nikolas's horse and steadied him for the two-block ride to Eva's. When they arrive, Eva greeted them. "A convalescent, I see. I hope the Germans paid more than you."

Johnny, still groggy, said, "Yes, ma'am. It cost them a railroad bridge."

"Excellent. Fine work. Now it is time for your just reward. Bring him to this bed and I will tend to him from here," she said, pointing to a doorway past her kitchen.

The nurse and Nikolas helped Johnny to the bed. As he hobbled by, Eva said, "You rest today, and I'll bring avgolemono soup. It is the best for healing. Tomorrow, when you feel better, we will talk about America and why American boys are so handsome."

Johnny gave her a woozy smile.

When Johnny was comfortable, Nikolas thanked the doctor and nurse, gave them three sovereigns, and made ready to mount his horse. The doctor tried to refuse the money, but Nikolas folded the doctor's hand around the coins. Nikolas said, "It is yours. You have earned it, and the people want you to have it."

With the invocation of "the people," the doctor knew the offering had the weight of EAM-ELAS. He acquiesced. Nikolas mounted and headed for Chómori, leading Stavros's horse.

Chapter 46

Stavros offered the two American cigarettes that now were his toll for passage to the schoolhouse. Yiorgos beckoned at the doorway. Stavros nodded to the sentries, then went inside. Yiorgos sat behind Dimitra's desk and Stavros in front, the usual configuration. The only difference was that Stavros noticed a hand-drawn map on rough brown paper with creases and fold marks splayed on the desk. Yiorgos saw Stavros glance at it before he folded it in half and returned it to the drawer. Stavros knew better than to ask.

Yiorgos began, "Nikolas said your mission was a success. Congratulations. Were you satisfied with your men's performance?"

"They were fine. It took longer than I planned to rig the bridge because the scouts didn't notice the rail and tie structure. They won't make that mistake again. The riggers did an excellent job and the bridge rests now at the bottom of a river in four pieces. No trains to Missolonghi for a while. I wonder how long it will take the Germans to make repairs," said Stavros.

"What do I know? They may not repair it at all. They are thinking now of leaving Greece, no? Still, your men are finding their way, no?" asked Yiorgos.

"The men are fighting well. They set up the ambush on the roadway in a matter of minutes, held their fire until ordered, then improvised when they needed to. We had one casualty, did Nikolas tell you?"

"Yes. He said a man fell on the bridge and broke his leg. He said he lost his rifle in the river. Do you need another?" asked Yiorgos.

"No. We have replacements. But thank you. We were lucky that no one else got injured on the bridge. It was tricky and dark."

"Yes. Luck is always part of success. It sounded like the Germans had some bad luck on their patrol, no?" asked Yiorgos.

"Bad luck or bad leadership," answered Stavros.

"How do you mean?"

Stavros said, "Their commander patrolled in two segments and sent one truck south and the other north. That meant the big, clumsy, noisy diesels had to turn around in the middle of the roadway. We were lucky to position where we did, but when the first truck tried to turn around, it gave us a broadside target stopped dead in the road. The BARs ripped it apart. The troops were trapped with the side curtains down. They had to dismount by the tailgate. They were obvious targets. The curtains should have been up, and they could have jumped over the side to cover. And the men in the back were unaware. They could not have seen us even if we were not hiding.

"If they had patrolled both trucks together and let them range the entire six kilometers in tandem, their Jeep could have acted as a spotter. The Jeep was nimbler and quieter. They could have radioed our location to the trucks and the Germans would have been on us in minutes. Then when they dismounted in tandem with the curtains up, their men could have found cover and advanced. They split their forces and allowed us time to maneuver and flank them.

"Oh, your man Nikolas is great. He had no hesitation. He said, *Attack*. It is the Greek way. He said the Germans would scatter, and they did. He knows his stuff."

Yiorgos nodded with Stavros's after-action assessment, impressed with the American's tactical reasoning. He said, "The Germans are stiff; they do not bend. Sometimes that is good. But if ambushed, bend. Their infantry has no heart to be in Greece. This we can tell. They have become this way over the past year. They are turning into Italians.

"What of your injured man?" asked Yiorgos.

"Nikolas took him to a doctor in Platanos. They set his leg, put him in a cast, and said he should be ready to maneuver in five to six weeks. They left him with Dimitra's mother to rest and recuperate. We expect him to stay there for a week, maybe two.

"Is that a secure location, Yiorgos? I worry about my man without OSS security. Should I send someone?" asked Stavros.

Yiorgos waved his hand. "There is no need. The Germans have other fish to fry. We have good reserve fighters there. Some have been with us since the Italians came. Dimitra and her father, God rest his soul, have known these fighters for. . . ." Then Yiorgos shrugged his shoulders.

Yiorgos went on, "Dimitra's mother is a good caretaker. She has nursed other fighters, and she is a joyful woman with much life. She has been walking with the spirit of her husband for two years now. But I am told she is coming back to the world."

Stavros wanted to know more about Dimitra's father, but he didn't want to intrude. He bit his lip and remained silent.

He asked instead, "Should we send someone to check on Johnny and maybe take Dimitra's mother some sovereigns?"

"No. No. No sovs," Yiorgos said, waving both hands. Then he went on, "Send someone to check, maybe. In a day, maybe two, but not before. Your man will be fine. He will live the life of a prince with Eva."

"Eva is Dimitra's mother's name?"

"Yes, Eydokia. And it is easy to tell mother and daughter. Peas from the same pod," answered Yiorgos.

Stavros nodded, intrigued by the mother and daughter sketch. He also noted Yiorgos had been practicing his American idioms. First the frying fish and now the pea pods. He wondered about the Greek fascination with American slang.

Yiorgos said, "Today you rest your men and tomorrow we can talk about other missions, no?"

Stavros nodded. "Great. That sounds like a plan."

Stavros approached the Hantzis home on his walk back to the monastery. He noticed the green front door was open. He saw to the right of the courtyard an old man tending grape trellises with pruning shears. He snipped at the smallest twigs and tendrils in the way the Japanese tend bonsai plants. The old man stood with a slight stoop. He wore a black cape over a white T-shirt and baggy black pants. He had a full white beard and wore a black lamb's wool cap. A long shepherd's crook leaned against a pillar of the trellis.

Stavros decided now was as good a time as any. He took the steps down from the roadway into the courtyard and crossed to the far side and the trellises. The old man's eyes followed him all the way. Stavros stopped on the stones of the courtyard, not entering the plot where the grapes grew. With the old man three meters away, he raised his voice and said, "You have a lovely crop of grapes coming, no?"

The old man remained silent, staring at Stavros. Stavros noticed the man's grip on the shears tightening.

Stavros tried again. "Are you Demitris Konstantinos?"

Again, the man said nothing.

"Sir, I believe our families are connected. I am Stavros Theofanis from St. Louis in America,"

With the mention of Stavros's surname, a glint of recognition flashed in the old man's eyes. The old man began walking toward Stavros. Stavros continued to note the shears in the man's right hand. He carried them like a weapon. Stavros remained relaxed with a wary eye.

When the old man was a meter away. He stared into Stavros's eyes, and Stavros saw in the old man a century of experience and caution. "I am Demitris Konstantinos Hantzis. You are the son of my son's friend in America. Your father's name is Alex. Is he still alive?"

"Uh, yes, sir."

"Good," replied the old man.

Then he gathered his crook and made his way past Stavros into the courtyard, leaving Stavros gazing to the mountains beyond.

Stavros turned to watch the old man take a seat on a bench in the courtyard opposite the green door. He moved to the far end, and when he sat, he stamped his crook twice on the stone paving and looked up at Stavros.

Stavros took that as a summons and went to sit next to him.

Before Stavros could say anything, the old man began, "I lost my son George last summer. The Italians killed him in action. Now the Italians are gone, and we have only Germans to kill."

Stavros waited to make sure the old man finished with his thought. "I'm very sorry your son died, *mními aiónia*."

The old man spoke again after a silence. "I have two more sons. Both are in America, in Indianapolis. I have two daughters, but they are married. And I have my grapes."

Stavros remained respectful. "Your son Harry helped my father."

The old man said, "Yes. I remember. Harry wrote to me. Did you know Harry was a boxer? A good one. He toured with Jack Dempsey. Did you know that?"

Stavros said, "Yes. My father told me."

There was silence. Then Stavros went on, "Sir, thank you and your family for the help in America."

The old man considered this. "Your mother's family helped my son Harry. He would have died in Epirus if your mother's brother were not brave. He died in Harry's place. The bond was formed when the bullets entered his body. It is a bond that can never be broken."

Stavros nodded, and again, silence followed.

Stavros sensed an end to the exchange. "Sir, our unit is staying in the old monastery. If I can be any help to you, please let me know. I will do whatever I can. May I visit again and perhaps we can talk more?"

The old man nodded.

Stavros rose from the bench. "You have a beautiful home. Best of luck with your grapes, sir."

He left the old man sitting on the bench with his crook.

Chapter 47

"No, ma'am. My family is not from Mount Olympus."

Eva's complimentary ribbing sailed over Johnny's head.

"Dad's family is from Poros and Mom's from Galatas. They met on a water taxi. There was a fire in a church. So, the people from one town had to cross the bay and go to the other church for some holiday. They met on the boat. My father gave his seat to my mother. That's how they met. She was with her family, and they liked what they saw.

"They came to America in the 1920s, stayed in New York for a while, then ended up in West Oakland, California. That's where I was born. Dad worked on the Southern Pacific Railroad, then he opened a little grocery on Seventh Street. Then he bought a kafeneion next door. Dad runs the kafeneion and my mom runs the store."

Thus did Eva's interrogation begin.

Johnny was feeling better. The day after his doctor's visit, he slept late and didn't wake until early afternoon. Propped up in bed eating pastry from the Platanos baker and drinking a sweet cup of Greek coffee, he smiled a broad infectious grin. Johnny, however, was slow on the uptake this afternoon and did not catch Eva's joke about Mount Olympus.

Eva tried again. "Are you certain about Mount Olympus? With your blond hair and good looks, you might be mistaken for the offspring of gods?"

Johnny said, "Oh. Thanks, ma'am. But no, Poros and Galatas."

Eva thought, *This will be fun.*

Eva sat with Johnny for the next half hour asking about his family, where he went to school, how he got into the Army, and why he was not married. Then she excused herself and went to make Johnny skordalia, a garlic and potato puree, to go with his avgolemono soup. Eva chose this simple but delicious dip, heavy with garlic, because she knew garlic inhibited infection and inflammation. This she had learned from her mother.

When Eva took the lunch to Johnny, he perked up and put two and two together, "So, you are the Kapetánios's mother, right?"

Eva answered, "That is right."

Johnny said, "I see the resemblance."

Dimitra was ready to leave Koryschades. The National Council met every day following her election. They finished the charter, and Dimitra found the follow-up meetings concerning the Mountain Government's relation to the Greek government in exile unmoored from reality. Everyone had a grand idea about what the Mountain Government should demand from the king and the new prime minister, Georgios Papandreou. In Dimitra's mind, it was posturing and puffing out of chests.

Mountain Government President Alexandros Svolos and Stephanos Sarafis, standing for ELAS, left for Lebanon the day following the National Council elections. The fate of the Mountain Government and hopes of unifying Greece were in their hands, not the National Council.

The Lebanon Conference looked to bring together the Greek government in exile, political parties, and the resistance. The resistance included the Mountain Government and royalist supporters from EDES. The goal was a National Unity government. The Conference was a British initiative designed to allow British troops to occupy Greece after the Germans left. They wanted Britain to take charge without fighting EAM-ELAS.

Dimitra found Vasilios smoking a cigarette in the hallway after an excruciating lecture by an Athens academician. He had droned for ninety minutes on Macedonian belonging to the Slavic family of languages. He proclaimed Macedonians could not call themselves Macedonians because four thousand years before, Macedonians had spoken Greek and still speak Greek. The lecture had Dimitra ready to fall from her chair.

Dimitra told Vasilios, "I am leaving here tomorrow. You can stay if you like. I will take only half of the detachment if you stay. Return to Chómori when you have had your fill."

Vasilios said, "We should travel together. It is safer that way. I have had my fill. We have reached the bottom of the barrel. What remains are middling actors in search of stages."

Dimitra nodded.

Vasilios said, "Perhaps on our return trip we can talk about Maria Svolos. You have her confidence, and she is an important person, no?"

Dimitra said, "We can talk. She is an important person, and her ideas have weight."

Dimitra was thinking about Maria's proposition. She was unsure how much to share with Vasilios. The young man was a staunch KKE supporter. While she trusted him and they had been through tough times together, she feared KKE discipline might trump their friendship.

Chapter 48

"So, if we hit all these targets, do we win the pot?" asked Gus. "Is it like a royal flush? No better hand?"

Stavros just finished reading out loud a mission's scorecard drafted by OSS HQ in Bari and given to him before leaving Italy. The list read:

Trains Attacked
Locomotives Destroyed
Train Cars Destroyed
Armored Cars Destroyed
Convoys Attacked
Trucks Destroyed
Bridges Destroyed
Roads Mined
Yards of Rail Blown
Garrisons and Pillboxes Attacked

Bari did not include sinking a ferry. He remembered Yiorgos telling him of EAM-ELAS attacks on mines and forestry operations, too.

Stavros called together the four squad leaders, two section leaders, and Yanni for an OG review of actions to produce suggestions for their next mission. The men sat and squatted in a circle on the monastery courtyard this warm morning. Stavros stood at the head of the circle.

They discussed shortcomings. The tone was professional, and no one took comments personally. The OG had performed well on their two encounters, encouraging Stavros and the other leaders. But every man in the group offered constructive suggestions for improvement. Stavros raised the scouts failing to note the difficulty of maneuvering on the bridge surface. Then he said they could improve their bazooka and BAR placements for an ambush. OG II knew German standard procedures and knew the distance between vehicles prescribed in their field manuals. The bazookas and BARs needed to place at those intervals during ambush for maximum advantage.

Then the focus turned to the next mission, and Stavros read the Bari scorecard. He knew Bari had drafted the card from British SOE reports. The Brits had been picking off Italian and German targets for a year and a half before the OSS arrived. The card reflected SOE's reported actions.

Gus piped up, "Two out of ten ain't bad for only being here a month. In a year, we'll be playing with house money."

This drew a few muted chuckles in the circle.

Yanni spoke without removing his cigar, "We're already playing with house money; it belongs to Uncle Sam."

Stavros said, "Dealer's choice, I'm open to suggestions."

Yanni removed his unlit cigar. "Bari wants us to inhibit German movement out of Greece to Western Europe. We can do that either by killing them here in Greece or slowing them down. That sounds to me like convoy ambushes, mining roads and railroads, blowing up locomotives. All actions that the Greeks find not to their liking. We're supposed to be activating the Greeks, right? Gentlemen, these are small potatoes, low risk, low reward. The Greeks seem like high risk, high reward folks."

Yanni's comments drew nods around the circle.

Stavros said, "I agree with Yanni. We need to think big. But we're still green. We could use another training mission. Something where we maneuver with the Greeks. We need to talk to Yiorgos and get an idea of what the Greeks are thinking. Let's pull off something coordinated before we try to take Athens. Remember, we are down to twenty-two men."

Gus asked, "What's the word on Johnny, Lieutenant?"

Stavros recounted his doctor visit and his recuperation in Platanos with Dimitra's mother. "I will visit him tomorrow and make sure he's behaving. Gus, you're his squad leader. Do you want to come?"

"Sure thing, Lieutenant. I get a horse, right? Not a donkey?"

"I'll talk to Yiorgos and see what we can borrow. We'll ride whatever he offers. The only mounts we can lay claim to in Greece are mules."

Gus said, "Too bad we don't have a motorcycle like those German BMWs. They seem to explode whenever we're around. If I capture one, can I keep it, lieutenant?"

Yanni and Stavros walked to the schoolhouse to see Yiorgos, but the sentries told them he had gone to Kato Dafni. Yiorgos left Nikolas in charge, and the OSS men went inside to talk after Stavros paid the two-cigarette toll.

Nikolas greeted Stavros and Yanni. "I see you are no worse for our mission. That was a long walk home, Lieutenant, something a noble officer should never endure, no?"

Stavros said, "OSS officers are noble in deeds only."

Nikolas smiled.

Stavros went on, "We've been talking about another mission, and we want to coordinate with you and plan something together."

Nikolas said, "This is good. But you will have to wait for Yiorgos. He is stratiotikós. I cannot speak for him. He will be back tomorrow, maybe the day after."

Stavros knew better than to ask what Yiorgos was up to. He held his tongue but remained curious.

Stavros asked, "May we borrow two horses tomorrow? Me and Johnny's squad leader would like to ride to Platanos and check on him?"

"Yes, yes. We have no movements planned for tomorrow. Please tell your young fighter that I pray for his speedy recovery. I know about leg injuries. It is best to let them heal before testing them. I was foolish with my injury and marched with the others to Gorgopotamos before I should have.

I had to ride a mule back to Chómori, and I've been living with the shame," answered Nikolas.

If Stavros had known of Nikolas's bravery at the Italian pillbox, he would have laughed at Nikolas's suggestion that he lived with shame.

Stavros asked, "Is there anything we can do for you? We'll be at the monastery for the next few days with little to do. We plan to spruce things up a bit, clean out the cobwebs, and sort our gear. Do you need any fighters for perimeter rotations or other security assignments?"

Nikolas shook his head. "Our fighters know well their assignments, and we are at full strength. Tell your men to watch for German planes. While we were away, they overflew Chómori but did not attack. Still, best to watch and listen. Take cover at the first sound. Don't wait.

"The Germans will not come here on foot, and their planes cannot hold territory, but they can kill all the same. We have nothing to defend against airplanes, no weapons. Hiding is all we can do."

Then Nikolas continued in English, "Tell your men to free their ears."

Stavros nodded, smiled, then added, "Keep their ears open."

"Yes, yes. That is what I meant to say. Keep their ears open," said Nikolas with a smile.

Chapter 49

"Do you see how the river flows, Vasilios, how it moves from east to west only where the mountains allow? Evinos is as old as the mountains, but it is only there because of the mountains. That is the appearance, no?

"Do you see this valley just before the little church? Can you see?" Dimitra pointed due south to a V-shaped gap in the river's course through the hills. "The gap is five hundred, maybe six hundred meters, no?"

Vasilios nodded.

"This is where a dam should rise. If we dam the Evinos, we create a reserve for drought, make electricity, and catch fish. This will bring jobs to the mountains, and people will prosper.

"But how do we amend six hundred meters of Gia? It is a small span of earth, and Gia will not mind. But how do we move the rocks and boulders and pour the concrete and install the hydro generators? Can we do this without capital? We must have money to invest. And where will that come from? Can we expect the Soviet Union will help?

"The Soviet Union receives aid from the United States. Yes, we are all allies today—the Soviets, the British, and the Americans. But after the war? The Soviets are brave fighters and have carried a burden fighting Germany, unlike other nations. Still, we were told in Koryschades, were we not, that after Germany invaded, the United States gave the Soviets fifty million dollars.[87] And we were told that the United States sent thousands upon thousands of tanks and planes and trucks and railroad locomotives and rolling stock and tons of food and medicine. And the United States sends food to Greece, too. This we all know.

"Again, look at the mountains. They control the river, no? That is an illusion! The river is there because it has cut through the mountains drop by drop over a scale of time we cannot imagine. Greece is the River Evinos; we must be patient. And these tall mountains, here and here, are America and Britain. The small one over there is the Soviet Union."

Dimitra and Vasilios stood on a rise north of the River Evinos while the detachment watered and grazed their mounts in the valley below. Dimitra did not like to lecture Vasilios, but his arguments for aligning Greece with the Soviet Union struck her as narrow and ideological. Yes, the communist movement supported women's liberation. And, yes, the movement was a rising force for national independence. And, yes, imperialism is wrong. Capitalism has systemic flaws.

Dimitra was a practical person. In her judgment, the USSR would be of little aid to poor Greece after the war. Greece would need all the help she could get. But try as she might, Vasilios remained in the KKE camp. He was young, idealistic, and not without reason to support the party. The party and its leading role in EAM-ELAS was why there was a Free Greece and a Mountain Government.

Dimitra never mentioned leaving the party to Vasilios. She couched their discussion as a *diálogos*, an investigative method familiar to Greeks since the days of Socrates. But Vasilios was smart. He knew Dimitra argued with more than academic curiosity. He had concerns.

Dimitra said, "We are four hours from Chómori. It will be good to sleep in a familiar bed, no?"

Vasilios said, "And good to be away from pretenders."

Dimitra smiled. "Vasilios, be careful. You sound like me."

Chapter 50

"They say these things are smart. I'd rather have a motorcycle. This guy's too smart. He's got a mind of his own."

"Talk to them in Greek, Gus. They are Greek horses, not American," suggested Stavros. "The mules, they're a different story. The ones branded with US ARMY . . . you talk to them in English."

The two men arrived at Eva's house in Platanos to check on Johnny. Nikolas had given them good directions, and the house near the town center was easy to find. The stone and terracotta home was set back from the street with an ancient fir tree in the middle of the front yard. Around its thick trunk was a five-meter square raised bed planted with herbs and flowers and ringed with a short, well-tended hedge. Planting beds edged the front yard with herbs and flowers and trees much older than the beds. There was an iron fence and a gate on the street, and the OSS men looped the reins of their mounts around the top railing.

A stone-paved walkway ran from the gate to the entrance on the right side of the house. Stavros and Gus opened the gate and walked to the door. The door was open, and they heard a woman singing inside. Stavros rapped on the doorframe but got no response. He rapped again, harder this time. The singing stopped.

Eva came to the door, wiping her hands on a white apron. She stared at Stavros and then Gus. She greeted them, "A fine morning to go riding, no? You must know my guest. Are you from the same group of American tourists?"

Stavros smiled. "Yes, ma'am. We came by to make sure he wasn't causing too much trouble."

"Trouble? Trouble? He is better than a movie. He can tell tales all day. A movie lasts only two hours.

"You are a lieutenant, I see. Since you do not have a cigar, you must be the commander. Your name is Stavros?" asked Eva.

"Yes, ma'am."

Then Eva gazed at Gus. "You, I do not know. You are a sergeant. You might be Johnny's squad man. I don't recall your name. Was it Joe?"

"No, ma'am. Gus."

"Yes, yes. That is what Johnny said. Gus.

"Please, where are my manners? Gentlemen, come in, or if you like, come sit on my humble plateia. I will tell Johnny you are here. The doctor brought crutches yesterday, and he can walk with them. But the doctor told him to not do much for a week, maybe two. Let me make you some coffee. I will tell him you are here. Come sit."

Eva directed the OSS men to a tidy iron table under a trellis of wisteria. Honeybees buzzed above, darting in and out of the early blooms. Theirs was the business of nectar, not of bothering men.

Eva went inside, and Gus said to Stavros, "Boy, can you see the resemblance? They could be twins. I mean, her mother is older and a little shorter, but . . . Hey, do you think we'll ever see Johnny again? If I were him, I'm not sure I'd want to leave."

Eva came to the door. "Maybe you should come this way and help Johnny to his feet so he can sit outside with you. It will be good for him to take the mountain air. We won't let him walk, so he should be safe. Just help him to the plateia." Then she pulled a stool around in front of an iron chair.

Stavros and Gus followed Eva into the bedroom, and Johnny greeted them. "Lieutenant and Sarge, good to see you guys."

"How are you feeling, soldier?"

"Great, Lieutenant. Eva is an angel and an incredible nurse. She sings like a nightingale. And boy, what a cook," Johnny said with a smile.

Gus said, "You look good, brother. In fact, you look so good we brought some potatoes for you to peel. May as well get started, Corporal."

Johnny said, "Ah, Sarge."

Stavros said, "We'll help you to the porch. We can chat there. How's that?"

"That would be great. It's a beautiful day. The doctor told me to stay off the leg for a week before I try walking with the crutches. I can hop around now, but that's about it. The leg feels better. Not so much pain. And I think the swelling is down. Eva says it's because of the garlic and the mountain tea," confided Johnny.

Stavros said, "She knows her stuff. I'd listen to her."

Johnny swung himself over the side of the bed and grimaced. His two OSS comrades steadied him under his shoulders. The threesome made their way to the plateia, and Johnny sat in the iron chair with his cast propped on the stool.

Johnny asked, "Have we got another mission?"

Stavros said, "Not yet. We need to talk to Yiorgos and coordinate with his fighters. He wasn't around yesterday. We'll talk when he gets back."

Johnny nodded.

Gus asked, "Is Eva married?" Gus wasn't in on the scuttlebutt about Dimitra's father.

In a hushed tone, Johnny said, "He's dead. He died two years ago. She talks about tending his garden. I've seen her tear up twice. Then she seems to snap out of it."

Gus nodded.

Stavros asked, "Is there anything we can do for her? Yiorgos told me not to offer sovs. I guess it would be an insult."

Johnny thought for a second, "She complains about that old tree in the backyard that has fallen over on her plants. I think they had a storm this winter. That's when it fell over."

"Maybe we can put together a detail to clean it up. Do you think she'd like that?"

"Yeah, I think she'd love it. Bring a squad up here and she'll feed them and know all their family members' names and birthdays by the time you're finished. She likes to ask questions. She's asked a lot about you, Lieutenant."

Stavros looked puzzled. "Like what?"

"Ah, normal stuff. Where are you from? What does your family do? Where did you teach college? Are you married? I think Dimitra must have said something to her about you," answered Johnny.

Gus nodded to Stavros, "You're getting the once-over, Lieutenant."

Stavros just shook his head. Then, hoping to change the subject, he said, "We can get a squad together and get up here tomorrow. Should we warn her in advance?"

Johnny said, "Sure. That would be polite. That'll let her plan how she can feed the men."

"All right. I'll ask her about it when she brings the coffee," said Stavros.

She brought not only coffee but pastry, cheese, and olives. She didn't serve Johnny coffee. He got a blend of dried flowers, leaves, and stems from a local herb called sideritis brewed into Greek mountain tea. Johnny liked the drink with its oily and earthy appeal. Eva served it with a spoonful of honey taken from hives tended by the busy bees buzzing above.

Eva placed the coffees and tea on the table, then set the treats in the middle. She returned the tray to the house and rejoined the men. As she sat, she asked, "Next time you visit, you must let me know and I will have a proper meal for you."

Stavros said, "This is wonderful. This is a treat."

Gus said, "This is the best pastry I've had since leaving New York. It must have taken days to make."

Eva said, "It took me twenty minutes. That is the time to walk to the baker at the village center. I like to cook, but baking, not so much."

Gus said, "One way or the other, it's great. Thanks for sharing it with us."

Eva said, "It is Dimitra's favorite pastry, galaktoboureko. Do you know it? She has loved it since she was a little girl."

"No, ma'am. I don't think so. But it's good," said Johnny.

Then Eva looked at Stavros. "Commander Stavros, why do your men not salute you?"

"Um . . . we're not like that, ma'am. We hold different ranks, but we're a small group. We all train together and work side by side," answered Stavros.

"Yes. But are you not the commander?"

"Yes, ma'am."

"Then you have a bigger mount and a nice bed and an office desk, no? Did you bring slippers?" asked Eva.

Stavros caught on. Eva was toying, trying to embarrass him. She was playing to Gus and Johnny, who were snickering at her inquiry.

Stavros ignored them, "We were wondering if you would let us help with the fallen tree in your yard? Johnny told me it needs to be cleared. I can bring a group of men with saws and axes. We'll turn it into firewood for you."

"Commander Stavros, I approve! I accept your generous offer. You must tell me how many men so I can prepare a suitable meal. And I hope you will return with your men, so we may talk more about your unusual American ways."

"Right," said Stavros. "Is tomorrow good?"

Johnny and Gus were finding other things to look at than Stavros.

On the ride back to Chómori, Gus said to Stavros, "She's checking you out. She's got plans."

Stavros said, "She's curious. She doesn't have much else to keep her entertained. You heard her. She likes Johnny because he keeps her entertained. That's all it is. And don't go spreading anything around camp. That's an order. Got it?"

"Yes, sir." Gus snapped a salute.

The two rode in silence, then Gus asked, "Do you want to use Squad Two for the tree? They'll like to see Johnny. Four working on the tree should be enough. I'll gladly come back tomorrow for the meal. I've eaten more dehydrated mutton than should be legal."

"Sure. That sounds good. I told Eva we would bring five or six men. Have your men find axes and saws. I'll see if they can borrow mounts. Muster at 0900 tomorrow morning. I'll go with you. I'll send Yanni to meet with Yiorgos if he's back," said Stavros.

"Lieutenant. Stavros. Some friendly advice, okay?" confided Gus.

Stavros looked over at his friend.

"If Eva is interested in you, so is Dimitra. These mother–daughter bonds run deep. I've got two sisters and I know. Believe me, I know, brother."

Stavros bucked up. "We're here to fight a war, Gus. Not look for wives."

Then Stavros realized he'd jump to a conclusion of his own. Nobody had said anything about marriage.

Gus said, "Fighting a war does not mean you can't look at the scenery."

Chapter 51

"This is good. She has worried about that tree since December. Thank you for helping her. And your man? Is he doing well?"

"He seems fine. I only worry about him coming back. I'm not sure he'll want to leave your mother's house."

"She has cared for many fighters. She pampers them, talks to them, asks them questions. Some have been in worse health than your man, Johnny. Most have recovered and left fatter than when they arrived," confided Dimitra.

"Has she asked many questions?"

"Johnny said that they talk a lot," answered Stavros.

"She is a one-woman intelligence service. Perhaps your OSS needs a professional interrogator, no?" Dimitra chided.

Stavros smiled. "Is it all right to borrow five of your mounts for the day? And do you know where we can find a forestry saw? One of those two-man types?"

"The horses are no problem. We have no movements planned for today. I have yet to talk with Yiorgos. Nikolas thinks he is in Kato Dafni. There's been no word from him for two days. But we have no movements planned.

"The saws you will find in the toolshed next to the stable. Take what you need. And please tell my mother hello and that I will visit her soon. Give her my love. And, before you leave, come back, and I will give you a letter to take to her," said Dimitra.

"Right," said Stavros. "Oh, and how did your conference go?"

Dimitra rolled her Cimmerian eyes and exhaled in exasperation. "It is a long story and a short one. We can talk about it when you return. We founded a government for Free Greece. They elected me to the National Council, one of five women out of two hundred and eight."

Stavros nodded. "Congratulations. Very impressive. You made history, no? A woman elected to national office in Greece. You are a historic figure."

"Only a professor of history would call me historic. Good luck with the tree." Dimitra dismissed Stavros.

Stavros stammered, "Um . . . I'm sorry. I didn't mean that you are only historic. I mean . . . you are an impressive person. An impressive woman . . . ah, congratulations."

Dimitra nodded and caught herself before she waved her hand to shoo him out of the schoolhouse. Instead, she looked up and offered, "Thank you."

Stavros replayed his awkwardness on the ride to Platanos. He wondered why he was tongue-tied around Dimitra and why it was so hard to be himself. She was a beautiful woman, but he had known beauties before. She was smart, and he had known smart women. But Dimitra was a military commander and now a political official. She commanded more men than him. She outranked him . . . if anybody was keeping score. Was he? Keeping score? Was he intimidated? Did she remind him of Marta, the woman who had raised him? His psychological prospecting proved too deep for the moment.

The OSS men arrived at Eva's house before noon and set to work on the fallen ash. The old tree was near the end of its growing zone when the December winds lashed it, and it had given up one hundred years of bountiful life to undeniable Gia. Johnny sat propped on a chair with his cast raised on a stool, watching his squad mates and sharing in the friendly banter. Stavros was supervising when Eva approached him. "They will be fine, Commander. Come with me and we will talk. Let's have some coffee." Then she tugged at his elbow.

Stavros followed Eva to the plateia. She motioned for him to sit, and he took one of the iron chairs. She held up a finger, then went into the kitchen. A few minutes later, she returned with two coffees. She put Stavros's drink in front of him. Before she sat, she asked, "Tell me why you are not married, Professor Commander?"

Stavros laughed. If anyone else had asked him, he would have clammed up. But there was something infectious about Eva. He recognized her disarming directness in her daughter.

He gathered himself. "Well, that's kind of personal."

Eva pounced on his hesitation. "You are in Greece. You are fighting a war. There is nothing personal, everything is communal. Everybody knows everything. Common knowledge, no? But if you insist, I can hold my tongue. If you tell me, I will tell no one else."

Eva's argument didn't sway Stavros. He doubted her confidentiality. He said, "I've been busy. My studies and teaching took a lot of time."

Eva knew the dodge. "I think you are a perfectionist. The perfect form obsesses you. Like Plato in the cave. You fear the light of day will bring imperfection to your ideal world, no?"

Stavros smiled. "Which form? A wife or marriage?"

"Do not toy, Professor. Marriage is not a form. You are waiting for the perfect wife. The perfect woman. You will wait as long as the ash tree your men are now chopping into firewood. Still, you will not find perfection. And like the ash, you will fall from grace as an old derelict, blown from your roots by winds of time," countered Eva.

Stavros knew now he was bested.

He said, "I've just been busy. But you are right. I've been picky."

Eva was right, Stavros had been picky. He was a catch. He was good-looking. He had a good job and a bright future, and he had played the field. An unforgiving estimation might have called him selfish. Or at least self-centered. He knew it.

He went on, "I didn't come to Greece for a wife. We're here to fight the Germans. This is what I think about, not wives."

Eva pursed her lips. "Hum . . . I believe you tell the truth. But not to yourself. Still, I like you, Professor Commander. Do you know something else? I think my daughter likes you."

She had Stavros's full attention. He almost spit out his sip of coffee.

At the mention of Dimitra, Stavros remembered her letter. He said, "Oh, Dimitra sent this. I talked to her this morning."

"How is she?"

"She seems fine. She's back from her conference." He considered telling Eva about Dimitra's election, but thought he should let mother and daughter share that moment.

Stavros regained his footing as Eva opened the letter. "Thanks for the coffee. I better go check on my men."

Eva said, "We will talk more. You are not off the hook. But now I must finish our lunch preparation. How long before the men are ready to eat?"

"They are always ready to eat. The tree should take an hour, not much longer."

Eva seemed eager to go inside. Stavros assumed she wanted to read the letter in private. He said, "Thanks again for the coffee."

Eva nodded, and Stavros pushed his chair away from the table. Stavros walked to the backyard and saw his men had everything under control. When he was sure Eva was inside, he walked to the front gate and mounted his horse. It was a quick ride to the baker.

Chapter 52

Stavros was all smiles, walking through Chómori to the schoolhouse the following morning. He had his wrapped pastry in hand and a new attitude about Dimitra. Fifty meters from the building, he sensed something wrong. There was too much activity, too many fighters moving about. Mounts from the stables were arriving, then tied to the schoolyard fence. He counted fifteen with more coming.

When he reached the school, he asked the sentry what was going on. The fisherman from Nafpaktos said, "Big trouble. They have Yiorgos."

Stavros asked, "Can I go in?"

The big man shrugged. Stavros took that as permission and went inside. What he found was not chaos, but something that could have been mistaken for it. Nikolas and Dimitra were at the center of a dozen fighters. Everyone wanted to voice an opinion. Arms were waving and fingers pointing. It was loud. Then Dimitra raised her voice. Her tone was as sharp as a knife. She said, "We will get him. We will go to the jail and free him. Should we go now, in daytime? Or should we wait until night? That is the question. One at a time, please. Tell me your thoughts."

A big man near Nikolas said, "We cannot wait. They might transfer him to the Germans. Then we will have no chance to free him. I know this building in Nafpaktos, the jail. It is not well-fortified, and the guards are only gendarmerie or Security Battalion swine. We should go now."

Another fighter said, "If we wait until dark, there will be fewer guards and we can surprise them. They will be drunk by midnight."

There rose again mumbling in the group, and the volume increased. Stavros, standing on the periphery, set the pastry on a school desk and raised his hand. He looked out of place, but his gesture got everyone's attention. Dimitra looked in his direction. She said, "Quiet, everyone. Let us hear from the American. Lieutenant, you train for such missions, no?"

Stavros asked, "Can you tell me what is happening?"

Dimitra nodded to Nikolas. "Yiorgos is in the Nafpaktos jail. The lady who provides meals to the prisoners saw him there last night. She is from Kato Dafni. She knows Yiorgos and his family. Her husband rode here overnight. It was 2100 hours when she saw him."

Stavros asked, "How many guards at the jail?"

A man to the left of Stavros said, "During the day, maybe ten. It is not a big place, maybe twenty cells. Not big at all. It is the headquarters of the chorofylaki. The local police and the Security Battalions come and go. It is impossible to know how many will be there in the daytime. At night, the police go home, and the Security Battalions get drunk and steal."

Nikolas said, "If they identify Yiorgos as EAM-ELAS, he is dead. They will torture him for information, then hang him."

Stavros said, "Then we better go soon."

Heads began nodding. Only Dimitra and Nikolas seemed reserved. Dimitra said, "Go make your men ready. We will leave in one hour or sooner. We need two dozen fighters. We will ride fast. We can be there in four hours. Bring an extra mount for Yiorgos. Is this understood?"

There was a round of "Yes, Kapetánios!" and the fighters filed out of the schoolhouse.

Dimitra turned to Stavros as they filed out. "Lieutenant, can you bring men? Maybe ten men?"

Stavros said, "Of course."

Nikolas said, "You should bring your bazooka men and your BAR men. You should bring explosives. We may want a diversion."

Stavros said, "Right. Good thinking. Can we get somebody inside to make sure he is still there? Can the meal lady come and go without suspicion?"

"We will see. I will have two men dress as shepherds so they can scout. There is a hill north of the jail, open land. We can stage over the rise out of sight from the jail. We will make a cavalry charge of one hundred meters for the attack. We will plan on the ride. For now, let us get the fighters ready," said Nikolas.

Stavros said, "Roger. I'll get my men."

Stavros left the wrapped pastry sitting on the desk and jogged to the monastery to muster his detachment.

Chapter 53

The cell smelled of vomit, urine and Papastratos cigarettes. Yiorgos sat slumped in the middle, tied to a wooden chair. Blood matted his long hair. Bruised and swollen, his face was unrecognizable. A deep cut seeped over his left eye. Three Security Battalion men hovered around him like jackals around a carcass. A bloody wooden truncheon rested next to a bottle of clear liquor on a table against the concrete wall.

A tormentor upended the bottle for a slobbering drink. An explosion rocked the parking area south of the jail, interrupting his refreshment. The six chorofylaki guarding the jail left their posts and ran into the parking area where a truck was aflame. The Security Battalion men left the cell without locking the door and ran to the jail's entrance.

The diversion worked. Before the chorofylaki and Security Battalion men knew it, they were under fire. Seconds after the first explosion, a BAR opened on the crowd in the parking area outside the jail. The cavalry charged with the first explosion. The fighters on horses covered the one hundred meters downhill in seconds. Andarte guns cut the exposed guards to pieces.

Gus's bazooka round smashed into the side entrance, blowing the metal door off its frame. Two OSS men entered the smoldering side door and made their way in a crouch to Yiorgos's cell. The Security Battalion men retreated into the jail. They spotted the commandos in the smoky hallway outside Yiorgos's cell. But before they could bring their weapons to bear, the OSS men felled all three with their Thompsons.

The commandos brought C2 to blow Yiorgos's door but didn't need it. Two more commandos rushed in behind the lead team and cut Yiorgos free, then helped him to his mount. Yiorgos was too weak to ride. An OSS man swung into the saddle and andartes heaved Yiorgos up behind. They placed Yiorgos's arms around the commando's waist and tied them overlapped with a web belt. Then the tandem bounded north and over the hilltop.

Andartes walked among the wounded, quelling those still moving. When Dimitra saw Yiorgos safely over the rise, she shouldered her carbine and pulled the Very pistol from her bandolier. She commanded, *"Upsilós!"* Obedient Diávolos reared to his full height and Dimitra fired the signal for retreat. The raid lasted less than ten minutes.

They retreated north into the low hills of Marmara and stopped outside the small settlement of Lefka Vomvokous. They took a defensible position on high ground with a 360-degree view. Andartes helped Yiorgos from the mount and laid him on a sheepskin on the sandy ground. The OSS medic kneeled over him to check his vital signs. His pupils were not responsive, and his breathing was labored. Yiorgos wore his shepherd's disguise, and the medic unwrapped the thick cape and shirt, then put his ear to his chest to listen to his heart. Then he felt for a pulse. Dimitra, Stavros, Nikolas, and Yanni watched as the young medic examined Yiorgos.

The medic looked up. "He needs a doctor. I think he has a broken rib. It might have lacerated a lung. He's banged up and may have a concussion but it looks like no other broken bones. He needs a doc. I'll clean up these cuts and bandage his head. Then we can move him."

Yiorgos moaned and struggled to open his right eye. His left eye was too swollen to open. Dimitra asked, "How do you feel, Yiorgos?"

The battered man licked his lips and tried to form words. Then, barely above a whisper, he said, "Thank you for coming. They were holding me for the Germans. They will be coming. We need to move. May I have a drink?"

The medic held his canteen to Yiorgos's mouth.

Dimitra asked, "Yiorgos, do they know you are from Kato Dafni? Do they know about your family?"

Yiorgos formed words painfully. "They know nothing. I am a shepherd from the west. That is what they know."

Then Dimitra, looking up at Nikolas, Stavros and Yanni, said, "It will be dark in three hours. We should take him to his family, and they can care for him. It is too long a ride to Chómori. If we ride to the east, we can stay away from motor roads. The trails will not be easy, but we'll be out of sight. We can leave a detachment with him and his family. When he is better, we can bring him to Chómori."

The three leaders nodded. Stavros said, "If we cannot get help tonight, our medic and a couple other OSS men can stay with him."

Dimitra nodded. "There is a doctor in Kato Dafni. Yiorgos's family is known there. They will watch after him. But we need him in Chómori as soon as he can ride. Kato Dafni is too close to the Germans. It is not safe.

"When we are close to Kato Dafni, the main force will go north around the village. Only a small detachment should go to his home. We will attract too much attention with all the fighters. Lieutenant, your medical man should go with the detachment."

Stavros looked at Yanni. Yanni said, "We can send the medic and another OSS man. They can ride to Chómori once they've contacted the doctor. Will the main force ride to Chómori tonight?"

Dimitra said, "Yes. We will return tonight. It is safe there."

They reached the route to bypass Kato Dafni two hours later. It was dark. The waxing crescent moon, just two days from new, shone with a vaporous glow. Nikolas sent five men with Yiorgos, and Yanni sent the medic and another man from Squad Three. Those with Yiorgos veered to the east for the road to Kato Dafni, and the larger force turned north.

Dimitra took the less-traveled route to Chómori, what the locals called the "Back Road." The ride took seven hours. This route was rough and impossible for motorized travel. Washed-out sections made the raiders travel single file around the danger. Fallen boulders blocked other parts. This way was longer, but safer. Dimitra knew the Germans would look for them. But the Germans moved with trucks, not on horseback. The darkness and highway treachery were tonight their friends.

The raiders reached Chómori just after sunrise. It was 0900 hours by the time the OSS men stabled their mounts, had some chow, and sorted their gear. Stavros told his men to get some rest. They would hold an after-action brief that evening. Stavros bunked down in his monastery alcove with the lingering image of Dimitra rearing on Diávolos.

Chapter 54

Gus started with, "We got lucky. That building was custom designed for a raid. That side door was everything. If we had to fight our way through the public entrance, that could have cost us. Big."

The BAR man from Squad Three, a tall Greek national, said, "We were fortunate to position the bazooka and the BAR as easily as we did. The alley to the east of the jail gave excellent cover, no? And we were lucky that the chorofylaki had no sentries outside the jail. They are lazy and untrained. They assume Nafpaktos is their territory. It is theirs no longer."

The sapper from Squad Four said, "We were lucky the andartes knew C2 and pencil timers. The two men disguised as locals planted the diversion like pros. No panic, no tip-off. We could never have gotten that close in American uniforms in broad daylight."

Gus piped up, "Hey, is there a cavalry charge on our scorecard, Lieutenant? Maybe we'll get bonus points."

This drew a few chuckles.

The medic and the other man from Squad Three arrived late in the afternoon. They reported Yiorgos was at his family's house and the doctor was with him. The doctor said he had a concussion but no fracture. He didn't think the broken rib had punctured his lung. He said Yiorgos might ride in a week, but the rib would be painful for months. He said the best thing for him now is to rest.

Stavros asked the medic, "Did Yiorgos say anything about his capture? Why he was there? What he was up to?"

The medic said, "No, sir. He was in and out of it. He said something about a priest a few times, but nothing that made sense."

Chapter 55

"Lieutenant, you have a visitor," announced a man from Squad Four.

Stavros looked up at the commando from the small desk inside of the monastery entrance where he was reading a map. He stepped into the courtyard, surprised to see Dimitris Hantzis. The old man wore the same black cape and dark wool hat Stavros had seen before. He held the shepherd's crook in his right hand.

Stavros said, "Sir. Mr. Hantzis. I'm surprised to see you. Would you like to sit? Can I get you some coffee or water?" Stavros pointed to a pair of wooden chairs against the outer wall of the monastery.

As a handful of curious commandos looked on, Dimitris walked to the chairs and sat. Stavros joined him and asked again, "Would you like some water or coffee?"

Dimitris shook his head and intimated, "I have brought you something to share."

He reached inside of his cape and withdrew a faded yellow envelope and handed it to Stavros. Stavros saw it was a letter postmarked from America in 1914. The paper was brittle.

Dimitris said, "You can read the letter. It is from my son Harry."

Stavros carefully opened the envelope and removed a single page. He unfolded it, hoping not to tear the weathered sheet. The letter read:

Trinidad, Colorado, USA
3 June 1914

Dear Father,
*   I write to tell you of the matter in Colorado and the debt our family owes. I will leave for Indianapolis in*

a few days. Our obligation is paid in part, and the rest will resolve in time. Of this, I have no doubt.

The poor woman Eleni, sister of my savior in Epirus, is avenged. Memory eternal. They murdered her in her tent with her baby near. We found one of the two murderers. This we could not have done without my friend Dimitri and Eleni's husband, Alex. These two men and other friends helped our search. The man we found was a Greek with no honor. He fell by the hand of Eleni's husband. The other man is more difficult. He is a soldier with the militia and difficult to reach. In time, we will reach this man and he, too will pay. But for now, we must all find work. I will bring with me to Indianapolis my friend Dimitri and see if I can find work for him. He is strong and smart. He will not be a burden on Nick and I. Eleni's husband, Alex, will stay in Colorado and care for his son. He plans to find work in a town north of the manifestation. It will be difficult for him to raise his son, but he is fortunate that a good family lives near and can help.

I will write when I am again with Nick and I know better of my job and my boxing. Nick and I are fortunate that Indianapolis is not like Colorado. Colorado was much like Epirus.

Your obedient son,
Epaminondas Dimitris Hantzis

Stavros was speechless. It took him a full minute to gather his thoughts. Dimitris sat next to him in silence, recognizing the effect on the humbled man.

Stavros finally said, "Sir, thank you for sharing this. There is much in this letter I did not know. I am in your debt."

Dimitris waved his crook, "There is no debt. This letter belongs to you as much as it does to me. You are the infant my son writes about. This is your story."

Again, Stavros fell silent. Then he said, "Sir, is there anything I can do for you? Our food is not so good, it is army rations, but you are welcome to it if you like."

Dimitris used his crook to help himself from the chair. Stavros stood with him. Then the old man left the courtyard, saying nothing. Stavros still held the letter, and he called, "Sir? The letter?"

Dimitris shook his head and kept walking. Stavros caught up with him and asked, "May I walk with you?"

Dimitris nodded, and the two men started up the hill to the Hantzis home.

Chapter 56

Dimitra, Nikolas, and Vasilios sat on the Chómori plateia on a pleasant morning in late May. The sun warmed the stonework, and the vines above buzzed with bees. Small porcelain cups of coffee sat before them on the iron table.

Vasilios started the meeting. "The Lebanon agreement is called the National Contract. Churchill has approved. It is a Government of National Unity. Georgios Papandreou is the prime minister. There are twenty-four ministers, and six will be EAM. No fighters will disarm. That is what the British demanded.

"EAM faced accusations of murder and thievery. The charges came from collaborators and cowards, those who have shed no blood for Greece. Now we have a government."

Nikolas asked, "What became of the Hellenic Army mutineers in April? They are the reason the British and the king sat for a conference, no?"

Vasilios said, "The British have sent the Greek soldiers and officers from Egypt to camps. Some say they are in Libya. Some say Egypt. Others say South Africa. Five thousand EAM supporters, our brothers, are under British guard.

"The king has organized a unit of royalists, the Third Greek Mountain Brigade. Their officers and enlisted men have pledged loyalty. Tsakalotos commands them."[88]

Dimitra said, "Then they are royalists. Tsakalotos is a powerful commander. He led the Three/Forty Evzone Regiment against the Italians. They captured the Hundred and Forty-First Blackshirt Battalion at Mount Kuç. The Evzones advanced far into Albania and had the Italians running before the Germans invaded. I have respect for his military skills. But he is a royalist with a deep hatred of EAM."

Vasilios said, "Sarigiannis will serve as Vice-Minister of Military Affairs. He is your colleague on the National Council,

Kapetánios. He is an EAM supporter and will be above Tsakalotos."

Dimitra said, "That is good, Vasilios. But give me a brigade before a title and we will see who is obeyed."

Nikolas finished drinking his coffee, "I must leave. I must check the mounts and make certain the fighters are tending the stables. The horses had a hard ride to the jail, and they deserve time to recover."

Dimitra said, "I checked on Diávolos yesterday and he seemed no worse for the wear."

Nikolas said, "He is a powerful mount, Kapetánios. A horse in his prime. How long have you owned him?"

Dimitra said, "He was my father's horse. I have ridden him since long before the Italians."

Nikolas left. When Dimitra and Vasilios were alone, Dimitra asked, "Tell me what you know of the Soviet directive for our members attending the conference in Lebanon."

Vasilios said, "Kapetánios, there are rumors. But I have no direct knowledge. . . ."

Dimitra cut him off. "This is not Koryschades, comrade. Do not play politics when a straight answer is best."

Vasilios hesitated. "The Soviets directed KKE to not disrupt the Allies. I heard this from a member of the Central Committee."

"Thank you, Vasilios. I appreciate your honesty. I too have heard this. I also heard the Soviets said we should disarm," she added, not disclosing her source.

Vasilios said, "This I have not heard, comrade. Only that KKE should promote unity in the alliance with Britain."

Dimitra's source was Maria Svolos. Maria's account had come from a member of the KKE Central Committee in Athens. Maria wrote to Dimitra about switching her affiliation. After disclosing the Soviet directive, she wrote, "Mother bear swatted her cub."

Chapter 57

"See, right here?" Yanni pointed to the map in front of Stavros. "Just east of Amfilochia. The road makes two sharp turns. The west turn is damn near a horseshoe. That's where the Germans slow down. That's where we set the ambush. Three days there, three days back. Two days on target."

Stavros said, "The andartes say the Germans run thirty and forty-vehicle convoys, both directions every day. Do you think we have the firepower to take advantage?"

"Setting charges will be tough. Our sappers will be exposed. So, we'll have to work at night. We will need to camouflage the charges and wires. The Germans will be suspicious. And there are no bridges along this section.

"That road is the main line of communication in Western Greece. When they aren't running convoys, they patrol. And they overfly. I'm not sure of the cover and retreat. But if we want big German targets that hinder resupply and movement, this is the location. The rest of the road is straight, and the convoys move fast. Once they form up, they travel fifty miles per hour, or better. These turns slow them to five . . . ten . . . sometimes they come to a complete stop . . . or so I'm told," answered Yanni.

Ionia Odos was a German lifeline. Over it moved the men and matériel necessary for Nazi occupation of Western Greece and projection of German force into the Adriatic and Ionian Seas. Yanni was right. Along the 276 kilometers from Igoumenitsa to Patras, the turns outside Amfilochia were the only section where traffic slowed.

Stavros didn't think the andartes would take part, since there were no weapons to seize and the number of probable German casualties small. This was a harassment and psychological operation. Stavros needed to talk to Nikolas and get his thoughts.

Stavros asked Yanni, "How's the resupply drop coming?"

"Wednesday, weather holding eleven hundred hours. There's a small clearing over the hill, past the stables, across from Saint Charalambous. We'll set some fires, and if the flight crew is good, they'll hit the mark. It's a small zone, but we should be okay."

"Do we know what's coming?" asked Stavros.

"More rations, sugar, cigarettes, coffee, meds. Probably ammo, charges, detonators, sovs. That's my guess," answered Yanni.

"Right. Anything else we need to worry about?" asked Stavros.

"Nothing on my list. The men are in high spirits except for living on rations. The men on the raid detachment are lording their cavalry experience over the rear guard, but it's all friendly. They're ready for another mission. Oh, and somebody needs to check on Johnny. He's been in Platanos for a week. I think you should go, Lieutenant. From all reports, you have a good rapport with the mother of the Kapetánios. OSS directive number something says make nice with the locals," answered Yanni.

"What reports, Lieutenant?" asked Stavros.

"Oh, just reports, talk in camp. You know," answered Yanni.

"You mean, Gus," said Stavros.

Yanni shrugged and didn't answer.

Stavros said, "Let's see if we can track down Nikolas and get his opinion on the ambush. We can discuss how many weeks of KP for Gus later."

Yanni gave a lopsided smile with his unlit cigar dangling from his lips.

When Yanni and Stavros arrived at the schoolhouse, the big fisherman sentry from Nafpaktos took the proffered cigarette. He added, "Thank you for the pastry." Stavros thought for a second, then put two and two together. He said, "Hope you liked it."

The big fisherman smiled.

Yanni gave Stavros a puzzled look. Stavros just shook his head.

Nikolas and Vasilios sat in front of Dimitra at her desk. When Stavros and Yanni entered, Dimitra motioned for them to pull chairs from those lined along the wall. Stavros sat to the side of Vasilios and Yanni alongside Nikolas.

Dimitra said, "We were discussing why Yiorgos was in Nafpaktos. Can either of you shed light on this mystery?"

Both Americans shrugged and shook their heads. Stavros said, "We were hoping you might fill us in."

"We are sending two riders to Kato Dafni tomorrow. They will check on his recuperation and perhaps return with some clues."

"We have one other business item. Vasilios, how is the telephone line to Chómori coming?" Dimitra looked at Stavros and Yanni. "Vasilios oversees our communications and infrastructure projects. EAM is wiring all Free Greece for telephones."

Vasilios referred to a set of notes in his lap. "The trunk line is already in Platanos. That is where we will connect. As you know, Kapetánios, the municipal building has a telephone connection to Nafpaktos. From there, we can reach Athens. They store the wires and poles for connecting Chómori at the junction of the Nafpaktos Road and the road to Chómori. We need to run the wires from there to Chómori. That may take another two weeks, quicker depending on the labor and the weather. Where do you want the line to end in Chómori, Kapetánios?"

Dimitra said, "It should end somewhere the people have access. Here in the schoolhouse or the taverna? Probably the schoolhouse is best for now."

Stavros said, "We have men qualified in signals. We can help."

Dimitra looked at Vasilios, who responded, "That might be useful. The challenge is not the technical work but the physical labor of setting poles in this rocky terrain."

Yanni said, "Would C2 help? It might be quicker than pick and axe."

Vasilios answered, "I will let the project foreman know. It may speed things along. Thank you for your offer."

Dimitra said, "That is all of our business. Now for the American concerns."

"Thank you," said Stavros. "We are planning an ambush on the Ionia Odos and need your thoughts and suggestions. Your fighters are welcome to join, but we know your EAM-ELAS directives."

"Where on the Ionia Odos?"

Stavros looked at Yanni, "Amfilochia. The turns in the road."

Dimitra said, "Nikolas knows the area well."

Nikolas said, "The Germans run large convoys on that road, thirty trucks, sometimes more. I know the turns. There are two sharp curves and the trucks slow for them. It is a suitable ambush location, but it has drawbacks. The Germans only run the large convoys in the daytime. Nothing at night. And the land around the curves is sparse and offers no cover. There are hills to the east, but your retreat in daylight will be over unprotected ground, no cover. At what range do you plan to attack?"

Yanni said, "Our bazooka men are deadly at fifty meters and fair at one hundred meters. We sight them for four hundred meters, but accuracy drops at that range. For accuracy and effect, we need them within eighty to one hundred meters."

Nikolas thought for a moment. "That is close. Better they advance after the attack begins. Position your riflemen at eighty meters . . . better one hundred meters. That will be the closest you can hide in the daylight. What of mortars? Are you so equipped?"

Stavros nodded. "We have two, an eighty-one-millimeter and a sixty-millimeter."

"Are your men good with them?" asked Nikolas.

Yanni said, "We have yet to fire them in Greece, but we were good back in the States."

"What are their range?" asked Nikolas.

Yanni replied, "The eighty-one is good to twenty-five hundred meters. The sixty about half that. The eighty-one throws a bigger shell, five kilos, and it must be at least two hundred meters away from target. The eighty-one is a bigger weapon, sixty kilos. It fires bigger shells, hard to transport. But it's almost as good as artillery."

"How rapidly can your men fire?" asked Nikolas.

"Once on target, fifteen, maybe eighteen a minute," said Stavros.

Nikolas was lost in thought, then he ventured, "These two weapons require further investigation. The larger shell is better. But you will need to retreat quickly. The bigger weapon may slow you. We must consider both."

Then Nikolas continued, "You should attack a southbound convoy and position on the east curve. The trucks will slow before they enter the turn. You must wait and attack the trucks at the end of the column. The last ten? What do I know? They will slow and give you a target, then when your mortar and bazookas find their marks, the wreckage will block the lead trucks from reinforcing those under attack.

"Still, your retreat and cover will not come easy. You will be in olive groves and sand and the fields of farmers. If you can, plant charges along the roadway to stop the Germans from advancing on you. Launch the attack, then detonate the charges when the German infantry advances. Kill an officer, and they will be a snake without its head. They will whip and flail but go nowhere.

"We will need to talk about sending our fighters. When do you plan to leave?"

Yanni looked at Stavros, then back to Nikolas, "Two days from now, maybe three. We expect a resupply drop Wednesday."

Dimitra said, "We will talk about sending fighters. How many if we do?"

Yanni said, "Ten to twenty and someone who knows the area. We'll use a section and a squad of our men, seventeen with officers. Sixteen without Johnny."

Dimitra asked, "How is your recovering commando?"

Stavros said, "If we can borrow two mounts, we'll check on him this afternoon."

Dimitra said, "I will travel to Platanos this afternoon. I need to check on the telephone wiring. Vasilios will ride with me. We will take a detachment of four. You are welcome to join us, Lieutenant. Bring a sleeping roll. My mother is preparing dinner, and it will be late and dark when we finish. We will spend the night."

On the return walk to the monastery, the men talked about Yanni going with Stavros to Platanos. But Yanni told Stavros he needed to ready the drop zone, and since Stavros would be with an andarte detachment, security should not be a problem.

Then Yanni asked Stavros, "What was that about the pastry?"

Stavros said, "I brought a pastry from Platanos for Dimitra. Her mother told me it was her favorite since she was a girl. I had it wrapped, and I meant to give it to her the morning of the raid. It got lost in the shuffle, and the big fisherman must have found it after everybody left. He saw me carry it into the meeting."

"Flattery by food. Good strategy. I approve," Yanni said, nodding.

"It was a friendly gesture. Help smooth relations with the locals. Just like the directive says," answered Stavros.

"You're the commander. You don't owe me an explanation," said Yanni.

Stavros realized he had answered defensively.

Then, after a moment of silence, Yanni continued, "You know if she were any other woman, I'd say you follow the sweets with flowers. But in her case, a couple bars of C2 might do the trick."

Chapter 58

Dimitra, Stavros, and two female fighters reached Eva's house in the late afternoon. Along the way, Dimitra inspected the telephone storage site to check on the poles, copper wire, handsets, and insulators. She had concerns. She counseled Vasilios at length away from the others, ordering him to increase security at the site. She knew the value of copper wire. She worried about pilfering and thievery that would cause ELAS to waste time hunting bandits and delivering their deserved punishment. Better an ounce of prevention.

"Vasilios, you are to stay here and guard these materials until you are relieved," ordered Dimitra. Then she looked at the two fighters in the column's rear, motioned them forward, and ordered them to stay with Vasilios.

When the party arrived at Eva's, Dimitra ordered the two remaining andartes to post at the entrance to her yard. The women tied their mounts, shouldered their Enfields, and took posts at both ends of the fence. Stavros thought they looked sharp, well drilled.

Eva met them halfway down the walkway. "My sweetness, I am so happy to see you. You look better in your uniform than the peasant disguise. And you, Professor Commander, nice to see you."

Dimitra chuckled at Eva's salutation.

Stavros said, "It is good to see you, ma'am."

Eva gave Dimitra a robust hug, then nodded to Stavros.

"Come, come, sit on my plateia. We will drink and talk. Then I will finish the meal," insisted Eva.

As they walked, Stavros asked, "How's Johnny?"

"See for yourself," answered Eva.

When they reached the doorway, Stavros could see into the kitchen where Johnny stood at the sink peeling potatoes. Stavros said, "Corporal, have you been disciplined?"

"Lieutenant, great to see you. No, no, Eva said I could help. This was all I could offer. I'm getting good at it," answered Johnny.

"Are you feeling better?" asked Stavros.

"Oh yeah. The pain's almost gone. The swelling is down, and I can stand on the leg for a few minutes. I'm better. I don't know about riding a horse, though. The doc says I need another week of rest. But if you need me in camp, I'll report for duty," Johnny said with a smile.

"At ease," said Stavros. "Get your rest, and we'll check in next week. Just take it easy."

Eva stuck her head around the kitchen doorway. "He is a dutiful apprentice, no? He is good with the peeler. I will teach him to carve chicken as he advances in my course work. For now, his marks are exceptional."

With Eva gone, Johnny lowered his voice. "Heard about the raid in Nafpaktos. The doc told me. Did we help?"

Stavros nodded. "We were there. We took ten men. We were lucky. Things went well, no OSS or andartes casualties. We busted Yiorgos out of jail. I wonder how the doctor knew?"

Johnny said, "They've got a lively scuttlebutt network, Lieutenant. Eva talks to three or four people a day. They swap rumors. They get a lot of news over the telephone in the municipal building. I think the hotel has a phone, too. The rest is over the radio. BBC is a big hit. Did you know Dimitra's dad worked in the municipal building? He was the head guy. He oversaw records for the municipality and this entire region. I still don't know how he died. Eva doesn't talk about it. But he was an important man.

"Have we got any other missions set?"

"We're working on one," said Stavros, and left it at that.

Eva looked around the doorway again. "Professor Commander, come sit. We can talk for a few minutes, and then I need to continue my instruction of the apprentice chef. He will leave here with another stripe for his shoulder boards."

Johnny smiled.

Stavros sat at the little iron table in the plateia under the vines. The bees still buzzed. Eva brought two fruit glasses of rhoditis wine and set them before the couple. She said, "With love from Patras."

Stavros looked at Dimitra. "Thanks for inviting me. It's a genuine pleasure to visit with your mother. And Johnny looks good."

"Yes, your man looks good. My mother, however, is a pleasure until she isn't. She is my mother, so I love her. But she is an inquisitor. She would have fit well with the Spanish Catholics in 1478, no?"

Stavros smiled.

Dimitra said, "Do you think it harsh to leave Vasilios guarding the wire?"

This surprised Stavros. Dimitra was second-guessing. She was always so confident and poised. "If he is under your command and the task was necessary, then no."

"He is so young. I have told him before not to temp thievery with the people's property. He thinks everyone believes as he does . . . the revolution comes first, the people will prevail, upright party members set sterling examples for the masses. He is not so practical. I will leave him there tonight. We can retrieve him tomorrow. The andartes will protect him.

"If we temp banditry and someone steals the wire, then we will search for them, find them, and punish them. All of this is a waste of time, fighters, and blood. I tell Vasilios he cannot trust that everyone is resolute and dedicated like him. I tell him he must be practical. I have preached this for years. Still, he lives with his head in the clouds."

The last comment made Stavros think about Yiorgos and his thoughts of a priest. Stavros asked, "What do you think Yiorgos was doing in Nafpaktos?"

"It was a secret. He was there to plan something he has not shared with me. Yiorgos is a headstrong man. He hates the

Germans. I think he was working on a plan. Something big. But why he went to Nafpaktos, I could not say. You have been there with him. Can you say?"

Stavros shook his head. But in the recesses of his memory, he pictured the lengthy conversation Yiorgos had with the priest at Antirrio. "Nothing, only speculation."

"Then speculate."

"Well . . . he talked with a priest in Antirrio. They talked for a long time. He left the priest three sovs so we could use the church bell tower to watch the ferry operation. Yiorgos left me with the impression he thought sinking a ferry was a fantasy, but. . . ." Stavros shrugged.

"It *is* a fantasy. The operation is well guarded, and there is no way to deliver a charge powerful enough to sink the boat. Are you still thinking of making an attack?"

"I would like to make an attack, yes. But I have yet to find the vulnerability. Yiorgos may have seen something and not shared it with me," answered Stavros.

"Humph. . . ."

She sipped her wine, then added, "Thank you for the galaktoboureko."

"Sure. My pleasure. I didn't know you saw it. I thought your sentry ate it. He thanked me for it this morning," said Stavros.

"He did. And he got an extra watch for his indiscretion. I recognized the baker's wrapping in all the chaos that morning. When you came in, I noticed. I didn't think about it until we returned to Chómori. Then it disappeared. I asked Ajax, and he confessed like a schoolboy."

"Ajax, so that's his name. Thanks, I'll remember. He's a big guy. It is fitting," said Stavros.

"He's a good man. He has been with us since the days of fighting the Italians in Epirus. Before EAM-ELAS. He knew my father," said Dimitra.

Stavros nodded. He didn't want to pry.

"So, your father was a record keeper here in Platanos?"

"Yes. He was the municipal councilor. He kept all the records for the villages in this area. Birth records, military records, death records, marriages, family reports. Each village has a clerk who gets his information from the priest, then all the records come to Platanos where my father organized them. That is how I gathered the guerrillas who fought with the Hellenic Army against the Italians. He was meticulous and organized and respected for his thoroughness."

"How did he meet your mother?"

"They met at university, Aristotle, in Thessaloniki. My alma mater. Father was from here, from Platanos. My mother was from the city. She studied music, and he studied administration. They married upon graduation and moved to Platanos. Then I was born, an only child, and here I am. That is the story, very tidy," answered Dimitra.

"And you, Mr. Professor Commander. What is your story?"

He thought first about telling the harmless version where his mother dies in childbirth. Then he thought of Dimitris's letter and wanted to tell the truth. He demurred, "It's not a delightful story. It's depressing."

"If you don't want to tell it, I cannot force you."

"No . . . it is not that I don't want to tell it. It is hard. It is hard to tell."

Dimitra pinned Stavros with her stare. "We do hard things every hour of every day, Stavros. You and I live in a world where the things we say and the decisions we make can mean someone lives, or someone dies. No matter how difficult . . . I will listen." She reached across the table and squeezed his hand, her smile reassuring.

"Right. Okay, here's the condensed version. My mother and father are from Crete. They met in Piraeus boarding the boat to come to America. My father was alone, and my mother was traveling with an aunt and uncle. They courted in New York City.

My dad worked as a bootblack. Then, my mother's uncle heard of jobs in Colorado and moved West. My father followed. All the Greeks thought they could get cheap land in Colorado. They all wanted to be farmers.

"My father took a job with a mining company. They married, and I was born a year later. That fall, the miners went on strike, and the union built a tent colony. The workers lived in company housing, and when they struck, the company evicted them. So, they lived in tents."

Stavros struggled. She said, "It is a story like any other. Tell it and the telling will free you to see it as a story. It is *your* story but nothing more."

Stavros worried he looked ridiculous. He was the commander of an American OSS Operational Group, and he didn't have the courage to tell his story. He felt vulnerable. He worried Dimitra would see him as half a man. Yet something compelled him to continue.

"I was one. It was just after my first birthday. It was night, and my father was away in the hills with the other Greek miners. They were on patrol, armed. The strike was violent, and the miners defended themselves against the company guards.

"Two men came into the tent and attacked my mother. They killed her. Stabbed her. She fought them, but they overpowered her.

"My mother's sister wrote to Harry Hantzis. She had never met him. But she had received a letter from him. Harry is the son of Dimitris Hantzis. His name in America is Harry, Harry Hantzis. My mother's brother saved Harry while fighting the Turks in Epirus and died doing it. There was an honor bond between the families. My aunt knew Harry was the son of Dimitris, the lawgiver for Chómori.

"Anyway . . . Harry went to Colorado to avenge my mother's death. He searched for her killers with my father and their friend Dimitri. They found one, and my father killed him. The other is still alive. I will find him one day and end his life.

"The strike was violent. It lasted two years. There was a lot of bloodshed. My father, Harry, and Dimitri left the strike and returned to work. They were not rich men and had to make a living. My father began working for the railroad, and a year and a half later, he married Marta. Marta, my stepmother, was with her family in St. Louis and had been my mother's best friend in Colorado. She cared for two children, my stepbrother and sister. The children belonged to her brother, who died in the strike. Their mother died in childbirth. Marta is a wonderful woman and a great stepmother. I learned Italian from her.

"That is my story. The condensed version."

Dimitra's mouth went slack. She felt close to Stavros, attracted to his resolve. His story was more than she expected. She had a million questions. Instead, she only asked, "Have you spoken with Dimitris?"

"Yes. He showed me a letter from Harry that filled in some blanks."

Dimitra said, "They are a prominent family. The Italians killed his son, George, last summer."

Stavros nodded. "Maybe you are right. Telling the story makes it a story. That may be easier to deal with than vague thoughts and notions. Thanks for listening."

Dimitra reached across the table to touch Stavros's hand again. He touched her back.

As their touch lingered, Eva rounded the door with a pot of soup. She saw the intimacy and cocked her head, but said nothing. She set the soup on the table and returned to the kitchen. Dimitra and Stavros looked across the table at each other.

Eva returned and set places for four people. She said, "I am taking soup to your guardians, and then we can begin. Do you need more wine?" She refilled the two glasses from a tin decanter. "Professor Commander, will you please get the stool for Johnny's leg?"

Stavros retrieved the stool from a flower bed where Eva had been weeding.

Eva went to the kitchen and came back with two oversized bowls of avgolemono soup that she walked to the female andartes at the fence.

Johnny hobbled to the table on one crutch and rested his leg on the stool.

Eva returned. "No wine for you, my patient. Wine makes for swelling." Then she began ladling the creamy soup into the bowls, releasing the tang of lemon.

It was a wonderful meal. First came the avgolemono soup with fresh crusty bread and olive oil infused with ground oregano and parsley. The main course was roast chicken stuffed with lemons, garlic, and rosemary. The potatoes Johnny peeled were roasted with oil and lemon and garlic and served with a horta salad. Then Eva served coffee and a thick, velvety yogurt with walnuts and honey. Midway through the meal, Eva took overflowing plates to the female andartes on guard duty.

Stavros smiled and grinned the entire meal. Eva offered choice observations and played against the innocence of Johnny and Stavros. Eva was playful but relentless. Dimitra pursed her lips and rolled her eyes at her mother's jabs and parries. Stavros relaxed into the evening. The wine lightened his mood, and the telling of his family's story unburdened his soul. That Dimitra listened and consoled warmed his heart. In the candlelight of Eva's garden, Dimitra looked as beautiful as any woman he had ever met and more substantial than any in his life save Marta.

After dinner, Dimitra went to give the female andartes their instructions. They would rotate on two-hour tours overnight. The one not on duty could bunk on a bench alongside Eva's flower garden. She collected their empty plates and bowls and brought them to Eva. Stavros helped Johnny inside, where he insisted he could help with the cleanup. But Eva shooed him away like a pesky moth. Stavros and Dimitra cleared the rest of the table and then were alone on the plateia with the candlelight flickering under the wisteria.

Dimitra said, "Come with me."

She took Stavros's hand. They walked into the backyard where the OSS men cleared the fallen ash. They crossed to the far corner flower bed. Faint light from the waxing crescent moon shone outlines of plants.

Dimitra asked, "Can you tell the one that is special?"

Stavros's botany insights were middling. But in the center of a leafy cluster, a flower the size of his fist bloomed in pale yellow and red. The smell was sweet and strong.

Dimitra said, "To bloom at night is a special flower, no? Eva is proud of her nychtoloúloudo. Do you know it better in Italian? *Bella di notte?*"

Stavros shook his head.

"My father started this plant years ago. It delighted him by returning and blooming every year. This is not so common in the mountains. It is a better plant for the warm islands. So, fill your eyes with this because you will not see. . . ."

Stavros reached for Dimitra, pulled her close, and kissed her deeply. In the faint light of the garden, they formed a majestic unity of pent desire. When they stopped and parted to look at one another, they heard the light footsteps of Eva rounding the walkway into the yard. They separated like guilty children, hands caught in the candy jar.

Eva said, "Can I. . . ?"

She saw the proximate couple and knew in an instant their intention.

"Can I make some coffee?"

Dimitra said, "No, Mother, I think we should go to bed. We need to ride early tomorrow. Isn't that right, Lieutenant?"

Stavros stammered, "Uh . . . yes, ma'am."

Eva said, "Very well. I will leave you to your flower gazing."

Eva pivoted to return to the house and took one step, then she couldn't help herself. She turned back to the couple and cooed, in her sweetest voice, "The nychtoloúloudo is remarkably intoxicating tonight, no?"

Chapter 59

"I can hear him. Dead ahead. Three miles out," said Yanni.

"Yep, sounds like a Skytrain," answered Gus.

The two men were under cover, waiting for the resupply drop and eager to get the show underway. Gus gave Squad Two a flash signal from his light. One flash meant the Skytrain was inbound. The squad readied the bonfires.

A minute later a flat gray, twin-engine aircraft overflew their location two hundred meters north, swaying the treetops. The throb of the Pratt & Whitney fourteen-cylinder Twin Wasp engines concussed the ground. Gus said, "We've got a good one tonight, Lieutenant."

Yanni nodded.

As the plane passed, the aircrew flashed its marker lights three times, signaling the mission was authentic and not a German ruse. Gus flashed twice, and the commandos set ablaze three gasoline-soaked bonfires arranged in a triangle with sixty-meter legs.

The commandos heard the plane make a wide circle, and with the next pass, the flight crew offloaded twelve canisters. Tumbling two-meter-long containers tugged static lines deploying pilot parachutes to open main canopies. The drop was flawless, and welcome supplies floated to earth under billows of black silk. The plane flew so low that the parachutes barely filled. The pilot circled again, and again the crew dropped twelve canisters, all falling within or near the triangle. With the drop complete, the Skytrain doffed its wings and set a return course to Brindisi.[89]

Gus said, "That guy was good. Low and slow. Nerves of steel."

Yanni, his blacked-out face in an appreciative smirk around his unlit cigar, nodded.

Chapter 60

The lanky young andarte, Manolis, stood before Dimitra reporting on Yiorgos.

"He was grouchy, Kapetánios. His face was not as swollen, but he still wore the bandage. His chest, too, was bandaged. His mother said he was eating well. She was pleasant. She fed us. The doctor said it was too soon for him to ride and he should rest another week, maybe two. He said the broken ribs would not heal if he tried to ride."

Dimitra asked, "Did you find out why he was in Nafpaktos?"

"Kapetánios, I asked him. I told him you wanted to know. He said he would tell only you in person and that no one else needed to know. That is what he said."

"He asked about the Americans, and I told him they were taking another mission. Then he held up his hand and said he did not want to know more. I think it worries him he is too close to the Germans in Nafpaktos. He would not want to give up information if captured," offered Manolis.

Dimitra said, "He is right. He is too close to the Germans, and we cannot protect him in Kato Dafni."

Dimitra stood from behind her desk in the schoolhouse and walked to the doorway. She motioned Ajax into the building and returned to her seat. Ajax stood front and center next to Manolis at attention. She said, "At ease, Ajax. Both of you, at ease. I have a question for you, Ajax. Can you get a car or truck in Nafpaktos? We need an ambulance to move our wounded stratiotikós from Kato Dafni to Platanos."

Ajax said, "These I can requisition. They are easy to steal, no?"

Dimitra corrected, "Liberate, Ajax. We will *liberate* a vehicle to evacuate our comrade."

Ajax said, "Yes, Kapetánios. Liberate, that is what I meant to say."

"Good. Ajax, you are in charge. Manolis, you go with him. We will move Yiorgos to Platanos, where he can be safe and recuperate. He too can stay with my mother. She has cared for two fighters before, so she should have no problem. The doctor in Platanos will look in on him. Take one other fighter, then Ajax can drive to Platanos and the other two will ride behind. You'll leave the vehicle in Platanos because the road to Chómori is still impassable," ordered Dimitra.

Ajax said, "Yes, Kapetánios. May I suggest something?"

Dimitra nodded.

"The road to Chómori is blocked in only one place. That is where the rocks have fallen across the roadway. The rest of the way is passable. If we remove the rock with charges, then we can drive all the way to Chómori. Then, if we like, we can use another charge to block the road again," said Ajax.

"Better we take him to Platanos for now. If we use charges on the fallen rocks, we may undermine the roadway and then it will be impassable until we reconstruct it. Let us wait until the Americans can help. They know the charges better. We will wait."

Ajax and Manolis nodded.

Dimitra dismissed them.

Chapter 61

The white-over-red Bedford sat parked at a gravel pit north of Kato Dafni on the banks of the Mornos River. Ajax knew these British trucks to be indestructible and easy to start. He pulled the ignition wires from under the dashboard and twisted together the voltage leads. Then he tapped the starter lead to the hot wire, and the engine turned over but didn't fire. Ajax depressed the cold-start knob on the firewall. The motor caught and spun to life. It ran rough for a minute, but smoothed as the engine heated. It was 0100 hours when he left the gravel pit with the means to evacuate Yiorgos. Three horses and two andartes followed.

The Bedford was a sturdy vehicle with a three-ton frame. It would never win a race, but it had the power and gearing to negotiate the hills to Platanos. Its tandem rear wheels offered plenty of grip. Its flat open bed would be Yiorgos's berth for the night.

It was a quick drive to Yiorgos's house. Yiorgos awoke, surprised and groggy. His mother didn't want to see him go, but she knew it was for the best. She made a pallet in the truck's bed and the andartes helped Yiorgos up and into his mobile resting place.

The ride into the mountains was rough. The Bedford was sturdy. But what it offered in ruggedness, it lacked in suspension. Yiorgos felt every pothole and bump. For the next two hours, Ajax listened to Greek curses flying from the cargo bed. After every curse, Ajax leaned his head out of the window, and offered to the darkness and his commander, "Sorry."

Chapter 62

The way to Amfilochia was the route they followed with Yiorgos, from Parga to Chómori. Now, in reverse, it was familiar if not ingrained. Only the final five kilometers were new to OG II. It comforted the Americans to have Nikolas along. He knew every inch of this land, every goat trail, and every shortcut. Nikolas and Dimitra talked and decided he should go and take two other andartes. If asked, they would tell EAM-ELAS command this was a training mission. Their fighters went along to learn the 81mm mortar. With Yiorgos away, there seemed no reason to thin the Chómori force further or flaunt the orders of EAM-ELAS command.

The detachment was twenty-one men, Nikolas plus two officers, two section leaders and Squads Two, Three, and Four. Squad Two was short Johnny. They moved out with three mounts and six mules. They traveled by daylight through Thermos and along the northern shore of Limni Trichonida. Then they veered north of Agrinio into the Turk Mountains and camped outside the small settlement of Pirgi. The officers dismounted and the commandos sorted their gear and unburdened the mules. It was nearing dusk, and the rest of their movement would be in the dark. They would camp until 0200 hours before moving on.

Gus walked into the woods and unzipped his pants to relieve himself. He heard something sizable stirring in the bushes behind him. He heard grunts and rooting and turned to face a sow boar not over twenty meters away. Gus, the city boy, had never seen a boar in the wild and the sight mesmerized him. The boar looked up, snorted, pawed the forest floor, and signaled no intention of giving ground. Gus estimated the pig at two hundred pounds. It was ugly, mean, and its stubby tusks menaced.

Gus drew his .45 and shot the beast in the head. It fell in its tracks. With the sound of his shot, eight striped piglets the size of footballs scrambled in every direction. Four OSS men and Nikolas also scrambled.

Nikolas was first on the scene. He sized up the commotion. "No rations tonight. Tonight is boar."

Nikolas told an OSS man to bring rope and an axe. The man returned to camp and brought both items. Nikolas chopped a straight, stout limb about two meters. He rolled the boar on its back and tied the rear legs spread apart to the limb. He tied the rope to the far ends of the limb and threw the ends over a firm branch above his head. He and two commandos hoisted the beast full length upside down. It was as long as they were tall. He drew a ten-inch knife from an ornate sheath on his bandolier and cut the skin around a hind leg, then he paused. He looked at Gus and asked, "Do you want the honor, Meleager?"

Gus shook his head. He didn't recognize the name, and the biggest game he had ever killed was a rabbit at Area B in Maryland. Even then, a Greek national had dressed that animal.

Nikolas set about his work, and in a matter of minutes, he heaved the dressed carcass over his shoulder and walked back to camp.

There was no time to construct a spit and rotisserie, so the men roasted cuts of meat on branches over the fire. As darkness drew on them, Nikolas asked Gus, "Have you been offering to Artemis? She has favored you tonight. You have slain the Calydonian Boar. Or his junior cousin."

Gus was clueless. "Calydonia? I thought this was Agrinio?"

Nikolas laughed. An andarte with Nikolas, a lean young man named Lambros, interjected, "This is myth. Calydonia is ancient. It was a kingdom between Missolonghi and Nafpaktos. There the goddess Artemis sent a boar, a huge male boar, a solitary boar, to wreck the harvest and punish the people."

"Why would she do that?"

Lambros explained, "That year, the king, Oeneus, failed in his offering, and this offended her. She was a god. They get offended. What do I know? That is what they are good at."

Gus asked, "Did they kill it?"

Nikolas said, "The king's son, Meleager, hunted the boar as did the woman, Atalanta. Atalanta was no ordinary woman. Her parents abandoned her at birth because she was a girl. Bears found her and raised her. She was a deadly hunter. She took the first shot, and her arrow wounded the boar so Meleager could kill him. This made Meleager fall in love with her."

Gus said, "So the young couple saved the day, got married, and lived happily ever after?"

Lambros shook his head. Then Nikolas spoke. "That is not a Greek ending. That is an American ending. In Greece, the killing must go on.

"Meleager fights with his uncles, who were also hunting the monster. They feel they should share in the glory. Meleager kills them. Then he gives the boar's pelt to Atalanta.

"Then Meleager's mother, Althaea, the wife of Oeneus, whose brothers her son has just killed, burns a magic stick given to her by the Fates. This seals Meleager's destiny, and he dies. Then she kills herself. Atalanta keeps the pelt. There is more, but I cannot remember."

Gus asked, "So what is the lesson?"

Both Lambros and Nikolas shrugged. Nikolas said, "It is myth. For lessons, you must go to school."

Stavros chuckled. The image of Atalanta suggested Dimitra, but he quickly put her out of his thoughts. He was on a mission. What mattered were his men and success. His thoughts of Dimitra lingered when Nikolas turned to him and Yanni.

Nikolas said, "Tonight we will march to Lepenou. That will position us on the east side of the Petalas range. The easier way is to the west, but there runs Ionia Odos. We will rest tomorrow during the day, then march to the ambush. A night's march. Then we can scout and plan weapons placement. Your explosives men will plant their charges the following night, and the next day we wait. When a long convoy travels south, we will spring the trap."

Stavros and Yanni nodded.

Nikolas asked, "How long will it take to ready the mortar?"

Yanni said, "Once we find a firing position, it only takes ten minutes to set up. The problem comes in registering the position."

Nikolas shrugged. Yanni said, "Registering is zeroing the weapon, establishing a position from which we make aiming changes. Since we can't lob practice rounds before the attack, this will be seat-of-the-pants."

Nikolas asked, "Seat-of-the-pants? This is a new slang to me."

Stavros said, "Right. Yanni means we will eyeball the target."

Nikolas again looked puzzled.

Yanni said, "Eyeball, seat-of-the-pants, they both mean we'll be guessing."

Nikolas said, "Yes. The firing will be more exact after the first round, no?"

Yanni and Stavros nodded.

Yanni went on, "We've got some eagle eyes in Squad Three. They are the mortar specialists. They guess range with the best of them. We'll be close. It shouldn't take over three rounds to walk it in on the Germans. We brought the eighty-one-millimeter, so we only packed two dozen rounds. Hit-and-run, right? But once we're on target, those shells will leave an impression."

Nikolas asked, "How many men for the mortar?"

"The Marine Corps manual says five. We've trained with four, but we can operate with three," answered Yanni.

"Three is good," said Nikolas. "We will need men forward to cover the bazookas when they advance. I do not know the land, only that it will not give much cover. We will see when we arrive. I hope your men are good at hiding."

Stavros and Yanni looked at one another and smiled. Yanni said, "They are flesh-and-blood ghosts."

Chapter 63

"Bearing three-zero-niner. Range nineteen hundred to two thousand meters. Set two kilometers. We're firing dead into the wind. The chop on the bay looks steady at five to ten. Correct fifty meters positive for the wind. The elevation adds twenty meters range negative, so correct thirty positive net. That should put us on the road at the apex of the curve. And let's hope that's where they stop."

Elias, the Squad Three leader, recited the estimations to Lambros, who wrote them on a notepad. It was early morning, and the team lay prone with the rising sun at their backs. Camouflaged head-to-toe in brush and webbing, their faces and hands smeared with olive drab camo paint, the men were the ghosts Yanni bragged about. The commandos peered through powerful binoculars from a three-hundred-meter rise above their target, two kilometers distant. Elias pushed a Y-shaped branch into the earth to mark the firing position. The site was as near the ambush as possible but allowing cover from overflights and prudent retreat. With the readings recorded, the men crawled back into the cover of the nearby low-growing brush.

That night, their second on target, Squad Three and the two andartes assembled the 81mm mortar. They carried the components two kilometers east from the staging area where the mules and mounts remained tethered under heavy cover. In the inky darkness, the squad lugged the thirty-six-pound barrel, twenty-seven-pound mount, and twenty-nine-pound baseplate plus the sight unit to the firing position. Then they retrieved the twenty-four rounds of M45 ammo, each weighing ten pounds. These they transported in protective metal cases of three rounds each.

The squad dug a depression for the baseplate to keep it from inching backward with each firing. They stamped the baseplate into the depression, making certain its spikes sunk deep into the earth. Stabilizing the weapon was key to exact aiming corrections. Lambros lowered the breech plug at the closed end of the barrel into the baseplate socket and twisted the barrel a quarter of a turn to lock it. Then he held the barrel straight up, and another squad man fitted the bipod legs and secured them to the barrel. He pushed the pointed bipod legs into the earth fifteen inches toward the target astride the line of fire. Then Elias, who would be the squad leader and the gunner in a truncated three-man team, removed the sight unit from its padded wooden case. He attached it to the left side of the weapon facing downrange. Once secure, he set a deflection of 3,200 mils and an elevation of 1,100 mils and leveled all the bubbles. Lambros laid a square swab over the end of the upright barrel and dribbled oil onto the cloth. Then, with a purpose-built plunger, he twisted the swab around the end and pushed the oily rag into the barrel. He withdrew the rag, turned it over, twisted it around the plunger, and again pressed it into the barrel. With the weapon assembled and lubricated, and the ammo staged, the squad built a hasty lean-to over the firing position. They covered its frame with webbing and branches from the shrubs that dotted the hillsides.

A kilometer and a half north, the bazooka teams, BARs, and riflemen dug in and camouflaged their fighting holes. The sappers worked through the night to lay mines and charges in a protective line to discourage German pursuit. They lay the mines randomly, as near the roadway as possible. The C2 charges awaited infantry advancing beyond the mines. Wired for manual detonation, these charges formed a defensive picket. The sappers covered the wiring and dusted their footprints in the sandy loam. As the sun rose on the morning of June 3, 1944, sixteen commandos and their weapons were indistinguishable from their surroundings and waiting to spring like a well-oiled bear trap.

Stavros, Yanni, and Nikolas took a command position on elevation halfway between the mortar and infantry. They used handheld Motorola SCR536 radios to communicate with the squad and section leaders. Nicknamed *Handie-Talkies,* these five-pound units worked to about six kilometers. Their attack formation separated the detachment by less than three. If the radios failed, they would revert to Very pistol signals.

The commandos were in position and ready as the sun rose over the hills behind them. The riflemen and bazookas held a 130-meter elevation advantage, and the mortar was 300 meters above the roadway. At about that time, 0630 hours, a German supply convoy mustered at the Port of Igoumenitsa. In its thirty-three vehicles moved troops, ammunition, fuel, and rations. In tow were eight 7.5 cm Gebirgsgeschütz 36 mountain artillery pieces, six destined for Italy's Po Valley. With the Allies on the outskirts of Rome, Germany was bolstering its defenses in the northern mountains. The artillery would slow the top speed of the convoy to forty miles per hour. After a stop in Ioannina to deliver two of the field pieces, the convoy was underway southbound at 0900 hours.

At 1100 hours a pair of Messerschmitt Bf 109s overflew OG II north to south. The fighters were overhead without warning, flying low and fast. All was quiet. Then the ground shook with the exhaust drubbing of the Daimler-Benz V-12s. They flew low enough that Stavros saw their 20mm gondola cannons hung under their wings. He knew these to be potent weapons for ground attack missions.

Stavros keyed the radio twice and received a series of clicks, signaling all positions ready. Nikolas said, "The planes come before the convoy. They are approaching."

At 1137 hours Stavros spotted the first vehicle two kilometers north of the turns. He keyed the radio with the ready command. The mortar team pulled back the lean-to and cleared their firing angle. The riflemen in their fighting holes responded to their team and section leaders. The two bazooka teams loaded rounds. The sapper team wired the first picket charge and raised the plunger on the Livens detonator.

It all happened quickly, just as the plan required. The convoy slowed as it entered the first turn, then slowed again a thousand meters later as it entered the second turn. Halfway through the procession, the vehicles came to a stop in the firing zone. Stavros keyed his radio and commanded, "Fire."

The next sound was a dull *pumpft* to his left as the first shell launched from the mortar. Then he heard the BARs open with their deep cadence to his right. Next came the M1s of the riflemen sniping at truck drivers and officers in their open cars. The mortar shell fell twenty meters short, and Elias corrected. His second shell found a troop carrier with a direct hit. The vehicle exploded and burst into flames, blocking traffic in both directions. Now that he had his range, Elias began walking the shells along the line of vehicles at thirty-meter intervals.

German troops dismounted and took cover behind their equipment. Two trucks at the far end of the convoy began backing away from the fight and tried to turn around in the roadway. They were trailering artillery, so their backing was slow and cautious. This gave time for the bazooka teams to advance and fire from eighty meters. The first team missed wide, but the second team, with Gus at the trigger, found its mark on the second truck. A few seconds later, the lead truck exploded in flames as the first bazooka team found its range.

By now, the mortar team had lobbed half of their shells onto the sitting ducks. A detachment of German infantry formed behind the wreckage, waiting for leadership to advance on the OSS riflemen. A German officer held his pistol aloft and pointed toward the OSS fire. The first squad to cross the roadway climbed over the drainage ditch and into the sparse hillside. They were fifty meters up the slope when a man flew into the air, propelled by a mine. The squad stopped dead in its tracks, knowing better than to lie down. They were easy targets for the BARs and M1s of the sharpshooters as half of their number fell to OSS bullets.

Another squad formed and advanced, and this time cleared the mines, but they didn't clear the C2. One hundred meters beyond the minefield, a picket of C2 charges awaited. As the German squad approached, a sapper fell on the plunger and detonated the first line. They rewired for the second picket and waited for targets.

Elias and the mortar team finished with their ammo and began disassembling the weapon. Without ammo, they were out of the fight. They packed the components and began their retreat to the staging area.

Stavros noted the bazooka teams had advanced as far as they could under the cover of riflemen and BARs. The bazookas were taking longer range shots, most of which were off target. Stavros counted twenty vehicles damaged or in flames, and he saw thirty German bodies scattered. With the sound of the final C2 picket detonating, he ordered retreat. The bazookas fell back first, covered by the infantry. All fighters were into heavy cover in a matter of minutes, and Stavros saw no organized German ground pursuit. It was the pursuit he didn't see that laid him low.

The canopy above and the ground below erupted like the earth was coming apart. Then he heard the cannon's report and the V-12s signature. This all happened in the longest second of his life. Stavros dove under a rocky ledge. Nikolas and Yanni joined him, and the three men huddled together. For all its sophisticated armaments, the detachment had little to use against planes. The BARs were it. The detachment reported under cover and invisible from the air. Stavros thought the Messerschmitts may have been strafing blind, hoping to draw fire. Any fire would give away their location. He radioed the detachment to hold fire and stay in cover. Then they waited for another pass.

The earth again erupted. This rip in the canopy came perpendicular to the first. The planes had circled only ninety degrees, then stenciled a giant X on the landscape. Stavros looked at Yanni and Nikolas. Nikolas said, "They are hunting. They want us to fire."

Stavros keyed his radio and again told his men to hold fire and stay under cover.

The detachment was spread out. Stavros, Yanni, and Nikolas were in the middle of a hundred-meter long column with the mortar team nearest the mounts and the staging area. Again, they waited, and this time the strafing came from the south, dead ahead to their line of travel. The tree canopy erupted, and the earth spit chunks of debris over their heads. But with this pass, Stavros keyed the radio and ordered the detachment forward, prepared to cover before the next pass. Yanni looked at his watch and held up two fingers. The detachment moved and when two minutes passed, Stavros ordered everyone to take cover. This time the pass came east to west again, making a gigantic X cross behind their line of travel. The detachment was out of their target zone. Again, the men moved and again they took cover after two minutes. But this time was different. Instead of the silent eruption, then the sound of the warring Messerschmitts, the commandos heard the launch of artillery. The shells fell behind the detachment, and Stavros gave the order to move forward to the staging area.

The staging area was over three kilometers from the ambush. Under heavy cover and on the opposite side of the hills, the men packed the mules. It was 1330 hours and without the cover of darkness, movement would be chancy. They were invisible to the artillery spotters on the far side of the hills. But if the planes returned and found them, their situation would deteriorate. The detachment was two and a half kilometers from favorable guerrilla terrain, forested hills with full cover and defensible redoubts.

Stavros ordered the men forward, and the column moved out in good order. The trickiest part of this retreat was a dry riverbed they had to cross to get to the better cover. The artillery couldn't spot them, but a plane might. Stavros sent lookouts one hundred meters up and down the creek bed. Getting across would be a matter of luck. They couldn't hear the planes flying low and fast until they were right on top of the men. Still, the Germans were firing as though the detachment was on the other side of the hilltops and north of their position. The five minutes it took to move the train across the riverbed and into the cover were terrifying. But everybody did their job and pulled their weight. After the tense crossing, the detachment was into friendly territory and, so far, suffered no casualties.

They marched for half an hour, then the column rested. Stavros talked with Yanni and Nikolas. Nikolas said, "If we keep moving, we can reach Kompothekla by sundown. This is a friendly village. Even if we do not enter, we will not worry about the Germans there. There, we can decide if we want to move on or rest for the night."

Stavros asked, "Should we worry about the Germans following?"

Nikolas answered, "They will not. They have their orders telling them to move their convoy. Their officers will not want to enter the mountains after dark. We should be careful, but it is not likely that they will follow. They used their artillery and airplanes, and in their reports to headquarters, that will be enough. They will report dozens of Greeks killed in their counterattack. Then, days from now, they will send their murderers to savage some poor village miles from the ambush. The Germans want to leave Greece. Fighting here, they have no heart. As I have said before, they will soon be Italians."

Chapter 64

On the afternoon of June 4, 1944, a day after their ambush and unknown to the retreating commandos, General Mark Clark and the American 5th Army entered Rome. It was the first Axis capital to fall. Two days later, with the OSS detachment on the last leg of their retreat to Chómori, General Eisenhower launched D Day. When troops went ashore at Normandy, the Greek Operational Groups realized they would not be part of a European invasion via the Mediterranean's soft underbelly. They were disappointed.

The regression of Greece as a military priority began in May 1943 with the defeat of Rommel in North Africa. When El Alamein fell, the need for an Axis line of communications through Greece vanished. Then, with the invasion of Sicily in July 1943, the Germans began doubting that the Allies commanded sufficient landing craft in the Mediterranean to invade Crete or the Greek mainland. D Day confirmed German guesswork, and the military backwater of Greece became a theater whose only importance was securing land routes of retreat and redeployment.

While the Germans were receding in Greece but still present and deadly, the conflict between political movements intensified. The battle for the future of Greece was, at its core, a clash between Churchill and the Greek communists.

Through it all, the OSS mission remained and the American bond with the andartes grew. By mid-July 1944, seven of the eight OSS Operational Groups were in Greece. The eighth group would parachute into Macedonia in early September. The OGs established bases in Epirus, Roumeli, Thessaly, Olympus, Mount Paiko, Peloponnesus, and Macedonia. One hundred and eighty-one OSS commandos fought in Greece.[90]

Chapter 65

Yanni leaned against the doorsill and surveyed the monastery courtyard. He said, "It's good to have Johnny back. He's moving well with the cast. That kid never complains. He's been on KP for two weeks and not a peep. When does he get the cast removed?"

Stavros, seated at his desk proofreading an action report, spoke without looking up. "Next week will be two months. We'll take him to the doc in Platanos and get him checked out. The last word was he should be good to go. It'll take some time before he can keep up on a march. We'll give him a mount or assign him to home guard until he gets his strength back."

"He looks like he gained ten pounds,"

"Eva," said Stavros.

"Did you see Yiorgos yesterday?" asked Yanni.

"No. But I hear he's still favoring his ribs and not a pleasure to be around. I need to talk to him and see what the big secret is. I'm sure Dimitra knows why he went to Nafpaktos. But she hasn't said. Do you want to take a walk and see if we can get it out of him?" asked Stavros.

"Sure. Hey, did you see what came in last night's supply drop?" Yanni held out a flat gray stone the size of a deflated basketball.

Stavros said, "You're kidding me? Bari is sending rocks? We've got plenty of those."

"It's a mine. Set it on the road and hope the Germans run over it. They also disguise them as donkey and horse crap."[91]

"Right. Drop them in the road and hope Germans run over them and Greeks don't? How many did we get?" asked Stavros.

"A dozen."

"Bring it along and we'll show Yiorgos. It might cheer him up."

On the way to the schoolhouse, Stavros and Yanni passed the Hantzis home and Dimitris waved from his grape trellis. Yanni said, "That old guy's your buddy. How did you get to know him?"

"He's a friend of the family."

Yanni waited for more. When Stavros didn't offer, he dropped his inquiry.

It was true, Dimitris was a friend of the family. Stavros spent hours talking with the man and learning the care of grapes. Dimitris shared family letters and stories. Now Stavros had a fuller picture of the Hantzis family and Harry's help to solve the murder of his mother. Dimitris was circumspect. But his occasional insight illuminated dim notions where Stavros sought clarity.

Perhaps every son feels less than his father. Stavros commanded trained and vetted soldiers, elite without equal. They drilled and honed their fighting skills. They all expected death and injury upon entering Greece. All had volunteered for lopsided odds and outgunned encounters. But when Stavros thought of the hardship, perseverance, and bravery of his father, he felt lazy and undeserving.

Stavros had nothing resembling a deprived childhood. His father and Marta worked hard, taught Stavros to work hard, and supported him. But the mystery that descended on young Stavros at age sixteen, when Alex told him of this mother's murder, opened a blank chapter in his life's story. Stavros strove for completeness. He was an accomplished person. He had completed his academic life. He had completed his OSS life. Now, at thirty-one, he searched for a personal completeness. Dimitris Hantzis helped with that search. But as that void filled with emerging narrative, another, Dimitra, was blank and mysterious.

They performed the greeting routine at the schoolhouse entrance. Ajax lit his complimentary cigarette and looked pleased. Yanni showed Ajax the rock mine and the big man stepped back. Yanni chuckled and showed him it was unarmed. Ajax stood at ease.

Yanni and Stavros entered, and Dimitra and Yiorgos seemed pleased to see the OSS men. The two Americans pulled chairs from the wall to sit alongside Yiorgos in front of Dimitra. Stavros looked over and smiled at Yiorgos. "It's good to see you, stratiotikós. How do you feel?"

Yiorgos grimaced, "I am fine."

Dimitra said, "He is fine until he laughs, breathes deeply or mounts a horse. Then, not so good."

Stavros said, "Yep. Ribs take a long time to heal."

Yiorgos said, "Thank you and the other OSS men for coming to the jail. I am in your debt."

"You have already paid any debt with your wisdom and leadership. We are the ones in *your* debt."

Yiorgos said, "A bazooka for the jailhouse door? That was an inspired choice, no?"

Stavros smiled.

Yanni said, "We American Greeks are a practical people."

This produced smiles all around the room.

Then Yanni showed Dimitra and Yiorgos the rock mine.

Both were skeptical about its use with the same concerns Stavros had. They agreed it might be handy, but in restricted areas where only Germans traveled.

With the mood light, Stavros asked, "Yiorgos, can you say why you were in Nafpaktos? It is a mystery of some bearing, no?"

Yiorgos looked at Dimitra. She nodded. Then he said, "It is your fault."

Stavros looked at Yanni, puzzled.

"You and your American idea to sink a ferry. An idea too grand for humble Greeks, but not for Americans. Your idea infected my thoughts. But what do I know?

"I was only passing through Nafpaktos to meet the priest in Antirrio. He agreed to watch the German convoys to see if there was a pattern to their movements. If we have their pattern, then we might fashion an attack. It is that simple."

"Did the priest have anything?"

"He did. He had the days, times, numbers of vehicles, and other notes. I read it quickly. It was too much to memorize. I folded it and put it in my boot. I wore my old shepherd boots with the holes and tatter, so the Security Battalion pigs were not interested in taking them. They didn't search. I still have the paper, but I see no pattern. The priest is still watching, but I will need more sovs to keep him interested."

Stavros said, "Sovs are not a problem. But how will we get them to the priest?"

"The swine did not see me with the priest. They stopped me in Nafpaktos on my return. I was riding a donkey at night on a back street, and a party of the pigs were leaving a whorehouse and had fun with the poor old shepherd. Then they found my knife, the British dagger. They decided I must be an andarte, for no other Greek would carry a British knife. I told them I had traded a Britisher for the knife, my lamb for his knife. They didn't believe me and hauled me to jail. Then I saw the neighbor lady from Kato Dafni. She told her husband. I am lucky the Germans were busy, or they would have come sooner. Then. . . ."

Dimitra interrupted, "Then you would have died a horrible death and been of no use to any of us. You should have told someone about your trip. Your secret would have been safe, no?"

Yiorgos said, "Yes, Kapetánios."

Stavros asked, "Yiorgos, are you still interested in the ferry attack?"

"Perhaps. But it would be impossible without the German schedule. I have had other thoughts about getting a bomb aboard. But without a schedule, there can be no plan," said Yiorgos.

Stavros asked, "Have you ever heard of a limpet mine?"

Chapter 66

Politics is the prelude to war. The Government of National Unity, which the Mountain Government joined in mid-May, was a work in progress. Its political construction was like piling sand for a castle on a stormy Greek beach. Each bucket was well-intentioned but washed away by the inexorable swell.

In early July 1944, Papandreou remained prime minister with unwavering support from the king and Churchill. EAM-ELAS felt bold. They were the largest constituent of the Mountain Government, and they pushed forward a demand for seven of the fifteen cabinet seats instead of five. They also demanded that EAM-ELAS armed forces stay independent of British command. By the end of July, they demanded Papandreou resign. That didn't happen. Negotiations broke off, and Svolos, president of the Mountain Government, announced their withdrawal from the Government of National Unity.

With politics unraveling, the British and Papandreou began planning military options. In the summer of 1944, the British increased supplies to EDES, the anti-communist forces in Epirus. EDES, under commander Zervas, had twelve thousand fighters concentrated in a small area along the western coast.[92] EAM-ELAS commander Stephanos Sarafis divined the British strategy. Sarafis believed the British wanted EDES to eliminate EAM-ELAS west of the Arachthos River. With EAM-ELAS gone, Papandreou and the British could land Greek National Army units from Egypt and supporting British invasion forces on the Ionian Coast.

Sarafis's divination came to life on July 1, 1944, when EDES attacked the 24th Regiment of EAM-ELAS in Preveza with no British objection. EDES wanted control of Parga and its landing beach. But it wouldn't be a Greek story without overreach and hubris. EDES also attacked the Germans.

On July 3 through 6, EDES took ten kilometers of coastline near Parga, displacing German occupiers and landed five thousand reinforcements from the British-controlled Greek units in Egypt.[93] It took the German command a few days to verify that Zervas had betrayed them, and when they did, they decided to destroy EDES. On August 5, The Germans set the XXII Mountain Corps upon EDES.

EAM-ELAS, now with forty thousand fighters, also decided to eliminate EDES. The problem was that EDES was well-supplied by the British and, until their betrayal, received small arms and ammunition from local German commanders.[94] Attacking EDES was further complicated because the Germans controlled much of EDES territory. The western cities of Igoumenitsa, Ioannina, and Arta were major bases of German operations.

While Sarafis was inspecting his forces and organizing for an attack on EDES, the Germans launched mopping-up operations. They attacked the 9th ELAS Division along the Haliacmon River Basin in Northern Greece, inflicting two thousand casualties.[95] They plundered villages, burned them to the ground, and hauled off crops and cattle. EAM-ELAS fought off the Germans and the Security Battalions. But the question of arms and supplies remained. EAM-ELAS requests for supply drops from the British to fight the Germans went unanswered. In the summer of 1944, EAM-ELAS needed supplies and weapons.

On the night of July 25, 1944, following the Soviet recall of their ambassador to the Greek government in exile, a Soviet "training flight" took off from an Anglo-American airbase in Italy. The flight landed in Yugoslavia. and ten members of the Soviet Military Mission boarded. They left Yugoslavia for the British-built aerodrome in Thessaly. Two Soviet officers parachuted over Macedonia, and the remaining eight under the command of Colonel Popov reached EAM-ELAS HQ the morning of July 26.[96] They landed without British knowledge. The British found out when they intercepted a telegram from

Operation Pericles, three Greek American OSS spies who had infiltrated EAM-ELAS.[97]

On July 28, the Soviet delegation met with EAM-ELAS. The Greeks argued that, with Soviet support, they could eliminate EDES and strengthen their political position. The Soviets said they had no authority to order supplies, but they would return to Moscow with a list. The Greeks might have foreseen their request for gold, arms, and ammunition would go no further when the Russians could not supply the conference with vodka.[98] Sarafis gave them a list two days later, and that was the last they heard from the Soviets. No supplies or weapons came their way.

Stalin and Churchill had a tacit agreement. The Soviets would control the countries to the north, and Greece would remain in the British sphere of influence. This geographic distribution became formal with the Percentages Agreement concluded on October 9, 1944, by Churchill and Stalin in Moscow.

EAM-ELAS, friendless and undermined, sought a political compromise. Svolos, representing the pacifist wing of the Mountain Government, announced they would agree to the five cabinet seats offered before their withdrawal. EAM-ELAS agreed to nominal subordination to British command. On September 2, 1944, the Mountain Government ministers joined the Government of National Unity in Cairo.

Chapter 67

Dimitra's world churned. By the end of July, she no longer thought of KKE as her political home. Maria Svolos was right. The Soviets were not trustworthy, and the KKE still bent to their will. The Soviets had bigger fish to fry than fomenting a revolution and liberating Greek women. But leaving the KKE was neither simple nor safe.

Dimitra saw America as Greece's natural ally, and she found one American much to her liking. Stavros excited her. They had spent enough time together since the night in Eva's garden for her to know that he was not a passing fancy. He was solid, smart, complex, and honest. All qualities that lured her down a path of romance. But the war complicated things. Theirs was a path not of choice but of fate. She knew he was torn like her. How could he not be? He had men under his command whose lives were in his hands. She had the same, men and women and innocent villagers. Her responsibilities overshadowed her desires and fancies. She knew Stavros could disappear with a single communiqué from OSS command, a command unmoored, tossed in the tempest and fortunes of war. His pending departure disheartened her, but this she did not control.

She had Germans to fight and now EDES. Chómori was well east of EDES territory, but Sarafis had ordered Dimitra to ready a detachment to attack Zervas upon command. She sent Yiorgos, who had friends and former Hellenic Army comrades in EDES, to open a channel of communications. This outreach was risky, as it bypassed the EAM-ELAS chain of command. When Yiorgos returned with a disappointing report, her premonition darkened. EDES was under strict British command with no intention of accommodating EAM-ELAS. This meant only one thing. The bloody horizon for Greece was Greek killing Greek.

Dimitra sent word to Maria that she would like another meeting in Platanos. Dimitra needed a plan for shedding KKE discipline. Dimitra knew the twists and turns of KKE and the ins and outs of Central Committee politics. The KKE presented high-profile defectors as collaborationist conspirators, and the penalty was but one. No figure, no matter how high in the party's leadership, was immune. She hoped that her elected position as councilor for the Mountain Government offered some protection. But this was a flimsy notion, a clutching at straws. Still, a conversation with Maria, a woman with political resources at her command, was vital.

The two women met on a sweltering summer day under the shade in the Platanos courtyard. Maria again arrived in the old Austin flying Red Cross flags. This time she had with her a driver and a bodyguard. She was the wife of the President of PEEA, the Mountain Government, and herself an elected councilor.

Dimitra arrived in the Bedford truck Ajax liberated for Yiorgos's evacuation. Since then, the andartes and Americans had cleared the road to Chómori, and it was now passable for motor vehicles. They took the precaution of pre-wiring a boulder above a narrow section with C2 in case they needed to block it again. Ajax drove, and two armed female andartes rode in the truck's bed for security.

Maria dressed in the same simple dress and belt combination that Dimitra knew from many encounters. And still Maria wore no wedding ring. Dimitra decided this must be a security measure and not a political statement.

Dimitra was again in her village disguise. As the two women sat in the courtyard, they comforted themselves with folding fans when the mountain breeze was at bay.

After greetings, Maria began the conversation. She asked, "What are your thoughts on the Soviet denial of EAM-ELAS's request for arms, comrade? You, I'm sure, have heard the news, no?"

"Yes, I have heard this from my reluctant politikós. Even he cannot explain the denial. I think his blind allegiance to Mother Bear is fraying."

"There is little to explain," said Maria. "The Soviets have a deal with Britain. The British will receive Greece as a token of victory over the invaders, and the Soviets will have everything to our north. The Turks understand this. They will cut relations with Germany next week. Even the Bulgarians know this. Did you know the Bulgarians are ready to surrender? They joined with the Germans to gain Thessaloniki, and now they fear losing Eastern Macedonia, which they stole from Greece. When their friends of convenience leave, they will face Greece and the Turks, both hungry for retribution and land. They will withdraw from the Axis by September, no doubt. These are swift currents we swim in, comrade. Change is upon us, and the future is ours to call. What are your thoughts on your political affiliation?"

Dimitra leaned forward, "The KKE offers no easy separation. They will denounce me as a collaborationist. I will face a people's tribunal. They will sentence me to death or permanent exile. This is my future from a discipline I once respected but now fear. Do you have thoughts on my way free?"

Maria was studied. "We must consider the problem. You are a prominent woman. If you leave, the KKE will need to save face. Otherwise, they will do as you say, label you a traitor, then make an example of you. We must let them save face or silence your exit.

"My husband and the forward-thinkers in the PEEA are ascendant. The Soviet snub and the German offensive and the EDES attacks have tempered the KKE. Now that PEEA has ministers in the Government of National Unity, we may have a way out. But I need to speak with Alexandros. What are your thoughts? What are your demands?"

"There should be no trial, no public denunciation, no retribution. In Chómori, I am defended by the andartes, and my only opponent will be Vasilios. But he is becoming less KKE every day. The Americans, too, will defend me. But they are under orders not to engage in politics. The andartes can remain under EAM-ELAS discipline. I will remain Kapetánios, and I will obey the commands of Sarafis and Aris. But I will not be a member of KKE."

Maria thought for a moment, "My husband told me Greeks dislike being treated as schoolboys by their big nation headmasters. He said in Cairo, during the meetings, he felt the British treated the PEEA delegation as accused persons. He said this made him realize he was Greek first and a politician second. He said in all the names, PEEA, EAM, ELAS, EDES, and even KKE, the _Es_ stood for Greece.

"Yours, Dimitra, is a reckoning many will face. We are Greeks first. Outside control of any type, military occupation, or foreign ideology insults us all. Our independence, our timeless history of fighting invaders, elicit ideologies, and agonistic religions—these struggles unite us. I will talk to Alexandros soon. In the meantime, stay safe in Chómori."

Dimitra watched as Maria's Austin chugged away over the cobblestones of the courtyard, issuing a thin cloud of gray smoke. She went to the kafeneion and bought five servings of galaktoboureko, three of which she left with Ajax and the andartes, and two she carried with her to her mother's house.

Eva was kneeling over a flower bed along the side fence of her front yard. Dimitra called to her as she opened the gate. Eva looked up, surprised, "This is a pleasant development. Thank you for saving me from this heat and the stubborn weeds that bedevil my lonely life."

The two women hugged, and Dimitra looked at her mother, "Are you sad for Father's passing?"

"Well, of course I am, but that is not why I'm lonely. I am lonely because you took from me my two charges. Johnny, I miss like a son. Yiorgos, I miss like a cantankerous old goat."

Dimitra laughed, "I am sorry for your displeasure, but it is better for us that no fighters need rehabilitation."

Eva said, "My burden as a healer and a puller of weeds makes for trifling conversation. Come sit on the plateia. I will bring some lemonade, and we can eat the pastry. Then we can talk of indispensable matters. How is Professor Commander?"

Chapter 68

"What's it look like, Yanni?" asked Stavros.

"I see a German armored train in the siding with four eighty-one-millimeter mortars, eight fifty-caliber machine guns, two Flak thirty-eight auto-cannon twenty-millimeter antiaircraft guns. Check that, I see eight barrels, two quads. Six cars in the cut and a double-gang locomotive and tender setup. Both locos are fired. Coal smoke and steam issuing from each.

"I've got twenty ore-haulers in a small switching yard to the west. Looks like two switch engines and road power. In the vehicle pool, I see two armored troop carriers and thirty assorted trucks and transport.

"I see barbed wire and minefields around the mine face, armored train, and barracks. The barracks are big enough for at least a thousand troops. There are officer quarters to their left and I'd say they house fifty to one hundred.

"I see pill boxes north and south at both ends of the approach, two guns in each. Guard towers with searchlights and snipers, three of them.

"See for yourself,"

Yanni handed Stavros the powerful field glasses.

Stavros saw the same thing as his second. "They are taking no chances. I guess Bari and the AMM were right. This must be the German's last chrome mine. No chrome, no airplanes."

"No planes, no trucks, no cars, no locomotives, no ships. Makes it tough to fight a war," offered Yanni.

Stavros handed the binoculars to Nikolas. He peered into the switching yard.

"Among the rail cars, I see two klouves."

Then he handed the glasses back to Stavros.

Stavros looked at the switching yard and spotted the hostage crates. He'd heard of these wire-enclosed wagons filled with innocent Greeks that the Germans pushed in front of trains to discourage attacks, but he had never seen one. He nodded and handed the glasses to Yanni.

Yanni spotted the crates. "Those sons-of-bitches."

Nikolas said, "They may have hostages already in the compound."

The three men lay together on their bellies with a covered vantage of the Golines Chrome Mine. Dawn was upon them after a night of hiding. Now the view two kilometers to the southeast was obstructing with the rising sun. They made notes of the compound's defense, the mines' layout, drew a sketch of the perimeter, and decided it was time to retreat. Just as they were gathering their kits, the German public address system blasted to life broadcasting reveille. It was 0600 hours sharp.

Yanni asked, "Do you want to stick around for a count?"

"Sure, we've waited this long," said Stavros, settling back prone.

Each man made a silent count as the Nazi flag inched up the pole at the center of the assembly area. Its red background, centered white disk, and black swastika unfurled in the morning breeze. All three men gave the same estimate: one thousand troops plus officers. The conclusion of their reconnaissance was unavoidable. The Golines Chrome Mine was unassailable by an OSS ground attack. The three officer scouts and their men waiting in the hills to the west would need another approach.

The Germans needed chrome. The dark-gray mineral formed the hardened plating on aircraft engines and control gear. You could build an airplane without chrome, but it wouldn't fly long. When applied to a cast iron engine block at a thickness of one-ten-thousandth of an inch, and bathed in the right oil or lubricant, pistons in cylinders traveled reliably. Otherwise, they heated uncontrollably, fused, and had their utility reduce to that of a boat anchor. Every ball or roller bearing used to mount a crankshaft, or any rotating component, was made of chrome steel.

Chrome reached everywhere in industry and manufacturing. Stainless steel is 18 percent chrome. Chrome plates the breechblock dovetails on firearms, from rifles to Howitzers. Chrome plates machine tools and gauges, instruments needed to make precision components. Chrome-treated milling copy plates reduced the friction between the tool and the plate, another indispensable process in manufacturing.[99] The Germans needed chrome. In the summer of 1944, Greece was their last hope and the Golines Chrome Mine was their last source.

Turkey was a neutral nation during the occupation of Greece, but the Allies pressured her to take their side. In the spring of 1944, the Allies asked Turkey to stop chrome exports to Germany. Turkey balked, and the Allies threatened a blockade. Then, with the Germans on their heels and ready to leave the Balkans, Turkey relented on April 20, 1944, and cut off chrome shipments.[100]

Meanwhile, in March 1944, a four-man OSS Operational Group parachuted first into Bulgaria before coming to Greece. They trained 220 communist partisans. In May 1944, they blew up the Svilengrad railroad bridge in Bulgaria and the Alexandropoulos bridge in Macedonia curtailing Turkey's export of chrome. In May, they destroyed the Larymna mine in Greece, wrecking railroad stock and a loading wharf. And in June, they destroyed the mine shafts at Larima.[101] Now, in late July, Stavros and his commandos were tasked with cutting Germany's chrome lifeline.

The three scouts walked west, four kilometers from their vantage near the ancient town of Domokos, then into the Tsamadoráchi hills. The open plains of Thessaly made daytime travel dangerous. But into its flat fields jutted rising hills, fingerlings of the impenetrable mountains to the west. This wooded land offered the only cover for daylight travel. Staying in the wooded land was not the direct route, but it was the safe route.

They reached camp two hours later. After rations and coffee, Stavros called the thirty-man detachment together. The OSS had Squads One, Three, and Four, plus the two section leaders. There were ten andartes with Nikolas.

Stavros began, "We can't attack the mine. It's too well defended. If we had a battalion, we would still be outmanned and outgunned." Then Stavros asked Yanni to read from his notes. Yanni detailed the defenses and equipment.

Stavros went on, "The logical target would be the rail line connecting the mine to the station at Dereli where the ore cars transship to the mainline before traveling north.

"Elias, what's your report from Dereli?"

Elias, a Greek national and the OSS Squad Three leader, had reconnoitered the railway station with another OSS man and an andarte. "The station is well defended. The Germans have burned all the homes around the station, and the villagers live in hovels of brushwood and straw. There is no cover to approach the target. This area, too, has a Panzerzug. The train sits in a siding off the mainline north of the station. It is armed like the one at the mine compound. There is a vehicle pool north of the Panzerzug.

"We estimate eight hundred to a thousand soldiers in the area. And like the compound, there are minefields, towers, and pillboxes. Three hundred meters east is a crane and a switching yard where the Germans transfer the ore into the larger cars for the mainline trains."

Stavros asked, "Is the crane guarded?"

Elias said, "We were only there for two hours. When they transferred the ore, the Germans brought many troops. Otherwise, they left only a few. But their reinforcements are only minutes away. There were no towers or minefields that I could see. But mines are easy to hide."

Stavros asked, "Did you see any work lights? Lighting that they would need to load at night?"

Elias shook his head.

"Tonight, return to the station and watch the crane overnight. See how the Germans guard it and see if they use it in the dark. I doubt they do if there are no work lights. Take two men with you," said Stavros.

"Yes, sir," answered Elias.

Stavros went on, "We can blow up a section of the railroad from the mine to the mainline. That's eleven kilometers, and they can't guard every inch. We might even get lucky and wreck a locomotive or some ore cars. But those are small potatoes. Easily repaired and replaced. If we take down the crane, that'll put their operation out of commission for much longer. Does anybody have any ideas?"

"A diversion, then crane demolition would be textbook," said Yanni.

Stavros said, "Elias, take a sapper with you tonight and estimate how long to rig the crane, okay?"

Elias nodded.

"Elias, do you have a sketch of the station?" asked Stavros.

"Yes. Right here." Elias handed Stavros a pad with his sketch and notes.

"W-T is water tower?" asked Stavros.

"Yes, sir."

"How far is that from the station? And how well guarded?"

"One hundred meters south of the station and no dedicated guards. But many soldiers in the station. There are foot patrols and searchlights and machine-gun nests at both ends of the station."

"How close can we get a bazooka under cover?" asked Stavros.

"There is a tree line fifty meters to the west. But the approach is open land, and a team would have to cross the motorway to get there," replied Elias.

"Okay. Double-check that tonight. If we can target the water tower with a bazooka round or two, we might have our diversion. If we damage the tank, all the better. If we don't, we keep them busy chasing ghosts. We need to make sure there is a safe retreat for the bazooka team. Got it?"

"Yes, sir," replied Elias.

Stavros thought for a moment that he should have brought Squad Two and his buddy Gus. Gus had proved to be a bazooka sharpshooter. The thought was fleeting. He told himself all the OSS men were bazooka-qualified. If they used the water tower as a diversion and the shot was from fifty meters, they would score. The biggest problem for any bazooka team would be their concealment, approach, and retreat.

The crane was a different story. It was twelve meters high and built on a solid concrete base fifteen meters square. This would be a job for C2 shaped charges set on the four iron beams rising at the corners to form the tower. At its heart, the crane was a derrick, but it was not a simple machine. The derrick controlled two conveyor belt systems, each twelve meters. The lower conveyors carried the ore from the bottom hatches of the meter gauge ore cars, up to a hopper high on the crane. Then, from the hopper, the machine transferred the ore onto another conveyor. The second conveyor angled up and over the top of the standard-gauge ore carriers and delivered the mineral into the open-top cars. Once in the larger, standard-gauge rolling stock, the ore moved north to the industrial heart of German manufacturing. But the complicated machinery rested on four iron beams carrying the weight of the machine's superstructure. The beams were thick, but no thicker than the OSS sappers had cut before.

The Dereli Railroad Station was half a kilometer south of the intersection of two roads. The Central Greece Motorway ran north and south just to the west of the station. The smaller Xiniadas–Makriachis road ran east and west. The layout was that of a cross with the station on the lower right section, with the water tower below it. The transfer yard was on the upper right section, four hundred yards from the station. The approach to both targets would force men to cross roads where traffic was an uncontrollable factor.

The next morning, Elias and his team returned with their report. They saw only two guards for the transfer crane after the last operation at sundown. They stationed at its base and relieved at two-hour intervals on the hour starting at 2000 hours. The water tower received no dedicated guards, but it was close enough to the station that roaming patrols were a constant threat.

The sapper reported it would take four men ten minutes at the base of the crane to plant the C2. They could use timed charges and not need to wire the explosives. Stavros let the report sink in, then sat with Yanni and Nikolas to form a plan.

Chapter 69

"Can we approach Thanasis Hadzis about her resignation, her departure from KKE discipline? He and the party are looking for friends now, no?" Maria questioned her husband.

Alexandros inhaled his cigarette, leaned back into the overstuffed chair, and released the smoke, "The KKE is writhing in one of its endless ideological contortions. The party knows it needs ELD. We socialists have utility. They need us for legitimacy and to make the EAM appear broad and representative of all progressive outlooks. Still, they are fighting within to maintain their proletarian purity, or what they present as their purity. I suppose we might play on Dimitra's non-proletarian background and see if the KKE might agree to a silent, voluntary purge. She is prominent. They will notice her departure."

"What if she said she wanted to return to her academic studies?" asked Maria.

"Perhaps," answered Alexandros. "Whatever fiction we invent, there will be a political price. The KKE will want something. We have negotiated all the ministers for the cabinet. We might have room to discuss deputies. It depends on what they want.

"Are you certain she is worth our efforts?"

Maria answered without hesitation, "She is. She is a remarkable woman with honed leadership. She is confident and poised, and she will be an asset to ELD. I know. Women listen to her. She can speak to the villagers as well as to women of the city. She can hold her own with the academics. Yes, she is an asset."

"The KKE is in a constant struggle over how to use the minor parties," explained Alexandros. "They want the ELD for its public cover to present the fiction that EAM is a composite of equal parties. ELD is a fig leaf, but not without value. This spring the KKE began smearing the minor parties as conservative, and reactionary, and some even as traitors. This was the sentiment among the middle and lower cadres. Thanasis Hadzis, as General Secretary of EAM, was one of the chief proponents of this purity movement in public. Privately, he and Georgios Siantos, the General Secretary of the KKE, reassure the minor parties. They even tried to recruit royalists into EAM. That caused the reaction within the KKE cadre and the demand for purity they now both fan and try to put out.

"I say this only so you understand that we, the ELD, are in a sound position. But we cannot impose our demand on the KKE, especially regarding one of their star kapetánios."

"Yes, yes," said Maria. "That you try is all I can ask. If we trade for Dimitra a vice-deputy in agriculture, it is a bearable price, no?"

"It may be more complicated than that. The KKE will want to save face, especially after Stalin's rebuke. They are a large organization still gaining members. Their leaders jockey for influence, and their fights are confusing. Do you know they have over four hundred thousand members?" asked Alexandros.

Maria shook her head.

Alexandros went on, "They started with two hundred members in Greece when the Italians invaded, and by December 1942, they had fifteen thousand. They print sixty thousand copies of their newsletter. ELD is a minnow to the KKE whale.[102]

"In a growing organization there are always fights, rising political stars bumping shoulders, establishing dominance. But in the KKE they are vicious and often deadly and revolve around ideological notions impenetrable to outsiders.

"I will talk with General Secretary Siantos. If he agrees, the Central Committee of KKE will go along. If he says no, we may have signed Dimitra's death warrant."

Chapter 70

Stavros had orders to interrupt chrome ore shipments to Germany. Otherwise, he would have backed away from this mission. The problem was concealment. The terrain around the Dereli Railroad Station was flat and open. The nearest hills and woods were four kilometers west. The only cover the OSS detachment could count on was darkness. The rest would be wits and dumb luck. Nikolas and Yanni recognized the problem, too.

The three men sat near the fire, pushing twigs into the map fashioned in the ground before them. The dirt diagram was the cross configuration, with stones placed for structures. Yanni chewed on his unlit cigar and used a fir branch to point out a movement for the bazooka team. The detachment had both bazookas with them, but the three leaders agreed only one team should create the diversion. Yanni summed it up. "It is better to keep one weapon in reserve. We may need to shoot our way out of here if the wheels fall off this rickety wagon of an attack."

With Yanni's use of a wagon metaphor, Stavros asked, "Can we go mobile? Can we move with vehicles? The diversion team could damn near shoot the water tower from the roadway."

Yanni said, "Look at this," and he held up Elias's map. "From the road to the water tank is one hundred meters, too far for an accurate shot. I'd put our chances for a bullseye at maybe fifty-fifty. But look. If we had a vehicle, the team could dismount, rush to the tree line, take the shot, maybe two, then remount.

"Now look at this. Just south of the water tank, maybe two hundred meters, there's a storage shed of some sort. Elias couldn't tell what it's used for. This is well within the range of a vehicle, only fifty meters from the road. So, if the vehicle is moving southbound to exfiltrate the team, they could set a second diversion on their way out of town. That would put the Germans in motion away from our primary target.

"The diversion team will have to outrun the Germans for four kilometers. Then they will be in the hills south of Perivoli, right here."

Yanni jabbed his pointer into the earth at the base of the cross south of the stone designating the water tank.

Stavros thought for a moment. Then he looked at Nikolas. "It would take four men and a truck, something that will move fast but not draw attention."

Stavros said, "So we need a truck."

The other men nodded.

Stavros said, "What about the crane, our primary target? We've got the same problem. No cover. And we'll need four sappers, six for cover, and two scouts, maybe four, depending on the number of guards. That's fourteen men to move, plus us."

Nikolas said, "Domokos. There, the Germans have a maintenance garage where they repair vehicles. Greeks run it. They have a dozen trucks there on any day. Sometimes more. They would not miss two or three since they are there for repair."

Yanni said, "We don't want to steal broken trucks."

Nikolas shook his head, "No. The Greeks fix them, then don't tell the Germans until the Germans threaten them. The Greeks use them to move crops for local farmers, it's all black market. Two sovs or a goat will get you a truck for the night, and you can move your pigs to another town. The Greeks return the trucks to the facility before dawn, wash the shit out of the bed, and the Germans are none the wiser."

"Isn't that risky for the Greeks?" asked Stavros.

"Oh yes," said Nikolas. "But the Germans patrol little at night. When they stop the Greeks, the Greeks say they are driving the truck to test it. The Germans think the Greeks are crazy because we keep late hours anyway, so there has never been a problem. I'm certain the Germans know what goes on, but they allow it because their trucks need repair, and their commander likes the sovs that find their way into his tunic. But what do I know?

"How many sovs do we have?"

Stavros said, "Forty, right? Twenty with me, twenty with Yanni."

Nikolas said, "This should buy us three trucks, no problem. We'll tie the Greeks up and make it look like a robbery."

Yanni asked, "Are the Greeks collaborators?"

"No, no, no," said Nikolas. "They are businessmen. Domokos has no love for Germans. This is a town with much history, a Greek bastion. In the year 1897, the town fought to the death against the Turks. And do you know who was at our side?"

Yanni shook his head.

"The Italians! Ricciotti Garibaldi, son of Giuseppe, commanded two thousand countrymen, volunteers. It was a valiant effort, but the Italians proved no better fighters than they are today. The town fell, and the Turks were merciless. But it is a Greek town to its bones. They have no love for Germans or Turks. And they don't like Bulgarians, either."

Yanni said, "Then let's do some business."

The two sentries never knew their fate. OSS scouts emerged from the darkness unseen and unheard just as the first explosion ripped a giant hole in the water tank. The surprised guards turned toward the mayhem, and it was the last voluntary movement of their young lives. Fairbairn-Sykes fighting knives as sharp as razors sliced their tracheas and carotid arteries in less than a second. They both died in a paralytic ballet, crumpling in heaps against the cold concrete of the crane's base.

The sappers moved up and shaped their charges. Just then, a second explosion rocked the water tank and Stavros thought, *Get the hell down the road.* The bazooka team wanted to finish what they started.

Less than a minute later, Stavros heard another explosion, and then another. He knew the diversion team was attacking the storage shed since the report was distant. But the second explosion came too soon. It takes at least ten seconds to reload and aim a bazooka. Then he could have sworn he heard cheering. Faint, but cheering like Americans at a baseball game. He put it together in his mind. The diversion team must have hit something in the shed for a secondary explosion.

Then he heard another explosion, and another. The fireball on the southern horizon was bright enough he saw the hijacked German lorry racing away a kilometer distant. The diversion team had an excellent head start, and the Germans were just getting organized.

The sappers fell back from rigging the crane after only eight minutes. With the four shaped charges wired in parallel, the team leader stomped the heal of his boot on the end of a pencil detonator. This broke a glass vial containing cupric chloride and started a chemical reaction. In ten minutes, the reaction would sever the lead alloy wire retaining the spring-loaded striker poised to impact the blasting cap.

The ground activities finished, the remaining detachment fell back to their two illicit German trucks and raced four kilometers west to the town of Makrirrachi and the wooded hills beyond.

There was nothing glorious or glamorous in the way he died. As the following truck raced through the intersection at the center of the cross, a German machine gun at the north end of the station fired a burst. Most of the rounds tore through the canvas covering the bed too high for impact. But it only took one. The andarte slumped to the truck bed with half his skull missing. It was Ajax's friend from the schoolhouse, Dimitra's number two sentry.

The Germans gave pursuit, but the detachment had a head start. Once through Makrirrachi, they left the trucks and disappeared into the hills over a scouted path. It was a trail they wanted the Germans to find.

The scouts had planted mines and wired the trail with C2. As the first German squad entered the darkness, C2 charges rigged at chest level cut the unit down. The scouts seized the plunger detonator and followed their comrades into the darkness. Seconds after the first detonation, they heard a mine explode, then another, and the German pursuit ended.

In the stillness of the woods, the detachment heard a massive explosion and the sound of toppling, contorted iron.

Chapter 71

"We buried him at Agios Ioannis in Paliá Giannitsou. A priest presided, and the fighters were his honor guard. Nikolas said he had no family nearby, so it seemed the respectful thing to do," Stavros told Dimitra.

"He has a family, but they are in Thessaloniki. I will write them," Dimitra assured.

"I'm sorry. I didn't know his name until he died," said Stavros.

"His name was Konstantinos. He was the youngest in a family of four brothers. Two are in Egypt with the Third Greek Mountain Brigade, and I don't know of the third. I assigned him to my security detail because of an action in the early days. We went against an Italian convoy. He stood in the roadway with a Bren to block the trucks when our trees didn't fall as they should have. After that, I told him he had earned his name, Konstantinos, steadfast. He was a dutiful man."

Stavros nodded.

"Is this the first man you have lost under your command?"

Stavros nodded again.

"It is a burden, no? You are responsible for his death. You didn't fire the shot that killed him. But you ordered him into a position where the bullet met him. He was where he was because of your insistence.

"It is a weight that never recedes. You will carry it, borne as a debt, one you can never retire. That is our burden. It is the price of freedom and leadership."

Stavros took this to heart.

"Very well, then. It is done. The past is behind. We must advance to our fate, whatever comes.

"Now, I have something to tell you and you must keep it secret. No reports to Bari. Is this understood?" instructed Dimitra.

Sitting alongside the stream beyond the OSS camp at the monastery, Stavros looked up to make certain no others were present. "Go ahead. I can keep a secret."

Dimitra leaned back on her arms, seated on the big rock overlooking the stream. Just as she was about to speak, a trout breached in the rippling waters, taking a dragonfly from the air. He returned to his watery home with a soft splash. She said, "For a moment he flew like a bird, no? Something he is not. Now he returns to his world satisfied with a full belly and a taste of freedom.

"What I must tell you is also about freedom, only I hope to leap and stay in the air. I intend to leave the party. Do you understand?"

Stavros said, "Sure. But what does that involve?"

"It involves me casting my fate with politicians I do not trust."

Stavros asked, "Do you want to tell me why you want out of KKE?"

"It is less important. My mind is made up, and I will follow," said Dimitra.

Stavros shrugged and gave the beautiful woman a puzzled glance. She relented. "Have it your way. I believe the Soviets dominate the KKE, and their pathway is less their own and more that of Stalin. There, you have it."

Stavros made a slow whirling motion with his hand, showing he wanted to hear more.

Dimitra rolled her dark eyes. "I believe the war will end and the Greeks will need friends, good friends. We will need money and support. I do not believe the Soviets will provide either. I doubt the British and their intentions, and I believe the United States is our only friend. The KKE will never see things this way.

"I tell you this because I do not know what will come next. If I must leave Greece, I want you to know . . . I want you to know that I will miss you. I have grown fond of you."

"Wait a minute," said Stavros. "You might have to leave Greece?"

"You are impossible, American! A woman just told you she is fond of you, and what do you say? You ask a stupid question. Impossible," spouted Dimitra.

"Uh, yes . . . I mean, I'm fond of you, too. I mean, I like you. Ah. . . ." Stavros stumbled.

Dimitra shook her head. "It is no matter. I may have to leave quickly. I need to know how we can be in touch, so I may continue your education in all matters of war and love."

The mention of loved stunned Stavros. He sat on the streambed, his eyes unfocused, jaw gaping.

With a quick shake of his head, he refocused. "Right. Get in touch. Well . . . there's always the OSS APO address. But the best way will be to write to my family in Saint Louis. I mean, if you're talking about getting in touch after the war. After the war, I don't know what I plan to do. So, my parents are the best contact.

"Tell me, why is this so dramatic? Can't you just resign from the party?"

"You do not understand. The KKE is not a party like yours in America. The KKE formed as an army, a secret army. We do not organize to win elections but to win wars. This requires discipline. I am not opposed to the discipline. When in battle, it has served us well. But KKE extends the discipline to all matters. You cannot simply leave the party. It is a breach of discipline. Very senior members, prominent personalities, have been ridiculed as traitors and some shot. This is a fate I wish to avoid. Do you understand now?" asked Dimitra.

"Sure . . . I think so. How can I help?"

"This I do not know, not now. Perhaps in a week, I will know more. There are people talking in Athens, and I may know soon."

Stavros prodded, "Your position in the Mountain Government offers you some protection, right?"

"That is uncertain. It complicates matters. My position makes me prominent, and prominent people are more likely to receive scrutiny from the Central Committee. It is all complicated, far too complicated for your simple American mind. And I mean no disrespect. Your simplicity is charming."

Had she insulted him?

Dimitra asked, "How long will you be in Greece? And do not worry, I will not give this information to the party."

Stavros shook his head. "I don't know. I assume we will leave when the Germans leave . . . in the fall from the look of things. We have no orders . . . no timetable."

"Then we should act on the things we can in this moment."

Dimitra leaped from her stone onto the riverbank. She ordered Stavros to his feet. Then she kissed him.

Chapter 72

"Then she will be released from party discipline the first week of September so she can return to her academic studies. Is this agreed?" inquired Alexandros.

"We agree with the proviso that the KKE will receive two deputy appointments," answered Georgios Siantos, General Secretary of the KKE.

"Two deputy appointments. But not within the Ministry of National Defense. These we have already negotiated," responded Alexandros.

"Yes, yes. Two, but not in the Ministry of National Defense," came Siantos's reply. Jovial and personable, Siantos was a hard man not to like. But this was politics, and a deal was in the making. Like all politicians, Siantos saw the request for Dimitra's resignation from party discipline as an opportunity to receive something in return. A quid pro quo. Siantos knew of Dimitra, but his was the world of Athens, not the mountains. He thought of the woman as a rising star in the KKE and a potential asset. But she was an asset he did not know. She was not a friend and supporter, only a notable leader commanding a band of armed fighters. His unwillingness to jettison her from the party without a show trial was a ruse. He was happy to see her go. She was a potential force in his political future, one that he did not control.

Alexandros sensed as much and bargained the General Secretary's original request for five deputies down to two.

The motivation and reasoning of Siantos ran even deeper. Siantos was a placeholder for Nikos Zachariadis. Zachariadis had led the Greek Communist Party in the dark years of the Metaxas dictatorship. He was the soul of the party. Metaxas arrested Zachariadis in 1936 and sent him to prison. In 1941, the Germans moved him from Greece to their Dachau concentration camp. Zachariadis's smuggled letters were an inspiration to the party cadre, like encyclicals to the faithful.

Zachariadis was not a supporter of Aris Velouchiotis. He saw the mercurial battlefield leader as unreliable and unretainable, someone willing to buck party discipline for laudatory gratification. Dimitra was in the Velouchiotis camp. Aris liked and respected the woman, and she respected him. Ridding KKE of an Aris supporter was an additional gain for Siantos and, by extension, his benefactor, Nikos Zachariadis.

Thus, in late July 1944, Dimitra had her pathway out of the KKE. In September, she would take up her archaeological studies. But as in all matters Greek, time can bend even the truest path.

Chapter 73

"The church in Arta, Saint Dimitrios, they have also been watching for the German convoys. The church is only three hundred meters from Ionia Odos. From their report, we compare the times and the number of vehicles moving southbound. Their travel during the week is random; some days there are two convoys, other days there are none. The Germans are good at this deception. But what they allow us to predict is the time to travel the hundred forty kilometers to Antirrio, and this is always two hours, a little more but never less. The count remains the same in both places, so we know they make no stops along the way. A convoy that passes Dimitrios with thirty vehicles arrives at Panteleimon with the same.

"When the convoy reaches Antirrio, it takes thirty to forty minutes to board. Then the passage is twenty minutes, no more. At Rio they leave the ferry, muster, and are on their way to Patras," Yiorgos reported.

Yiorgos, Nikolas, Stavros, and Yanni sat at the Chómori taverna halfway between the schoolhouse and the monastery. The taverna was a small open-air affair on a raised deck opposite the plateia. Wisteria, in full bloom, trellised over the men with its squadron of busy bees. The men sat with coffee, Yanni chomping on his unlit cigar, Nikolas smoking an American cigarette from Stavros, and Yiorgos intent as ever. It was midmorning, and the area was clear of all but the four men and the taverna owner.

Stavros asked, "So if we have a radio at Arta and one at Antirrio, we can determine when the Germans will be on the ferry. Once on, it's a twenty-minute ride, and we will have only two hours to prepare a surprise."

Yiorgos nodded.

Stavros went on, "And we will have to position our teams, whatever we do, days in advance and wait on their movement."

Yiorgos nodded again.

"And the attack will all take place in daylight," continued Stavros.

Yiorgos said, "That is right; the Germans only travel in the daytime, never at night."

Yanni said, "We can get limpet mines from Bari, but they may not be our ticket."

Nikolas and Yiorgos looked at each other and shrugged toward Yanni.

Yanni said, "They design limpets for sinking boats. They attach to the hull underwater with magnets and detonate by timer. The Australians used them in Singapore against the Japanese and the SOE in Bordeaux against the Germans. We, the OSS, have seen them, but we've not trained with them.

"Those other attacks were at night. The commandos infiltrated under cover of darkness in small canoes, dove with respirators, attached the mines, and swam away to watch the fireworks. We won't have that luxury at Antirrio."

Stavros asked, "How far does the ferry sink when it's loaded?"

Yiorgos said, "We have not studied this. I'm sure a meter, at least. Thirty vehicles is a full load, no? Why does this matter?"

"The mine should be at least two meters below the waterline when it explodes. I only ask because it could change how we approach attaching it," answered Stavros. "Yanni, make sure Bari knows we need four limpets in the next drop. And when is it?"

Yanni said, "This week, Wednesday, depending on the weather."

Stavros said, "Right. Send them a code when we get back to the monastery."

Yanni said, "Roger."

"Oh, and Yanni, have Bari send a couple pairs of diver fins and masks, too," said Stavros.

Yanni nodded.

Nikolas asked, "How large is the mine?"

Yanni said, "It's the size of half a basketball. It contains two kilos of explosives and weights about six kilos."

Nikolas asked, "How long does it take to attach the mine to the hull?"

Yanni said, "You dive in, swim to the boat, dive under and the mine sticks to the hull. Then you set the timer. It doesn't take long if the hull's clean. If it's covered with barnacles, the diver has to scrape off a small area so the mine will stick."

"Yes. Does a swimmer need a diving suit?" asked Nikolas.

"Not really," answered Yanni. "If he can hold his breath for three minutes, he can do the job. Do you know someone?"

"Perhaps. Have you met Lambros?" asked Nikolas.

"The bright boy who lectured Gus on the boar?" asked Yanni.

"Yes, he is a sponge diver from the Dodecanese. He was an Italian prisoner until they surrendered. He joined us soon after. The Italians arrested him when he tried to bomb an outpost on Kalymnos, an island stolen from Greece in 1912, as were all the Dodecanese.

"He is a young man. Only the young can hold their lungs long enough to gather sponges at thirty meters," answered Nikolas.

"How can he swim to thirty meters?" asked Stavros.

"They do not swim down. They strip naked and hold a stone of fifteen kilos and sink to the bottom with their net. There, they gather the sponges and swim to the surface. Sometimes they are down three, maybe five minutes. The longer they can hold their breath, the more sponges they gather, the better their pay."

"Okay. If we have Lambros attach the mine, then how do we get him within swimming distance of the ferry, just as the Germans are arriving? In daylight." asked Stavros.

This silenced the dialogue with no obvious ideas percolating among the four. Stavros sought another tact. He asked, "Maybe we should bring Dimitra in on our planning. She might have another approach."

This generated nods all around.

Yiorgos said, "She is with her mother in Platanos this morning. Ajax drove her there last night. I am uncertain when to expect her."

Stavros said, "Let's think about it. We can get the mines. We know the timetable. We may have a method of attachment. It comes down to delivery and timing, no? It comes down to ten minutes, right? If it takes the ferry twenty minutes for a crossing, we want the blast to hit in the middle of the Gulf for maximum damage. So, that's ten minutes on a timer that is not your grandfather's pocket watch. I mean, the timers are close, but they aren't exact.

"Let's put some thought into it. Yanni, maybe you can brief the section and squad leaders, get their ideas."

"Right. Will do," answered Yanni.

"Yiorgos, do you want to brief the kapetánios when she returns?" asked Stavros.

Yiorgos nodded.

The men left the taverna with more of a concept than a plan. Still, sinking a ferry in the Gulf of Corinth was a compelling notion. For Stavros, it was a historical statement and a crowning triumph for the OSS in Greece. For Yiorgos, it was blood retribution and redress for the massacre of his family members in Kommeno. Whether egos and emotions were overruling military prudence remained as open as the buzzing canopy above.

Chapter 74

"But, Mother, you love Thessaloniki. You talk about it all the time—its sophistication, its culture, the university. You like to see women dressed in style so you can comment. You like the kafenios and cafés. Why would you not want to move there? We still have Giagiá and Pappoús's house in Ano Poli. The sun retreating over the Gulf of Therma? Watching the ships entering and leaving the port? You love to make up stories about where they are bound or where they have traveled, no? What is it that keeps you in Platanos?"

The two women seated on Eva's plateia were a mixture of relief and nerves. Dimitra told her mother about her plan to resign from KKE and return to her studies. But Dimitra wanted her mother to move with her to Thessaloniki, and Eva was dragging her feet.

Eva said, "It's your father."

"What? Father is dead. We buried him in the churchyard, where he will remain eternal. I will miss him, too, Mother, but we will visit and always have him in our thoughts, no?" said Dimitra.

"No, no. This is his garden. All these green and flowering things. Every tree, every bush. All these beautiful species and all their persistent pests. All of it, the good and the bad. These are the things he loved and tended, and I must keep them for him. It is the way of love. That is all," answered Eva. "If I leave, who will tend to them and honor your father?"

"Mother, we will find someone who loves these things as you do. They can rent the house or buy the house, and the plants will start a new life. Just as we must start a new life.

"If all the Germans left tomorrow, there would no longer be a kapetánios in Chómori. So, we would need to start anew, anyway. That day will come, and Dimitra the kapetánios will be no longer. Dimitra the archaeologist, she will come if not sooner, then later. You know that. And you know we should be together. In Thessaloniki. Don't be stubborn. You loved Father as did I. We still love him, and he would want us to be smart and do the smart thing. Correct? He would want us to advance and not dwell in the past. He loved his plants, as do we, but they are only plants. We are people. We have feet, and we can move. We can change. You may have tended the earth for too long, and now you believe you have roots instead of feet," said Dimitra.

"Don't be silly, Daughter. I have practical concerns and sentimental anchors," answered Eva.

"The anchors we will weigh. Together," said Dimitra. "We will take a flat in September and give your renters notice that we will move back into our house in Ano Poli. We will find a respectable renter or buyer for this house. Someone who will honor the landscape. I will study at Aristotle, and you will find work teaching or tutoring music. You will tend the rooted things in Ano Poli, and there we will live and respect Father. That is all. It is decided. You will tell the school you are leaving, and I will tell the KKE. Then we leave."

"What of your professor commander?" asked Eva.

"What of him?" asked Dimitra.

"He is a marvelous man for you, no? He is smart and handsome and, yes, a little slow, but he is American, that is expected," answered Eva.

"Mother, he will return to his base in Italy when the Germans leave Greece. Then who knows? The American OSS may send him to another battlefront. That is what they trained him for. Because the Germans leave Greece does not mean that the war is over. The Americans will still fight in Asia.

"I will stay in touch with Stavros. I am fond of him and I have told him so. And he is fond of me. But when all the blood of war has washed from our lives, he lives in Missouri in America, and I am Greek. It is here that I want to study and here that I want to live. But these matters lie in a future we cannot reckon. Even a pilgrimage to Delphi would not show us the future. For now, we will stay in touch, and that will be all," said Dimitra.

Eva noted a faint wavering of resolve in her daughter's voice. She knew this telling sign from Dimitra's earliest days. Dimitra had made a hard decision, one that she had weighed and pondered and was determined to see through. And she would. It was the same conclusion that Eva would have reached had she been Dimitra.

Eva said, "I will begin looking for someone to rent this house and write to the couple in Ano Poli. They are students, so moving will be not too much of a burden. Classes will begin in September. Have you enrolled?"

Dimitra shook her head.

Eva asked, "Is Professor Petropoulos still the department chair?"

"I think so," answered Dimitra.

"Then you should write to him soon. I'm certain he will want you back. You were his favorite before the Italians came, right?" asked Eva.

"I am no one's favorite, Mother. You speak of me like the cutest kitten in a litter. I was his best student, not his favorite," answered Dimitra.

"And his proudest, too," said Eva.

"Mother. . . ." said Dimitra, pinning Eva with her stare.

"Yes, yes, yes. . . ." Eva raised her coffee cup as her words trailed off into the ether of a lived-together lifetime.

Chapter 75

"We need to know more about the docking, loading, and launch operations," said Gus. "If we know the details, we might sneak a diver into the mix. Someone needs to go to the church in Antirrio and watch two or three convoys come and go.

"As to the structure of the ferry, we didn't build those at the Brooklyn Navy Yard. But I know they are not deep-V hulls, more of a dory or flat-bottom type of design. How many mines will it take to sink one?"

Yanni shrugged and rolled his unlit cigar. No one else in the circle of section and squad leaders squatting in the monastery courtyard ventured a guess. Then Yanni said, "One, maybe. Two, we're in business. Three, they go to the bottom. That would be my uneducated guess."

"So, we need either three divers or one diver to make three trips," said Gus.

Yanni nodded.

After a moment of silence, and no ideas percolating into conversation, Yanni said, "Gus, take Lambros and reconnoiter at Antirrio. See what you need to see and report back. Got it? Take some sovs for the priest, and you may be away for a few days. Kit accordingly."

"Yes, sir," replied an eager Gus.

"The rest of us should keep this close-held until we know what we're up against. Is that understood?" asked Yanni.

"Yes, sir," rose all around.

Chapter 76

"So, we're two visiting priests who have binoculars and machine guns. That's our cover?" asked Lambros.

Gus said, "You got it. That's as good as it gets, Sponge Man. Put on this cassock, and act priestly. If the Germans show up, grab your gun, and let 'em have it."

Thus began three days of reconnaissance from Saint Panteleimon in Antirrio. Over the three days, Gus and Lambros watched three German convoys, nothing on the first day, two on the second, and one on the third. The first was thirty-one vehicles, the second twenty-five, and the third twenty-three. Some vehicles towed artillery, some trailed ammo carts, but most were the common Borgward B 3000 utility trucks loaded with troops or supplies. All three convoys arrived in the daylight hours, with the earliest reaching Antirrio at 1100 hours. Yiorgos was right. The Germans were good at mixing things up. The three convoys offered no predictable pattern.

But, once the Germans mustered at Antirrio to board the ferry, movements became more predictable. The ferry arrived and made fast to its dock. The arriving passengers and vehicles disembarked through a corridor of Germans who split their vehicles into two columns to form a channel by which the travelers left Antirrio.

During the unloading of civilians and the loading of Germans, a Schnellboot—what the Allies designated an E-boat—patrolled a watery perimeter of five hundred to a thousand meters. Thirty-three meters long and armed with 37mm Flak guns, machine guns, and a 40mm cannon, the boat was fast and sleek with a top speed of forty-eight knots. The boat's only weakness was its maneuverability. It could turn fast and sharp, but not in the way of a smaller craft. Still, the Germans could outrun and sink any boat in a matter of minutes, no matter how maneuverable. The waters of the Gulf were deep, and a smaller boat could not escape into the shallows.

The boarding process was slow. The ferry was not a pass-through design. All vehicles backed onto the deck, even the ones towing artillery and ammo. The vehicles parked close together, with officers barking orders at the enlisted drivers. The boarding took between thirty-five and fifty minutes, depending on the size of the convoy.

The only craft within the E-boat's perimeter were dinghies and small fishing vessels. Gus and Lambros saw half a dozen interceptions of larger vessels fishing in the Gulf, drifting too close to the ferry operation. A burst of machine-gun fire across their bows warned them off. One hundred meters northwest of the loading pier, beyond the German sentries, fishermen dabbed their long poles into the Gulf hoping to hook branzino, mackerel, or flounder for lunch. Or perhaps if the flathead mullet were running, a batch would become *avgotaraho*, sun-dried, salted roe sealed in melted beeswax.

Southeast of the loading pier was the Antirrio Fortress with its permanent German garrison. In 1499, Sultan Bayezid II fortified the location following the Turkish defeat of Venetian defenders at Nafpaktos, then called Lepanto. The fortress was a massive stone monument to the strategic importance of the narrow strait. A similar fortress rose across the Gulf at Rio, two kilometers south.

The Germans began deploying extra guards and patrols an hour before the convoy's expected arrival. During normal operations, when moving civilian traffic, the Germans maintained a lighter presence and no patrol boat. They allowed small craft near the ferry at the dock, and dinghies maintained mooring balls and channel markers nearby. Fishermen on the seawall could stand anywhere northwest of the loading ramp and civilians on foot clustered at the end of the ramp waiting to come aboard. Vehicles waited in the open area preceding the ramp where they turned around and made ready to reverse onto the ferry.

Looking through binoculars at the harbor, Gus asked Lambros, "How far can you swim underwater with a mine strapped to your belly?"

"With good diving fins, perhaps one hundred meters. Much farther with an *anapnefstíras*. But then I would need to swim near the surface to take a breath and they might spot me. I will be slow with a mine attached to my stomach. Yanni said, it is like being pregnant," answered Lambros.

"A what?" asked Gus.

"Anapnefstíras, a reed. In English . . . maybe breathing pipe. The Greeks have used these since time before Christ," answered Lambros.

"Oh, you mean a snorkel," said Gus.

"Perhaps. But the word sounds German, and I prefer anapnefstíras," replied Lambros.

"Okay. So, see that buoy tender northwest of the ferry with the three men? The men in that seven-meter skiff. The one just out from the fishermen. That's about seventy-five meters away from the ferry, no?" said Gus.

"Yes, that is accurate," answered Lambros, peering through his binoculars. "But the tender is under the harbormaster's direction. It is an official vessel. We could not imitate one without the cooperation of the harbormaster. The Germans would intercept us."

"Where do the buoy tenders launch?" asked Gus.

"Look to the northeast of the fortress. The marina, there. Do you see? They launch from the far seawall in view of lookouts at the fortress, only one hundred meters distant," said Lambros.

"Could we commandeer a tender in broad daylight?" asked Gus.

"Better to buy them off," offered Lambros.

"Do you think that's possible?" asked Gus.

"With enough sovs in Greece, anything is possible," said Lambros.

"How would we find them and cut a deal without tipping off the Germans?

"We are wearing the answer to that question. We go as priests," said Lambros.

"Okay, let's make sure we're seeing everything. What about the Rio port? It looks like the Germans muster security over there when the ferry leaves Rio. That gives them about an hour and forty minutes to get set up for the return to Rio. So, that's a tell. From the time the ferry leaves Rio until the Germans board at Antirrio and leave again takes about an hour and twenty minutes. Agreed?" asked Gus.

Lambros nodded. "They can take longer, depending on the size of the convoy."

"Right. So, what are we missing? There's got to be a gap.

"How long will it take for you to set three mines from a distance of one hundred meters, Sponge Man?"

Lambros, who didn't mind the friendly nickname, contemplated. "Thirty minutes, minimum. And only then if the water is calm and nothing goes wrong, and I have fins and an anapnefstíras. The mines will slow me."

Then Lambros had a thought. "But what if the mines are already at the ramp? The ramp is not deep, ten meters, maybe less. What if we take the mines to the ramp at night, tether them to the bottom, then I can swim in quickly, attach them, and swim away?"

"Now you're thinking, Sponge Man. We can sink those babies at night when the ferry doesn't run, and the Germans are sleepy time. We need twenty-four-hour surveillance. You know what this means? We're pulling an all-nighter."

Lambros looked puzzled.

Gus said, "It's American college slang for staying up all night."

Lambros nodded and repeated, "All-nighter."

The ferry stopped running at dusk and no German convoys arrived later than 1800 hours. With the ferry docked and darkness upon the landing, the Germans maintained a foot patrol that circulated in the loading area and did not appear to have a set route. But, around midnight, a small skiff with two men arrived near the dock with a lantern hanging from a long pole on its bow. One man rowed, and the other leaned over the freeboard, peering into the water. They drifted in the shallow water just beyond the seawall. The German guards paid them no mind.

Gus nudged Lambros and whispered, "What are these guys up to?"

Lambros said, "They are fishing for octopus."

The man leaning over the side of the boat sprinkled something on the surface of the calm water.

Gus asked, "What's he doing? Is that a religious offering?"

"No, no," whispered Lambros. "He is making it easier to see the bottom. The olive oil cuts the surface reflection of the lantern.

"Watch him, he's got one now."

Gus looked on in amazement. The fisherman plunged his arm into the water up to his shoulder and retrieved a writhing octopus with its eight arms wrapped around the Greek's forearm. Gus was slack jawed when the fisherman raised the creature into the boat, grabbed its hood, and sunk his teeth into the back of its neck, severing its spine. The animal went limp, and the man heaved it into a bucket.

"Well, I'll be damned. I have never seen anything like that," said Gus.

"It is the Greek way, Meleager," said Lambros.

Without taking his eyes from his glasses, Gus said, "Right. And it will be *our way* to deliver mines, Sponge Man."

Chapter 77

"Gus and Lambros are in Antirrio watching the Germans come and go. They should be back today, maybe tomorrow. We need more information on the ferry operation to fashion an attack. We'll debrief as soon as they arrive," reported Stavros.

"Yes, Yiorgos told me about your far-fetched dream of sinking a ferry. I too, would love to send the Germans to the bottom of the Gulf. But the precision and detail required may not conform to the chaos of Greece. Ferries, water, tides, storms, Germans—these all stir the cauldron and make a tempest of your devil's brew, no?" intoned Dimitra.

Stavros nodded, then asked, "How is Eva?"

Dimitra leaned back on her arms and stretched out on the flat rock by the stream. She gathered her thoughts and pronounced, "My mother is fine. She is missing my father. She honors him by tending his plants. She believes her proximity to his grave shows her devotion. She is not wrong in these beliefs; neither is she correct.

"We will sell or rent the house in Platanos. I told her we would find someone who respects the garden and will carry on the loving attention. Then we will move to Thessaloniki in late August. I will study and she will tend the plants there. It is done. The decision is made.

"I have a tricky task ahead. I must talk with Aris about my decision. He must be the first to know I am leaving the KKE. The Central Committee may already know. But Aris, I respect and must tell him face-to-face, in the way of fighters. He has shot people for less."

"Wait. You don't have to tell him. The word will come down through EAM-ELAS chain of command. That's good enough," said Stavros.

"But he is my direct commander. And, he is, if not a friend, someone I have known in this fight since the beginning.

He organized EAM-ELAS. Without him, there would be no resistance, not an army of thirty thousand with fifteen thousand reserves. Without the army, we would not have held the elections, and women would never have voted. There would be no Mountain Government and no hope for Greece. We would have only the royalists and corrupt politicians that have weighed on us since liberation. His is a chapter I must close on my own, in person. That is all."

Stavros knew the woman well enough that nothing he could say would shake her.

"Okay, but let me come, too. Just in case. He won't harm you if an American is present. He'll be on his good behavior," said Stavros.

"Do you hear the words you speak? Do you not know the meaning of honor and respect? Some roads we must walk alone, our fates never to be denied."

"Always with the philosophy," said a frustrated Stavros. "I'm offering a little American practicality. I want you to be safe. What do you gain by taking a bullet for honor?"

"You don't know where you are. You look at a map and say, oh good, I'm in Greece. You point to the map and think, this is where I am, this little spot on this piece of paper. But Greece is a way unto itself. It differs from America. People are different. Life is different. We have lived this way for unimaginable eons. Our life today is a distillation of all we know and all we have ever been. But no. You, an American, an educated American, cannot see beyond the map."

Then she calmed and continued, "I appreciate your offer of help. I know it is because you care for me and I for you. But talking to Aris is something I must do on my own, in my time."

"What if you take Yiorgos? Does that offend you?" asked Stavros.

"I will take Ajax and my security detail. That is all. This meeting will be only a routine meeting. Nothing more, nothing less."

"Let's hope," said Stavros. Then he picked up a walnut-sized stone, tossed it in the air once, then threw it into the stream. He watched the concentric ripples spread from the impact. Their predictability comforted him.

After a full minute of silence, Stavros asked, "When do you leave?"

"Tomorrow."

Chapter 78

"Let me get this straight. You want to sink the mines near the boat ramp, wait on a convoy, then attach the mines in broad daylight using a swimmer from one hundred meters off? Is that the plan?" prodded Yanni.

"That's about it, Chief." answered Gus.

"What's with the *Chief* talk?" asked Yanni.

"Sorry, Lieutenant. I thought since we're about to become Operational Group II's navy, I should use navy-speak," Gus answered sheepishly.

"Well, navy or not, your plan has some holes in it big enough to sink it before we launch. First, where do we get the octopus fishing boat? Second, where do we get the buoy tender boat? How do we get the buoy tender boat onto the water within swimming distance of the ferry? How does the swimmer see well enough underwater to set the timers at whatever time we need? How do the swimmer and boat crew exfiltrate? How big is our support detachment, and where the hell will they position? Those are just the obvious questions. I'm sure Stavros, Yiorgos, and Nikolas will have more. Have you got answers?" asked Yanni.

"Some," said Gus. "I'm sure we will come up with something, Lieutenant. With all that brain power and officer pizzazz, we'll come up with something."

Yanni shifted his gaze to Lambros. "Young man, what do you think? You will do the hard work."

"Sir, I believe we can do it, as Meleager has said. But you are correct. There are questions we need to answer and a plan we must refine. But, yes, I can swim the distance and work the mines if they are already near the boat. With a mask and fins and a breathing tube, I can make the swim," answered Lambros.

Yanni rolled the unlit cigar in his lips. "Who the hell is Meleager?"

Chapter 79

Aris was happy to see Dimitra. "Come in, come in, Kapetánios. How good to see you! We have not spoken since your ascension to the Council. It is proper I address you as Councilor, no? Comrade Councilor, no? The Mountain Government is lucky to have such an intelligent and forward-thinking voice in its contemplative body. And the party is fortunate. Your voice will keep our fledgling government on a correct path, no?"

He was all smiles and courteousness, and his lightheartedness made Dimitra's purpose even more contrasting.

Dimitra returned the smile, "Commander, I thank you for your kind words. I am honored to be a councilor, but we have not met since Koryschades, so I'm uncertain what effect my opinions have on Mountain Government policy."

"Your election—a woman elected to such a body in Greece—this is the biggest effect. Not on policy, but on history. Do you remember the days when we had no fighters, no political power? We were mistaken for brigands, and if the truth be told, we looked the part, no? But we organized and prevailed. Ours was a force of history and will be more so when the Nazis turn tail and run like scalded dogs. Then we will take back Greece, this time for the people."

Aris's florid preface was making Dimitra's announcement more difficult by the minute. He was in an expansive mood. Dimitra feared she would be the one to burst his bubble and pay the price. Aris was mercurial. It was his strength, and like Icarus, would be his undoing.

Dimitra said, "Comrade, I need to tell you something difficult, but something I hope you will respect."

Aris cocked his head, his black beard and deep-set eyes peering into Dimitra's stare. His mood changed, and he stiffened for dire news.

Dimitra continued, "I will leave the party in September to return to my studies in Thessaloniki."

This elicited a guttural "Um. . . ."

"I asked for this meeting to tell you in person, face-to-face. I respect your leadership, and our friendship, comrade."

Aris reflected, then asked, "Tell me this, *comrade*. . . ."

Dimitra noted a change in tone. She perceived a hardening of Aris's attitude and a regression to military formality. The change worried her, and she hoped Ajax and her detail were standing by as she instructed.

"Is your departure from the party so you may resume your academic studies, or are you dissatisfied with KKE politics?" asked Aris.

"Commander, I am leaving because I want to continue my studies. As you know, the Italians interfered in 1940, and I have always planned to finish my work at Aristotle. Now, with the Germans ready to leave Greece, it seemed like an opportunity to return this coming semester. But, in my respect for our friendship and my respect for the party, I must tell you I am disappointed in the party's subservience to the Soviets.

"I believe Greece will be better off with a future linked to the Americans. For this I have my reasons, but we need only discuss them if you wish. I am here to tell you of my departure from KKE discipline and hope you will respect my decision," concluded Dimitra.

"This is the Svolos line, no? This is what the socialists preach, no?" asked Aris.

"Yes, I believe it is, comrade," answered Dimitra.

"You understand that leaving party discipline in an ongoing military action is punishable, no?" asked Aris.

"Yes, comrade."

"Are you under my command for an ongoing military action?" asked Aris.

"No, comrade. The last direction I received was to make ready a detachment to battle EDES when called upon. General

Safaris gave me this instruction two weeks ago. This I have done. The fighters stand ready at Chómori," answered Dimitra.

"But they are not in action, no?" repeated Aris.

"No, comrade," answered Dimitra.

"It looks like the Germans will beat you to the punch. They have an offensive operation planned against EDES starting early August," confided Aris.

Aris went silent for a tense moment. Then inhaling from his cigarette and returning it to the tray at the front of his desk, he said, "Sit down, comrade."

Dimitra took a seat in the simple wooden chair. She sat erect, knowing not to prejudge. She wondered how many sat where she sat in their last moments.

"I will now tell you something that you must pledge on your honor to never speak of to anyone, Dimitra."

Aris surprised Dimitra. Was she out of the woods regarding punishment? She said, "Comrade, I hope our bond of friendship and respect remains intact."

"Yes, yes, I'm certain that it will," said Aris.

Then he continued, "I too am displeased and concerned with the KKE attachment to Soviet coattails. It is simple; we are Greeks, and while we have international obligations of solidarity, that obligation must go both ways, no?"

Dimitra nodded. She worried Aris might be setting her up for a charge of duplicity or another transgression to justify her punishment. He wasn't. Aris had doubts. His reputation, the lore that allowed him independence within the party, would be the leash on which he would hang. He spoke from his heart.

"For the KKE to take power and establish a people's government, we must have the support of a major country. The Soviets are the only country for that outcome. And I know they have sold Greece to the British for all the countries to our north, the countries where the Red Army is amassing troops. I hope that EAM-ELAS can take enough power that we will force the royalists and conservatives to acknowledge progress, reform agriculture, women's rights, workers' rights. . . .

"But all of this will not amount to a revolution. The KKE will not control Greece. It is impossible, but the Central Committee and the Soviet lovers seated there believe otherwise. They have weathered the occupation in Athens, reading glowing Russian propaganda and reveling in the Red Army's advance. And this is true, the Soviets have made remarkable contributions to defeat the Nazis. But there it ends. The Soviets will not risk a war with the British and perhaps the Americans to save poor Greece. And even if they did, what of it? Russia will be destitute by the end of the war. Today, they depend on the Americans for much of their arms and supplies. Their citizens eat bread baked with grain grown in America and Canada. I too see the contradiction, but I am, as the British say, in for a penny, in for a pound."

Dimitra couldn't believe her ears. This man was the soul and embodiment of EAM-ELAS military prowess. This was the unvarnished testimony of a Greek hero. A hero who would face the tragedy of so many Greek dramatic protagonists.

Aris continued, "I dismiss you, comrade. Go in peace. Know my heart is sad for your departure. You are a worthy Kapetánios and a fighter I will miss in battle. Perhaps one day we will meet at an academic conclave, you as the noted archaeologist and me as the humble agronomist. The future may surprise us, no?"

Dimitra nodded and fought a tear that rose in her eye but never reached her cheek.

Chapter 80

"We need another radio. Have Bari package one for the next drop. We'll pack one to Arta and one to Antirrio and share the andartes' set here in Chómori until the other units return. Did we get what Lambros needs, the fins, mask, and snorkel?" asked Stavros.

"Roger, we've got four limpets, and Bari sent double the fins and swimming gear. Their last code asked what we were up to? Should I send them the details?" replied Yanni.

"Not yet. We don't know the details. Tell them we're making ready for a possible sabotage attack on a floating vessel. Leave it at that. Oh, and tell them the attack will be coordinated with EAM-ELAS forces stationed Chómori. They'll like that," said Stavros.

Yanni nodded.

"Have you talked to Yiorgos about Gus and Lambros's report?"

"Not yet. He was busy yesterday with the detachment they are sending to fight EDES. Dimitra should be back today, so maybe we brief both tomorrow. Let me get this code off to Bari. That'll give us a better idea of our timetable. We've got to sink these Germans before they leave Greece. Bari intel reports they are already moving support troops north. Bari expects the full retreat in October. When they leave, I guess we'll leave, too?" asked Yanni.

"Who knows? We'll know when we get orders. It's the last week of July, so we still have time to put a ferry on the bottom. German traffic will increase as they retreat. They'll use Patras as their point of departure. It's a bigger port and deeper water. But that's just a guess.

"Have you thought about staffing?" Stavros asked.

"Just ballpark. I'd say a squad with each radio. Then a squad in reserve here in Chómori. And the other squad as backup somewhere near the Mine Team. And I'd say the Mine Team might be Gus, Lambros, and Ajax. Ajax is the only true fisherman in the lot. And he's a big guy who can handle the oars and weight. They'll all have to be in disguise. I've asked Lambros to get the fishing boat and the buoy tender. He was confident he could find a way so long as we have the sovs. I told him to talk it over with Ajax, since he knows the Nafpaktos fishermen and their boats," said Yanni.

"Where are we going to stage in Antirrio? We might have to be on site for days. I don't think the church will work. We'd be too obvious there, a squad plus the Mine Team, plus us and Nikolas and Yiorgos. That's a big group," said Stavros.

"Yep, we've still got to work that out. We need to ask the priest if there's a place near the church. Somewhere close enough that we can distract the garrison if the Mine Team needs a diversion for retreat," answered Yanni.

"What else? Are we forgetting anything?" asked Stavros.

"We're painting with a broad brush at this point. But it feels like a plan coming together. What worries me is the tight timeframe. We're depending on the Germans to be . . . well, Germans. They must travel from Arta to Antirrio at a certain speed, load the ferry at a certain rate, get halfway across the Gulf, blow up, and sink. We must be accurate almost down to the minute. The new timers for the limpets, the MK Three Clockwork Delay Devices, are British made and reported by the British to work well. They are waterproof down to seven meters. Now, that wouldn't be a problem if we were attaching the mines straight to the hulls at two meters. But we need to sink 'em to an unknown depth, retrieve them, set the timers, then hope they work. There are lots of variables, lots of what-ifs," said Yanni.

"A devil's cauldron," said Stavros.

"I think we have our codename for this operation," said Yanni.

Chapter 81

The schoolhouse steamed in the late July heat, and the closeness bore on the assembled. Absent a morning breeze, Dimitra suggested, and all agreed, a retreat to the open air of the plateia was the first order of business. There, the security detail cleared a handful of early rising villagers enjoying their coffees, smoking Greek cigarettes, and chatting of the day. The villagers registered no imposition, gathered their coffees, and trundled to the taverna.

Dimitra was in a pleasant mood. She smiled and made light of Ajax's grumbling about the heat. Stavros assumed the meeting with Aris had gone well, but he hadn't talked with her since her return. That she was there with them, alive, was proof of success. He was relieved.

They pulled the metal chairs into a tight circle. Stavros, Yanni, and Gus sat together across from Dimitra, Yiorgos, Nikolas, Ajax, and Lambros. Dimitra began by looking at Stavros, "I understand, Lieutenant, that you have a plan to sink a ferry load of Germans. You would like EAM-ELAS support, no? Perhaps you can explain the operation."

Stavros said, "Thank you, Kapetánios. Here's the outline. We can get into the details later.

"We know the time it takes the Germans to move between Arta and Antirrio. We will position one radio in Arta. When that detachment spots a convoy, they will count the vehicles, note the time and types of vehicles and anything unusual, then call it in to the detachment at Antirrio. That will give the detachment and Mine Team in Antirrio a timetable.

"We know how long it takes the Germans to load the convoy onto the ferry, based on how many vehicles it contains. And we know that a typical ferry crossing takes twenty minutes.

"We will position the mines near the ferry ramp at night. We'll take them in a small boat disguised as fisherman looking for octopus. The mines are slightly buoyant. We will attach them to a weight that sinks to the bottom and allows them to float so they rise to maybe five meters below the surface.

"Once we position the mines, the next convoy to arrive at Antirrio will be the target. We know the Germans only move in the daytime. So, the Mine Team will stand ready to deploy when radioed that the convoy is past Arta. We will disguise the team as buoy tenders working about one hundred meters from the ferry. They will drop Lambros with his swimming gear when the ferry lands and just before the Germans arrive. We know it will take the Germans at least thirty minutes to load. More if it's a big convoy.

"Lambros will swim in, attach the mines, set the timers, and swim back to the buoy tender. Then the Mine Team will motor away like they have finished their work and come ashore at the marina opposite the garrison from where they launched.

"That's it in a nutshell. The support detachment will be close by in case we need a diversion to extract the Mine Team. That would be hit-and-run tactics. We can't hope to match up with the numbers and firepower of the garrison."

Dimitra considered for a moment, "Lambros."

"Yes, Kapetánios."

"Can you accomplish this feat of swimming?" asked Dimitra.

"Oh yes, Kapetánios. With the fine equipment from the Americans, I could swim to Italy," answered Lambros.

"And the mines? Do you feel confident you can attach them to the hull and set the timing mechanisms?" continued Dimitra.

"Yes, Kapetánios. I have practiced with the explosives and worked the timer. With the swimming mask I can see to do the work. I will set the timers at the interval as instructed. If the Germans are true to their character, they will be halfway to Rio and on their way to hell before the surprise."

"You sound confident, young fighter. I have no reason to question your swimming ability. But have you considered what might go wrong?" asked Dimitra.

"Oh yes, Kapetánios. There are many things to go wrong when it is you against the sea. Many things. These I know from diving for sponges, work I began when I was eleven years old. So, yes, I have seen the sea trick many divers and kill some. But I will not be deep. I should only have to dive to fifteen meters, maybe less.

"I will paint my skin green, and this will make it hard for the Germans to spot me underwater. And, on the port side of the ferry, there are outlets for the bilge pumps above the waterline. Their discharge disturbs the water's surface, and it is there I will place the mines. The German lookouts will not see me through the disturbance.

"The anapnefstíras I will also paint green and cover it with moss. It will only be visible for a few seconds while I take a breath, and the Germans will not tell it from driftwood. Yes, Kapetánios, I have considered many problems. But also, I know well that it is the problem not considered that threatens the most, no?"

"You are wise beyond your years," said Dimitra.

Dimitra returned her gaze to Stavros. "And you, Lieutenant, have you considered unexpected problems?"

"Kapetánios, I expect many unexpected problems. But first, can we discuss the expected one?" asked Stavros.

Dimitra nodded.

"First things first. Where do we get an octopus fishing skiff? Second, where do we get a buoy tender? Third, how do we get permission from the harbormaster to work on the buoys? Fourth, where will the support detachment position in Antirrio?"

Glances were traded around the circle before Ajax spoke. "The octopus boat, I can get. It must come from Nafpaktos, so it will take time to get it to Antirrio. Also, the tender craft, this we may also *rent*. But it, too, will have to come from Nafpaktos. My mother is related to the Antirrio harbormaster. I have met him. He is no friend of the Germans.

"These boats and the harbormaster will cost many sovs. But what do I know? We must negotiate before the attack. We will abduct the owners of the octopus boat and the tender craft until after the mission. It is the only way to ensure their silence. For this, we will need a place for their detention and fighters to guard them. Perhaps we can take them to Kato Dafni?"

Ajax looked at Yiorgos who nodded.

Ajax went on, "It is trifling, no? But better their silence than they spill words at a taverna."

Dimitra asked, "And what of the harbormaster? Will he remain silent? He will have to be working to permit our craft, no?"

"Yes, Kapetánios," said Ajax. "Perhaps we will take his wife? But from what I hear, for that he may be grateful. He has a son, a boy who helps at the marina. Perhaps. . . ."

"If he is a member of your family, Ajax, then he should be trustworthy, no?" asked Dimitra.

"Perhaps," answered Ajax. "The sovs may be all he needs. We will pay only after he has done his part. Sovs for silence, no?"

Stavros asked, "Where will we position the detachment and the Mine Team in Antirrio?"

Nikolas said, "There is another church, Saint Nikolas, near the ferry. We can position the Mine Team there. This too will require sovs. The detachment will require a bigger building, somewhere close. But not so close as to draw attention. All movement will have to be at night, in disguise."

Dimitra said, "There is an engineering university only half a kilometer from the ferry. It will be August, and the staff and students will be away. Perhaps they would welcome a group of short-term renters, no? Universities are always begging for money."

Stavros asked, "Do we know anyone there?"

There were blank stares all around the circle.

Then Yiorgos spoke. "We could send a delegation to speak with the headman. But again, if we tell him we need his building, he will know we are planning something. Then he can tell others. Better that we show up and take what we want, no? We can leave a few sovs as a token of our respect for higher education upon departure. That is the Greek way."

Stavros heard "the Greek way" offered many times. It meant boldness before caution and bravery before contemplation. He was skeptical of Yiorgos's plan. Then he judged the other Greeks' reaction, and none found fault. Stavros looked to his right at Yanni, who rolled his unlit cigar and raise his eyebrows.

Stavros said, "Yiorgos, will you command the team that secures the university building?"

"Yes, yes, this is not a problem," said Yiorgos.

"Okay," continued Stavros. "We've got radio number one in Arta at the church. We've got radio number two in Antirrio at the university. The Mine Team will be at Saint Nikolas with a Handie-Talkie. So that's our communication chain.

"We've got the boats and the harbormaster. We've got the support detachment at the university. Now all we need is a way out."

Yanni said, "We will fall back from the university after the Mine Team is clear. The movement will be away from the ferry, already underway, in daylight, so the Germans shouldn't be too alert. We must be in disguise and leave in small groups headed in different directions.

"How long will it take, Lambros, for you to swim back to the tender boat after setting the mines?" asked Yanni.

"Perhaps five minutes," answered Lambros.

"So, we will need to set the timers for five minutes. Plus, the time for the tender to dock at the marina. Plus, the ten minutes to put the Germans halfway across the Gulf. Plus, whatever time to arrive and load. Is that about right?" asked Yanni, of no one in particular.

The question received some nods and shrugs. Only Dimitra and Stavros silently critiqued his timetable.

Stavros said, "That may take some refinement, but I think you're on the right track. When the convoy passes Arta, we will estimate the time of explosion. Two hours, plus the loading time, plus ten minutes. Our movements will work backward from that. It will be best to attach the mines as soon as we have the estimate.

"If things go as planned, Lambros should be able to set the mines and return to the tender well before the convoy is on site. Then the tender can return to the marina before the Germans arrive. That assumes the ferry is docked at Antirrio and not in transit or loading in Rio."

Dimitra said, "To rely on the timeliness of Greeks is to misplace a confidence. What goes onto paper as crisp, clear numbers, minutes, hours, and seconds comes to life as an inky blob. It is the track of a meandering octopus you pretend to hunt. May hungry Kronos, his appetite sated with offspring, smile, and look past this tempting operation."

The meeting ended. Yanni and Gus went to the monastery. Lambros, Nikolas, and Yiorgos went to check on the detachment, making ready to attack EDES. Dimitra and Stavros stood at the railing overlooking the valley below and the peaks in the southern distance. The sun, now nearing noon, blazed in the crystalline blue sky on the last day of July. A thermal breeze rose from the cool valley floor, offering momentary relief. Both commanders gazed into the distance. Then Stavros said, "I see Aris let you live."

"He is a complex man in a complicated time. But yes, he let me live. And in his intricate ways, he blessed my departure. He too dreams of a life in academia, but he knows he is too far into KKE and EAM-ELAS, and from this, he may never pull away.

"And none of this can go to your headquarters in Bari. Is that understood?" stated Dimitra, her voice rising.

Stavros nodded.

A few villagers drifted back to the plateia. Dimitra smiled at them and lowered her voice. She went on, "My mother and I will move to Thessaloniki in early September. My studies begin the second week of September. I promised the Socialist Party I will speak on campus to support their plans for Greece. This will be my only political commitment. Otherwise, it is trowel and trug for me."

Dimitra paused. The gap emphasized the finality of the couple's separation. Both she and Stavros had known the day would come when they would part. But until she said it to Stavros, it seemed avoidable. Now it didn't, and both felt the emptiness.

Dimitra looked around the plateia, making certain the villagers could not overhear her. Then she went on, "When do you begin the operation?"

Stavros answered, "We need to work on the boats and the harbormaster soon, in the next couple of days. I'm guessing, but we should be operational by the second week of August.

"Oh, and in your honor, we've codenamed the operation 'Devil's Cauldron.'"

"You Americans are so dramatic, so Hollywood," said Dimitra. "Let me ask you, Lieutenant, what chance of success do you give your Devil's Cauldron? And speak as a military professional, not a head-in-the-clouds romantic professor of world history."

Stavros shrugged, "I'd say forty-sixty. But I think the reward is worth the risk. We've got the fighters. We've got the tools. But the Germans have the timetable. We must be precise, down to the minute. That's the key.

"And your professional opinion, Kapetánios?"

Dimitra said without hesitation, "I am not in your shoes. Our fighters are in reserve, awaiting the liberation of Greece and the destruction of EDES. I am not so bold as to dream of sinking a ferry. But you are American, and you think Greece is your Hollywood film, no?

"You may use our fighters. I permit this. But don't get them killed. To die for this fantasy is too great a price."

Stavros replied, "Ajax and Lambros and Gus are the most vulnerable. We'll cover them. The rest is war, and there are no guarantees. I promise to be cautious. That is all I can offer. If that is not enough, we'll call it off and go blow up some telephone poles."

Dimitra turned to look at Stavros. "I know you cannot guarantee anything. And you're right, this is war. What I meant to say is. . . ." Dimitra paused. "What I meant to say is, don't get yourself killed. You will be near a lot of Germans, under their noses. They are armed to take a city. You will be no match. I love you, and you are of no use to me dead."

Stavros fumbled. Then, remembering his earlier lesson, when Dimitra told him of her fondness, he said, "I love you too. And yes, Kapetánios, I promise not to get killed."

Dimitra said, "Good. It would be a shame to waste all my educational efforts now that you are matriculating."

Stavros wanted nothing more than to kiss the beautiful woman on the plateia. But it was neither the time nor the place. Stavros wondered if Greece would ever be the time and place.

Then Dimitra surprised him. She said, "I'm going with you."

Chapter 82

Devil's Cauldron simmered. Yiorgos and Ajax and a detachment of andartes rode to Kato Dafni to secure the skiff and buoy tender from Nafpaktos. They would meet with the harbormaster last, just before the Mine Team, support detachment, and Arta radio team deployed.

Gus and Lambros traveled with them to Kato Dafni, then on to the small fishing settlement of Monastiraki fifteen kilometers east of Nafpaktos. The Germans cared nothing for the sleepy village, and the two men practiced working as a team. They handled the mines and timers and got Lambros into and out of the water over the freeboard of a skiff. They devised an anchoring system and learned the depth of the water at the ferry ramp, then fashioned an anchor line. Lambros astounded Gus, who couldn't swim. The youth was as lithe as an eel, even without the American swimming gear. With the mask and fins and snorkel, he moved like a dolphin.

Gus enjoyed this assignment. At night, Gus and Lambros returned the seven kilometers to Kato Dafni, where Yiorgos's mother prepared amazing meals and doted over the fighters like long-lost nephews. Their orders were to practice and wait for the rest of the operation to position. Gus thought it was a week in heaven.

On the western shore of the Mornos River, dry as a bone this time of the year, Yiorgos's family owned a small honey bottling plant. Locals prized the rich amber nectar as the best in Western Greece. The diverse flora of Greece, over 7,500 species of herbs, plants, wildflowers and trees, and its mythological aura, made honey a staple in Greek kitchens and medicine cabinets. Yiorgos's family had done well in the business. But August was a slow month, with many of the flowering plants struggling in the arid heat. No nectar, no honey. The captives would wait out their inconvenience under EAM-ELAS guard in the honey plant.

In Chómori, Stavros and Yanni went over details. They decided that when the support detachment in Antirrio received the radio transmission from Arta noting the German convoy, they would estimate a time when the ferry would reach mid-Gulf. This they called T-Time. If a thirty-truck convoy passed Arta at 1300 hours, then the estimated time to Antirrio would be two hours. They would add fifty minutes for loading, plus ten minutes on the ferry to mid-Gulf for three hours total. The T-Time would be 1600 hours. Then, depending on when Lambros could attach the mines, he would set the timers to the difference between the present time and T-Time. They notified Bari that they would immediately need a waterproof diver's wristwatch, an item they had overlooked.

Stavros and Yanni designated the remaining four OSS commandos in Gus's Squad Two as the Arta radio team. Two andartes familiar with the route and Arta would accompany them. The Arta radio team would deploy first since they had the longest travel to location.

The Antirrio support detachment would be Stavros, Yanni, Dimitra, Yiorgos, Nikolas, and three female andartes, all disguised. Two female fighters would dress as nuns. The oldest-looking female fighter would dress as the abbess of the Monastery of Saint Nikolas in Patras visiting the sister church in Antirrio. Dimitra would travel with the women, also dressed as a nun. Once Yiorgos secured the university, all would stay there with the radio until time to retreat or create a diversion.

Squads One and Three would position in the low hills five kilometers north of Antirrio with the 81mm mortar. They would communicate with a Handy-Talkie and engage only if needed to assist the Mine Team and support detachment. Squad Four would remain in Chómori with the EAM-ELAS radio to monitor the operation and secure the monastery.

With the request for a diver's watch, Bari replied they would like more information on the operation. Stavros instructed Yanni to radio back, "Coordination with EAM-ELAS forces

Chómori nearly complete. The attack will be on a watercraft within our operational zone. Send watch ASAP. Critical to operation success. Also, send sovs, as many as the United States Government can spare."

Chapter 83

Aris was right. On August 5, 1944, the Germans began an offensive, but not against EDES. Operation Kreuzotter enlisted XXII Mountain Corps, the LXVIII Corps, and SS troops under the direction of Army Group E Commander, General Loehr.[103] Kreuzotter was to unfold in three phases, the first against EAM-ELAS in southwestern Greece, the second against EAM-ELAS east of the Pindus Mountains in Boeotia, and the third against EDES. Kreuzotter was ambitious. Had it succeeded, it would have disrupted and disarmed if not eliminated the resistance in Roumeli and Western Greece.[104]

On August 6, Dimitra's andartes, waiting in reserve to attack EDES ,instead rushed to attack the German 3rd Battalion, 18th Police Regiment in Amfissa. This diversion slowed the Germans and forced them to send troops to defend their battered police unit.

The German advance from Agrinio to Karpenissi continued. But instead of bottling up EAM-ELAS forces into concentrated targets, the guerrillas battled, then dispersed. The Germans burned crops and villages, killed innocents, and carried out mopping-up operations along their route. The second German task force advancing on Karpenissi from Lamia to the east fought the same ghosts. When the German task forces met at Karpenissi on August 15, the Germans declared phase one complete.

The second phase east of the Pindus Mountains produced the same partial results, and the Germans declared a conclusion on August 21. The third phase, the attack on EDES, evaporated. By mid-August 1944, the Germans were worried about Hungry and Bulgaria. EDES was spared.[105]

Operation Kreuzotter and troop movements to Bulgaria and Hungary meant traffic, some of it destined for the ferry crossing at Antirrio. And it meant the garrison at Antirrio was smaller because of German manpower requirements, leaving the guard force stretched thin and overworked.

When Devil's Cauldron deployed on August 9, the likelihood of an early convoy target was high. The Germans were distracted, and their guard force dulled. But Devil's Cauldron was a Swiss watch in a sandbox. Countless grains of complication awaited, and it would only take one to jam the works.

Chapter 84

Squad Two radioed in position from Arta the evening of August 13. The night before, Ajax and his andartes had confronted the two-man crew of the buoy tender and the owner of the octopus fishing skiff with sovs and Mannlichers. The three men agreed it was best that they volunteer for a few days' compensated retreat in Yiorgos's honey plant.

The motorized buoy tender chugged along with its rhythmic single-cylinder diesel, towing the octopus skiff from Nafpaktos to the marina at Antirrio. There they were tethered to mooring balls like dozens of other similar boats. Ajax, Gus and Lambros came ashore clothed as locals. The Mine Team walked to Saint Nicholas for Sunday service, indistinguishable among the faithful to the over-scheduled German patrols. When the faithful left, they stayed.

While Gus and the andartes were securing the boats, Ajax approached the harbormaster in Nafpaktos. The lure of sovs and the implied threat of EAM-ELAS displeasure assured his cooperation. The harbormaster hated the Germans and their high-handedness. They treated his duties as petty and him as a contemptible underling. Ajax did not tell the harbormaster of the mission. Ajax let him believe that something less grand was in store. The harbormaster reasoned that since the andartes would be in disguise, no blame would fall on him.

The harbormaster gave Ajax a blue-over-white pennant to fly on the buoy tender. This showed they were an authorized vessel on official business. He warned Ajax that they could still be stopped and boarded and asked for papers. Those the harbormaster could not produce without authentication from his German overseer. He gave Ajax an outdated set of authorization papers and warned the big andarte that, though they would never fool the Germans, they might confuse things and buy some time.

The Support Team and Squads One and Three left Chómori on mounts on the afternoon of August 13. Ten hours later, they were in the hills north of Antirrio. The eighteen fighters brought along three extra mounts for the Mine Team. Squads One and Three emplaced the 81mm mortar and established a perimeter. With a range of fifty-seven hundred meters, the garrison, fort, marina, and ferry dock would be within their field of fire. And, given their four-hundred-meter elevation, their high-explosives shells could reach halfway across the Gulf.

Then the Support Team split into three components. Yiorgos, with the andarte vanguard, advanced on the university and, in the early morning hours, breached the facilities building and confronted one sleepy maintenance man. He radioed the all secure code to Stavros. The remaining fighters approached in twos and threes along separate paths. At the break of dawn, the four nuns left to join the fighters and traveled along the most obvious route. Three were on foot and the abbess rode a donkey; their flowing habits concealed Stens and pistols. The Support Team was at full staffing by 0700 hours. They radioed in position to the Arta Team and used Handy-Talkies to contact the Reserves and the Mine Team.

On August 14, they waited. Late that night, Ajax and Lambros manned the octopus boat and rowed to position along the seawall north of the docked ferry. They had onboard netting to cover the three mines and their brick anchors. They fished along the wall, drifting closer to the ferry with each minute. They looked the part. Ajax was a fisherman by trade, although he didn't fish for octopus, preferring his time on the water to be in the daylight.

About one hundred meters from the ferry, a single German soldier shined a high-intensity light on the craft and asked what they were doing? Ajax at the oars replied in his deep but humbled voice, "We are after the octopus, Commander."

The German shouted back, "Come no closer to the ferry. It is forbidden. You have been warned." Then he chambered a round in his Mauser.

Ajax replied, "But, Commander, it is nearer the ferry we find the octopus. Tonight, we have only this one to show for our work." And with that plea, Ajax nodded to Lambros, who reached into a wooden bucket in the bow and lifted a limp dead creature.

"Perhaps we can share this one with you as a token of good faith, no?" continued Ajax.

The young German looked puzzled.

Ajax continued, "You see, Commander, the animals are drawn to the lighting around the dock. They, like us, are hunting, and the light makes for them easy work. If we can move closer, we can fill our bucket. Please, if you will, take this animal so we might catch more?"

The weary German had been on watch for ten nights straight, and his attention to detail was flagging. He had seen the octopus fishers many nights, and they were harmless. He yelled back, "You may fish, but only to the first piling. If I see you beyond that point, I will fire. You and that disgusting animal will be food for crabs."

Ajax again in his most humble voice replied, "Oh, thank you, Commander. We will be no problem."

Then the German's radio crackled, and a voice on the other end ordered him to another section of the dock. He walked away, unimpressed with the fishermen.

The first piling was within thirty meters of the ferry. The distance added time to retrieve the mines and more time to attach them, but the mission was still possible.

The duo drifted closer to the big boat and when they reached the piling; they brought the bow toward the ship, and Lambros eased the mines and their anchors over the low freeboard on the starboard side. They slipped in without a splash, and in the lantern light from the skiff's bow, he saw them submerge. They had made a good guess about the water's depth. The mines floated three meters under the surface. Lambros triangulated their position, sighting the piling in line with the steeple of Saint Nicholas and the bilge outlet on the port side of the ferry. He estimated a twenty-meter swim from mines to ferry.

By 0200 hours on August 14, the components of Devil's Cauldron were in position. All that was missing was a German convoy.

Chapter 85

Arta Team reported the lead motorcycles of a thirty-four-vehicle convoy past their position at 1137 hours on August 15. They transmitted, "Delta Charlie, this is Alpha Tango. How copy?"

The Support Team, Delta Charlie, responded, "Lima Charlie (Loud and Clear), Alpha Tango. Standing by."

Arta Team then broadcast, "2637, 68, 66, 40, 28, 2200, over." The first number was the time of day, plus the date added to the hours. The following numbers were products when multiplied by prime numbers in order, beginning with two. They stood for the number of vehicles (34 x 2 = 68). The number of standard trucks (22 x 3 = 66). The number of trailering trucks (8 x 5 = 40). The number of motorcycles or automobiles (4 x 7 = 28). And the estimated number of troops aboard (200 x 11 = 2200). It was a simple code and one the Germans would break, but not within the next two hours.

The Support Team repeated the numbers back to Arta Team. Arta Team replied, "Good copy." And with that transmission and a bit of grade school math, the clock started running.

T-Time calculated to 1442 hours; two hours for transit, fifty-five minutes for loading, and ten minutes to the middle of the Gulf. The code went to the Mine Team and the Reserves over the Handy-Talkies.

The Mine Team had been at their buoy tending since 0800 hours. Their tender puttered around the distant buoys onto which Gus slathered paint and gathered rode like a long-lost deckhand. With the code of an approaching convoy, they moved toward the inner buoys to give Lambros a shorter swim to the mines. Lambros lay out of sight in the low cuddy cabin of the tender, waiting for the ferry to be in the right place for attaching the mines. They had yet to spot the E-boat. They expected its patrol to begin when the convoy neared.

The ferry was in use. It was just then docking at Rio on the southern shore. It had made three round trips already that morning. The Mine Team would wait until they were certain that the convoy would be the next load. If the convoy arrived before the ferry, they would add the time to load to the T-Time.

Yiorgos watched the buoy tender through binoculars from the third floor of the university building. Yiorgos, Dimitra, Nikolas, Yanni, and Stavros passed the powerful glasses around and tried to divine the Mine Team's intentions. The tender maneuvered two hundred meters from the ferry dock and six hundred meters from the Support Team. From what Yiorgos could see, the nearest buoys to the ferry were less than fifty meters. But he doubted the Germans would allow any craft that close to the loading of a convoy. He spotted two other buoys farther away from the ferry and estimated their distance at one hundred meters. He thought it was from these buoys that Lambros would launch to avoid suspicion.

He handed the glasses to Dimitra, and just as he did, the group froze at the penetrating sound of three Daimler-Benz MB 501 twenty-cylinder marine diesel engines firing to life on the seawall north of the marina. The E-boat's 3,960 horsepower and elongated hull gave it a speed advantage, but the boat would never sneak up on a target. The thunder of the E-boat meant the convoy was on its way and that the Mine Team was sitting ducks, praying to go unnoticed.

With the E-boat idling at the seawall, its massive exhaust ports churning the placid Gulf, the nuns and the abbess walked to Saint Nikolas church. They did not hide their movement. The church was only a block from the ferry loading dock, and if Devil's Cauldron needed a diversion, the nuns would cause havoc in the center of the Germans. It was a suicide mission and one that Stavros argued against. But as Yiorgos contended, it was the Greek way.

The E-boat crew uncovered weapons and made ready to shove off. Before they left the dock, Ajax decided it was time to move from the outer buoy ring to the closer floats from which Lambros could launch. He pointed the bow of the tender toward the ferry dock and began puttering toward a channel marker one hundred meters from the mines. As Ajax began his move, the E-boat cast lines and pulled away from the seawall, revealing a menacing black panther insignia below the wheelhouse cockpit. Once clear of the marina, the helmsman opened the throttles and made a sharp 180-degree turn toward the open Gulf. The Germans were showing off the big boat's power and maneuverability. Ajax remained steady on his course to the inner buoy. They were on official business, the blue-over-white pennant fluttering in the headwind.

Yiorgos, peering through the glasses from the third floor of the university, watched the E-boat get underway and Ajax make his move. Then he said to no one in particular, "There is nothing impossible for him who will try."

Stavros heard the words and recognized the quote from Alexander the Great. They had come on the eve of the India Campaign in 326 BCE. They were inspiring words. But Stavros, ever the student of history, knew that India was as far as Alexander had gone. The Greeks had battled their way into Punjab and east to the Indus Valley against armies numbering five times theirs. After two years and with his troops exhausted and homesick, the ruler of the known world turned back west. Alexander had reached the limit of his power and persuasion in India. To Stavros, Yiorgos's words were an inspirational caveat.

At 1250 hours, there was no sign of the convoy. T-Time said fifty minutes to arrival. The ferry loading at Rio would take at least forty minutes to arrive at Antirrio. So this was it. If the convoy was on time and the ferry operated as usual, Lambros would launch upon the next docking at Antirrio. The young andarte would retrieve the mines, plant them two meters below the ship's waterline, then swim back to the tender. With Lambros aboard, the Mine Team would motor away to await the surprise.

The E-boat prowled east of the ferry dock in the open water of the Gulf. Ajax watched as it intercepted a small fishing skiff with two young Greeks a kilometer away and no threat to the ferry. A seaman on the bow loosed a six-round burst from a tripod-mounted MG34 machine gun. The fusillade stitched an arc in the Gulf ahead of the flimsy wooden skiff. The youth at the oars came about and rowed, his back bent in desperate strain. But the skiff faced a stiff northeasterly and its progress was negligible. The seaman again took aim and a second before Ajax expected the weapon's report, an officer stepped on deck and admonished the seaman. The seaman lowered the weapon and strapped it into its standby position. Ajax knew the youths had that day been lucky. He hoped the same for the Mine Team.

The ferry sounded its horn and backed away from the Rio dock, reversing in a large semicircle once in open water. Ajax saw the E-boat on the far side of the channel reposition to escort the ferry. Ajax hoped this was good news. With the E-boat on the far side of the ferry, the Mine Team might go unnoticed. But as the ferry backed away then reversed direction, the E-boat changed course, crossed aft of the ferry, and moved to the west with the tender full in its sights. It was 1305 hours, with the convoy thirty-two minutes away and the ferry twenty minutes from Antirrio. Lambros could attach the mines after the ferry docked at Antirrio. But the best estimate for when it would be loaded with Germans and mid-Gulf would come after they noted the convoy's time of arrival. T-Time would be fifty-five minutes for loading and ten minutes for travel to mid-Gulf.

Ajax approached the inner buoy, but he didn't want to launch Lambros, only to wait in the water for the convoy. He decided it was best to stall until the convoy was in sight. He raised the engine cover on the tender and dropped the prop into neutral. He would fake a clogged diesel fuel filter if asked. The boat drifted west at a steady two to three knots, borne by the current and the northeasterly wind. Ajax noted their movement to be certain they could cover the distance for a good launch.

The Germans were early. The four lead motorcycles advanced in formation down the street to the loading dock at 1329 hours. A minute later, the ferry began unloading local farmers and Greek travelers, and the Mine Team revised T-Time to 1434 hours. Lambros would make the final calculation underwater as he set the three timers for the difference between the current time and T-Time. Ajax noted the time, then made for the inner buoy.

When the tender reached the buoy, Gus tied off with a mooring hitch, a quick-release knot he'd practiced for the past week. Ajax thumped the cuddy cabin three times and Lambros crawled up the companionway onto the deck. Ajax saw him first, then Gus and both men's eyes widened. Lambros was green, a dirty shade of tan-green with jagged chestnut brown stripes around his limbs and torso. And other than his fins, mask, and a belt with an odd metal disk over his stomach, he was naked.

Lambros pulled the mask and snorkel over his face and slipped a large, serrated knife into a sheath on the belt. He looked up at Ajax, pointed to his waterproof wristwatch, and said, "Fourteen thirty-four?"

Ajax nodded.

Then Lambros reached over the freeboard, cupped his hand to wet and cool the wooden railing, and slid into the Gulf of Corinth like a mythical sea creature.

The world Lambros entered was alien. Tides in the Gulf of Corinth are not extreme. A complete cycle takes about twelve and a half hours, and the differential is less than a meter. But the strait between Rio and Antirrio amplifies the speed of the current as all the water squeezes between two kilometers of land. And tide is not the only force moving water. During the summer months, a continuous cold-water bottom current flows west from the Gulf of Corinth into the Gulf of Patras. An upper-level warm current flows the opposite direction.[106] The wind also moves current. Taken together, the sea is a place of mystery, power, and surprise. A 155-pound swimmer, no matter how well-equipped, is at its mercy.

When Lambros slipped into his dangerous domain, the tide was rising but not yet full. The wind was moderate and variable from the northeast, and the upper current of warm water aided his progress. As he swam east, he had the tide working for him, the warm current on his side, and the wind pushing water against him. He swam deep enough to avoid detection, but not so deep to require extra effort to surface for air. Lambros could hold his breath and swim in full gear for four minutes. He could cover one hundred meters on full lungs.

He rose for air just before reaching the submerged mines. The instant his mask was above the water, he lined up the landmarks for the triangulated position. The next second, he saw the first German vehicles reversing onto the ramp of the ferry. Again submerged, he looked at his watch and noted the time; it was 1337 hours. He moved T-Time up two minutes to 1442 hours.

Lambros wore an odd disk over his stomach attached to his belt. The thin metal was the size of a pie dish with a fabric backing pad to fit against his body. It restricted his abdominal movement and slowed him. But now the accessory would prove its worth.

Lambros found the sunken mines. Grabbing the nearest, he cut the anchor line with the knife and centered it onto the keeper plate on his stomach. With the mine magnets clinging to the plate and its buoyancy near neutral, Lambros swam naturally, if burdened. To observant fish or octopus, Lambros, the mythical creature, was pregnant with half a basketball. He covered the twenty meters to the ferry's hull in seconds and there, under the steady downfall of bilge water expelled from the pump outlets, he was invisible.

He scraped away the barnacles with his knife, placed the mine to the hull, then set the timer for sixty-two minutes. He surfaced under the bilge flow, just enough to clear his snorkel, took a deep breath and returned to the anchored mines. He repeated his moves twice, adjusting the timers with each placement. He took his last breath and visualized a dead reckoned course back to the buoy tender. Halfway to his salvation, Lambros broke the surface to get a fix on the tender. It had vanished. He submerged and treaded water and removed his mask and snorkel. The reflection from the glass could be a dead giveaway to any sentry. He surfaced again, and this time with only his bare head above the water; he rotated 360 degrees. Nothing, no sign. He wondered if the Germans sank the tender or took it in tow.

A moment after Lambros launched, the E-boat, now on the west side of the ferry, spotted the buoy tender and made a full-ahead interception. The fast craft covered the kilometer in less than a minute.

Ajax and Gus saw it coming. Gus began slathering paint on the channel marker and pretended to tend to its frayed rode. Ajax stayed at the helm and tried to calm his demeanor. This time, the E-boat did not fire warning shots but pulled alongside the small tender. A boarding officer with his five-man team, all armed with Maschinenpistole 40s, their retractable butt stocks tucked for close range encounters, hailed Ajax. He said, "What is your business on these waters?"

Ajax, in his most humble voice, replied, "Commander, we are here to refresh these markers and make certain they are properly anchored. It is our job, sir."

The boarding officer looked over the tender and all he saw were tools and lines and items that anyone would expect. He saw the blue-over-white pennant, typical for an official craft.

As the tender bobbed like a cork next to the E-boat, the boarding officer weighed the inconvenience of an inspection against the boat's threat to security. The tender could not intercept the ferry, which was already nearing the Antirrio dock. He had boarded these boats before. Not only were they cluttered and ill-organized, but they invariably had aboard a bucket the

Greeks used for a head, and always it smelled of human excrement.

The boarding officer called to Ajax, "Give me your authorization papers."

Ajax glanced to Gus and saw the fear in his eyes. He said to the boarding officer, "Yes, Commander."

Ajax reached under the helm station and retrieved the out-of-date papers given to him by the harbormaster. Maybe it was chance, luck or pure atmospheric coincidence. Ajax reached to hand the papers up to the boarding officer on the E-boat's deck. The officer made no effort, expecting the subservient Greek to do the work. As Ajax balanced on the freeboard with one hand fast to the cabin, a gust from the northeast ripped the papers from his fingers. The two pages stapled together fluttered like an oversized butterfly landing aft of the two craft fifty meters away.

The exasperated boarding officer cursed the clumsy Greek. Then he stood with his hands on his hips like a pouting schoolmaster and considered retrieving the papers. But it was too much trouble, and the documents sunk beneath the surface. He commanded Ajax, "Leave here immediately and return to your mooring. I prohibit operation of this craft for the rest of the day. Is that clear?"

Ajax nodded and replied, again as humbly as possible, "Yes, Commander. We will leave immediately."

And with that, the E-boat boarding team released the grappling poles they had used to secure the boats. Gus tugged the quick-release knot. Ajax advanced the diesel's throttle and came to a heading to return to the marina. The E-boat made a sweeping 180-degree turn and sped off toward the ferry.

As the thunder of the German craft faded, Gus said, "I hope Sponge Man remembers the plan."

Chapter 86

"*Epanénosi*, epanénosi, epanénosi." With the E-boat out of sight and the ferry nearing the dock in Antirrio, Gus retrieved the Handy-Talkie from under the mass of buoy rode stored in the forward hatch. He repeated the Greek word for reunion three times. Yanni with the Support Team at the university pressed the rubber transmission bar on their Handy-Talkie three times, breaking squelch to acknowledge message received. It was a well-chosen codeword. If the Germans intercepted the transmission, they might believe it was a traditional greeting on this Assumption Day. A reference to the reunion between Mary and her son, Jesus. Also receiving the message, Dimitra waited the proscribed thirty seconds, then keyed her unit twice. Thirty seconds after that, the Reserves in the hills to the north keyed once.

Gus looked aft to Ajax at the helm. "They copy." It was 1341 hours, and the convoy began loading.

Dimitra spoke to the three nuns. They knew codename reunion. She said, "We need a priest's vestment, something fitting for the holiday. But for a young priest, not an old one. Pack it in a bag with my Sten. I will go to meet Lambros, and when he and I are together, we will leave Antirrio by the plan. Are we clear? Questions? You three leave Antirrio by the plan when you receive the all-clear on the radio."

The Kapetánios received nods of acknowledgment all around. Three minutes later, her bag was ready, and she left the church for the meeting place.

Yiorgos and the Support Team watched the buoy tender return to the marina. It was a little more than a kilometer from the E-boat interception to the mooring ball, and the tender's top speed was seven knots. Bucking the northeasterly headwind, the tender only made five knots, and the trip took seven minutes. Once tied to their mooring, Gus and Ajax rowed the octopus skiff to the north wall of the marina, the wall opposite the garrison encampment. There they made fast to a cleat and walked away from the craft with Ajax hauling a stringed canvas sack, secreting their Handy-Talkie and Stens.

The two men walked along the street leading to the loading dock lined with German vehicles waiting to reverse, then back aboard the ferry. They kept their eyes forward and moved deliberately. Two blocks north of the marina, Gus grabbed Ajax's arm. "Over there," he said, nodding to his right toward a shed. Leaning against the building was a small motorcycle, one that Gus recognized from their training in Maryland. The British called it a Flying Flea. The bike was a lightweight motorcycle dropped with parachute units. Most were a sandy brown color, but this one was red, painted with what Gus assumed was a hand brush. The British dropped these in Crete, and Gus assumed this one had found its way to Antirrio through the ever-resourceful Greek black market.

Gus looked at Ajax. "I've always wanted a motorcycle."

Ajax swiveled his head and saw the Germans in their vehicles waiting to load, but no foot patrols. The bike was on the opposite side of the shed from the queuing Germans.

The two men sauntered behind the shed. Gus kicked the two-cycle motor to life and motioned for Ajax to climb on. The big andarte tried to get comfortable on the metal carrier behind Gus in the saddle seat. He slung the canvas bag over his shoulder and grabbed Gus's waist with his left arm. Gus juiced the tiny 126cc motor, and the bike eased away from the shed and onto the road in a cloud of oily smoke. Overloaded to the rear, Ajax balanced with his legs spread wide. But not a soul took notice. Soon they were beyond the waiting Germans and on their way to rendezvous with the Reserves. Gus had gotten his wish. It was 1358 hours, forty-five minutes to T-Time.

Dimitra left Saint Nikolas for the quick walk to Tavérna Michális. The restaurant was on the swimming beach five hundred meters north of the ferry loading dock, and today,

Assumption Day, it massed with celebrating Greeks determined to escape the August heat. The crowd provided cover for Lambros but a problem for Dimitra. Even in her expansive habit, Dimitra was a stunning woman trying to remain unnoticed. The heads and bodies bobbing in the salty Gulf made it hard to spot Lambros, who she could only hope was executing his part of reunion.

In the Gulf, one hundred meters southwest of the loading ferry, Lambros embraced reunion. Unable to spot the buoy tender, the young swimmer reoriented to his secondary landmark. Not a simple task. He looked six hundred meters to the northeast for two palm trees and a flagpole flying the Greek cross and stripes. Many Greeks flew flags today, and he had only spotted this landmark in the middle of the night as he and Ajax pretended to fish for octopus. He got what he hoped was his bearing, then submerged.

Underwater, he removed the mine keeper from his belt and let it sink to the bottom of the Gulf. This would make swimming the six hundred meters to the beach easier. Then he rose to take a breath and began a steady pace.

The tide had yet to peak, so he swam against it and the upper warm water current moving into the Gulf of Corinth. And there was another characteristic of the Gulf, making his journey hard. The Gulf of Corinth is saltier than ordinary ocean water. Its salinity can be over thirty-eight parts per thousand, higher than the thirty-five parts per thousand of typical ocean water.[107] When Lambros jettisoned his mine keeper, he increased his buoyancy. The saltier water also increased his buoyancy. So now, as he headed into the tide and current, he had to swim downward to keep from floating to the surface. In the clear waters of the Gulf, German lookouts peering through powerful binoculars could spot him even at two meters' depth.

It was 1406 hours, thirty-six minutes to T-Time.

The first four hundred meters went well. Lambros, equipped with diver's fins, made steady progress against the tide and current. But his training with the fins had been at the one-hundred-meter distance. When the hamstring muscle in his left leg cramped, he knew he was in trouble. The big muscle locked up like concrete set to stone. The pain made him want to gasp. Had Lambros been diving for sponges, he would have surfaced and leveraged himself back into his skiff. There, he would have worked the cramp, massaging the muscle with olive oil until he could stretch without pain. Then he would have continued his collection. Now, in the expanse of the Gulf with nowhere to retreat, he began the only treatment available.

With his buoyancy, he could surface, float on his back, and work the muscle tissue. But that would be suicide. The Germans would spot him in less than a minute. The E-boat would come, and he would be shot, run down, or taken prisoner again. His only remedy was to fight the buoyancy, remain underwater, and stretch and flex his muscle. Lambros knew that if he were in his skiff, his recuperation from a cramp like this would take at least ten minutes. So, with his arms his only propulsion, he stayed down, breathing through his snorkel, and hoped for the best. If he couldn't ease the cramp, he hoped to at least mitigate the pain. Meanwhile, he drifted at a relentless two knots on the tide and current back toward the Germans at Antirrio. He thought of the irony that he might drift back to the ferry in time for the explosion.

It was twenty-nine minutes to T-Time.

Dimitra arrived at the beach and searched the swimmers. But the glare off the shimmering water made finding Lambros impossible. The sun was at an angle, in midafternoon, when its reflection and the breeze from the northeast ruined her vision. There were hundreds of bodies in the water. Picking out Lambros would be guesswork, if he were there at all. Her instructions were to leave the rendezvous at ten minutes before T-Time. That would give her a head start on the Germans, who would be on high alert when the mines detonated.

She made herself visible, hoping Lambros would see her. She was a nun, a tall woman of stature, standing in a crowd of beach-attired swimmers. She would never have done this in any other operation. She made herself the focus of attention. Greeks stared at her. She was lucky the German guards were ignoring the swimmers and clustered near the ferry to secure its boarding.

At 1429 hours, three minutes before she had to leave and thirteen minutes to T-Time, she saw a young man with a green face and chest. He waved to her with both arms twenty meters from the beach. It was Lambros. He had jettisoned his fins, mask, and snorkel and was motioning to Dimitra to join him. She walked to the water's edge and his motions became more animated. Swimmers near Lambros were standing with the water only above their knees. Dimitra raised her habit and, without removing her shoes, she waded into the water to Lambros. Now the crowd was interested. When she was near, Lambros said, "I need the clothes."

Through the clear water, Dimitra saw his predicament. He was naked. She looked at him, puzzled and embarrassed.

He said, "I swim faster in the flesh."

Dimitra took the priest's cassock from her bag and handed it to him in the water, soaking the heavy black garment. Lambros rose slowly, wrapping the cassock around him like a robe. He came to his full height with a face painted green and the tang of his knife protruding. He covered the weapon, but the swimmers nearby saw full well.

Dimitra began crossing herself and kept crossing until the couple were out of the water and beyond Tavérna Michális. Lambros limped on his left leg and Dimitra tried to help him, but he waved her away. A plump woman under a beach umbrella crossed herself as the couple passed. Then she asked, "Sister, is there a blessing the priest can offer on this holy day? I have never seen such a ritual as he has just performed, but it is moving. Mary be forever blessed. Is this ceremony special?"

Dimitra looked at the woman, "The priest is of a rare order . . . the Order of Assumption Redress. Their monastery is far from here on Antikythera. They are silent, and this is their penance for impure thoughts."

The woman nodded at the explanation and crossed herself as the fighters walked away.

Clear of the crowd, Lambros asked, "Impure thoughts?"

Dimitra said, "You are dressed such. And cover that knife."

It was nine minutes to T-Time.

Chapter 87

Stavros, Yanni, Yiorgos, and Nikolas watched the beach reunion from the top floor of the university not three hundred meters away. They had released the andartes five minutes before and told them to make for the Reserves in small groups and indirect routes. The nuns and abbess left the church for the hills at the same time.

Yanni spoke to the group. "We're finished here. We should split up and cover Dimitra and Lambros for their retreat."

The three others nodded agreement.

Stavros said, "Yanni, you and I will follow them. Yiorgos, you, and Nikolas try to stay parallel to our movement."

Yiorgos said, "I need to visit the maintenance man."

Stavros looked at Yanni. Both men showed concern.

Yiorgos saw their reticence. "I will leave him some sovs. Not to worry, I will not slit his throat. Sovs for silence. It is the Greek way. Had we no sovs, his fate. . . ." Yiorgos shrugged.

"Okay. But make it fast. We don't want to lose the holy procession," warned Stavros.

As the four men left the rear entrance of the university, they heard the deep horn of the ferry announce its departure. Stavros checked his watch. It was 1433 hours, nine minutes to T-Time.

Dimitra and Lambros walked east from the taverna, then turned north on the first major road away from the ferry dock. They planned to enter the olive groves a half kilometer distant, turn back east, then work their way into the hills and to the reserves. Stavros and Yanni spotted them and trailed at fifty meters. Yiorgos and Nikolas had no choice but to trail Stavros since no paths paralleled theirs. The Greeks stayed back a hundred meters. The biggest weakness in the plan was that all six had to cross Ionia Odos in broad daylight just when the Germans were most agitated.

Sound travels four times as fast underwater as in the air. Submerged swimmers at the beach were the first to hear the limpets, save those aboard the ferry. The muffled sound from the explosions on land were hardly audible. The German garrison paid no attention. The ferry was two-thirds of the way to Rio, a kilometer and a half from the fort and two kilometers from Stavros and the retreating fighters.

Lambros had placed the mines well. The ferry was built with bulkheads that transect their longitudinal beam. These watertight compartments can seal in case of a serious leak. Had Lambros placed the mines near each other, the crew might have been able to seal one compartment and save the ship. But Gus had coached Lambros, and the young fighter was diligent. He placed the first mine near the bow, the second midship, and the third he attached far aft to what he knew to be the hull of the engine compartment. It was all in his plan. When he finished with the third mine, he swam for the tender already clear of the Germans ashore. The three mines were on separate timers, so they didn't explode at the same time. But their sequence was fortunate; lending credence to the American idiom "better to be lucky than good."

The British Mk III Clockwork Delay Devices did their jobs, but they were not precision timepieces. The ferry was two minutes late leaving Antirrio, and the timers were late in their detonation. The first mine to detonate was the aft mine. Its two kilos of high explosives punched a hole the diameter of a basketball in the unarmored stern of the ferry. Salty water poured into the compartment and soon began shorting out electrical connections. The engine room crew of two Greeks were unharmed, but scared to death. They left the compartment only half securing the bulkhead on their way to the deck. The engines died two minutes later.

Just before the ferry lost power, another explosion jolted the craft. This one came near the bow. The boat started listing to port. With their craft overloaded at German insistence, the second hole in a remote compartment went unsecured. The Greek crew didn't want to go below and risk their lives for a boatload of Germans.

The third explosion came thirty seconds later, and another hole erupted midship. By now, the boat was listing at an uncorrectable angle and the vehicles on deck were moving on their own. German soldiers piled out of their troop carriers to add to the confusion. With no power and no way to stop the listing, the Greek captain ordered abandon ship. He was the last Greek off the vessel, with his crew of six already in the water, clinging to life vests and making for shore half a kilometer away.

The Germans were not so lucky. They required commands, and their officers froze. There were no vests for the troops, save a paltry few stored aboard the tilting deck. The officers broke into the vest lockers but found most were waterlogged and offered negative buoyancy. When the first enlisted man jumped without orders, an officer commanded him shot in the water. But that failed to stop the stampede as one after another panicked German jumped. Without vests and wearing heavy boots and ammunition belts, not even the salty Gulf buoyed their fate.

On the starboard side of the ferry, three officers tried to launch a lifeboat. But the listing ship was now taking water over its deck, and the lifeboat couldn't reach the Gulf, landing instead on the rotating hull.

It was a rewarding sight. One that Ajax and Gus took in from five kilometers north in the hills with the Reserves. They watched the sinking unfold like a grim fairytale. Each man elbowed the other for a turn at the glasses. Soon, all the andartes and OSS men were elbowing for their turn.

They saw the E-boat race to the sinking ship. But the fast patrol boat was ill-designed for water rescue. As the E-boat approached the sinking vessel, they slowed to avoid running down desperate Germans. The floating survivors were an unintended picket, preventing the boat from getting close. And the ferry was a lost cause. She rolled to port, then went down stern first. The fighters in the hills begged each other for the glasses to witness her last gasp. At the end, it was Ajax with the glasses. He watched, spellbound. As the bow slipped below the surface, he said to no one in particular, "For Greece and the revolution. Only Arion's dolphins can save you now."

Chapter 88

The E-boat's siren shrieked as it sped to the rescue. Its piercing call told Stavros and the others that the Germans had an emergency. They didn't hear the limpet blasts, and they couldn't see the Gulf from their route. But with the mighty boat's scream, spirits lifted. Operation Devil's Cauldron may have worked. Now, the only missing piece was a safe retreat.

Dimitra and Lambros walked into the olive groves on a narrow cobblestone roadway and started their journey east. Stavros and Yanni, then Yiorgos and Nikolas followed at a discrete distance. They had to avoid the Germans. Outnumbered and outgunned, they would be no match. Lambros, save for his knife, was without a weapon. Dimitra carried a Sten under her habit, the same weapon the trailing fighters carried in two canvas sacks with the Handy-Talkie. They had sent the bulky BC-1306 HF field radio to the Reserves earlier. Two andartes left the university with it soon after the Support Team received the coded convoy transmission from Arta.

Once in the olive groves, homes were more spread out than in Antirrio. As she and Lambros passed a small stone dwelling, she saw a farmer tending his trees. Lambros was limping, slowing their progress. He had no shoes.

Dimitra called to the farmer, "Brother, would you have shoes for my poor priest? He lost his in a ceremony and finds these paths rough on his tender flesh."

She glanced back at Lambros, and he gave her a questioning look.

The old man walked to the edge of his grove. "I have only these shoes. But perhaps with a payment, I could buy another pair."

Negotiations ensued.

Dimitra would have toyed with this exchange, but she had no time to waste. She pulled from inside her habit a pouch with a dozen sovs. She took one from the holder, not allowing the farmer to see how many she had. She held it before her penetrating stare, "With this sov, you can buy another pair and go with God's blessing."

The shrewd farmer answered, "Sister, with one sov, I can buy only one shoe."

That was a lie, but this was a Greek transaction. No harm, no foul.

Dimitra removed another sov. When offered to the farmer, he pulled the worn shoes from his feet and handed them to the priest with the green face. Dimitra nodded to Lambros, and her stare prompted him. The young swimmer nodded to the farmer, crossed himself, and faked a blessing.

Dimitra said, "The priest is silent. That is his vow. *Now, you* must remain silent as well. Is this understood?" Then she opened her habit to show the buttstock of the Sten.

The farmer's face drained of blood, and he nodded.

Stavros and Yanni saw the interaction and waited at a distance. When Dimitra and Lambros resumed at a faster pace, so did they.

The narrow road to the sleepy village of Molykreio wove through farms and groves before reaching Ionia Odos. When Dimitra and Lambros saw the main road, they stopped at an orange grove and motioned for the four followers to move up. They were out of sight. An occasional farmer passed with his laden donkey. But there were no Germans on this road.

Stavros and the others caught up with Dimitra and Lambros. The six moved into the grove and huddled away from the road to fashion a plan. Ionia Odos was busy. The metallic signature of straining diesels was constant. But luck was with them. The road to Molykreio was among the few that crossed under the major highway. There was no intersection, only an underpass. They would be exposed, but only on their approach and departure. Still, it was broad daylight. The Germans were wary, and the risk was high.

They discussed waiting until dark to cross. But time was not on their side. Soon, the Germans would organize and begin searching. With reinforcements and vehicles, the German grid would expand fast. The fighters' head start was only a matter of minutes.

The German garrison at Antirrio radioed Ioannina HQ after the third limpet detonated. HQ ordered mobile units near Antirrio to reinforce the garrison without delay. The relentless diesels were troop transports rolling south.

The din of diesels masked the plaintive singing and footfall of hoofs on stone until the farmer and his wagon were only meters away. Lambros was the first to hear. He and the others moved closer to the road to investigate. Thirty yards away, a preoccupied older man sang a sweet Greek love song as his ancient dapple gray self-navigated a road trod countless times. By his side was a half-finished bottle of local wine.

Lambros looked to Dimitra and then to Stavros, who both nodded. Then he stepped from the grove into the roadway, surprising the horse more than the farmer. The wagon stopped and Lambros walked to the farmer, who quit singing and began crossing himself. Lambros looked like a young priest, except with a green face. This was enough to make the farmer fearful he may have come upon the devil in one of his deceptive forms.

As Lambros drew closer, he heard the man mumbling a prayer and reassured, "No, brother. No need for prayer. I paint my face for a ritual. Fear not. But with all humility, I must ask you and your fine steed for a favor. Can you grant this to our small procession on the holy day for Mary?"

When Lambros asked for a favor, Dimitra first, then the others, walked from the grove into view.

"Are you going to Molykreio?" asked Lambros.

The first words from the farmer's mouth were mumbled. But Lambros understood him to say, "yes, Father. I go for fodder and straw, but no further."

"Then, brother, may we come along for the ride? It will save us walking and be a godly deed for your ledger this holy day," said Lambros.

The farmer mustered a more sober continence now. It was obvious to Dimitra that the composition of their band worried him. Before he could equivocate, Dimitra said, "Brother, today we have been fortunate and blessed with tithings. For your time with us on this holy day, I believe God intends you a gold sovereign." Then Dimitra withdrew one piece from her pouch.

This confused the farmer. He grew more so when the band, not waiting for his agreement, climbed aboard the small wagon. As Dimitra and Lambros sat on the bench on either side of the farmer, the gray turned his head to watch the loading.

The sideboards of the wagon were red and colorfully painted with amateur floral artwork and elaborate geometric designs. The tall wooden wheels were a pastel blue. The bed of the wagon held three large empty woven baskets with lids. The bins were for the fodder. Yiorgos and Nikolas climbed onto the bed and into the baskets. It was a tight squeeze, especially for Nikolas. Stavros was too tall for the baskets, so he crawled onto the bed of the wagon. Stavros withdrew a Sten and Yanni placed the carry bags and fallen branches from the grove over Stavros. With Stavros mostly concealed, Yanni climbed into his basket and pulled the lid over him. Stavros thumped the wagon bed three times, and Lambros said to the farmer, "Thank you for coming to our aid. May God be with us. It is time to go."

Dimitra crossed herself.

And with that, the shell-shocked, tipsy farmer flicked the reins, and the gray turned his head toward Molykreio.

Unterfeldwebel Müller was six days in Greece from northwest Poland and already on notice of a pending transfer to Bulgaria. He sat with his platoon on the hard bench in the back of an Opel Blitz 6700A troop carrier bounding for Antirrio. He sat in the last position, first out of the truck, on the driver's side facing the road embankment. The truck sped along at fifty miles per hour. As it passed over the road to Molykreio, he saw a horse and wagon with a priest and nun. That did not register as unusual. Then he saw a basket in the rear whose lid came loose, then somehow realigned itself. This gave him pause. But he was under orders to muster with his men at the garrison in Antirrio without delay. He knew better than to be the fly in the ointment. He stayed silent. Silence was how you survive the German Army.

The Church of Saint George sat on the tallest peak in the foothills two kilometers northwest of Molykreio. The farmer rode the fighters up the hill to its courtyard, where Lambros thanked him and told him never to speak of his good deed. As the fighters walked away, the old gray whinnied and started down the hill. This was the meeting point for reunion.

The view of the Gulf captivated the six fighters as they dismounted. From the church's elevation, they saw the E-boat circling near the Rio dock, and with the binoculars, they saw smaller inflatable craft pulling bodies from the silvery blue. They took turns passing the glasses.

Just as Yanni was about to retrieve the Handy-Talkie, a familiar voice called. Ajax stepped around the stone wall of the churchyard. "Devil's Cauldron boils with the blood of Germans. Congratulations, Lieutenant and Kapetánios, your mission is a triumph. I watched the sinking from our redoubt. It was glorious. All is lost for the Germans. They have gone to the depths, and may God save their souls."

There were smiles now on every face. Stavros had lived his history and added his battle to the lore of Lepanto. Yiorgos felt the deep satisfaction of retribution for the massacre of his family on this holiday with over three hundred others in Kommeno. And all remembered the sinking of the cruiser *Elli* at anchor off the island of Tinos on this day in 1940. The intervening four years and a world at war had forged this band of brave fighters. They were authors of redress. And Ajax was right. It was glorious.

Yiorgos looked to Stavros, "Thank, you, Lieutenant for being American and teaching us humble Greeks to dream like Hollywood." It was a friendly joke. Stavros saw the suppressed tears in the hard man's eyes.

Stavros nodded. "We better leave. The Germans have plenty of men and plenty of trucks. It's only a matter of time before they come looking."

The six fighters and the detachment of nine andartes turned to the hills and began walking, Ajax with his arm around Lambros. The Stens were out of the bags and Ajax had one for the young swimmer. It was a kilometer to the Reserves and the mounts. From there, the detachment could make a swift retreat to the friendly territory north and be in Chómori by early in the morning.

An hour had passed since T-Time, and shadows cast in the valleys. The path, an unused dirt road into the mountains, twisted and turned every twenty meters. They walked in low hills with tree cover and although they were hard to see, they were not invisible.

Upon arriving at the garrison, Unterfeldwebel Müller informed his oberleutnant of the odd sighting on the road. He reported the priest, the nun, and the wagon with baskets and the odd incident with the lid. His lieutenant passed this information up his chain of command. Fifteen minutes later, two platoons were sent to investigate. HQ ordered aircraft out of Corfu to search the hills.

Two Messerschmitt Bf 109s arrived thirty minutes after the order. They began circling above Molykreio, widening their search with each orbit. Lambros was again the first to hear them, then Stavros, who remembered the terrifying sound from the Arta ambush. Stavros gave the signal for everyone to take cover. By then, all could hear the unmuffled V-12s.

The detachment was fifteen fighters and no mounts, all andartes save Stavros and Yanni. They strung out on a fifty-meter train, and the last two in line were in the open. The

Messerschmitts were on them before they could hide. The pilots wasted no time identifying their targets. They fired their 20mm gondola cannons and shredded the bodies of the last in line. The aircraft banked right to circle for another pass. In mid-turn, the lead pilot radioed their location. The fighters were still half a kilometer to the Reserves and a defensible location. They had poked the German wolf, and now the pack was upon them.

Chapter 89

With the Messerschmitts in a tight circle and only seconds from another pass, an andarte alongside Nikolas rose to run to his dead comrades. Nikolas grabbed his shoulder. "Leave them for now. If we move the bodies, the pilots will know there are more of us. Stay under cover. Their next pass will be a guess, and our chances are better this way."

Stavros withdrew the Handy-Talkie. He keyed the transmission strip. "Reunion under attack. Half a kilometer south of your position. Send BARs and remain undercover from air."

The heavy BARs were the only guns that could serve as antiaircraft weapons. The OSS didn't train commandos for this because it was rare. But the OSS selected its men for weapons handling and improvisation. Gus, his section leader, and two men from Squad Two shouldered the two weapons and grabbed their ammo boxes. The four OSS men started down the trail to the others.

The second pass of the Messerschmitts was indeed guesswork, and they missed. Everyone stayed under cover and thanked their stars. The leaf canopy offered no protection from the leaden storm.

Stavros caught the scent first. A fire smoldered to the east of their location, where the airplanes strafed. August in Greece is dry as a bone. Careless shepherds or lightning strikes typically started forest fires. This one had begun with a Brandgranatpatrone 151, an incendiary round loaded among every ten antipersonnel rounds for the 20mm gondola cannons. The northeasterly wind on the water came around to the south in the hills. The smoke blew up the mountain parallel to the fighters' path. But the fire would spread fast and force the fighters to move.

Dimitra said to Stavros, "The fire will move on the wind as if primed with gasoline. I have seen it before. We must let the smoke build, then use it to mask our movement. Have everyone wet their face coverings and hold them to their noses. We will duck under the smoke and move toward the Reserves. Up the mountain are outcrops where we can shelter from the strafing."

Again, the Messerschmitts passed, this time correcting their fire too far west. Their next pass would bring fire right down the middle and chew the fighters into unrecognizable bits of flesh. Yanni overheard Dimitra's suggestion and when she finished, Stavros nodded and Yanni passed the word down the train.

Dimitra and Stavros led the way into the smoke. It burned their eyes and nostrils and denied their lungs oxygen. It was hell on earth, but it was their only hope. They stayed as low as possible and made slow progress. When the aircraft returned, they fired into the vacated cover.

Two hundred meters up the mountain, they came upon an outcrop and the thirteen fighters packed under it. It gave shelter from all directions but east. If the Messerschmitts took that approach, they would all die. The smoke still hung over the site, providing cover but leaving them breathless and blind.

Crouching, otherwise undefended, they heard the planes pass low but not fire. Then they were out of earshot for thirty seconds. When the andartes reacquired the drumming of their engines, it was from the east. There was nowhere to run. The only hope was that the pilots had not spotted them, and the strafing was still guesswork. But by the approaching sound of the mighty motors, Stavros feared they had a fix. He looked at Dimitra holding the bandanna across her face and thought how lucky he had been to know this wonderful woman.

The planes approached low at a perfect firing angle, with the lead plane followed by his wingman to his right. Stavros steeled himself for the cannon onslaught. Then he heard two weapons, but not aboard the airplanes. He looked to his left. On the mountain pathway, just visible through the roiling smoke, he saw hazy apparitions.

Seventy meters up the mountain, Gus and the section leader stood side by side, shouldering the heavy BAR rifles. They set the firing selectors to automatic and fast fire. The deep penetrating cadence of the .30-06 shells leaving the muzzles at five hundred rounds per minute was fearsome but friendly. Both Messerschmitts peeled to their right, and Stavros saw a trail of smoke from the rear plane. Cheering erupted in the outcrop and Stavros thought, *Are those guys that good, or was that luck?*

The lead Messerschmitt tailed his wingman to the east. The aircraft was in no shape to return to Corfu. The lucky or good shooting of the BAR men had severed an oil line and soon the Daimler-Benz DB 605A-1 would melt. The wingman ditched in the Gulf, and the lead pilot flew alongside for support. The BAR gunners reloaded.

Dimitra said, "Quickly! Now we move up the path. There are more outcrops the higher we go."

Stavros whistled to Yanni and waved his arm forward. Yiorgos did the same.

When they reached Gus and the section leader, the two OSS men were arguing about who hit the Messerschmidt. Stavros said, "Thanks for your help. Have I interrupted anything important?"

Gus was ready to plead his case and pointed to the smoking aircraft. Then he thought better. He said, "This way, Lieutenant. The flyboy will be back. No time to waste. Tell the train to follow in our footsteps . . . *only!*"

They traveled under heavier cover now, with rocky escarpments along the way. As they continued north, the dirt path disappeared. Five minutes passed. Then they heard the single Messerschmidt pass without strafing. The plane was searching to the south of their position. He had lost his fix on the fighters, and now the smoke obscured the hills.

Unterfeldwebel Müller with his platoon and one other reached the Church of Saint George and dismounted their vehicles. They were just in time to see the Messerschmidt make its smoky retreat. They started up the path on the double with twenty-four men. The fire raged to their east and the mountain breeze, ever unpredictable because of thermal currents, folded in on them.

The Reserves redoubt offered cover, clean air, and a vantage from the Gulf all the way up the mountain. But its biggest advantage was its fast escape north. When Stavros and the detachment reached the Reserves, there was a cheerful hero's welcome for Lambros and jokes about him naked and painted green. There was a quick meeting of the leaders as the Reserves broke down the mortar and retrieved the mounts. When the mounts arrived, Dimitra announced to her andartes, "There are bodies of our comrades on this trail. The fire may consume them. But if not, they deserve our respect and a proper burial. I ask for two volunteers to hide in the woods with their mounts until dark, retrieve their bodies, and return the remains to Chómori."

The hands of every andarte flew into the air, even Lambros. Dimitra picked two andartes dressed as nuns. Their disguise, she thought, might provide cover.

As the entire detachment mounted and made ready to ride, Gus said, "We got company."

Through the intermittent smoke, he saw the Germans making double time toward them. They were five hundred meters down the pathway.

Stavros said, "Time to go."

Yanni motioned the OSS men to the north, and Yiorgos did the same for the retreating andartes. The nuns took another path to the east, there to hide in the dense woods.

Gus circled Stavros on his mount and Dimitra on Diávolos. He called, "Hey, I got my motorcycle. And I put it to good use."

Stavros looked at Dimitra, puzzled. Dimitra shrugged. And with that and the two leaders at the head of the train, the mounts started off at a trot.

There was a reason Gus insisted the train follow his footsteps. When he veered off the dirt path for fifty meters into the scrub on their way to the redoubt, the fighters knew better than to question his route. The Germans had no such insight. Their point man stopped to clear the beaten red motorcycle from the path. He squared his Mauser back onto his shoulder. He raised the overturned bike to push it off the path, lifting its weight off the Mk2 grenades' safety lever hidden under fallen leaves. From then, the German soldier had four seconds to live.

When the grenade exploded, the others in Unterfeldwebel Müller's platoon scattered to the sides of the path for cover. There awaited them more tripwires and C2 charges. The charge that killed Müller was strung shoulder-high to the trunk of an ancient chestnut tree. And, although the German never saw it, the block of explosive contained an epitaph. It read *Bye-Bye*.

Chapter 90

OSS Operational Group II received orders to leave Greece a week after Devil's Cauldron. They were to board an LCI on the beach in Parga and leave the way they came. The connection between Devil's Cauldron and their premature departure went unstated. They were the second group in the country but the first OG to leave Greece.

Devil's Cauldron was a success. With German casualties in the dozens if not hundreds, thirty-four vehicles destroyed, and high-level coordination with EAM-ELAS, it was one for the win column. It denied the Germans a critical line of communication during a strategic redeployment of their forces. By the grizzly scorecard of war, the Allies suffered acceptable losses. But the OSS, however unconventional and adventurist, was still a bureaucracy. It valued control.

Stavros had not lied to Bari about the operation, but he had not detailed the complexity or scope. From the start, he and Yanni transmitted what they thought Bari wanted to hear. Perhaps not the complete picture, but a comfortable caricature. And Greece was fading from the Allies' focus. The Germans were leaving, and hotter zones of operation like Yugoslavia and China, Burma and India pressed.

It was late afternoon, and Yanni had just decoded the message from Bari. He found Stavros in the monastery's courtyard talking with Gus and Johnny. Gus was still trying to claim the downed Messerschmitt. Johnny was nodding, and Stavros had heard it all before.

Yanni said, "You need to see this." And he waved the decoded message at Stavros.

Inside the monastery, Stavros read the order. It was a terse message. Translated from OSS-speak, it read, "Discontinue offensive operations immediately. Muster at Parga 2300 hours September 5 for transport to Bari."

Stavros looked at Yanni, and no words passed. The moment was bittersweet. Relief and regret fell upon both men.

Stavros walked to the schoolhouse, where Ajax stood at the door. The men greeted one another warmly, and Stavros offered the token American cigarette. This gesture brought a smile to the big man. He held the prize before his grateful gaze, then put it in his shirt pocket. Ajax said, "Thank you for everything, Lieutenant. The cigarettes are enjoyable, but it has been even more a pleasure fighting with you."

Stavros said, "You are welcome. The pleasure of fighting together is all mine. Is she busy?"

"She is talking to Vasilios. But she will not mind the interruption," replied Ajax.

"Thanks," answered Stavros. Then he pushed open the wooden door far enough that he could see Dimitra with Vasilios seated before her desk.

Dimitra looked over her shoulder at the doorway and smiled. "Do you have something for me, Lieutenant?"

Stavros asked, "Fishing? Nineteen hundred hours?"

Dimitra knew the code. She nodded, and Stavros closed the door.

Chapter 91

Rocks and stones sculpted the stream marking serene detours. Eddies gurgled and the scent of sideritis lay thin on the evening air. She came on him like a cat. He was easy prey with his mind elsewhere.

Dimitra said, "No man ever steps in the same river twice, for it is not the same river and he is not the same man."

Stavros turned to watch her approach. He admired this woman, her skills, her intellect, her leadership, her presence. His love had grown to universal and immutable agápe, a bonding of spirit. A bond to be tested by time and distance. A test not of choice but of fate.

He turned on the soft stones of the stream bed, and the sandy mix shifted under his boots. He said, "Heraclitus."

Dimitra nodded, "Very good, Professor. You pass the exam."

The couple embraced and kissed. Then during their lingering hug, Dimitra said, "Bari is calling you home, no?"

For a second, Stavros wondered if EAM-ELAS had intercepted and decoded his orders or if Dimitra was prescient. It didn't matter. He said, "We'll leave Chómori on the first. We exfiltrate Parga on the fifth."

Then he waited. He had nothing more to say. He could not form his feelings into words.

Dimitra led him by the hand to the flat stone, her perch by the river. The couple sat close together and stared into the soothing waters. After a moment, Dimitra said, "My mother and I will leave soon after, probably on the second or third."

Another silence passed. Then Stavros asked, "What about us?"

Dimitra sighed, "We are what we make of ourselves. Nothing changes. Today you make of yourself an OSS Lieutenant. I a Kapetánios. Tomorrow will be different."

"Right, I get it. Heraclitus and all that," replied Stavros with a note of exasperation. "But what about us?"

"Always the practical American. You have no mind for philosophy. Your constructs must be bing . . . bing . . . bing. This comes before that. Everything falls on a straight line. At the end there is a meeting, a wedding, a funeral. Who knows? Impossible!

"*This* is the thing. We will separate. We will miss each other. We will write. You will take another lover in America or wherever the OSS sends you. I will study in Thessaloniki. That is all. My nails will grow dirty searching for relics of an ancient past, clues to my country's greatness and misfortune.

"Why is *this* not enough?"

"I want you in my life. I want us to be together," answered Stavros.

"Impossible! Will you stay in Greece? I can arrange an interview at Aristotle. Perhaps you are smart enough to be a Greek professor. Perhaps? But we must hope they have no philosophy examination, no?

"Or should I come to America? Can I bring Eva? Two of us, both fish out of water."

And on cue, with perchance Dimitra's perpetual companion, a trout launched into the air in midstream.

"There," she said. "That is me. Falsely free, then forced by gravity and fate back into my world. You see now? These are the moments of *us*. This rock, this stream, this village. This is *us*. There may be *us* someday, somewhere, but now it cannot be said."

Stavros processed the pain in silence. She was right. Then he relinquished. "We will leave behind all that we don't need for our trip to Parga. I'll give Yiorgos a list. Should we leave it stored in the monastery?"

Dimitra said, "Yes, for now. Yiorgos can arrange things to his liking when he takes over as Kapetánios. He will accede to that position September first, the day you leave. We will send a detachment with you to bring back the mules from Parga."

Stavros asked, "Who will become stratiotikós?"

"Nikolas," answered Dimitra. "Vasilios will remain politikós. That will keep the KKE happy for now."

Stavros veered from questioning Dimitra's political entanglements as the OSS forbid. He trusted her to handle the complex personalities, affiliations, and doctrines.

He asked, "Can I say goodbye to Eva on our way to Parga?"

Dimitra smiled. "I will ride with you to Platanos, and we will both visit her. You will keep your goodbye short because you will be commanding. That is good. My mother can stretch such moments into a three-act play."

Stavros smiled, and the two fighters stared at the swirling water as the gently falling curtain of night erased their dreams.

Chapter 92

Women and children buzzed about the grape vines like worker bees. Demitris stood to the side of the trellises nearest the house and supervised, leaning on his shepherd's crook. Stavros descended the steps from the roadway into the courtyard of the Hantzis home and walked to the patriarch. Demitris looked at Stavros, then back to the vines. Just as Stavros was alongside the old man, he raised his staff, pointed to a cluster, and called to a child.

Stavros said, "Sir, am I interrupting your morning? It looks like you have important business this day, no?"

"It is the early harvest. These grapes we take to the priest for blessing. He waves his hand, and all is made right in the world. This is how it is always done.

"In days before, I harvested myself. Now, I must have the women and children do my work. I should feel shame, no?

"But a man must live his fate. That can never change. Mine is to grow old and tell children what to do. And you, Stavros, son of Alex? What is your fate?" asked Demitris.

Stavros thought about the man asking the question. He knew of Demitris's life; his father had told him much, and the village of Chómori told him more. Demitris was lore.

In the days before the Turks fled Greece, the village looked to Demitris as the lawgiver, the assassin. This man wrote Greek justice as a subscript to Turkish occupation. He was the keeper of eiréné, Greek wholeness.

Demitris earned a living at this, good enough to send two of his sons to America. Harry returned in 1912 to fight the Turks. When he left in 1914, it was the last Demitris saw of either son. Letters, photographs, and memories were what he had left. The death of his remaining son, George, to the Italian occupation toppled another pillar of his life. But that was war.

Demitris never lost bearing, never wavered. Stavros suspected that this man saw himself as much more than a boss of children. Stavros said, "Sir, I know better than to predict three women."

Demitris smiled at the reference to Clotho, Lachesis, and Atropos, the three Fates.

"But, sir, this much I know. Our group will leave Greece soon. That is why I came to visit you. I owe you a debt that I can never repay. You have helped me understand my mother's death and the challenge of my father and your son. Now it is a part of me. For this, I can only offer thanks. When I return to America, it would be my honor to take a message to Harry. I do not know when we will return. But when we go, I can tell him anything you wish. Or perhaps I could deliver a letter?"

Just then Stavros saw Johnny and Gus returning from the taverna. Johnny was a shutterbug. On a lanyard around his neck hung the OSS-issued Kodak 35 US Army PH-324. Stavros said, "Excuse me, sir."

He ran to the roadway, and after conferring with Johnny, the two men returned to Demitris. Stavros explained, "Johnny will take our picture together and photographs of the grape harvest. These I can take to Harry. Would you like me to do that, sir?"

Demitris thought for a moment. Then he said, "Yes, Stavros, son of Alex. That will make Harry happy. But one thing you will need to do for me."

Stavros cocked his head.

"You must send to me our picture together."

Chapter 93

Stavros handed the list down to Yiorgos from the saddle. He said, "Two grenades. That's all we couldn't account for. Otherwise, it's all in the monastery, compliments of Uncle Sam."

The grizzled fighter smiled. "I trust you can find your way to Parga. From there to Italy. Let us hope the Germans have no sponge divers with big ideas."

Stavros smiled. "It's been an honor to fight alongside of you, Kapetánios. I have learned a lot. I will forever think of you as a friend and comrade."

Yiorgos nodded. There was emotion in his eyes. He said, "Go with God, American."

The fighters clasped hands, and their grip lingered. Then Stavros rose and looked to his right at Dimitra. He asked, "Ready?"

The poised woman astride antsy Diávolos nodded.

Stavros looked over his shoulder at the OSS train and at Yanni mounted next in line. He nodded to Yanni, and Yanni raised his right arm, then motioned forward. As the horses took their first hesitant steps, Dimitra said, "You believe you have seen challenges in Greece. You are about to face the most difficult. Saying goodbye to my mother."

Chapter 94

It was, as Dimitra said, the beginning of a three-act play. When the OSS train reached Platanos, they stood down in the courtyard while Johnny, Stavros, and Dimitra went to visit Eva.

Eva was out of her element. Her home was in crates and boxes, and she didn't have the service to offer coffee or anything to eat. Dimitra, instead, had brought galaktoboureko and the foursome ate the sweet pastry sitting under the wisteria-laden pergola. After Eva explained her frantic effort to corral her belongings and meet the emotional demands of moving, she said, "Listen to me. I think only of myself. I am a diminished host, not for want of service but for attention to my guests. Please tell me, Professor Commander, do you know what will happen next? How long will you be in Italy? Will they send you somewhere else? When the war is over, will you return to America or perhaps you will stop here in Greece and take with you something left behind?"

Dimitra rolled her eyes.

Johnny, who had finished his pastry and sensed a private moment, said, "Eva, I have to go back to the courtyard and check some gear. I just wanted to see you and say I cannot thank you enough for helping heal this leg."

Then Johnny handed Eva a small, wrapped bundle. She carefully removed the covering to find a potato peeler, US Army issue.

Eva was speechless and touched. Johnny said, "I'll send you something nicer when we get to the States. I've got to go."

The young man rose from the table. Eva rose a second later. They hugged, and she looked up into his innocent eyes. "My student and son, you must be careful in your travels and in this war. We have invested many hours in your training. Make certain you return safely home, and your knowledge will grow with time."

And with that, Johnny left with a nod to Stavros.

"Now, you two. . . ." Eva began once Johnny was out of earshot.

Dimitra cut her off. "Mother, this is unnecessary. Stavros is here to say goodbye. He does not need a lecture or encouragement. He has men waiting for his command. This parting needs to be short and sweet."

"I am forever sorry for impeding the war effort," replied Eva. "But this needs saying. I will be brief."

Dimitra shook her head, and a smothered scowl came over her lips.

"You two are meant for each other. But not for this time. That is all I have to say. Go with God, Professor Commander. You will be in my prayers until. . . ." Then Eva teared and her words trailed.

Dimitra walked with Stavros to the gateposts of Eva's yard. There, out of sight of her mother and any OSS commandos, she kissed Stavros. They embraced everlastingly, and when they separated, his tears were of overwhelming joy. This was a moment, a woman, a country that would forever own his heart.

Epilogue

The Germans had no sponge divers or E-boats or submarines. At least none between Greece and Italy in early September 1944. The Germans did, however, have big ideas, all of which the Allies were now blowing up on two fronts. Stavros and OG II arrived safe and sound. Stepping onto the pier in Monopoli, the Operational Group looked as wild as the mountains they had haunted for the past five months. Every man was skinny, wiry, and ready for a bath, a haircut, and a new uniform. A big plate of pasta was foremost on their minds. They were lucky. Johnny's broken leg was the only long-term debilitating injury. Bouts of dysentery, sprains, cuts, and bruises had plagued the OG, but they suffered no killed in action. Of the 185 OSS commandos in the eight OGs that fought in Greece, three were killed in action and twenty-three wounded.[108]

The mountains of Greece forged lifetime bonds and habits. Greece changed both the way they looked and the way they looked at the world. Cockiness lived on, but their depth of awareness and resolve and confidence grew. It would serve them well. There was more fighting to come.

Stavros rested in Italy until November. He wrote Dimitra at the university, worked out and regained his normal body weight. The Germans left Greece in October. They evacuated Athens on the twelfth and the Papandreou Government of National Unity arrived on the eighteenth. This opened a chapter in Greek, British, and American history that will not see the depth it deserves in this book. From October 1944 through 1949, Greece was a tale of bloody politics, imperialism, and great power skullduggery. Personal sacrifice and hardship beset the population, unprompted by occupiers. Stavros returned to Greece for the latter years of this chapter. His position at Park College provided cover for a succession of America's secret services and the CIA. And yes, he and Dimitra reunited.

In November 1944, Stavros shipped out with an OSS French OG to China. They landed in Calcutta, then trained in the provinces of Bengal and Assam. An overloaded C-47 flew them into a remote province north of Chongqing, China's wartime capital. There Stavros and his team trained guerrillas to retrieve downed pilots and radio weather forecasts to Allied forces. He returned to the States in October 1945.

Stavros left India aboard the *General Fitzpatrick* with a shipload of GI railroaders, men who ran logistic support in the China–Burma–India Theater. He left the ship in New York and routed his return to Missouri through Indianapolis, Indiana. There he visited Harry Hantzis, shook the hand of the son of Demitris, and presented the photos from Johnny's camera work in Chómori. Stavros thanked Harry for pursuing his mother's killers and pledged to complete Eléni's requite. Harry counseled Stavros that some obligations require patience. Eléni's requite would take twelve years.

They ate a celebratory meal at the Hantzis Brothers Restaurant in the Loraine Hotel near Union Station. That's where he met James Hantzis, Harry's son, himself back from India and the 721st Railway Operating Battalion. The next morning, Stavros left on a train to St. Louis.

His reunion with Marta and Alex was tearful and joyful and featured endless Lombardy delights: *cotoletta, cassoeula* and osso buco. He stayed with his parents for two weeks, trying to decide what should come next in his life. He was still on the OSS payroll, and Park College had assured him he could resume teaching the coming spring semester.

Dimitra studied. She enrolled in the archaeology master's program as a second-year student. She loved the science. She especially loved the field work. She was a natural. She sensed and rationalized locations and structures and took pride in the smallest recoveries.

She missed Stavros. She wrote to him, and he was always in her thoughts. But she had her work, and she had Eva. Dimitra backed away from politics and spoke for the Socialist Party at university events only a handful of times. The socialists migrated farther from the KKE as civil strife grew. The KKE miscalculated. They overplayed their political and military strength and grew isolated. Their dogmatic adventures modeled on the Soviet Union, their elusive supporter, were disastrous.

As the Germans fled north, Stalin and Churchill met secretly in Moscow and signed the Percentage Agreement. Postwar Europe took shape. Rumania and Bulgaria fell into the USSR's sphere of influence, and Greece belonged to the British. They confirmed the agreement in February 1945 at Yalta. The KKE was on its own and no match for the British. When the British ran out of money in 1947, the Americans stepped in.

Dimitra completed her master's and stood for a doctorate degree. She lived out the Civil War years in Thessaloniki with Eva. She attended and presented at graduate seminars, colloquia, and conferences. After six semesters, she successfully defended her thesis, *Material and Social Dimension of Pottery Style: The Handmade Pottery of Bronze Age from Tombs of Thessaloniki.*

Eva taught music at a nearby lyceum. She tended and expanded the garden and never failed to prompt Dimitra on Stavros and her plans. She liked Thessaloniki. Platanos had a special place in her heart, but Thessaloniki was a city, much more in tune with Eva's sensitivities. She relished the buzzing markets, discursive coffee houses, stylish cafés, and vibrant social scene. She took up painting. She worked in oils, her subjects, the plants she tended. Soon the walls of their home teamed with her work. Dimitra grew used to finding her mother in the garden wearing her paint-spotted smock, keenly focused on mastering a detail. Eva was happy. And Dimitra was happy. When Eva painted, she didn't bombard Dimitra with questions.

Aris Velouchiotis was too revolutionary for the KKE. He was a legend and founder of EAM-ELAS. But the KKE couldn't control him. After the KKE failed to oust the British from Athens in December 1944, they agreed to demobilize EAM-ELAS. Aris signed off along with General Sarafis, but Aris reneged. The KKE accused him of treachery and denounced him as a "suspicious and adventurous element."

Aris retreated into the mountains of Agrafa, north of Chómori, with a band of true believers to reorganize the resistance. An informer betrayed him. Before a paramilitary unit of the Athens' government could take him prisoner, he committed suicide. His would-be captors cut his head from his body and hung it from a pole in the city of Trikala.

Yiorgos, too, fell out with the KKE. He was never a member, aligned instead with the Popular Democratic Union. As the Germans left, the KKE elements in EAM-ELAS predominated and ordered active resistance to the returning British. This didn't sit well with Yiorgos. He defied EAM-ELAS orders and marched the Chómori andartes to Patras to greet the British 2nd Airborne Brigade landing on October 4. This force eventually reoccupied Athens.

With the Government of National Unity installed, Yiorgos's mission ended. He knew the future for Greece would be stormy, and he wanted none of it. When the KKE attempted to drive the British out of Athens in December, he quit. He returned to Kato Dafni to help his family in their business. He was a master apiculturist. Beekeeping had its perils, but they were not death, barbarity, and cruelty. Of these, he had a lifetime's fill.

Lambros returned to Kalymnos. In early 1945, the island was still Italian, only reverting to Greek administration in 1947. Lambros continued opposing the Italian occupation, but in less explosive ways than the plot that saw him arrested in 1941.

He dove for sponges, this time without painting his body. He met a lovely Greek Italian girl. They fell in love and married in 1946. But the war had undermined the sponge trade. In 1947, Lambros and his wife joined with hundreds of other Greek divers and immigrated to Tarpon Springs, Florida. He and Gus reunited when his ship docked in New York.

Gus returned to Brooklyn after his time in China with Stavros. He had matured, still cocky but aware that he needed to plan a future. Stavros inspired him. Gus returned to school and earned his degree in Naval Architecture from the State University of New York (SUNY) and continued to work at the Navy Yard. He never made it to Milos, and no one ever erected a statue of him in his family's village.

Vasilios was a deadender. He remained under KKE discipline through the Civil War. He was lucky he didn't burn to death in the hell of napalm that fell on Mount Grammos near the Albanian border in August 1949. After their defeat at Grammos, Stalin ordered the KKE to declare a ceasefire. Vasilios retreated to Albania, then Yugoslavia, then Romania. He finally landed in the Soviet Union in 1952 and made his way to Moscow.

In 1947, the Greek government enacted a law that stripped citizenship from Greeks who fought against the government in the Civil War. The law banned them from their country. In 1948, another law allowed the government to confiscate the property of those stripped of citizenship. In 1982, the government enacted an amnesty law, allowing for the repatriation of banned citizens.

Vasilios returned to Greece in 1983 and taught history at a lyceum in Athens. The KKE, their network still active, arranged his job.

When the OG returned to Bari, they rested but were soon told of their disbandment. The OSS offered the commandos a choice of volunteering for China–Burma–India or waiting for assignment to a combat unit in Europe. Johnny, along with Stavros and Gus, volunteered for China.

Johnny was an affable companion. His laid-back personality and California good looks always fit in. But Sichuan Province knew not what to make of him, or the other OSS men. The dusty hills of northwest China were not a world of interspersed nationalities, and Johnny was the strangest of all the strangers. Dressed in black peasant trousers, sandals, and a loose-fitting top, the locals called him *megwah*. The commandos interpreted this as *giant*. The curious peasants put bowls of tea on rocks where they knew the giant would pass and then hid to see what the *megwah* would do with them. It took the American a while to catch on to this friendly gesture. His light hair and blue eyes fascinated the illiterate peasants. They couldn't care less that he was Greek—of Greece they knew nothing—but they came to idolize his Adonis persona.

Johnny returned home after the war, enrolled in the University of Southern California, and earned a Bachelor of Arts degree in Cinematography. He worked as a cameraman on early television productions, notably *I Love Lucy*. Johnny married his childhood sweetheart, and they raised a picture-perfect family in the Hollywood Hills. Once back in the States, Johnny sent Eva a Parker 51 fountain pen with a card that read, "I will forever remember you and our lessons. You inspired me to enroll in college. Thank you for healing my wounds and pointing me in the right direction. You are a wonderful woman, a master cook, a talented singer, and an even better gardener. Please use this pen to write often. I hope you are happy in Thessaloniki. Yours always, Johnny."

Johnny was a valuable commando. In a firefight, he was as vicious and deadly as any in the OSS. But Johnny's easy-goingness sometimes translated into forgetfulness. When OG II left Chómori, it was Johnny who couldn't locate the two grenades missing from Yanni's inventory.

May 27, 2020
Nafpaktia News

Two Grenades were Found in the Yard of a House

A World War II grenade was found in the yard of his house this morning by an elderly man in Chómori, Nafpaktia, while he was cleaning. The grenade was stuck somewhere in wood and a stone package and when the old man picked it up, the grenade rolled and stopped at the entrance of his warehouse. The elderly man immediately alerted his children, who in turn informed the police. A few hours ago, a special team of pyrotechnicians from the Greek Army arrived at the spot where they found another grenade during a search of the spot. The pyrotechnicians collected them in a special bulletproof box to be safely transported to a place where a controlled explosion will take place. [109]

Acronyms

ACRONYM	NAME
AHEPA	American Hellenic Educational Progressive Association
AMM	Allied Military Mision
AOA	Antifascist Military Organization, Greek Air Force, left led
AON	Antifascist Military Organization, Greek Navy, left led
ASO	Antifascist Military Organization, Greek Army, left led
BAR	Browing Automatic Rifle
BMM	UK British Military Mission
CCC	New Deal's Civilian Conservation Corps
CIGS	UK Chief of the Imperial General Staff
COI	Office of the Coordination of Information, forerunner of OSS
EAM-ELAS	Greek National Liberation Front-People's Liberation Army, left led, abbr. ELAS
EDES	National Republican Greek League, right led, pro-king
ELD	Greek Union of People's Democracy, socialist party
EPON	Greek student Wing of National Liberation Front, EAM
FNB	Foreign Nationals Branch, division of OSS
G-2	US Army Intelligence
JCS	US Joint Chiefs of Staff
KKE	Communist Party of Greece
NATO	North Atlantic Treaty Organization
OG	OSS Operational Group
OSS	US Office of Strategic Services
PEEA	Greek Political Committee of National Liberation, the Mountain Government
SOE	UK Special Operations Executive
VESMA	UK Royal Greek Middle East Forces
WPA	New Deal's Works Progress Administration

Photographs

Photo 1 Cruiser Elli (Hellenic Navy History Service)

Photo 2 The explosion of one of the Italian torpedoes at the pier of the port of Tinos, on August 15, 1940. Elli can be seen on the right side of the pole. (Hellenic Navy History Service 424003)

Photo 3 Aris Velouchiotis, founder of ELAS resistance army (Creative Commons)

Photo 4 EAM-ELAS Andartes (Greek Ministry of Foreign Affairs - Photo exhibition of the Diplomatic and Historical Archive Service)

The original party of British officers and men who were dropped
into Greece in the autumn of 1942

Left to right, standing: Themie Marinos, Denys Hamson, Nat Barker, Chris
Woodhouse, Inder Gill, the author, John Cook, Arthur Edmonds and Tom Barnes;
Kneeling: Sergeants Len Wilmot, Chittis and Phillips.

*Photo 5 British SOE Team in Greece. Parachuted into Roumeli (Central
Greece) September 30, 1942. Haim Herzog Museum for the Jewish Soldier
in World War II.*

Photo 6 Photo Gorgopotamos railway bridge in ruins, following its destruction by Greek EAM-ELAS and Greek EDES partisans led by British SOE operatives, November 25, 1942. (Hellenic Army General Staff)

Photo 7 Klouve or crate. Germans began using hostage cages following Gorgopotamos (From the photographic archive of Spyros Meletzis)

Photo 8 Camp Carson World War II (US Army)

Photo 9 Liberty or Death, The Greek Battalion passing in review, Camp Carson 1943 (US Army)

Photo 10 OSS Greek Operational Group 1944 (OSS Society)

Photo 11 Village of Chómori (Hantzis collection)

Photo 12 Hantzis home. (Hantzis collection)

Photo 13 Demitris Konstantinos Hantzis. (Hantzis collection)

Photo 14 Photo taken by British liaison with EAM-ELAS fighters, John Emberson. This encounter took place in Crete near Krousonas on July 14, 1944.

Maps

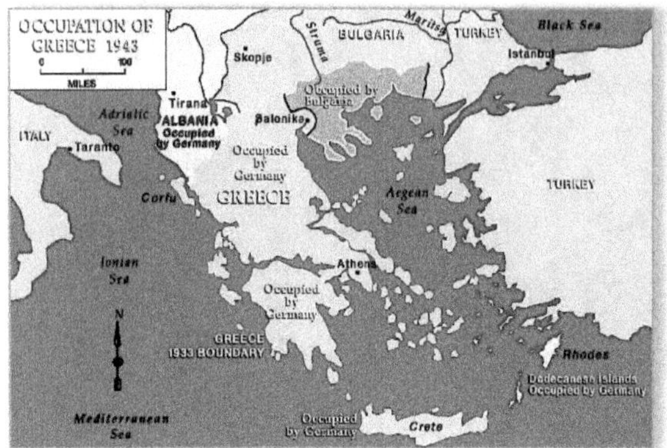

Map 1 Occupation of Greece 1943 after Italian surrender - United States
Holocaust Memorial Museum

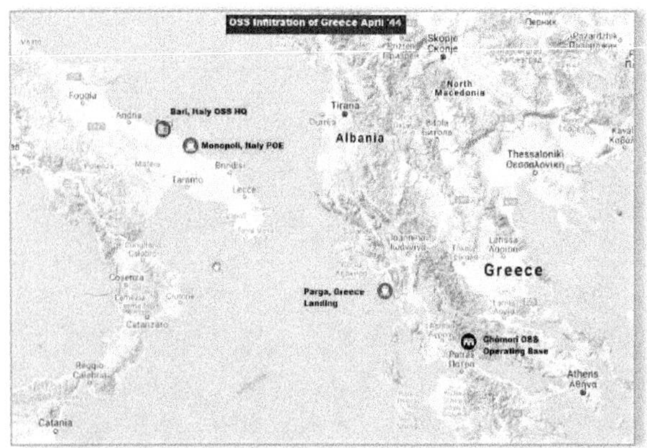

Map 2 Monopoli to Parga via Landing Craft (365 km or 226 miles) then
Parga to Chómori on foot (214 km or 133 miles).

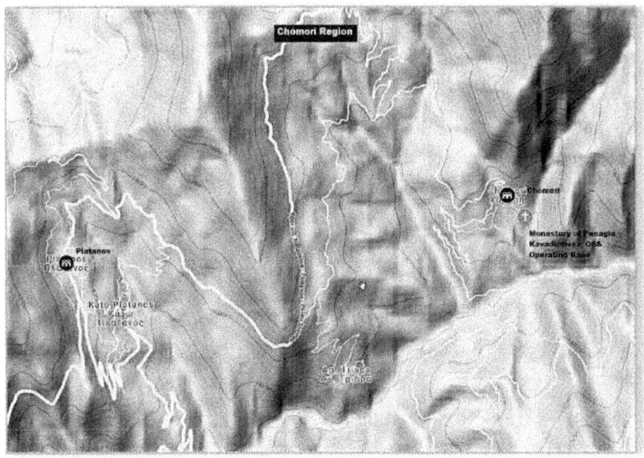

Map 3 Area around Chómori showing elevation in meters. Distance from Chómori to Platanos is 13.5 km or 8.3 miles.

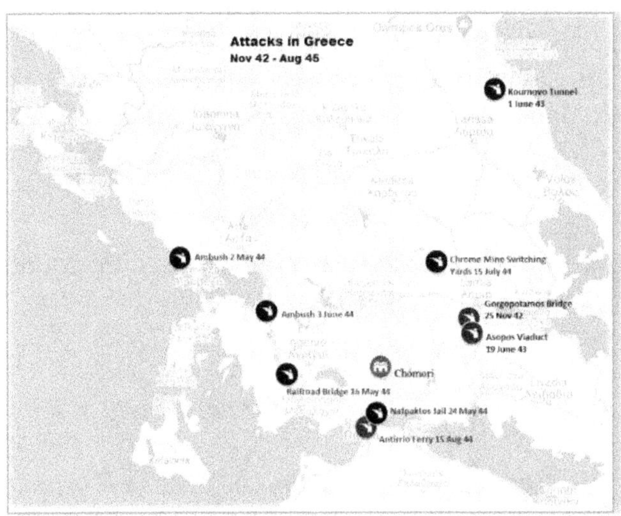

Map 4 Attacks in Greece. SOE-Andarte actions shown in red. OSS-Andarte attacks based on composite after-action reports but fictional per narration shown in blue.

Bibliography

<u>Books</u>

Clogg, R. (2002). *A Concise History of Greece*: Cambridge University Press.

Cramer, J. A. (1828). *A Geographical and Historical Description of Ancient Greece, with a Map, and a Plan of Athens*. Oxford: Clarendon Press.

Davis, P. K. (2001). *100 Decisive Battles: From Ancient Times to the Present*: Oxford University Press.

de Haan, F., Daskalova, K., & Loutfi, A. (2006). *Biographical Dictionary of Women's Movements and Feminisms in Central, Eastern, and South Eastern Europe: 19th and 20th Centuries*: CEU Press/Central European University Press.

Demetrios, G., & Huybers, J. A. (1913). *When I Was a Boy in Greece*. Boston: Lothrop, Lee & Shepard.

Fermor, P. L., & Bailey, R. (2015). *Abducting a General: The Kreipe Operation in Crete*: New York Review Books.

Forster, E. S., & Dakin, D. (1958). *A Short History of Modern Greece, 1821–1945*: Methuen.

Fourniotis, N., & Horsch, G. (2012). *Early Summer Circulation in the Gulf of Patras (Greece)*.

Giannaris, J., & Olson, M. K. C. (1988). *Yannis*: Pilgrimage Pub.

Helias Doundoulakis, G. G. (2014). *Trained to Be an OSS Spy*: Xlibris.

Hinsley, H. (2019). *British Intelligence in The Second World War* (Vol. 1).

Hinsley, F. H., & Thomas, E. E. (1979). *British Intelligence in the Second World War* (Vol. 2): H.M. Stationery Office.

Hunt, D. (1990). *A Don at War*: F. Cass.

Iatrides, J. O. (2010). *Greece at the Crossroads: The Civil War and Its Legacy*: Pennsylvania State University Press.

Iatrides, J. O., & McNeill, W. H. (2015). *Revolt in Athens: The Greek Communist "Second Round," 1944–1945*: Princeton University Press.

Kaloudis, G. (2018). *Modern Greece and the Diaspora Greeks in the United States*: Lexington Books.

Kent Roberts Greenfield, R. P., Bell Wiley. (1987). *The Army Ground Forces, The Organization of Ground Combat Troops*. Washington, DC: Center of Military History, United States Army.

Kosmidou, E. R. (2013). *European Civil War Films: Memory, Conflict, and Nostalgia*: Routledge.

Kouvaras, K. (1978). *Photo Album of the Greek Resistance*: Wire Press.

Kouvaras, K. (1982). *OSS with the Central Committee of EAM*: Wire Press.

Lulushi, A. (2016). *Donovan's Devils: OSS Commandos Behind Enemy Lines—Europe, World War II*: Arcade.

Mazower, M. (1993). *Inside Hitler's Greece: The Experience of Occupation, 1941–44*. New Haven: Yale University Press.

Moss, W. S. (1950). *Ill Met by Moonlight*: Harrap.

Mousalimas, A. S. (2018). *Co C 2671 Special Reconnaissance Battalion, Office of Strategic Services (OSS), Greek US Operational Group, World War 2: Memoirs*: North-Eastern Federal University Publishing House.

Myers, E. C. W. (1985). *Greek Entanglement*: Alan Sutton.

Neal, S. D. Y.-M. (2018). *50 Women Against Hitler: Female Resistance Fighters in World War II*: Books on Demand.

Neal, S. D. Y. M. (2018). *Places of Shame—German and Bulgarian War Crimes in Greece 1941–1945*: Books on Demand.

O'Connor, B. (2016). *Sabotage in Greece*: Lulu.com.

Paddock, A. H. (2002). *US Army Special Warfare, Its Origins: Psychological and Unconventional Warfare, 1941–1952*: University Press of the Pacific.

Perdue, R. E. (2010). *Behind the Lines in Greece: The Story of OSS Operational Group II*: AuthorHouse.

Rielly, R. L. (2013). *American Amphibious Gunboats in World War II: A History of LCI and LCS(L) Ships in the Pacific*: McFarland, Inc.

Rottman, G. L., & Dennis, P. (2013). *World War II Allied Sabotage Devices and Booby Traps*: Bloomsbury Publishing.

US Government. (1988). *OSS Foreign Nationalities Branch files, 1942–1945*. Washington, DC: Congressional Information Service.

Sutherland, I. D., & Sutherland, I. D. W. (1990). *Special Forces of the United States Army, 1952–1982*: R. James Bender Pub.

VanderLippe, J. M. (2012). *The Politics of Turkish Democracy: Ismet Inonu and the Formation of the Multi-Party System, 1938–1950*: State University of New York Press.

Woodhouse, C. M. (1950). *One Omen*: Hutchinson.

Woodhouse, C. M. (1951). *Apple of Discord: A Survey of Recent Greek Politics in Their International Setting*: Hutchinson.

Woodhouse, C. M., & Clogg, R. (2003). *The Struggle for Greece, 1941–1949*: I.R. Dee.

Book Section

Kalyvas, S. N. (2015). Rebel Governance During the Greek Civil War, 1942–1949. In A. Arjona, N. Kasfir, & Z. Mampilly (Eds.), *Rebel Governance in Civil War* (pp. 119–137). Cambridge: Cambridge University Press.

Conference Proceedings

Kotora, J. C., Major, USMC. (1985). *The Greek Civil War.* Paper presented at the War Since 1945 Seminar and Symposium, Quantico, Virginia

Discussion Forum

Hunt, D. (1995). Re: Greece in the Second World War. Message posted to https://catalog.hathitrust.org/Record/004977670

Government Document

Government, U. S. (1949). *Trials of War Criminals before the Nuremberg Military Tribunals under Control Council Law no. 10. Nuernberg, October 1946–April 1949.* Washington: US Govt. Print. Off. Retrieved from https://catalog.hathitrust.org/Record/000596400

Interview

Miron, A. B. *For That, It Deserves a Prize—The Story of a Two-Thousand-Year-Old Jewish Community in Ioannina, Greece: An Interview with Survivor Artemis Batis Miron/Interviewer: K. B. Liz Elsby.* The International School for Holocaust Studies, Yad Vashem, Israel.

Journal Articles

"Case Study in Guerrilla War: Greece during World War II." (1961). *Special Operations Research Office, American University, 1961.* Retrieved from https://catalog.hathitrust.org/Record/102113375/Cite

The Editors of Encyclopaedia Britannica. (2019). "Battle of
Lepanto 1571." Retrieved from
https://www.britannica.com/event/Battle-of-Lepanto

F. H. Hinsley, F., Noble. (1980). British Intelligence in the
Second World War: Its Influence on Strategy and
Operations. Volume 1. Assisted by E. E. Thomas et al.
New York: Cambridge University Press. 1979. Pp. xiii,
601. *The American Historical Review, 85*(2), 399-400.
doi:10.1086/ahr/85.2.399

Fleischer, H. (1978). "The Anomalies in the Greek Middle East
Forces, 1941–1944. "*Journal of the Hellenic Diaspora,
5*(3). Retrieved from
https://www.scribd.com/document/42305154/Anomalie
s-in-the-Greek-Middle-East-Forces-1941-44-Hagen-
Fleischer

Greekcitytimes. (2019). "Panagia of Tinos, National Patron
Saint of Greece." Retrieved from
https://greekcitytimes.com/2018/08/14/panagia-of-tinos-
national-patron-saint-of-greece/

Hionidou, V. (2019). "What Do Starving People Eat? The Case
of Greece Through Oral History." *Continuity and
Change*. Cambridge Core.
doi:doi:10.1017/S0268416011000014

Hood, M. S. F. (1957). "Archaeology in Greece, 1957".
Archaeological Reports (4), 3-25. doi:10.2307/581146

Keeley, R. V. (2010). "The Colonels' Coup and the American
Embassy: A Diplomat's View of the Breakdown of
Democracy in Cold War Greece."

Latrides, J. O., & Rizopoulos, N. X. (2000). "The International
Dimension of the Greek Civil War." *World Policy
Journal, 17*(1), 87-103. Retrieved from
https://www.jstor.org/stable/40209681?seq=1

Lindsay, J. H. (2010). "The Plating Industry in World War II:
Part Three, The Road to Victory." *Plating & Surface*

Finishing, 16-25. Retrieved from
https://www.nmfrc.org/pdf/psf2010/2010-05-16.pdf

Skalidakis, Y. (2015). "From Resistance to Counterstate: The Making of Revolutionary Power in the Liberated Zones of Occupied Greece, 1943–1944. *"Journal of Modern Greek Studies, 33*(1), 155-184. Retrieved from
https://muse.jhu.edu/article/581787

Stavrianos, L. S. (1952). "The Greek National Liberation Front (EAM): A Study in Resistance Organization and Administration." *The Journal of Modern History, 24*(1), 42–55. Retrieved from
https://www.jstor.org/stable/1871980?seq=1

Stevens, W. O., & Westcott, A. F. (1920). "A History of Sea Power." Retrieved from
https://archive.org/details/historyofseapowe00stev

Voglis, P. (2002). "Political Prisoners in the Greek Civil War, 1945–50: Greece in Comparative Perspective." *Journal of Contemporary History, 37*(4), 523–540. Retrieved from https://www.jstor.org/stable/3180758

Xydis, S. G. (1963). "America, Britain, and the USSR in the Greek Arena, 1944–1947." *Political Science Quarterly, 78*(4), 581-596. Retrieved from
https://www.psqonline.org/article.cfm?IDArticle=7688

<u>Newspaper Articles</u>

"US Army Forms Greek Battalion." (1942, 13 Dec 1942, Sun · Page 10). *Detroit Free Press*. Retrieved from
https://www.newspapers.com/image/97394655/?terms=US%2BArmy%2BForms%2BGreek%2BBattalion

Frangos, S. (2009). "The Creation and Fate of the WW II Greek Battalion." *The National Herald*.

Frangos, S. (2009). "Greek American Commandos of World War II: Behind Enemy Lines in Greece." *The National Herald*.

Hawkins, L. (1943, 7/11/1943). "Sicily Attack Only First of
     Series, Is Belief; Defending Force May Total 400,000
     Troops." *Fort Collins Coloradoan*. Retrieved from
     https://www.newspapers.com/image/588977443/?terms
     =Sicily
Maltezou, R., & Georgiopoulos, G. (2019, April 17, 2019).
     "Greek Parliament Calls on Germany to Pay WW2
     Reparations." *Reuters*. Retrieved from
     https://www.reuters.com/article/us-greece-germany-
     reparations/greek-parliament-calls-on-germany-to-pay-
     ww2-reparations-idUSKCN1RT1PL
Pennington, B. (2011, 6/13/2011). "When the Rounds were
     Ammo." *New York Times,* p. 1. Retrieved from
     https://www.nytimes.com/2011/06/13/sports/golf/when-
     the-rounds-were-ammo-at-congressional-country-
     club.html

<u>Pamphlet</u>

"The German Campaigns in the Balkans (Spring 1941)."
     (1953). In Department of the Army (Ed.), (Vol. 20-260).
     Washington, DC: Department of the Army.

<u>Web Pages</u>

"1943: Italian Dictator Mussolini Quits." *On This Day.*
     Retrieved from
     http://news.bbc.co.uk/onthisday/hi/dates/stories/july/25/
     newsid_3600000/3600649.stm
"An Account of the Blowing Up of the Asopos Viaduct in
     Greece in Which Don Stott Played a Prominent Roll."
     Retrieved from
     http://www.mackayresearch.com/uploads/1/0/9/8/10989
     841/asopos_viaduct.pdf

"Counter Intelligence Corps History And Mission in World War II." Retrieved from "https://fas.org/irp/agency/army/cic-wwii.pdf

Fort Carson a Tradition of Victory." Retrieved from https://www.carson.army.mil/assets/docs/pao/historybook.pdf

"German Antiguerrilla Operations in the Balkans (1941–1944)." Retrieved from https://history.army.mil/books/wwii/antiguer-ops/AG-BALKAN.HTM

"German Intelligence Service (WWII)," Vol. 1. Retrieved from https://www.cia.gov/library/readingroom/docs/GERMAN%20INTELLIGENCE%20SERVICE%20%28WWII%29%2C%20%20VOL.%201_0003.pdf

"History of Greece: Greece in the 2nd World War." Retrieved from https://www.ahistoryofgreece.com/worldwarII.htm

"Royal Air Force Historical Society Journal." *46.* Retrieved from https://www.rafmuseum.org.uk/documents/Research/RAF-Historical-Society-Journals/Journal_46_Seminar_N_Med_Ops_in_WW_II_Italy_Balkans_Greece.pdf

"Sara Fortis." Retrieved from https://encyclopedia.ushmm.org/content/en/article/sara-fortis

"Recommendations on Greece & Turkey: The President's Message to the Congress, March 12, 1947." (1947). Retrieved from https://babel.hathitrust.org/cgi/pt?id=uc1.31822019353960&view=1up&seq=1

"The History of Military Entrance Processing." (2008). Retrieved from https://www.mepcom.army.mil/Portals/112/Documents/Messenger/Messenger_Vol_30_No_4.pdf

"Organizational Development of the Joint Chiefs of Staff." (2013). Retrieved from https://www.jcs.mil/Portals/36/Documents/History/Institutional/Organizational_Development_of_the_JCS.pdf

"Fort Leavenworth Bridge." (2019). Retrieved from http://bridgehunter.com/ks/leavenworth/fort-leavenworth/

"Museum Spotlights Reception Center." (2019). Retrieved from http://www.ftleavenworthlamp.com/news/20190314/museum-spotlights-reception-center

"The Tehran Conference, 1943." (2019). *Milestones: 1937–1945.* Retrieved from https://history.state.gov/milestones/1937-1945/tehran-conf

"DOD Dictionary of Military and Associated Terms." (2020). Retrieved from https://www.jcs.mil/Portals/36/Documents/Doctrine/pubs/dictionary.pdf

The Editors of Encyclopaedia Britannica. (2018). "Greek Civil War." Retrieved from https://www.britannica.com/event/Greek-Civil-War

CIA. "Greek Hellenic Information Bulletin_0003." *Nazi War Crimes in Greece CIA Summary.* Retrieved from https://www.cia.gov/library/readingroom/document/519cd81c993294098d516444

CIA. "Greek Hellenic Information Bulletin_0004." *Nazi War Crimes in Greece CIA Summary.* Retrieved from https://www.cia.gov/library/readingroom/document/519cd821993294098d516e0b

CIA. "Greek Hellenic Information Bulletin_0005." *Nazi War Crimes in Greece CIA Summary.* Retrieved from https://www.cia.gov/library/readingroom/document/519cd81c993294098d516446

CIA. "Greek Hellenic Information Bulletin_0006." *Nazi War Crimes in Greece CIA Summary.* Retrieved from

https://www.cia.gov/library/readingroom/document/519
cd81c993294098d51644a

CIA. "Greek Hellenic Information Bulletin_0007. *Nazi War
Crimes in Greece CIA Summary.* Retrieved from
https://www.cia.gov/library/readingroom/document/519
cd821993294098d516e16

CIA. "Greek Hellenic Information Bulletin_0009. *Nazi War
Crimes in Greece CIA Summary.* Retrieved from
https://www.cia.gov/library/readingroom/document/519
cd81c993294098d51644b

CIA. "Greek Hellenic Information Bulletin_0010." *Nazi War
Crimes in Greece CIA Summary.* Retrieved from
https://www.cia.gov/library/readingroom/document/519
cd81c993294098d516448

CIA. "Greek Hellenic Information Bulletin_0012. *Nazi War
Crimes in Greece CIA Summary.* Retrieved from
https://www.cia.gov/library/readingroom/document/519
cd821993294098d516e14

CIA. "KKE Plans for Andartes, Politics, and Propaganda."
General CIA Records. Retrieved from
https://www.cia.gov/library/readingroom/document/cia-
rdp82-00457r001000530008-8

CIA. "KKE to Shift Blame for Failures to Markos." *General
CIA Records.* Retrieved from
https://www.cia.gov/library/readingroom/document/cia-
rdp82-00457r001800250002-7

Denezakis, A. (2020). "The Infernal "Cages of the
Occupation—Two Battles for their Liberation."
Retrieved from https://www.imerodromos.gr/oi-
kolasmenoi-kloyvites-tis-katochis-dyo-maches-gia-tin-
apeleytherosi-toys/

Frizzell, A. "Office of Strategic Services Operational Groups."
Retrieved from http://oss-og.org/overview.html

Gardner, H. H. (1962). "Guerrilla and Counter Guerrilla
Warfare in Greece, 1941–1945." Retrieved from

https://www.ibiblio.org/hyperwar/NHC/NewPDFs/UN/
UN%20Guerrilla%20Warfare%20Greece%201941-
1945.PDF

Greekacom. (2019). "Torpedoing of the Greek Warship *Elli* in
Tinos Island". Greeka.com. Retrieved from
https://www.greeka.com/cyclades/tinos/history/elli-
torpedoing/

Chambers, J. W., II. (2008). "OSS Training in the National
Parks and Service Abroad in World War II." Retrieved
from
https://irma.nps.gov/Datastore/DownloadFile/486417

Chambers, J. W., II. (2019). "A Wartime Organization for
Unconventional Warfare" (US National Park Service).
Retrieved from https://www.nps.gov/articles/a-wartime-
organization-for-unconventional-warfare.htm

Harris, W. D., Jr. (2012). "Instilling Aggressiveness: US
Advisors and Greek Combat Leadership in the Greek
Civil War, 1947–1949." Retrieved from
https://pdfs.semanticscholar.org/cb76/bfb9a8160afcc25c
1f719a7618ff6e0bdaf4.pdf

Kirwan, W. E. (1945). "Escape Tactics of German War
Prisoners." Vol 3, Issue 5. Retrieved from
https://scholarlycommons.law.northwestern.edu/cgi/vie
wcontent.cgi?article=3310&context=jclc

Kostopoulos, G. "The War Against the Goats in Interwar
Greece." Retrieved from
http://www.environmentandsociety.org/node/9011

Lord, V. M. (2019). "Oxi Day: The Day of No!" Retrieved
from http://ultimatehistoryproject.com/oxi-day.html

Mancini, J. "Bringing Down the Bridges." Retrieved from
https://warfarehistorynetwork.com/2016/07/21/bringing
-down-the-bridges/

Mousalimas, A. S. (2004). "Greek-American Operational
Group Office of Strategic Services (OSS) Memoirs of

World War II." Retrieved from
http://www.pahh.com/oss/toc.html

Oliver Z. Tyler, J. (1951). "History of Fort Leavenworth, 1937–1951." Retrieved from
https://apps.dtic.mil/dtic/tr/fulltext/u2/a437831.pdf

P. Psimoulisa, S. S. "Using Robotic Theodolites (RTS) in Structural Health Monitoring of Short-span Railway Bridges." Retrieved from
https://www.fig.net/resources/proceedings/2011/2011_ls gi/session_1e/psimoulis_stiros.pdf

Papaeti, A. "Music and 'Reeducation' in Greek Prison Camps: From Makronisos (1947–1955) to Giaros (1967–1968)." Retrieved from
https://pdfs.semanticscholar.org/5d49/810619d7eb63c6 9cd417dde684fc4aecdabe.pdf?_ga=2.145142260.15347 77187.1580596617-417118914.1580596617

Paschal, A. W. (1979). "The Enemy in Colorado: German Prisoners of War, 1943–46." *56, 3 & 4*. Retrieved from
https://www.historycolorado.org/sites/default/files/medi a/document/2018/ColoradoMagazine_Summer-Fall1979.pdf

Ray, J. (2006). 1941-1945 "Andartiko: The Greek Resistance." Retrieved from https://libcom.org/history/1941-1945-andartiko-the-greek-resistance

Reuben-Shemia, D. A. (2017). "Trade Unions in Greece between Crisis and Revitalization: Rebuilding Workers' Power from Below?" Retrieved from
https://pdfs.semanticscholar.org/004f/62ca4ee6d9e5cb2f ee8259a1851a2ec9d604.pdf?_ga=2.145152500.153477 7187.1580596617-417118914.1580596617

Robert R. Palmer, B. I. W., William R. Keast. (1991). "The Procurement and Training of Ground Combat Troops." Retrieved from
https://history.army.mil/html/books/002/2-2/CMH_Pub_2-2.pdf

Wikipedia. (2019). "Greco-Italian War." Retrieved from
https://en.wikipedia.org/wiki/Greco-Italian_War

Endnotes

---

1 Lord, V. M. (2019). "OXI DAY: THE DAY OF NO!". from http://ultimatehistoryproject.com/oxi-day.html.

2 Hinsley, H. (2019). British Intelligence in The Second World War, p 234

3 Wikipedia (2019). "Greco-Italian War - Wikipedia, The Free Encyclopedia." from https://en.wikipedia.org/wiki/Greco-Italian_War.

4 "US Army Forms Greek Battalion." Detroit Free Press (Detroit, Michigan), 13 Dec 1942, Sun · Page 10 1942.

5 Mousalimas, A. S. (2004). "Greek-American Operational Group Office of Strategic Services (OSS) Memoirs of World War II." Retrieved Jan. 8, 2019, from http://www.pahh.com/oss/toc.html., page 32

6 II, J. W. C. (2019). "A Wartime Organization for Unconventional Warfare (US National Park Service)." from https://www.nps.gov/articles/a-wartime-organization-for-unconventional-warfare.htm.

7 Sadkovich, James J. "Of Myths and Men: Rommel and the Italians in North Africa, 1940-1942." The International History Review 13, no. 2 (1991): 284-313. www.jstor.org/stable/40106368.

It was Rommel and his 'Germans' that prevailed over the British : Rommel ..... Ceva also notes that the Italians were the first to use self-propelled guns both in ..... with 1,037 guns, 3,986 serviceable vehicles, 2,806 camels, 4,658 quadrupeds.

8 Fort Carson a Tradition of Victory, Public Affairs Office, Fort Carson, Colorado, page 18

https://www.carson.army.mil/assets/docs/pao/historybook.pdf

The Enemy in Colorado: German Prisoners of War, 1943-46 BY ALLEN W. PASCHAL, THE COLORADO MAGAZINE 56/3 and 4 1979.

https://www.historycolorado.org/sites/default/files/media/documen t/2018/ColoradoMagazine_Summer-Fall1979.pdf

9 http://www.fortwiki.com/Fort_Carson

10 https://www.calisthenicsempire.com/the-history-of-calisthenics/

11 Frangos, Steve. "Greek American Commandos of World War II: Behind Enemy Lines in Greece." The National Herald (New York City, NY), 2009.

12 "Greek-American Operational Group Office of Strategic Services (Oss) Memoirs of World War II." Preservation of American Hellenic History, 2004, accessed Jan. 8, 2019, http://www.pahh.com/oss/toc.html. Part 1

13 William E. Kirwan, Escape Tactics of German War Prisoners, 35 J. Crim. L. & Criminology 357 (1944-1945)

14 Stavrianos, L. S. "The Greek National Liberation Front (EAM): A Study in Resistance Organization and Administration." The Journal of Modern History 24, no. 1 (1952): 42-55. www.jstor.org/stable/1871980. Page 43

15 Kalyvas, S. (2015). Rebel Governance During the Greek Civil War, 1942–1949. In A. Arjona, N. Kasfir, & Z. Mampilly (Eds.), Rebel Governance in Civil War (pp. 119-137). Cambridge: Cambridge University Press. doi:10.1017/CBO9781316182468.006, page 128.

16 Stavrianos, L. S. "The Greek National Liberation Front (EAM): A Study in Resistance Organization and Administration." The Journal of Modern History 24, no. 1 (1952): 42-55. www.jstor.org/stable/1871980.

17 Macintyre, Ben (2010). Operation Mincemeat. London: Bloomsbury. ISBN 978-1-4088-0921-1.

[18] Smyth, Denis (2010). Deathly Deception: The Real Story of Operation Mincemeat. London: Oxford University Press. ISBN 978-0-19-923398-4.

[19] https://en.wikipedia.org/wiki/Stefanos_Sarafis

[20] On May 19, 1943, the EAM-ELAS Central Committee appointed Sarafis to EAM-ELAS military chief. They appointed the long-standing guerrilla leader and KKE member, Aris Velouchiotis, as Kapetánios. They appointed Vasiles Samariniotes, also with KKE, as the EAM-ELAS representative. Thus, the power of ELAS, the military wing of EAM, rested with three men, two communists, and Sarafis. Decisions required unanimity.

[21] Woodhouse, Christopher Montague (1948). Apple of Discord: A Survey of Recent Greek Politics in their International Setting. London.

[22] German Antiguerrilla Operations in the Balkans (1941-1944), CMH Publication 104-18 page 24-25

[23] http://www.occupation-memories.org/en/deutsche-okkupation/Wichtige-Begriffe/index.html

[24] Brewer, David (2016). Greece, The Decade of War: Occupation, Resistance, and Civil War. London: I.B. Tauris. ISBN 9781780768540. Page 176

[25] Mazower, Inside Hitler's Greece, quoted in Dionysis Charitopoulos, Άρης ο αρχηγός των ατάκτων (=Ares, Leader of the Irregulars) (Athens, Topos, 2009), p. 545 (back-translated by contributor).

[26] Churchill's Ministry of Ungentlemanly Warfare, The Mavericks Who Plotted Hitler's Defeat – Giles Milton, page 206.

[27] Churchill's Ministry of Ungentlemanly Warfare, The Mavericks Who Plotted Hitler's Defeat – Giles Milton

[28] Myers, E.C.W. Greek Entanglement. Alan Sutton, 1985. https://books.google.com/books?id=NP1mAAAAMAAJ. Page 43

[29] Assessing Revolutionary and Insurgent Strategies, "Case Study in Guerrilla War: Greece during World War II, Revised Edition." United States Army Special Operations Command,   page 29

[30] Using Robotic Theodolites (RTS) in Structural Health Monitoring of Short-span Railway Bridges, P. Psimoulisa,b *, S. Stirosa, a Geodesy Lab., Dept. of Civil Eng., University of Patras, Patras, Greece – stiros@upatras.gr, b Geodesy and Geodynamics Lab., ETH Zurich, Schafmattstr. 34, Zurich, Switzerland – panospsimoulis@ethz.ch, page 1
https://www.fig.net/resources/proceedings/2011/2011_lsgi/session_1e/psimoulis_stiros.pdf

[31] Myers, E.C.W. Greek Entanglement. Alan Sutton, 1985. https://books.google.com/books?id=NP1mAAAAMAAJ. Page 44

[32] Assessing Revolutionary and Insurgent Strategies, , "Case Study in Guerrilla War: Greece during World War II, Revised Edition." United States Army Special Operations Command,   page 39

[33] Churchill's Ministry of Ungentlemanly Warfare, The Mavericks Who Plotted Hitler's Defeat – Giles Milton, page 218.

[34] German Antiguerrilla Operations in the Balkans (1941-1944), CMH Publication 104-18 page 19.

[35] Yada-Mc Neal, Stephan D. Places of Shame - German and Bulgarian War Crimes in Greece 1941-1945.N.p.: Books on Demand, 2018. Page 137

[36] http://www.occupation-memories.org/en/deutsche-okkupation/Wichtige-Begriffe/index.html

[37] http://www.occupation-memories.org/en/deutsche-okkupation/repressalien/index.html

[38] http://nzetc.victoria.ac.nz/tm/scholarly/tei-WH2-2Epi-c2-WH2-2Epi-j.html page 24

---

39 Yada-Mc Neal, Stephan D. Places of Shame - German and Bulgarian War Crimes in Greece 1941-1945. N.p.: Books on Demand, 2018. Page 55.
https://books.google.com/books?id=_T1RDwAAQBAJ&pg=PA54&lpg=PA54&dq=kourmovo+tunnel+greece&source=bl&ots=sHE082CrNj&sig=ACfU3U3nxE70oy290AQc2gPYLQcns7cUig&hl=en&sa=X&ved=2ahUKEwil5MHv99DmAhVJBcoKHSnuDG8Q6AEwDX0ECA0QAQ#v=onepage&q=kourmovo%20tunnel%20greece&f=false

40 Assessing Revolutionary and Insurgent Strategies, , "Case Study in Guerrilla War: Greece during World War II, Revised Edition." United States Army Special Operations Command, page 241.

41 Yada-Mc Neal, Stephan D.Places of Shame - German and Bulgarian War Crimes in Greece 1941-1945. N.p.: Books on Demand, 2018. Page 57.

42 Assessing Revolutionary and Insurgent Strategies, , "Case Study in Guerrilla War: Greece during World War II, Revised Edition." United States Army Special Operations Command, page 58.

43 Myers, E.C.W. Greek Entanglement. Alan Sutton, 1985.
https://books.google.com/books?id=NP1mAAAAMAAJ. Page 184.

44 Myers, E.C.W. Greek Entanglement. Alan Sutton, 1985.
https://books.google.com/books?id=NP1mAAAAMAAJ. Page 184.

45 Perdue, R.E. Behind the Lines in Greece: The Story of Oss Operational Group Ii. AuthorHouse, 2010.
https://books.google.com/books?id=RA-7DAcCXHsC. Page 7.

46 https://metaxas-project.com/alexandros-koryzis/

47 Kosmidou, E.R. European Civil War Films: Memory, Conflict, and Nostalgia. Routledge, 2013.
https://books.google.com/books?id=OucgI1cfauwC. Page 120

48 Fleischer, Hagen. "The Anomalies in the Greek Middle East Forces, 1941-1944." Journal of the Hellenic Diaspora 5, no. 3 (1978).

https://www.scribd.com/document/42305154/Anomalies-in-the-Greek-Middle-East-Forces-1941-44-HAGEN-FLEISCHER. Page 6

49 Fleischer, Hagen. "The Anomalies in the Greek Middle East Forces, 1941-1944." Journal of the Hellenic Diaspora 5, no. 3 (1978). https://www.scribd.com/document/42305154/Anomalies-in-the-Greek-Middle-East-Forces-1941-44-HAGEN-FLEISCHER. Page 10

50 Fleischer, Hagen. "The Anomalies in the Greek Middle East Forces, 1941-1944." Journal of the Hellenic Diaspora 5, no. 3 (1978). https://www.scribd.com/document/42305154/Anomalies-in-the-Greek-Middle-East-Forces-1941-44-HAGEN-FLEISCHER. Page 18

51 Hawkins, Lewis. "Sicily Attack Only First of Series, Is Belief; Defending Force May Total 400,000 Troops." Fort Collins Coloradoan (Fort Collins, Folorado), 7/11/1943 1943. https://www.newspapers.com/image/588977443/?terms=Sicily.

52 Myers, E.C.W. Greek Entanglement. Alan Sutton, 1985. https://books.google.com/books?id=NP1mAAAAMAAJ. Page 125

53 "1943: Italian Dictator Mussolini Quits." On This Day, accessed 2/13, 2020, http://news.bbc.co.uk/onthisday/hi/dates/stories/july/25/newsid_3600000/3600649.stm.

54 Woodhouse, C.M. Apple of Discord: A Survey of Recent Greek Politics in Their International Setting. Hutchinson, 1951. https://books.google.com/books?id=ObZongEACAAJ. Page145

55 Myers, E.C.W. Greek Entanglement. Alan Sutton, 1985. https://books.google.com/books?id=NP1mAAAAMAAJ. Page 230

56 Woodhouse, C.M. Apple of Discord: A Survey of Recent Greek Politics in Their International Setting. Hutchinson, 1951. https://books.google.com/books?id=ObZongEACAAJ. Page 151

57 Frangos, Steve. "The Creation and Fate of the WW II Greek Battalion." The National Herald (New York City, NY), 2009.

58 Frangos, Steve. "The Creation and Fate of the WW II Greek Battalion." The National Herald (New York City, NY), 2009.

59 Document INT-14GR-338; Documents INT-14GR-345; INT-33GR-25. United, States. OSS Foreign Nationalities Branch Files, 1942-1945. Title on Accompanying Guide: Us Office of Strategic Services, Foreign Nationalities Branch files, 1942-1945. Bethesda, MD: Congressional Information Service, 1988. //catalog.hathitrust.org/Record/002794272 page 5

60 Pages 22-430 is the section entitled *Index by Subject and Names*. Although the number of entries per page vary, by my count, most pages have an average of just over 100. Thus, the number of pages, 408, multiplied by the entries per page, 100, gives over 41,000 entries.

61 Mousalimas, A.S. Co C 2671 Special Reconnaissance Battalion, Office of Strategic Services (Oss), Greek Us Operational Group, World War 2: Memoirs. North-Eastern Federal University Publishing House, 2018. https://books.google.com/books?id=q6pdwAEACAAJ. Part 2

62 Pennington, Bill. "When the Rounds Were Ammo." New York Times (NYC), 6/13/2011 2011, D, 1.

63 Mark Mazower, Inside Hitler's Greece (Yale University Press, New Haven and London, 1993), at pages 191 to 197

64 Congressional Country Club 1924-1984 Hardcover – 1984, by Anne Reilly Dolan (Author), Joe Gambatese (Photographer), Guy Hooks (Photographer), Duane M. Neilson (Photographer), Tom E Ryan (Photographer), Kim Saal (Photographer)

65 II, J. W. C. (2008). OSS Training in the National Parks and Service Abroad in World War II Retrieved from https://irma.nps.gov/Datastore/DownloadFile/486417 page 54

66 II, J. W. C. (2008). OSS Training in the National Parks and Service Abroad in World War II Retrieved from https://irma.nps.gov/Datastore/DownloadFile/486417 page 74

67 Mousalimas, A. S. (2004). Greek-American Operational Group Office of Strategic Services (OSS) Memoirs of World War II. Retrieved from http://www.pahh.com/oss/toc.html part 2

68 Lulushi, A. Donovan's Devils: Oss Commandos Behind Enemy Lines—Europe, World War Ii. Arcade, 2016.

69 II, J. W. C. (2008). OSS Training in the National Parks and Service Abroad in World War II Retrieved from https://irma.nps.gov/Datastore/DownloadFile/486417 page 62

70 Giannaris, J., and M.K.C. Olson. Yannis. Pilgrimage Pub., 1988. https://books.google.com/books?id=w5i8PAAACAAJ. Page 52

71 "Oss Training in the National Parks and Service Abroad in World War II ", 2008, https://irma.nps.gov/Datastore/DownloadFile/486417. Page 55

72 https://www.nps.gov/cato/learn/historyculture/shangri-la.htm

73 Perdue, R.E. Behind the Lines in Greece: The Story of Oss Operational Group Ii. AuthorHouse, 2010. https://books.google.com/books?id=RA-7DAcCXHsC. Page 32

74 https://lyricstranslate.com/en/%CE%BA%CE%BF%CF%81%CF%8C%CE%B9%CE%B4%CE%BF-%CE%BC%CE%BF%CF%85%CF%83%CE%BF%CE%BB%CE%AF%CE%BD%CE%B9-koroido-mousolini-mussolini-you-fool.html

75 "The War against the Goats in Interwar Greece." accessed 3/20, 2020, http://www.environmentandsociety.org/node/9011.

76 Germany. Trials of War Criminals before the Nuremberg Military Tribunals under Control Council Law No. 10. Nuernberg, October 1946-April 1949. Washington: US Govt. Print. Off., 1949. Page 1310

77 Miron, Artemis Batis. "For That, It Deserves a Prize – the Story of a Two-Thousand Year Old Jewish Community in Ioannina, Greece: An Interview with Survivor Artemis Batis Miron." By Kathryn Berman

Liz Elsby. The International School for Holocaust Studies. https://en.wikipedia.org/wiki/Ioannina#cite_ref-55.

[78] Stevens, William Oliver, and Allan F. Westcott. "A History of Sea Power." [In English]. (1920). Page 106. https://archive.org/details/historyofseapowe00stev.

[79] Davis, P.K. 100 Decisive Battles: From Ancient Times to the Present. Oxford University Press, 2001. Page 199. https://books.google.com/books?id=nv73QlQs9ocC.

[80] Skalidakis, Yannis. "From Resistance to Counterstate: The Making of Revolutionary Power in the Liberated Zones of Occupied Greece, 1943–1944." Journal of Modern Greek Studies 33, no. 1 (2015): 155-84. https://muse.jhu.edu/article/581787. Page 166

[81] Skalidakis, Yannis. "From Resistance to Counterstate: The Making of Revolutionary Power in the Liberated Zones of Occupied Greece, 1943–1944." Journal of Modern Greek Studies 33, no. 1 (2015): 155-84. https://muse.jhu.edu/article/581787. Page 169

[82] Skalidakis, Yannis. "From Resistance to Counterstate: The Making of Revolutionary Power in the Liberated Zones of Occupied Greece, 1943–1944." Journal of Modern Greek Studies 33, no. 1 (2015): 155-84. https://muse.jhu.edu/article/581787. Page 170

[83] Skalidakis, Yannis. "From Resistance to Counterstate: The Making of Revolutionary Power in the Liberated Zones of Occupied Greece, 1943–1944." Journal of Modern Greek Studies 33, no. 1 (2015): 155-84. https://muse.jhu.edu/article/581787. Page 167

[84] Skalidakis, Yannis. "From Resistance to Counterstate: The Making of Revolutionary Power in the Liberated Zones of Occupied Greece, 1943–1944." Journal of Modern Greek Studies 33, no. 1 (2015): 155-84. https://muse.jhu.edu/article/581787. Page 160

[85] Renee Maltezou, George Georgiopoulos. "Greek Parliament Calls on Germany to Pay Ww2 Reparations." Reuters (Athens), April 17, 2019 2019. https://www.reuters.com/article/us-greece-germany-

reparations/greek-parliament-calls-on-germany-to-pay-ww2-reparations-idUSKCN1RT1PL.

[86] The three men hanged were Avraam Anastasiadis, Panos Soulos and Christos Salakos.
https://en.wikipedia.org/wiki/Dimokratias_Square_(Agrinio)

[87] https://www.historians.org/about-aha-and-membership/aha-history-and-archives/gi-roundtable-series/pamphlets/em-13-how-shall-lend-lease-accounts-be-settled-(1945)/how-much-of-what-goods-have-we-sent-to-which-allies

By the end of June 1944 the United States had sent to the Soviets under lend-lease more than 11,000 planes; over 6,000 tanks and tank destroyers; and 300,000 trucks and other military vehicles.

We have also sent to the Soviets about 350 locomotives, 1,640 flat cars, and close to half a million tons of rails and accessories, axles, and wheels, all for the improvement of the railways feeding the Red armies on the Eastern Front. For the armies themselves we have sent miles of field telephone wire, thousands of telephones, and many thousands of tons of explosives. And we have also provided machine tools and other equipment to help the Russians manufacture their own planes, guns, shells, and bombs.

We have supplied our allies with large quantities of food. The Soviet Union alone has received some 3,000,000 tons. Lend-lease has contributed about 10 percent of Britain's over-all food supply. This, together with a great increase in agricultural production in the British Isles, has helped to feed the British civilians and armed forces. Bread, potatoes, carrots, cabbage, and other common vegetables have been available to the British from their home gardens and farms. The United States has provided a high proportion of such foods as bacon, eggs, cheese, and fruit juices.

[88] https://en.wikipedia.org/wiki/3rd_Greek_Mountain_Brigade

[89] "Case Study in Guerrilla War: Greece During World War II." Special Operations Research Office, American University, 1961. (1961). https://catalog.hathitrust.org/Record/102113375/Cite. Page 133

90 Office of Strategic Services Operational Groups http://oss-og.org/greek.html

91 "Oss Training in the National Parks and Service Abroad in World War II ", 2008, https://irma.nps.gov/Datastore/DownloadFile/486417. Page 586.

92 "Case Study in Guerrilla War: Greece During World War II." Special Operations Research Office, American University, 1961. (1961). https://catalog.hathitrust.org/Record/102113375/Cite. Page 85

93 "German Antiguerrilla Operations in the Balkans (1941-1944)." Department of the US Army, accessed 2/2, 202, https://history.army.mil/books/wwii/antiguer-ops/AG-BALKAN.HTM. Page 38

94 "German Antiguerrilla Operations in the Balkans (1941-1944)." Department of the US Army, accessed 2/2, 202, https://history.army.mil/books/wwii/antiguer-ops/AG-BALKAN.HTM. Page 35

95 Kotora, Jeffrey C., Major, USMC. "The Greek Civil War." Paper presented at the WAR SINCE 1945 SEMINAR AND SYMPOSIUM, Quantico, Virginia 1985.

96 XYDIS, STEPHEN G. "America, Britain, and the Ussr in the Greek Arena, 1944-1947." Political Science Quarterly 78, no. 4 (1963): 581-96. Page 583

97 Kaloudis, G. Modern Greece and the Diaspora Greeks in the United States. Lexington Books, 2018. Page 141. OSS Operatives were Kostas Kouvaras, Kostas Papadopoulos, and Yiannis Kokosaios.

98 Woodhouse, C.M. Apple of Discord: A Survey of Recent Greek Politics in Their International Setting. Hutchinson, 1951. https://books.google.com/books?id=ObZongEACAAJ. Page 198

99 Lindsay, James H. "The Plating Industry in World War II: Part Three, the Road to Victory." Plating & Surface Finishing, Part Three

(May 2010 2010): 16-25. https://www.nmfrc.org/pdf/psf2010/2010-05-16.pdf. Page 25

100 VanderLippe, J.M. Politics of Turkish Democracy, The: Ismet Inonu and the Formation of the Multi-Party System, 1938-1950. State University of New York Press, 2012. https://books.google.com/books?id=7u_YRaL42K8C. Page 98

101 O'Connor, B. Sabotage in Greece. Lulu.com, 2016. https://books.google.com/books?id=TJvFBgAAQBAJ. Page 387

102 Iatrides, J.O. Greece at the Crossroads: The Civil War and Its Legacy. Pennsylvania State University Press, 2010. https://books.google.com/books?id=Vv1t3D_3vjkC.

103 "Case Study in Guerrilla War: Greece During World War II." *Special Operations Research Office, American University, 1961.* (1961). Page 260. https://catalog.hathitrust.org/Record/102113375/Cite.

104 "Guerrilla and Counter Guerrilla Warfare in Greece, 1941 -1945." Department of the Army Office of the Chief of Military History, 1962, accessed 2/2, 2020, page 181. https://www.ibiblio.org/hyperwar/NHC/NewPDFs/UN/UN%20Guerrilla%20Warfare%20Greece%201941-1945.PDF.

105 "Case Study in Guerrilla War: Greece During World War II." *Special Operations Research Office, American University, 1961.* Page 260 (1961). https://catalog.hathitrust.org/Record/102113375/Cite.

106 Fourniotis, Nikolaos, and Georgios Horsch. Early Summer Circulation in the Gulf of Patras (Greece). 2012. https://www.researchgate.net/publication/287587091_Early_summer_circulation_in_the_Gulf_of_Patras_Greece.

107 https://encyclopedia2.thefreedictionary.com/Ionian+Sea

108 There are discrepancies in the number of OSS commandos who served in Greece and the number of killed and wounded. Mousalimas, a corporal in OG IV, cites the following in his fascinating memoir but the citation is not specific. Mousalimas, A.S. Co C 2671 Special

Reconnaissance Battalion, Office of Strategic Services (Oss), Greek
US Operational Group, World War 2: Memoirs. North-Eastern
Federal University Publishing House, 2018. National Archives, Greek
US Operational Groups, Operations in Greece 1944, p. 11

<u>Report filed at OSS Headquarters, 24 December 1944</u>

No. of operations in Greece: 76

Results of Operations

Trains Attacked: 14

Locomotives Destroyed: 11

Train Cars Destroyed: 32

Armored Cars Destroyed: 2

Convoys Attacked: 5

Trucks Destroyed: 61

Bridges Destroyed: 15

Roads Mined: 5

Yards of Rail Blown: 9920

Garrisons & Pillboxes Attacked: 6

Enemy Killed, Wounded, Prisoners, est.: 2000

OGs Wounded: 23

OGs Killed: 3

The OSS Operational Group Organization at http://oss-og.org/greek.html lists a total of eight groups and 181 men. They show one killed in action and eleven wounded. They cite the following sources: *This summary of these Operational Groups was extracted from records of the National Archives provided through the courtesy of Lt. Col. Ian D. W. Sutherland. Attorney Sutherland is the compiler of the encyclopedic "Special Forces of the United States Army, 1952-1982"*

109
https://www.nafpaktianews.gr/%cf%87%cf%8c%ce%bc%ce%bf%cf%81%ce%b7-%ce%bd%ce%b1%cf%85%cf%80%ce%b1%ce%ba%cf%84%ce%af%ce%b1%cf%82-%ce%b4%cf%8d%ce%bf-%cf%87%ce%b5%ce%b9%cf%81%ce%bf%ce%b2%ce%bf%ce%bc%ce%b2%ce%af%ce%b4%ce%b5%cf%82/